PENGUIN BOOKS

COLLECTED PLAYS VOLUME TWO

Mahesh Dattani, born in Bangalore on 7 August 1958 studied in Baldwin's High School and St. Joseph's College of Arts and Science, Bangalore.

He has worked as a copywriter in an advertising firm and subsequently with his father in the family business. His theatre group Playpen was formed in 1984, and he has directed several plays for them, ranging from classical Greek to contemporary works. In 1986, he wrote his first full-length play, *Where There's a Will*, and from 1995, he has been working full-time in theatre. In 1998, he set up his own theatre studio dedicated to training and showcasing new talents in acting, directing and stage writing, the first in the country to specifically focus on new works.

Dattani is also a film-maker and his films have been screened in India and abroad to critical and public acclaim. His film *Dance Like a Man* has won the award for the Best Picture in English awarded by the National Panorama.

In 1998, Dattani won the Sahitya Akademi award for his book of plays *Final Solutions and Other Plays*, published by East–West Books Chennai, thus becoming the first English language playwright to win the award.

Dattani teaches theatre courses at the summer sessions programme of Portland State University, Oregon, USA, and conducts workshops regularly at his studio and elsewhere. He also writes plays for BBC Radio 4.

He lives in Bangalore.

COLLECTED PLAYS

VOLUME TWO

Screen, Stage and Radio Plays

Mahesh Dattani

PENGUIN BOOKS

An imprint of Penguin Random House

PENGUIN BOOKS

USA | Canada | UK | Ireland | Australia
New Zealand | India | South Africa | China | Singapore

Penguin Books is part of the Penguin Random House group of companies
whose addresses can be found at global.penguinrandomhouse.com

Published by Penguin Random House India Pvt. Ltd
4th Floor, Capital Tower 1, MG Road,
Gurugram 122 002, Haryana, India

Penguin
Random House
India

First published by Penguin Books India 2005

ISBN 9780143032762

Typeset in Sabon Roman by SÚRYA, New Delhi

Printed at Manipal Technologies Limited, India

www.penguin.co.in

MIX
Paper | Supporting
responsible forestry
FSC® C043100

This is a legitimate digitally printed version of the book and therefore might not
have certain extra finishing on the cover.

Contents

Contents

Introduction

The art critic Walter Pater said that all arts 'aspire to the condition of music'. I maintain that all drama 'aspires to the genre of the detective play'. Why after all, does the theatre audience come back to their seats after the interval? If not to try and find out why it is that the characters they see 'strutting and fretting' on the stage are so driven, and to wonder at the denouement and feel the catharsis of the resolution. If the resolution includes the unravelling of a dark and mysterious crime, then so much the better.

So I was particularly pleased when Mahesh Dattani, having seen his first radio play, *Do the Needful* through to a successful broadcast, told me that he was tempted to create a radio detective. Uma Rao has all the hallmarks of a successful sleuth. She is fiendishly intelligent (rather more so than her unfortunate husband), she is fearless, and her motivation is entirely honourable. She wants nothing more than to see justice done, and the guilty punished. She also has that quality, shared by Miss Marple and Sherlock Holmes, of being able to assume the mantle of invisibility when she so chooses. Not literally of course, but she knows that she can insinuate herself into situations where the uniformed police would be unable to go.

In his Uma Rao plays, three of which are contained within this volume, Mahesh Dattani can also be seen pulling the wool over the eyes of his audience. There is something apparently 'safe' about the detective play. The characters—the English aristocrat, or the Diva-like actress—are rather larger than life. So, we feel, these plays cannot be read as a commentary on the real world. But hold on a moment! The issues are far from superficial. Here, guided by the confident Mrs Rao, we are led to face up to questions of sexual identity, religious faith, family ties and the feelings of parents for their children.

All the issues in fact which Mahesh Dattani has made his own in his stage work. I remember seeing a production of *Bravely Fought the Queen* in London nearly ten years ago and thinking, as I waited for the revelations of the third Act, 'here is a writer who has seen and learned from the work of Tennessee Williams!'. The issues of maternal love are prominent in the two other plays in this volume, *The Tale of a Mother Feeding Her Child* and *Clearing the Rubble*, both of which are set around natural disasters.

The Tale of a Mother Feeding Her Child is a short, but powerful monologue, which manages to overlay the story of an English woman revisiting India for the first time in many years, with that of an Indian woman widowed during a savage drought. It is a bold and moving story which asks important and revealing questions about the relationship between two very different worlds. *Clearing the Rubble*, written as a direct response to the 2001 earthquake in Gujarat, also develops this theme. In *Clearing the Rubble*, an English journalist revisits Bhuj a year after the earthquake, desperate to trace a boy he helped free from the rubble. In both plays the English characters learn how to take an active role in the events in India, but both characters also learn that they are limited by their own background and outlook.

As Uma Rao says in *Uma and the Fairy Queen*, 'What a tangled web'. Taking her cue from Sir Walter Scott ('What a tangled web we weave when first we practise to deceive'), Uma could well be commenting on her creator's art. Mahesh Dattani does not seek to cut a path through the difficulties his characters encounter in his plays; instead he leads his audience to see just how caught up we all are in the complications and contradictions of our values and assumptions. And by revealing the complexity, he makes the world a richer place for all of us.

BBC Radio   JEREMY MORTIMER
October 2004   *Executive Producer,*
                                                    BBC Radio Drama

THIRTY DAYS IN SEPTEMBER

A Stage Play in Three Acts

A Note on the Play

My friend, Protima Bedi, once told me, that when she first saw the land on which Nrityagram now stands, it whispered to her, that it wanted to be a dance village.

Such is the stuff of dreams and Protima's wonderful, soaring imagination!

The plays closest to my heart, that have transformed and changed me in some way, happen in somewhat the same manner. They seem to have a voice of their own, a voice that *demands* that they be done . . . and I have no choice.

But then the oddest thing happens! The universe *does* conspire to make it so. (Together of course, with a team of very hardworking actors, artists and technicians plus the generous support of enlightened sponsors like the Tatas, who often support me on the strength of my passion!)

In August 2000, when I was shooting for *Monsoon Wedding* in Delhi, Mahesh met me and told me over a cup of coffee, that he had been commissioned by RAHI to write a play on child sexual abuse and would like me to consider producing it. I agreed almost immediately. It was the first time that I committed to doing a play, without even seeing an outline of the script! But RAHI's commitment, Mahesh's integrity and my own response to the subject, left me in no doubt that this was a play I had to do! My only condition was, that the play should work first and foremost as a piece of theatre, that the issues addressed should be organic to the plot and the message subliminal.

The 'tripartite' talks that followed as the script began to take shape, between RAHI, Mahesh and me were probably one of the most interesting aspects of the project. With RAHI striving to ensure authenticity (every survivor and psychologist who has seen the play is amazed by its veracity!), to me insisting on it being a strong stand-alone piece of dramatic work and Mahesh struggling to walk the delicate tightrope between both, while interviewing over a dozen survivors and moulding their stories to provide a framework of truthfulness for our tale, life was fraught with frantic phone calls and flying emails!

And then the actors moved in. Rehearsals, workshops and the individual inputs of the actors reshaped the material further and a slightly different avatar of the play was born.

The play turned out to be a liberating and learning experience for everyone involved. Especially for the actors, who had to delve deep into unexplored areas of themselves in order to connect truthfully with the material of the play, through intense workshops that often left them shaken and not a little disturbed. Especially for the actors who played the abuser—first Darshan Jariwala and later Amar Talwar—it was a process that took them into the heart of darkness! Their reward was the passionate dislike they evoked in the audience for their superb portrayals!

If rehearsing the play was a journey of discovery, the performance was a revelation! A dark piece, albeit powerful and immensely moving, its commercial success and critical acclaim took us all by surprise. We were amazed at the depth of emotion and strong outrage it evoked in audiences across the world from varied cities in India to Colombo (where we performed for an audience of over 900 to a five-minute standing ovation!) to the US and Malaysia (where the image of young Malay girls in their headdresses, watching wide-eyed, will never leave me).

Thirty Days in September has touched hearts and consciences everywhere. Sensitive and powerful without ever offending sensibilities, it manages to bring home the horror and the pain within the framework of a very identifiable mother–daughter relationship. (On a personal level, *that* was quite poignant for me as well, because *Thirty Days in September* was the first time I played 'Ma' on stage, to both my daughters, Neha and Ira, who played the title role at different times.)

After every performance, women have come backstage with their own traumatic stories writ large on their faces, grateful for the catharsis the play offers, but even more, I think, for the expiation of their own guilt which they have carried as a heavy burden for so long. Meeting them, alone, has made the play worthwhile. For through it they believe, their silent screams have finally been heard.

To do plays moored in a living social context provides a fulfilment of its own. And to do those which deal with subjects that simmer dangerously below the surface of our consciousness, even if the seeing of them discomforts us, is surely one of the aims of theatre.

Peter Brooks once said that if a play did not provoke and disturb the audience, it wasn't worth doing.

I don't think there could be a better way to put it.

Lillete Dubey
(Lillete Dubey is a well-known theatre personality and stage director. She has directed Dattani's Dance Like a Man, On a Muggy Night in Mumbai *and* Thirty Days in September.*)*

Thirty Days in September was first performed at the Prithvi Theatre, Mumbai, on 31 May 2001 with the following cast:

MALA	Nandana Sen
SHANTA	Lillete Dubey
THE MAN	Darshan Jariwala
DEEPAK	Joy Sengupta
Producer Director	Lillete Dubey
Light Design	Lynne Fernandez
Set Design	Bhola Sharma
Vocals	Ila Arun
Original Music	Mahesh Tinaikar
Sound	Nupur Goel
Puppet Design	Ramdas Pandhye

In subsequent performances of the play, the part of Mala was played by Neha Dubey and Ira Dubey. The Man was played by Amar Talwar.

The play was commissioned by RAHI, a support group for women survivors of incest. RAHI was supported by the John D. and Caterine T. MacArthur Foundation.

ACT I

The stage is divided into four acting areas. All the action moves without any set changes between scenes.

The first area has a comfortable chair and a simple table with magazines and a double seater. The chair is reserved for the counsellor whom we never see.

The second area, occupying the central portion of the stage, is the living room of Shanta and Mala's home in a suburb of Delhi. The dominant feature is a large picture of Shri Krishna. The furniture is basic and minimal, almost as if this is just a point of transition rather than a room where the family would meet and receive people.

The third area is the pooja room which is perhaps behind a scrim so that it is visible only when required. The scrim will go up in the last scene as specified.

The fourth acting area is the most flexible, representing several locations—a party house, two restaurants, Deepak's home. Since this area is more representational, it would suffice to have four cubes that could be configured by the actors before the required scene, in full view of the audience.

During Mala's taped conversation, we see the back of a life-sized doll of a seven-year-old girl propped on a chair. During the first conversation we only see the back of the head. With every subsequent taped conversation we see more of the profile. We only see the doll's full face after Deepak's taped conversation.

Optional: During Mala's taped conversation, the director could choose to have a video projection of Mala, but it is important that the image is disjointed from her conversation. The video should focus on close ups and/or her body language with the idea of providing a contrast to Mala's confidence and clarity after four years as seen in the sessions with the counsellor.

The lights come up on Mala seated at the counsellor's desk. This Mala is more at peace with herself. She has taken a journey and has arrived somewhere, psychologically. This could be reflected in her easy manner or body language.

Mala talks to the imagined counsellor in the single seater opposite her. She does not talk to the audience. There is a tape recorder on the table, but she is not self-conscious about the recording.

MALA. Mala Khatri. February 2004 . . . *(Listening to the counsellor.)* Why not? . . . I do not hesitate to use my real name now. Let people know. There's nothing to hide. Not for me. After all, it is he who must hide. He should change his name, not me. It is he who must avoid being recognized. In people's homes, at parties, hopefully even on the streets. He should look the other way when someone spots him anywhere on this planet. And I can make that happen. I have the power to do that now. If I use my real name . . . *(Sighing, thinking about it almost as if it were a pleasant memory.)* I wish he were here now, so I could see his face when I tell him I have nothing to hide. Because I know it wasn't my fault . . . Now. I know now.

Pause.

MALA *(saying it with a growing sense of joy).* But what is the point? He is dead. Today. February the 29th. He is dead. Today.

Fade to black. Mala's voice on tape plays in the black out. This voice of Mala's is more unsure and a great deal more nervous.

MALA. I–I don't know how to begin . . . Today is the 30th of September . . . 2001, and my name is . . . I don't think I want to say my name . . . I am sorry. I hope that is okay with you . . . I am unsure about this . . . and a lot of other things. But this . . . This is the first time you see that I . . . *(After a long pause, where we do hear her breathing.)* I know it is all my fault really . . . It must be. I must have asked for it . . . Somehow, I just seem to be made for it. Maybe I was born that way, maybe . . . This is what I am meant for. It's not anybody's fault, except my own. Sometimes I wish that my mother . . . *(It gets to be difficult for her.)* I am sorry but . . . I can only tell you more if you turn this thing off.

The tape continues to hiss for a while.

Fade in. Music. The lights fade in on Shanta, Mala's mother, in the prayer room. Shanta is singing softly to herself while she rings a bell. The music fades out. Late evening.

Shanta offers some flowers and picks up the bell once again while she sings.

SHANTA *(singing).* 'Mere to Giridhar Gopal, Doosro na koi Mere to Giridhar Gopal, Doosro na koi . . .'

The doorbell rings.

Shanta stops singing, puts the bell down, bows to the idol before getting up and moving to the living room area. The lights come up on that area as she picks up a notebook from a shelf or table and goes to the door. She appears to be doing all this on 'automatic'.

She opens the door and as a matter of routine opens the book. She looks up and is disconcerted to find a stranger before her.

DEEPAK. Namaste, auntie ji.

Shanta stares at him, not sure what to say or do.

DEEPAK. My name is Deepak. I spoke to you on the phone the other day.

SHANTA. Deepak?

DEEPAK. Mala's friend.

SHANTA. Mala is not at home.

DEEPAK. I know. I have come to meet you.

SHANTA. To meet me?

DEEPAK. If you recall, I spoke with you on the phone, about meeting you.

SHANTA. Oh!

DEEPAK *(repeating it now as if to someone who doesn't understand)*. I called to ask if I could come and see you.

SHANTA. Mala will be returning at seven o'clock. Please come then.

DEEPAK. But I came to meet you.

SHANTA *(pleading)*. Please come later.

DEEPAK. You are expecting someone else?

SHANTA. I–I thought you were the paper wallah.

DEEPAK *(patiently)*. Auntie ji, you said I could come and meet you. It is very important that I talk to you.

SHANTA. Why? Please go away before Mala comes.

DEEPAK. Why?

SHANTA. She was very angry when I said you were coming.

DEEPAK. I told you not to let her know. That was the whole point!

SHANTA. Please I beg of you! If she finds out you are here and I talked to you.

DEEPAK. What will she do? She can't kill you!

SHANTA. You don't know her.

The man walks in to the house and heads straight to the kitchen much to the surprise of Deepak.

The man as the paper wallah, wears a synthetic shirt and khaki trousers, with worn out chappals.

Shanta goes back to 'automatic' and steps back in, opening the book and looking at the accounts.

Deepak uses this opportunity to come right in.

MAN *(entering from kitchen)*. No gas smell now. I told you it was the tube.

DEEPAK. I thought he is the paper wallah.

MAN. That is right. I also help Madam with small things. There is no man in the house, that is why. If there is a man in the house, what is my problem whether her gas is leaking or her terrace is leaking. *(Turning to Shanta and speaking with the authority of a man.)* Hahn. Have you kept the money ready? Quickly.

Shanta has been looking down while the paper wallah made his comment on her situation. The man easily towers over her, pelvis thrust out in an imposing manner, making Shanta very uneasy.

SHANTA *(reading from the book)*. Six hundred and twenty rupees.

She offers the money to him which is between the pages of the book.

MAN *(giving her a bill)*. No. It is six hundred and eighty.

SHANTA. But I have written it down! Every day's account!

MAN *(snatching the book from her)*. Show.

The man shakes his head while reading. He returns the book back to her.

MAN. Some entry must be forgotten. Here is the bill.

SHANTA. But I write it as soon as I get the magazine or paper.

MAN *(very sure of himself, not at all threatening)*. You are wrong. It is six hundred and ninety. Look at the bill.

SHANTA. But I never forget to write it in the book!

MAN. I will come back later and take it from your daughter.

Pause.

SHANTA. No. No. Why trouble her? *(Rising.)* I will give you the balance money.

Shanta gives him the money in his hand and exits to get the rest.

Deepak sits down on the sofa.

The two men stare at each other.

DEEPAK. They must take a lot of magazines from you.

MAN *(without blinking).* Femina. Elle. Cosmopolitan. All . . .

Shanta enters and gives the man some more money.

The man exits.

DEEPAK. You shouldn't allow people to walk right in to your house. *(Laughing.)* Look at me. I just walked right into your house. At least you know the paper wallah. *(More serious.)* Let me not waste your time. I am here to talk to you about Mala. But first let me tell you something about myself. I am Deepak Bhatia . . . I am Colonel Bhatia's son.

Shanta looks at him now in a new light.

SHANTA. Deepak? Why did you not tell me you are Colonel Bhatia's son? I have seen you when you were so small!

DEEPAK. My father conveys his regards to you.

SHANTA. Why didn't you tell me on the phone?

DEEPAK. Didn't Mala tell you? *(Looking at Shanta's uneasiness.)* Looks like she hasn't told you a lot of things.

Pause.

Shanta gets up.

SHANTA. Just one minute.

Shanta goes to the phone and begins to dial.

DEEPAK. Are you calling Mala?

Shanta does not respond.

Deepak goes to her.

DEEPAK. She is not in her office. And she has switched off her cell phone.

Deepak takes the phone from her hand and puts it down.

DEEPAK. Please. Can I talk to you, auntie. For Mala's sake!

Shanta looks at him not knowing what to do.

DEEPAK *(gently).* Please.

SHANTA. She will be very angry with me. You must go now! What if she comes home and . . . please!

Deepak looks at her for a while, then takes charge by putting on the posture of the man, pelvis thrust forward, taking charge of the space.

DEEPAK. No. I will not leave. But I will make a deal with you . . . I won't tell Mala that you let me in. So—if you don't tell her we had a talk, she won't know. So she won't be angry with you.

Shanta looks at him, thinking about it.

DEEPAK. I promise I won't tell her. Scout's honour.

SHANTA. She may come home right now.

DEEPAK. Has she ever been home at this time of the day?

SHANTA *(after a while, a bit more sure).* Sit down.

Deepak sits down on the sofa.

Shanta sits at a little distance from him.

DEEPAK. Have you any idea at all where she is right now?

SHANTA. At the office.

DEEPAK. No she isn't, and you know it . . . *(Leaning forward.)* Look, didn't she say anything at all about me?

SHANTA. Yes . . . She does not want to see you.

DEEPAK. Before that. Did she tell you that we were . . . seeing each other?

SHANTA *(shaking her head)*. No.

DEEPAK *(really hurt by this)*. Oh.

SHANTA. When I told her you had called, she said she doesn't want to see you again . . . she told me not to let you inside the house.

DEEPAK. I just don't get it. I thought everything was going well. *(Upset.)* I thought she loved me. Maybe I said or did something to upset her. But what could it be? . . . *(Composing himself.)* Last week, I told her that she was the most intelligent, sensitive and dynamic woman I had met. She just stared at me and said, 'I have something to tell you. It is over. I don't want to continue with our relationship.' She doesn't want to see me ever again.

SHANTA. She said that?

DEEPAK. Yes.

SHANTA. There was nothing else you said?

DEEPAK. Like?

SHANTA. That you did not want to marry her?

DEEPAK *(shocked)*. No! On the contrary! . . . Did she say I did not want to marry her?

SHANTA. Yes.

DEEPAK. I thought she never told you anything about me.

SHANTA. She didn't say it like that. I thought—I thought that, something she said made me feel . . . that you did not want to marry her.

DEEPAK. But that's not true! . . . What did she say to make you feel that way?

SHANTA. After she said she never wanted to see you again—she said—'That is the way it is with men.' That is why I thought that you . . .

DEEPAK. That just doesn't make sense. I have never ever given her the feeling that I am only interested in a casual affair. In fact, I went out of my way to show how much I respect her as a person.

SHANTA *(gently, with hope)*. Do you want to marry my daughter?
> *Deepak nods.*

SHANTA. And your parents?

DEEPAK. Our fathers were friends. My parents would be happy to know that . . . *(Knowing this would get her on his side.)* But it doesn't look like it's going to happen. I guess that's the end of that.

SHANTA *(hastily)*. No don't say that! She is a very nice girl at heart. Sometimes she gets angry with me but . . . It is always my fault . . . I–I forget things. I am the one to blame. But she is a very nice girl at heart. If she settles down, she will be all right.

DEEPAK. What do you mean by 'all right'? Do you feel there is something wrong?

SHANTA. No, no. What am I saying? I mean that everything will be all right.

DEEPAK. There is something you are not telling me.

SHANTA. It is my fault only. I will feel easy once she settles down.

DEEPAK. Auntie ji, I want to continue to meet your daughter. You must help me.

SHANTA. I also want you to meet her and–and take her to meet your parents.

DEEPAK. But you know she won't. She has been avoiding my calls ever since we last met. Only you can help now.

SHANTA. Tell me what you want me to do and I will do it. How can I help?

DEEPAK. I don't know. By telling me what is worrying you about your daughter. There is something that you are not telling me.

> *Pause.*

DEEPAK. Trust me.

SHANTA. Promise me you won't tell her anything.

DEEPAK. You have nothing to fear.

Pause.

SHANTA. She tells me she is going some place, and she . . . Oh, why should I, her own mother, say all this to you? You will not like her then.

DEEPAK. I am here to help Mala, believe me.

SHANTA. About a month ago, she told me she was going on Holi for a picnic to Palam Vihar with her office friends. But the next day, I overheard her talking on the phone to her office friend that she had to spend Holi with me. Why? Why should she tell lies? To her friend and to me? As if I could stop her from going anywhere . . . She keeps on telling me lies. Sometimes she repeats the same lies, as if she does not care if I know she is lying . . . But please don't think bad of her. There are times when she is at home early from work and spends the whole evening reading magazines. She feels very restless then. That is when we quarrel. She is fine when she has work, or when she goes out. That is why I feel sometimes, thank God she is going out. At least then she looks—happy. But I am her mother. I must worry about her. I pray for her. I never pray for myself. Only for her happiness.

Pause.

DEEPAK. I know where she was on Holi.

SHANTA. She told you?

DEEPAK. She was with me.

SHANTA. With you? Oh! I always think the worst. But why so much hiding?

DEEPAK. We met at a friend's party a couple of days earlier. She smiled at me and wanted to dance with me. We got talking about her work. I dropped her here that night and we arranged to spend Holi together as we were both free. We were seeing each other every day after that. Very soon I wanted to meet you right away. But somehow, she didn't want it. She has other plans. God alone knows what they are. Last

Monday she told me in no uncertain terms that she . . . *(Shrugs his shoulders.)* I just don't understand it. What did I do wrong?

SHANTA *(thinking about something else)*. Monday?

Shanta opens the book once again.

SHANTA. She bought some magazines that evening. She was very depressed. She . . . There is something else.

Shanta gets up.

SHANTA. One minute. I will get it for you.

Shanta exits to another room.

Pause.

The phone rings. Deepak answers the phone.

DEEPAK. Hello?

A long pause as there is no response.

Shanta enters with a calendar. She looks at Deepak on the phone.

SHANTA. Who is it?

Shanta hands him the calendar and takes the phone.

Deepak looks at the calendar.

SHANTA *(on the phone)*. Hello?

DEEPAK *(looking at the calendar)*. There's a cross on last Monday's date!

SHANTA *(terrified, her pitch rising)*. Mala! . . . No. No! I tried to but he just came in! Mala! Please! I will tell him to go away! I will tell him to go away right now! . . . No. Don't say that! Come home! Mala please come home!

Deepak stares at the calendar. He flips the pages backwards and looks at the previous months.

Shanta sobs as she puts down the phone.

The music builds up.

SHANTA. Please go away. Please go away!

Black out.

Mala's voice on tape as before.

MALA. I don't know why. I just don't understand . . . Please don't ask me why I do it. It's just a game . . . not a game. No . . . it's . . . I know it's wrong. What I am doing is terribly wrong! But it means a lot to me. I like it. That is why I am a bad person. I have no character . . . I suppose it's these Western values, I wish I were more traditional then I wouldn't behave like this . . . no, no, that's stupid, I know, that's very easy to put the blame elsewhere . . . *(Listening to the counsellor.)* It has to end in a month's time. In fact I like it best when I can time it so it lasts for thirty days. I even mark it on my calendar. After that, I have to—move on, if you know what I mean . . . Well it means that it is no longer satisfying to me, and I don't mean the physical part of it, although that is usually the main attraction for me . . . not that I actually enjoy it when they are doing it to me . . . sometimes I do, with the right kind of people . . . the right kind of people are, let me see . . . usually older men thought not necessarily so, Deepak my fiancé, is only a few years older to me . . . I think I like it—I don't know how to put it . . . When they—sort of—you know—use me . . . *(Listening to the counsellor.)* I don't know. I can't explain it. The only person who can, who could have prevented all this is my mother. Sometimes I wish she would just tell me to stop. She could have prevented a lot from happening . . . Here are all the names of people whom I have been with. And the outline . . . well I just wanted a line that would put them all altogether. But if you ask me, whose face I think it is—it must be my mother's.

> *Lights come on a party in progress. Music. The man is seen talking to someone on his right. In the far corner, Mala is on her cell phone. She is dressed provocatively but not flashy or revealing. Although the room is full of people, we only see Mala and the man.*
>
> *Night.*

MALA. Hmm. I am not so sure whether it works.

Mala is talking to someone, presumably a colleague. She has her back to the Man who is talking with someone else.

MALA. To start with, I don't think she should be skipping rope with her daughter. That's not real freedom. It is still very gender constructed . . . If you ask me she should be playing cricket with her daughter and husband. You have to say it all in fifteen seconds. The important point is her physical ease and freedom. Start with her batting. A perfect hit. She makes two runs with her daughter. Then show her bowling while her husband is batting. He makes a snide remark about her being irritable because it is that time of the month. She bowls, hits him straight in the crotch. He runs yelping in to the house. She tosses the ball in the air. Freeze. Caption. A hit always. Perfectly in control, all through the month. Cloud 9—Sanitary napkins. That's enough . . . Oh, sure we could work on it together. I will come in early tomorrow. Okay? And one more thing—go easy on the cigarettes. *(Digging out her cell phone.)* Excuse me, I have to make a call.

Mala walks to a corner while she waits for someone to answer it. She stops, stunned for a while to hear Deepak's voice first and then her mother's.

MALA *(on the phone).* How could you let him in the house? What did I tell you? Why can't you just do what I tell you to do? I am not coming home! If I go away somewhere it will be your fault!

Mala puts her cell phone in her bag, takes a deep breath, and clears her mind of the conversation with her mother. She looks around and notices the man. Mala walks up to the man and stands next to him. The man as Ravi is wearing a business suit. He wears gold rimmed glasses. He notices her standing there. Their eyes meet. She looks directly at him with her eyes wide open almost in fear. She can't help but give the impression she is interested in the man.

MAN. Hi. Haven't we met before?

MALA *(not at all as articulate as before)*. I–I am Mala.

MAN *(smiling)*. The Bronze Beauty Campaign, right?

MALA. Right.

MAN. You deserved the IAAFA award. One of the best campaigns I have come across in my years in advertising. You are a genius.

MALA *(almost as if he has offended her)*. Shall we talk about something else apart from work? *(At once apologetic.)* I am sorry I didn't mean . . .

MAN. Oh don't be. We are at a party, so why talk shop . . . *(Changing the subject.)* Oh this is my fiancé, Radhika. *(To Radhika.)* This is Mala. One of our most . . . *(Checking himself.)* She is with our Delhi creative department.

MALA. Hello . . . Oh! This is my favourite tune.

Mala looks straight at the man. Her eyes telling him to dance with her.

MAN. Would you—like to dance?

MALA. I am not so sure, whether . . . If it is okay with you Radhika. *(Rising.)* Thanks . . . Would you mind my bag for me please? . . . Thanks.

Ravi leads Mala on to the dance floor. They move to the centre of the space. Ravi holds her, casting a quick glance in Radhika's direction. They dance.

MAN. You dance very well.

MALA. No, I don't. You are saying that just to please me.

MAN. No. Not at all–I–Oh yeah sure. I could teach you the salsa some time . . . So I hear a lot of things about you.

MALA. Oh.

MAN. From the office. Rahul was telling me . . . You have been with him for some time I think.

MALA *(sighing)*. So how long are you going to be in town?

MAN. For about a month I guess.

MALA. Perfect.

MAN. Huh?

MALA. How long have you known Radhika?

MAN. For about five years. We will be married in a few months. But–I would like to get to know you better.

MALA. Hold me closer.

The man moves closer to her, his arm slipping from her back closer to her waist.

MAN. Yes . . . You have a nice body.

MALA. Thank you.

They look at each other.

MALA. Hold me closer.

They dance for a while, with the man exploring her back more with his hand when it is away from Radhika's line of vision.

MAN. Look why don't I take Radhika home and you could— you know—come over to my hotel tomorrow? For a drink. Hmmm?

MALA. Take me to your room with you now.

MAN. No. No . . . I–I can't. I am with her tonight.

MALA *(pleading, looking up at him to be kissed)*. Do whatever you want with me, but take me with you now.

MAN. No, don't get too close. Later okay. Oh my God! She is coming here.

The man breaks away abruptly as Radhika presumably pulls them apart.

MAN. Radhika, no! I was just being polite and dancing with her.

Mala stands to one side humiliated.

MAN. I am sorry I . . . Look, don't be angry with me. She was

leading me on. I swear it was her fault. What could I do?
Radhika!

*The man follows Radhika in a hurry without even a
glance at Mala. Mala follows head held down like a
schoolgirl caught in the act. She looks around at all the
people who are staring at her. Mala fights her tears.
She covers her face, picks up her bag and leaves.*

Fade to the living room.

Later.

*Mala walks from the party area into the living room
area. The music fades out. Mala unlocks the door and
lets herself in. She drops her bag on the sofa and
stands there for a while, not knowing what to do. She
sits on the sofa and stares into space. The lights come
on and Shanta enters.*

MALA. What do you want?

SHANTA. Have you eaten? Shall I make some roti for you?

MALA. No. I am not hungry.

SHANTA *(whining)*. Eat something, no.

MALA *(sharp)*. Go to sleep! Go!

Shanta begins to leave, switching off some lights.

MALA. What did he say to you?

SHANTA. The man wanted extra money, I gave him.

MALA. I mean the man you let inside my house. The man I told
you not to let inside the house! What did he say to you about
me?

SHANTA. I don't remember. Please I have a headache.

MALA. You forget! As usual. You forget what you don't want
to deal with!

SHANTA. Please, Mala, I am not feeling well.

MALA. I don't care if you are not feeling well, mummy. Because
I don't know whether you are telling the truth or simply trying
to escape as always. What did he tell you?

Shanta turns to the portrait of Shri Krishna and does not respond to Mala's question.

MALA. Stop looking at that picture!

SHANTA *(still looking at the picture)*. He told me he wanted to marry you.

MALA. Always staring at that picture whenever you want to avoid something.

SHANTA. That boy wants to marry you.

MALA. One of these days I will throw that picture out of the house.

SHANTA *(looking at her, mildly)*. But you are the one avoiding the subject now.

MALA *(staring at her)*. I don't want to marry him.

SHANTA. No. You will have to. This is like my prayers have been answered. All these years I have been waiting for this. I have always listened to you for everything, but this. You must say yes.

MALA. I won't.

SHANTA. Why? He is such a nice boy and from a family we know. What more do you want? What more can anyone ask for?

MALA. I have my reasons.

SHANTA. What reasons?

MALA. I won't tell you . . . I don't have to tell you anything. Go to bed.

SHANTA. You can tell me what is troubling you. I am always there for you.

MALA. That's not true. You are never there . . . You never have been.

SHANTA. What have I done to deserve this?

MALA. You don't want me to tell you that, do you?

SHANTA. Please tell me where I have gone wrong so I can say sorry to you.

MALA. You forget. You forget so easily.

SHANTA. No. That is not true! Why are you punishing me like this?

MALA. It is true. It did happen, but you never believed me.

SHANTA (turning away). I don't know what you are talking about. I will prepare alu paratha for you tomorrow, you always like that for breakfast.

MALA. That is how you always pacified me and that is how I know that you believe me, deep down. Oh yes, you would remember that I always like alu parathas because that's what I got whenever I came to you, hurt and crying. Instead of listening to what I had to say, you stuffed me with food. I couldn't speak because I was being fed all the time, and you know what? I began to like them. I thought that was the cure for my pain. That if I ate till I was stuffed, the pain would go away. Every time I came to you mummy, you were ready with something to feed me. You knew. Otherwise you wouldn't have been so prepared. You knew all along what was happening to me, and I won't ever let you forget that!

SHANTA (turning to the portrait). I put myself at the feet of my God. He knows what I am going through. Only my Krishna knows . . .

MALA. That is the trouble! (Going to her.) That has always been the trouble! You were never there for me. You were too busy (Pointing to the portrait, saying the word with contempt.) praying!

　　Shanta closes her eyes and begins to pray.

MALA. For what? And for whom? Surely not for me! . . . (Yelling.) Stop praying! . . . I said stop that! (Turning Shanta around.) Look at me!

SHANTA. Go away! Go away or tell me what you want from me!

MALA. It's no use now. You should have said that twenty years ago!

SHANTA. Why this punishment? Why this punishment because you fell down the stairs and broke your leg?

Mala stares at her.

SHANTA. It is my fault that I should have simply asked you where it hurt and kissed you, put you in my lap and rocked you to sleep singing a lori. Instead I gave you sweets and went to my pooja. That is my fault.

MALA. I cannot believe it. I simply cannot believe that . . . Do you really think that is what I am talking about? Ask yourself honestly. Tell me if you honestly believe that is what I am talking about. Tell me. No don't look at your God, look at me, look me in the eye and tell me—'yes, that is all that you are talking about'.

SHANTA *(looking at her with a wide-eyed innocence).* What else are you talking about?

MALA. Ma, I am talking about what I had told you five years ago, but you said it wasn't true, it couldn't be true. But now I know that you want to believe it is not true.

SHANTA. Five years ago? You didn't tell me anything . . .

MALA. Five years ago, six years ago, I can't remember exactly when! We were in the kitchen and we were talking about that rape case that was in the papers. You said something about children also not being safe. Don't you remember anything at all? Then I told you about—what happened to me. But you changed the subject. At that time I wondered . . . Is it just me? Did I imagine it all? Surely not. No. It did happen.

SHANTA. Mala, I don't remember. Please forgive me. Maybe I said something in my foolish way and you took it seriously.

MALA. No. No, ma. I think it was the other way round. I said something serious and you took it lightly. Yes, yes I am sure you did that deliberately.

SHANTA. No, no Mala. Just forget all these bad dreams and . . .

MALA. I am not talking about a bad dream! I am talking about the time when uncle Vinay would molest me. When I was seven. Then eight. Nine. Ten. Every vacation when we went to visit him or when he came to stay with us. You were busy in either the pooja room or the kitchen. I would go to papa and cry. Before I could even tell him why I was crying he would tell me to go to you. You always fed me and—and you never said it but I knew what you were saying to me without words. That I should eat well and go to sleep and the pain will go away. And, and—Oh God! It did go away. But it comes back. It didn't go away for ever!

SHANTA *(really puzzled)*. Mala, my daughter. What all have you been thinking all these years? You have always been so bold and frank. But sometimes, you tell stories.

MALA. This is not a story I made up and you know it.

SHANTA. If it were true I would have said something. Now go to sleep and we will talk about this boy Deepak tomorrow. Such a good family he is from . . .

MALA *(screaming)*. Listen to me!

Shanta covers her ears more for the scream than not wanting to listen to her.

MALA. No. No . . . It is so easy for you, because you can hide behind *(Pointing to the picture.)* This! Just forget what you don't want to know and then pray. I won't let you get off so easily. There is only one way I can make you listen to me. By taking this away from you!

Mala takes down the portrait. Shanta tries to prevent her.

SHANTA. Mala, what are you doing? Please don't! No, no, don't—

MALA. I can't let you hide behind this all the time!

SHANTA *(hanging on to the portrait)*. I will do anything you say, but leave my Krishna alone!

MALA. Let me go—!

SHANTA. Please, no!

Mala finally manages to break free and takes the painting to the main door.

SHANTA *(aghast).* What are you doing? NO!

Mala flings the painting out of the door. We hear a crash and the breaking of glass. Shanta rushes out. Mala is slowly regaining her composure. She sits down on the sofa. Shanta re-enters with the portrait and the pieces of glass on the portrait. She begins to cry.

MALA. I am sorry, Ma. If I had done that a long time ago . . . Then maybe . . .

SHANTA. You don't know what you have done. You don't know what you have done!

Shanta places the portrait on a table and turns to look at Mala.

SHANTA *(going to Mala).* Yes. Yes, I remember now.

MALA. It's okay. We don't have to talk about it if you don't want to.

SHANTA. No, no. I want to talk. I remember, but what I remember is not what you remember. I had forgotten it, but now . . .

MALA. It doesn't matter now. I just have to learn to live with the pain.

SHANTA. Not just the pain. I remember, much as I was trying to forget, what I saw. Not when you were seven but when you were thirteen. *(Gently.)* Please don't misunderstand me, Mala. I remember, seeing you with my brother during the summer holidays. You were pushing yourself on him in the bedroom.

MALA. No! That's not true!

SHANTA. I remember, Mala. You want me to remember? You were telling him to kiss you.

MALA. No.

SHANTA. To touch you.

MALA. I didn't—

SHANTA. To pinch your—breasts.

MALA. Stop it!

SHANTA. You were forcing him to say things to you.

MALA. Stop it, I said!

SHANTA. To do things to you.

MALA. I did not! I did not!

SHANTA. That is why I forget. I went to the kitchen to vomit. Then I prayed. I prayed for you Mala. *(Pointing to the portrait.)* That is what I was praying to. To our God, so He could send his Sudarshan Chakra to defend you, to defend us from the demon inside you, not outside you. But you wouldn't let me. You don't let me.

MALA *(crying)*. No!

SHANTA. I remember other things also. When your cousin, your father's nephew came for his holidays.

MALA. He made the advances. He found out from uncle . . .

SHANTA. No Mala!

MALA. Why don't you believe me? He told me that I was uncle's reference! Those were his words! 'Your uncle Vinay has given me your reference!' Uncle told him, Ma! I didn't do or say anything to him. He came to my room! Once he said uncle's name, I just couldn't stop him!

SHANTA. Why should you stop him? You were enjoying it. Your cousin told me in private that he was concerned about you, that I should not send you out of the house.

MALA. That was after! He told you that after he molested me!

SHANTA. But Mala, I have seen it with my own eyes. You enjoyed it. You were an average child but you had my brother and your cousins dancing around you. That is what you wanted. Yes! How can I forget? I am trying to forget, please help me forget.

   Silence.

MALA *(quietly)*. Yes. You are right.

SHANTA. And please don't talk about trying to forget the pain . . . Try to forget the pleasure.

MALA. That is part of the pain, Ma. The pleasure is part of the pain. *(Composing herself.)* I–I will try, Ma. I can only try.

SHANTA. I forget. I forget everything. Be like me.

MALA. Yes.

SHANTA. You have been a very bad girl, you have gone astray. But Krishna will show you the way.

MALA. Yes, Ma.

SHANTA. And please meet that boy Deepak. I will invite his father next week to come and see you.

Mala looks at her helplessly.

SHANTA. That is the only way. Krishna has sent him for you.

Mala nods. Mala gets up.

SHANTA. And Mala . . . Don't say anything about all this to him. You understand? If I had known what those marks on your calendar meant, I would not have shown it to him. You are lucky he is so understanding. But this . . . nobody will forgive this. God help us if his father comes to know . . . This is your only chance.

MALA. How can I hide all this from him if I am to marry him, Ma?

SHANTA. If you forget it ever happened, then you won't have anything to hide.

The two women look at each other. Mala straightens up.

MALA *(speaking sharply as before).* Go to sleep. I don't want you complaining that I keep you up all night.

SHANTA *(subservient as before, switching off the lights).* Yes, Mala.

MALA *(exiting).* Where are the magazines that I had ordered?

SHANTA *(exiting).* In your room, Mala . . .

Fade to:

Music. A restaurant. Mala walks slowly from the living room area on to the special area, which is now a restaurant. Deepak is seated. He rises when he sees her. They sit down. The music fades out.

DEEPAK. Thank you for seeing me.

MALA *(formal)*. You are welcome.

DEEPAK. What will you have?

MALA. Just a coffee, please.

DEEPAK *(signalling to a waiter)*. One more coffee over here, please. *(Sipping his coffee, which is mimed.)* Are you okay?

MALA. Yes. I think.

DEEPAK. So what's with the thirty-day affairs?

MALA. I am not sure you will understand.

DEEPAK. I want to understand. Make me understand.

The Man walks in and sits at a table. Deepak ignores him. He is wearing a T-shirt and jeans, and a cap.

MALA. You know I have been . . . around.

DEEPAK. I gathered from your calendar. That was some collection of ticks, crosses and names.

MALA. Why do you like me? Why?

DEEPAK. You are talented, beautiful, intelligent, honest. You have a rare gift of honesty. I have yet to meet a person as honest as you. Mala, I am a very patient man. I am willing to do what it takes to win your trust and to get to know the real person in you.

MALA *(unmoved)*. I don't know. I should feel something, right? I should be thrilled. But I am not. It doesn't mean a thing to me.

DEEPAK. Then what do you want? What is it that you want the most?

The waiter presumably serves her coffee. Mala looks up. At the same time the Man catches the waiter's eye and gestures for the waiter to go to him.

MALA. Did you see that?

DEEPAK. What?

MALA. The man over there.

DEEPAK. What about him?

MALA. He was staring at my breasts.

Deepak is angry. He gets up and goes to the Man.

MALA *(startled)*. Deepak, no!

DEEPAK *(to Man)*. Excuse me.

MAN *(looking up)*. Huh?

Mala goes to Deepak and holds him by the arm.

DEEPAK. Were you staring at my girlfriend?

MAN *(horrified at the thought)*. No! That's not true!

MALA *(pulling him)*. Deepak let's go.

MAN. How dare you insult me like that?

DEEPAK. She said you were staring at her and that's good enough for me to know that you were.

MAN. Well, she is mistaken or she is lying.

Deepak raises his fist. The Man rises.

MALA *(shouting)*. I made that up!

Deepak looks at her.

MALA *(taking Deepak back to their table)*. I made it up. Sit down.

The Man walks out of the restaurant in a huff. Deepak sits down, taken aback.

DEEPAK. Did you say that just to avoid trouble?

MALA. No. He wasn't staring at me . . . I wanted him to . . . You want to know what I feel most? . . . If he had looked at me, I would have felt–I would have felt–truly alive.

Pause.

Deepak throws his hands up in despair.

DEEPAK. This is just too . . . This can't go on. It just can't go on.

MALA. I told you so. I know it won't work between us.

DEEPAK. No. It won't work between us because you are not even trying. Can't you at least try? Do something about it?

MALA. What do you want me to do? I am being honest with you about what I feel, but what can I do?

DEEPAK. I don't know. See a psychiatrist or somebody.

MALA. I am not mentally ill or anything . . .

DEEPAK. But you do need help.

MALA *(sighing)*. Maybe. Maybe, you are right.

Freeze. Slow fade out while the tape plays the same conversation as the first. Except this time, the sound is processed almost to a point of distortion. Some of the key words reverberate so they overlap over each other.

MALA'S VOICE. Today is the 30th of September . . . 2001, and my name is *(Reverberate 'name is'.)* . . . I don't think I want to say my name . . . I am sorry. *(Reverberate 'sorry'.)* I hope that is okay with you . . . I am unsure about this . . . and a lot of other things. But this . . . This is the first time you see that I . . . *(Reverberate 'first time'.)* I know it is all my fault really . . . *(Reverberate 'my fault' almost till the end of the tape.)* It must be. I must have asked for it . . . Somehow, I just seem to be made for it. Maybe I was born that way, maybe . . . This is what I am meant for. It's not anybody's fault, except my own. Sometimes I wish that my mother . . . I am sorry but . . .

Spot on Shanta in the prayer room.

Music

MALA'S VOICE. I can only tell you more if you turn this thing off.

The tape continues to hiss for a while. The lights brighten on Shanta as the music builds up. Quick black out.

End of Act One.

ACT II

The counsellor's office as in the first scene. Mala is seated in exactly the same spot in the same clothes as in scene one. In fact it is a continuation of that session. However, this conversation is interspersed with Mala's voice on tape four years ago. The doll is not visible in this scene, and there is no black out during Mala's voice on tape except at the end. The focus stays on the confident new Mala even when the tape is playing.

MALA *(self-assured and easy)*. I feel I want to tell it to people who would understand. It's like starting all over again. It's like you never had those scars.

MALA'S VOICE ON TAPE . . . My father left us, for another woman . . . I feel if I were more lovable he would have at least visited us . . . We continue to get money from him every month, and he pays the rent . . . but I haven't seen him in fifteen years . . . I . . . don't think my mother and he got along—that way. Again, because of me . . .

MALA. It's like taking off the bandages on your face after a bloody car crash that left your face all scarred beyond recognition, as if you didn't have a face at all. To wake up after many many years, as if from a coma . . . And to let the bandages come off . . . and suddenly discover a whole new face again. All of a sudden you feel that you are—entitled to life.

MALA'S VOICE ON TAPE. I have been so bad, I can't tell you where to begin! It's not just the men in the office I told you about, but before . . . much before! I—Oh God! I–I seduced my uncle when I was thirteen! I—slept with my cousin—and—anyone who was available . . . No, there is nothing to tell about my uncle, forget all that, please help me stop this behaviour.

MALA. I can smile again. I can be a little girl, again. Not again, but for the first time. At thirty plus I am the little girl I never was. I want to see movies, taste ice cream. Really taste it, feel the high from the sugar. Tell the difference between flavours.

I hear sounds I never cared to hear before—birds, temple bells . . . My senses are working again. I can touch this chair and feel the chair touch me. My whole body can feel! And for the first time I enjoyed sex. Truly enjoyed it for its tactile pleasure. Not as a craving for some kind of approval. I came alive and experienced what it means to be really loved. And for once I could look at Deepak in the eyes and say 'I love you' to him and believe it when he says the same to me.

Fade to black. Mala's voice on tape as before. The light comes up on the doll once again.

MALA'S VOICE *(she cries).* My uncle just went away. He left me. He said he was disgusted with me—my behaviour. He never returned . . . But now he is coming back. He is coming home . . . Please understand he is not a bad person or anything like that . . . I am so confused, I don't know what I feel for him . . . I know you are not supposed to tell me what I am to do, I am to figure that out for myself, right?

Fade in:

The living room. Shanta brings in two cups of tea. Mala is flipping through a magazine. Shanta places Mala's cup of tea in front of her. Shanta sits at the far end of the sofa with her tea, sipping it nervously. The nervousness spreads to Mala. She too sips her tea nervously.

SHANTA *(after a while).* He will be here for two days.

MALA. Maybe I should leave now.

SHANTA. If it is getting late for you . . .

MALA. No. It's okay. I can wait for a while.

SHANTA. There is no need. You can meet him in the evening.

MALA. You said he is coming to Delhi on work.

SHANTA. Yes.

MALA. Can't his company put him up in a hotel?

SHANTA. Mala . . . You said it was all right for him to stay with us. So—I told him to stay here.

MALA. Oh. Yes, yes. It is perfectly all right. There's no need to—avoid anybody.

SHANTA. Yes. After all, he has helped us so much after your father left us.

MALA. In what way has he helped us?

SHANTA. If you have finished with those magazines, I can give them to the ruddi wallah today.

MALA. I hate it when you avoid answering questions! What way has he helped us?

SHANTA. I don't know . . .

MALA. Tell me!

SHANTA *(looking away, more nervous than before)*. Mala, I am sorry I should have told you but . . . The money that we kept receiving after your father left us was from your uncle.

MALA. And father? Didn't he send us anything at all?

SHANTA. Nothing.

MALA. No communication from him?

Shanta shakes her head.

MALA. But you pretended it came from him. You lied. *(Imitating her.)* Oh look! Daddy has sent us some extra money for Diwali. He wanted to come to your school day celebration but he has sent you some money for a new dress for you! *(Shrugging it off.)* Oh what does it matter? It doesn't make a difference to me. *(Getting up.)* I don't think I am going to wait for him.

Mala walks to pick up her bag.

SHANTA. I lied for you. So that you will feel that your father was thinking about you.

MALA *(stopping)*. Oh no. Oh I won't let you get away with that. You know why he left us. So don't try to pretend you tried very hard to show me that he loved me, but at the same time giving me the impression that actually he didn't. He left you not me. I know he didn't care about me, but he didn't leave because of me. He left because of you. You didn't love him.

The only reason you shared my room was because you didn't want to sleep with him. All night long I had to listen to your mumbling saying you didn't want him near you. You didn't want him touching you. You even moved that horrible picture of your god into my room saying he will protect us . . . I remember daddy's last words to me. You know what he said. He said to me 'I married a frozen woman'. A frozen woman. So don't try to tell me that you were concerned about me by hiding the truth. The only truth you want to hide is your failure as a wife and a mother.

Shanta gets up slowly and begins to leave.

MALA. Am I right?

SHANTA. I have to wash the clothes and change the sheets.

MALA. I am right.

SHANTA *(turning around)*. Yes. You are right. I may not be a good wife or mother. But at least I am a good servant.

Shanta picks up the tea cups.

SHANTA. I have my God and that is enough for me. Krishna knows what all I have gone through. He knows.

The Man enters, as Vinay. He is dressed in a business shirt and tie, with his coat slung casually over his shoulders or over his arm. He carries an overnight bag. He notices Shanta and ignores Mala.

MAN. Hello Shanta! How are you?

He goes to Shanta and pats her on the arm.

MALA *(under her breath)*. Uncle!

The Man turns around to her.

MAN. Hello, Mala. Off somewhere. *(Turning back to Shanta.)* So how have you been my dear sister?

Mala walks towards him slowly.

MALA. No. I–I . . .

Mala turns around quickly and exits through the main door. Shanta looks in the direction of Mala. Music. Black out.

ACT III

The living room. The Man enters with a shirt in his hand.

MAN. Shanta!

Shanta enters from the kitchen.

SHANTA. Yes? Dinner will be ready in half an hour.

MAN *(tossing the shirt at her)*. I was just wondering whether you could iron this shirt for me. You know how I have always been hopeless at these things.

SHANTA. I will do it tonight.

MAN. I hate to trouble you two like this.

SHANTA. No trouble, bhaiya.

MAN. That is the only reason why I stay in a hotel when I am in Delhi.

SHANTA. You sit and read or watch TV. I will take care of it afterwards.

MAN. But why did you ask me to stay with you?

SHANTA. I told you. About Deepak.

MAN. Yes. Finally! I was getting worried about that girl.

SHANTA. Sit down, Vinay bhaiya.

The Man sits down. Shanta joins him.

MAN *(innocent)*. What is it?

SHANTA. Nothing. I just want to tell you that I want this to go through.

MAN. You mean, Deepak and Mala?

SHANTA. Yes. This is her only chance.

MAN. Yes I understand.

SHANTA. So, I want you also to help. By meeting the boy and his parents. It will be of help. They knew her father very well you see and I don't want that coming in the way . . .

MAN. Shanta, you know you can always rely on my help. That is nothing. Isn't she like my daughter also?

Shanta looks at him. The Man continues regardless.

MAN. Think nothing of it. I shall play the dutiful uncle tomorrow at dinner. In fact, I should interview the boy and see if he is suitable for our Mala. Isn't that right?

No response from Shanta. The Man waves his hand in front of her face.

MAN. You are off again. Ever since I can recall you simply start dreaming whenever . . . *(Making light of it.)* Remember when we were small, you would simply vanish into your own world . . . like when we were having dinner and you nearly choked. If I didn't know the Heimlich manoeuvre from school, God alone knows . . .

He looks at her. Shanta is staring at the spot where the painting was.

SHANTA *(as if it is a matter of grave concern).* I forgot to get the glass fixed.

The Man goes to where the picture is on the table. Lightning. Lights dim. Deepak's flat. Thunder can be heard at a distance. The lights come on to this side of the stage which is Deepak's living room. The lights also remain on the Man and Shanta. It is important the two scenes are played simultaneously without dimming or raising the lights. Mala's voice is heard, with the doorbell.

MALA *(offstage).* Deepak!

Banging on a door. Deepak enters slipping on a T-shirt. He is in pyjamas. He opens the door and lets her in.

DEEPAK. Are you all right?

MALA. I don't know. Can I stay with you?

DEEPAK. Of course. Come in. Can I make you some coffee?

Mala shakes her head sitting down. We see the Man examining the picture.

MALA. I–I don't know where to go!

The Man holds up the shards that are still on the picture.

MAN. How did this happen?

Deepak sits next to Mala.

MALA. Can I stay here?

SHANTA. What? Oh that. The picture just—fell down.

DEEPAK. Trust me Mala and tell me what is bothering you.

MAN. How can it just fall down? You must have pushed it while cleaning it.

MALA. Let's call it off, Deepak.

SHANTA. It's my fault. Yes.

DEEPAK. You are not giving yourself a chance. You are not giving me a chance.

MAN. You are too hard on yourself. It's nobody's fault.

DEEPAK. Help me connect with you!

Mala simply stares at him.

MAN. I will put these pieces aside for now. Be sure that the koodawali takes them away tomorrow.

Man begins to pick the pieces carefully off the picture and put them aside.

MALA. I am scared.

DEEPAK. Of what? Of whom?

MAN. I am glad you still have this picture. A memory of our mother.

MALA. I am scared to be home. I don't want to be home. Anywhere but home!

Lightning.

MAN. It's going to rain.

SHANTA. Yes.

Thunder.

DEEPAK. You can't go home anyway if it rains again. Why don't you stay here? I will fetch you a blanket. Hmm?

As Deepak gets up, Mala pulls him back.

MAN. There. Do you want me to put the picture back where it was?

SHANTA. Over there.

The Man puts the picture back on the wall.

MALA. There was a man following me.

MAN. There. No one can tell it's broken. But you better put the glass back soon.

MALA. I cannot stop them! I attract them.

DEEPAK. This is all in your mind.

MALA. You don't understand! I am doing something that attracts them to me.

MAN *(sitting down)*. What is the matter? Is something wrong?

MALA. I want to. I want them to come to me.

DEEPAK. No. No you don't.

MALA. It is true. If I were to let that man in to my house, I will allow him to do anything.

DEEPAK. Mala. I met your counsellor yesterday.

MALA. What, what did she say?

DEEPAK. She didn't talk to me about you. She said that's confidential.

MALA. Then why did you go there?

DEEPAK. For myself. To find out how I can help you . . . Are you upset because your uncle is visiting you?

MALA. No. No. What has he got to do with anything?

MAN. Why are you so silent?

SHANTA. Vinay bhaiya, I am worried . . .

MAN. About Mala? Don't worry. I will handle it all.

DEEPAK. I did mention this to the counsellor, just a hunch you see . . . She said nothing, but I could tell . . .

SHANTA. She is–she–how can I say? How can I say anything?

MAN. I think I know what you are trying to say.

MALA *(avoiding talking about her uncle)*. No. It's not my uncle. It's my mother.

MAN. Is it me? Is it something to do with me?

Shanta stares at him, clutching the cushion.

MALA. It's her. She doesn't want to see me happy.

DEEPAK. Why do you think that?

MAN. Tell me. Has it anything to do with me?

SHANTA. No!

MALA. She told you about my affairs, didn't she?

SHANTA. It's my fault. I should be more strict with Mala.

DEEPAK. I sort of got it out of her. Believe me she wasn't willing to talk.

SHANTA. It is so easy to slip into bad ways. I wish she would listen to me.

MALA. I wish she wouldn't be so lost in her religion. I wish she had been there for me!

DEEPAK. I am here for you now and yet you make yourself inaccessible to me.

MAN. If there is any way I can help, just let me know.

SHANTA. Yes.

MALA. It's no use. I don't want you coming closer.

DEEPAK *(offering his hand)*. Hold my hand.

MALA. You don't understand. You just don't understand!

MAN. I am waiting. How may I help?

DEEPAK. Hold my hand. Forget everything and just touch me.

MALA. I–I can't. I don't want to. I can't!

SHANTA. Just make sure that the marriage happens. Just be there as if you were her father.

MAN. I have always been there like a father for her, in spite of everything.

Lightning. Spot on Shanta, lost in the photograph.

Mala slowly and very hesitantly reaches out to hold Deepak's hand. As she holds his hand . . .

Thunder.

The Man quickly enters their area. There is something very furtive in his eye movement and a sense of conspiracy in his tone of voice. It is not sexual but somehow urgent as if the job has to be done secretly and quickly. His gaze is fixed on Mala, except for his furtive glances. He exists only for Mala and not for Deepak.

DEEPAK. You see? It wasn't that difficult.

MAN. Touch me here.

Mala withdraws her hand sharply, frightened.

MAN. You don't love your uncle?

DEEPAK. What's wrong?

MAN. You don't love your uncle, hmmm?

DEEPAK. Try it one more time.

MAN. Quickly before someone sees you. Touch.

DEEPAK. Please for my sake.

MAN. You said you loved me in front of mummy and daddy. Come on! Show it!

Mala hesitantly holds Deepak's hand.

DEEPAK. Thank you.

MAN. There! You feel that? It means I love you. Your uncle loves you.

Mala begins to cry.

DEEPAK *(stroking her hand gently).* It's okay. It's okay. Cry if you want to.

MAN. Shhh! Don't cry. You want to come here in your holidays, no? Then don't cry. This is your seventh birthday, no? You are seven now. Ready for a real birthday present. Lie down. Come on, quickly.

DEEPAK. Look into my eyes.

MAN. If they hear you they will say you are a bad girl. This is our secret. *(Like an order but in a whisper.)* Don't cry!

Mala restrains herself from crying as if someone will hear her.

DEEPAK *(kneeling beside her).* Let go and trust me!

Mala begins to cry again, silently, looking at Deepak terrified.

DEEPAK. Sit back and relax.

MAN. Hold your frock up. Up over your face! Shut up!

DEEPAK. Relax and look into my eyes. I am not going to harm you.

MAN. I won't hurt you I promise.

DEEPAK. Talk to me. Help me to help you.

MAN. Help me and I will love you more than your mummy or daddy.

DEEPAK. Please!

MAN. I said I am not going to hurt you, stop crying! Shhh!!

DEEPAK. I love you.

MAN. Think of your school. Be still and put your arms up, come on. Yeees! What did you learn in school today? Hmmm? What? Tell me.

DEEPAK *(massaging her arm gently, looking into her eyes)*. You want to be loved but you must trust me.

MAN. Very good. Then sing it. Come on. Sing. Sing!

DEEPAK. You are beautiful.

Deepak embraces her and rocks her as if she is a baby, in a non-sexual way.

MAN. Good. Good. Keep singing . . . Again, don't stop until I stop. See, I love you even though you are so ugly. Keep singing . . . Nobody will tell you how ugly you are. But you are good only for this . . . Only for this. See how much I love you. See . . . Now go away. Quickly.

MALA *(holding him tighter)*. No! Don't go away! Don't leave me!

DEEPAK. I won't. I won't.

Mala breaks away from Deepak and lies on the bed, taking her T-shirt over her head, so that her head is covered and her bra is revealed.

MAN *(now more moralistic than before, the furtiveness gone)*. You like it! You enjoy it. After four years, you have become a whore! At thirteen you are a whore!

MALA. I won't tell anyone. But don't leave me alone!

MAN. Bitch! Whore!

DEEPAK. Mala! No! That's no good! It's no good for you!

The Man leaves in a hurry even as the lights fade on them, but remain on Shanta and the picture.

Deepak pulls her T-shirt back in place and holds her face.

DEEPAK. Mala, you cannot abuse your body like this! I won't let you do it to yourself!

MALA. You don't understand! You cannot understand!

The Man comes back to Shanta's living room. Black out on Deepak and Mala.

MAN *(to Shanta, as if he has just said something important).* You always go into your own world when I have something important to say to you.

SHANTA. Huh?

MAN. I was saying, that I definitely will do my best to see that this marriage goes through. In spite of her loose ways . . . If only you had controlled her from the beginning. She has always been wayward. You know that.

SHANTA. Yes. I wish I had been more—careful.

Black out. Deepak's voice on tape plays in the black out.

DEEPAK'S VOICE. I really wish she would tell me what is on her mind. She doesn't trust me, and I find that very tiring. I am exhausted. I am ready to throw in the towel. If I tell her it's off she would simply look at me. She may not say a word but her eyes would tell me what she is thinking 'See. I told you it won't work. You are wasting your time with me. Go away and leave me alone'. But she doesn't want to be left alone. She seeks company. Desperately enough to offer sex in return. Does she really feel anything? I think she wants something else, I don't know what, she doesn't know what . . . it doesn't take our relationship anywhere though . . . I don't even exist for her. I–I am tired . . . *(Sighing.)* I will give it one last shot. I don't know about her uncle . . . I have a strong hunch . . . well if what I think is true, then . . . Well, there is only one way to find out . . .

Lights on. Lightning. The doll is fully visible now. We cannot see the doll's face, just its ragged limbs. The dress on the doll is lifted and pinned at the doll's forehead. The doll remains lit throughout the following scene.

A restaurant. Dinner in progress. Deepak and the Man sit opposite each other. Mala and Shanta sit next to each other. Mala is between her uncle and Shanta. Shanta is between Deepak and Mala.

Music in the background. Vivaldi's Four Seasons. *The cutlery and food are all mimed. Shanta and Deepak eat their tandoori roti with their fingers. Mala uses a fork occasionally. The Man uses a knife and fork for eating his chicken breast.*

MAN. . . . So, when I joined the IT industry, I was thinking of settling in the US. But the real stuff is happening right here.

DEEPAK. True. One can lead a better quality of life right here.

MAN. Yes. Also, we can live our lives the way we want to, without having to be Westernized.

DEEPAK. Yes. Good old Indian values. Where will we be without them?

MAN. In USA.

The Man laughs loudly at his own joke. Deepak laughs too. Shanta smiles. Mala sips her drink.

MAN *(pointing to Mala's empty glass)*. Waiter! Serve more wine here.

SHANTA. No. No. She has had enough.

MAN. You stick to your orange juice. Do you want another one?

SHANTA. No.

MAN. Then keep quiet.

MALA. It's okay, mummy.

MAN. See. She is a big girl now, as we can all see.

SHANTA. Bhaiya . . .

The Man puts his hand on Mala's shoulder and pats it first, then kneading it.

MAN. What? Have I said anything wrong? The whole world can see she is a big girl. What is there to hide?

Shanta shrinks and looks down at her plate. Mala straightens up.

MALA. Yes. I have been a big girl for fifteen years, uncle.

MAN. See. She can drink more wine.

The waiter presumably has come with more wine. Mala looks at him with a 'thank you'. The conversation does not stop for this.

DEEPAK. You really seem to be a man of this world, uncle. You don't mind me calling you uncle?

MAN. Not at all. If I am Mala's uncle, I can be your uncle, right?

DEEPAK. Right!

SHANTA *(muttering a prayer of thanks to herself)*. If everything goes right . . .

DEEPAK. Why shouldn't things go right? Things have been right so far, haven't they? Don't worry.

MAN *(pointing with his fork at Deepak)*. I like you. I like this young man.

DEEPAK. Things have been fine so far. We are all perfect.

Lightning, followed by thunder.

SHANTA. It will rain again tonight.

DEEPAK. You have a great mother and a great uncle.

MAN. Are you being sarcastic?

DEEPAK. As a matter of fact—yes.

MALA. Deepak, what are you getting at?

DEEPAK. Nothing my dear. Just a few questions that need answers over here.

MAN. Please explain.

DEEPAK. We all know that Mala has been seeing a counsellor. I have too, for her sake.

MAN. If you ask me that is not a good idea. These therapists try to create problems where there are none. It's their job. That is how they earn a living. They will say that, oh because her father left the family . . .

MALA. What has that . . .?

MAN *(restraining her with a raised hand)*. Then they will blame it all on her father, or her mother. That's what they always do—blame it on the parents and exploit the fact that most people carry some kind of resentment against their parents.

MALA. Just forget he ever brought it up.

DEEPAK. But there is one other person you haven't mentioned.

MALA. Stop it.

SHANTA. Deepak . . .

MAN. No, no. Let us talk about it, now that he has brought it up. If you mean that I have something to do with her depression, then you are wrong. Ask her. I have only given her love and attention, right from the start. I treat her like I would my own daughter.

DEEPAK. She isn't being treated for depression alone . . . It would be interesting to know what happened to her when she was a child. What kind of attention did you give her?

MAN. I am sure your therapist or whoever has set you up for this . . . No, no. It's okay. I understand. It is the fashionable thing to do, blaming whoever was closest to her. But you trust her mother at least. Ask her that question. She will tell you the truth.

MALA. Please! This is embarrassing. Stop it.

MAN *(to Shanta)*. Say something. They are insulting your own brother and you keep quiet.

DEEPAK. What do you have to say about this, auntie? Remember, the truth is important to me.

MALA. Stop it! Stop it or I will walk out of here.

DEEPAK. Darling, trust me.

MALA. No! I don't want this.

DEEPAK *(to Shanta)*. Do you have anything to say about this? Was Mala abused as a child?

Mala gets up to leave.

DEEPAK. I will take your departure and your mother's silence to mean that I have my answer to that question.

Mala stops and turns to Shanta.

MALA. Tell him, Ma.

Shanta looks at Mala and then at Deepak.

SHANTA. You are wrong. There is nothing like that. He is my brother and I know him.

MALA. There. Excuse me, I will be back in a moment.

Mala exits presumably to the ladies' room.

MAN *(calling the waiter)*. The bill please. *(To Deepak.)* I really appreciate your concern for Mala. I mean it. I really do. I think you will make a good husband to her. Believe me I am not angry with you, but grateful. All she needs is some love and attention and she will be fine. You have my good wishes.

DEEPAK. Thank you. I do apologize for any inconvenience caused to you.

The Man looks at Deepak to see if he is being sarcastic.

DEEPAK. I mean it. I really do.

MAN. Where is that waiter? *(Getting up, mumbling.)* Excuse me, I think I will settle this at the counter.

The Man gets up and exits. Deepak looks at Shanta. Shanta looks away.

DEEPAK *(gently)*. I wish you had remained silent.

Black out. Thunder shower.

The living room. Night. All four enter, a little wet from dashing out of the car and into the building. The sound of the rain can be heard.

MAN. A good end to a perfect evening.

SHANTA. I will get some towels.

Shanta exits in a hurry to get the towels. Mala puts her bag down and remains standing waiting for the towel.

DEEPAK. Well, that's great for me.

MAN. I am sure your car will be all right in the morning. But relax, we will call a cab for you later. Have another drink.

MALA. You might as well call that cab now. There's nothing in the house to offer you.

Mala goes to the phone and dials the cab service.

MAN. What? No booze? You should have told me, we could have . . .

DEEPAK. It's okay. I think I will be fine.

Shanta enters with the towels and hands them over, while they talk.

MALA *(on the phone).* This is 1316. Please send a taxi . . . Uday Park. Quickly.

MAN. But do stay for a while. If you have any more questions for us . . .

DEEPAK. No. No. I am sorry. I am embarrassed . . . *(Taking the towel from Shanta.)* Thank you.

MAN *(taking a towel from Shanta and rubbing his head with it).* Don't be, after all, it shows that you care for Mala.

SHANTA *(to Mala, rubbing her hair with a towel).* You will catch a cold.

MALA. Give it to me. *(Taking the towel from Shanta.)* Why don't you make us some coffee?

MAN. Splendid idea! Let's drink some coffee since that is all we will get in this house.

Shanta is about to disappear in to the kitchen.

MAN. No wait, Shanta.

Shanta stops.

MAN. I might as well do it now. While Deepak is also here.

SHANTA. What is it?

MAN. Sit down.

Shanta sits down.

MAN. You too Mala . . . Now, I will be with you in a minute.

The Man exits, while the others remain seated.

Thunder.

SHANTA. It will rain all night!

MALA. What do you think he wants now?

DEEPAK. What do you mean by that?

MALA. What?

DEEPAK. You just said 'what do you think he wants now?' As opposed to what he wanted then?

MALA. I wasn't thinking of what I was saying.

DEEPAK. That is why it is so telling, what you just said.

MALA (*sharply*). I don't know what you are talking about! I am not going to that counsellor any more!

DEEPAK. Since there is no problem, why should you go to a counsellor? Right?

The Man enters with an envelope.

MAN. Sorry to keep you all waiting. All I want to say is—I don't know where to begin . . . Shanta is my only sister. I know that life has not been very good to her. Our brothers say that she has brought it upon herself, the loneliness and the—rejection. Her husband left her because—of her . . . But she is my sister and I do have very fond memories of us growing up in our ancestral home. Which unfortunately was sold off by our brothers. So—we only have the pleasant memories to live with now, all of us. I am the oldest in the family and Shanta, the youngest, so I feel it is my responsibility . . . no—that is not the correct way to put it. It's more than a responsibility . . . It is my way of showing my deep and sincere affection to you, my sister.

The Man gives Shanta the envelope. Shanta opens it carefully and removes a legal document. Mala goes to Shanta and looks over her shoulder at the document.

MAN. The title deed. This flat is now yours.

SHANTA *(moved)*. Oh!

MALA. Why? I can pay the rent.

MAN. Yes. But you won't be living here for very long.

MALA. What do you mean?

MAN. I mean, you will get married to Deepak and live with him—elsewhere . . . I will be using your room as a spare room for myself when I want to visit Delhi on work. That is if Shanta won't mind. Do you?

SHANTA. Huh?

MALA. You are throwing me out!

MAN. What are you saying? Of course not. You can come and go as you please. It is your mother's flat after all.

Silence, except for the rain and thunder.

MALA. You are throwing me out.

DEEPAK. It's okay, Mala. We will have a home of our own.

MALA *(to Shanta)*. You knew it, didn't you? All along!

MAN. Be reasonable Mala.

MALA *(to the Man)*. You don't want me—*(Adding.)* Here . . .

MAN. You are a grown up woman now.

MALA. And no good to you . . .

MAN. This is the thanks I get for being so considerate. I didn't expect this response. Not even a thank you?

MALA. Thank you. Oh thank you . . . Thank you, mother.

The taxi driver honks.

SHANTA. I didn't ask for this, Mala. I did not.

MALA. Yes you did. He didn't just buy a flat. He bought you!

SHANTA. That's not true! Oh God!

MALA. He bought your silence. So that you can never tell anyone what he did to your daughter!

MAN. You have gone mad.

DEEPAK. Let her speak.

The taxi horn, longer and a little more insistent.

MAN. Your taxi is here. We can talk tomorrow.

DEEPAK *(not moving, staring at the Man)*. Go on, Mala.

MALA *(to Shanta)*. Where were you when he locked the door to your bedroom while I was napping in there? Where were you during those fifteen minutes when he was destroying my soul? Fifteen minutes every day of my summer holidays, add them up. Fifteen minutes multiplied by thirty or thirty-one or whatever. That's how long or how little it took for you to send me to hell for the rest of my life! Surely you must have known, Ma.

Silence.

MALA. You know, I couldn't say anything to you. You never gave me a chance to. If only you had looked into my eyes and seen the hurt, or asked me 'beta, what's wrong?' Then maybe, I would have told you . . . But ma, I did look to you for help, while you were praying, your eyes avoiding mine, and I knew, deep down I must have known, that you will never ask me that question. Because you already knew the answer. *(To Deepak.)* So. You have your answer. But so what? Where do I go from here?

MAN. You really have a wild imagination. That is all I can say.

DEEPAK *(to the Man)*. How could you be such a sick bastard?

MAN. You watch your tongue young man.

DEEPAK *(to Mala)*. It's over, done with. Come with me. Right away.

MALA. You can't really understand me, if you feel it's all over and done with.

Thunder. Followed by a long honk from the taxi.

DEEPAK. What do you mean?

MALA. It can never be over. It won't work between us.

DEEPAK. For God's sake give me a chance and it will. For your own sake.

MALA. For your own sake, forget me.

SHANTA. Go, Mala. Just go with him.

MALA. You know I can't!

DEEPAK. Why not?

MALA. You don't understand! YOU JUST DON'T UNDERSTAND!! I cannot love you.

DEEPAK. Why?

MALA *(looking at the Man)*. Because—because—How can I even begin to explain to you? I see this man everywhere. I can never be free of him. I am not so sure I want to be free of him. Even if I was, I am not sure whether I have the ability to love anyone . . . else.

Silence. Shanta is disturbed. She rises.

SHANTA. What are you saying? What do you mean? You can't love anyone—else? . . . How could you say such a thing? No!

DEEPAK. You don't know what is good for you.

SHANTA *(to Deepak)*. Take her with you. I beg you. Take her away from this hell. There is no love for her in this house.

MAN. Go Mala. Go with him. I don't want you. Think of your future.

SHANTA. Mala. You don't know what you are saying. You don't know. Go with him. Learn to love him. Learn . . . Forget. Forget. Remember what I told you. Forget!!

MALA. By staying silent doesn't mean I can forget! This is my hell. This hell is where I belong! It is your creation, Ma! You created it for me. With your silence!! You didn't forget anything, you only remained silent!

SHANTA *(defeated)*. Yes. Yes! I only remained silent. I am to blame. That is why God is punishing me today. I remained silent not because I wanted to, but I didn't know how to speak. I—I cannot speak. I cannot say anything. My tongue was cut off . . . My tongue was cut off years ago . . . *(To Deepak.)* Please save her. I did not save her. I did not know how to save her. How could I save her when I could not save myself? . . . *(To Mala.)* You say I did not help you? I could not help you. Same as you could not help me. Did you ever see the pain in my eyes? No. Nobody saw anything. Nobody said anything. Not my brothers, not my parents. Only *(pointing to the Man)* he spoke. Only he said, only he saw and he did.

The man backs away looking at Shanta with a warning.

SHANTA. I was six, Mala. I was six. And he was thirteen . . . and it wasn't only summer holidays. For ten years! For ten years!! *(Pointing to the picture of God.)* I looked to Him. I didn't feel anything. I didn't feel pain, I didn't feel pleasure. I lost myself in Him. He helped me. He helped me. By taking away all feeling. No pain no pleasure, only silence. Silence means Shanti. Shanti. But my tongue is cut off. No. No. It just fell off somewhere. I didn't use it, no. I cannot shout for help, I cannot say words of comfort, I cannot even speak about it. No I can't. I am dumb. *(To the Man, speaking like a mute person making unintelligible sounds.)* Uh, eh, oo, oo, aa, aa, aaaaaaaaaaa. *(Gesturing with her hands to say she will not tell anyone while making the sounds.)* Aaaaa, ooo eee oooo aaeeeeeeeee, aaaaaaaaaaaaaaaaaaeeeeeeeeee!

Shanta jumps to where the pieces of glass from the portrait are and picks up a sharp piece and jabs it in her mouth. It is all so quick that the rest are shocked.

Mala screams.

DEEPAK. No!

MAN. Shanta!

They try to stop Shanta from doing more harm to herself. Shanta moves away, blood from her mouth. Mala rushes to her with a towel and presses Shanta's mouth with the towel. Shanta looks at Mala with folded hands and falls on her knees. Mala kneels too and holds her. Shanta tries to continue to speak, we

*only hear muffled sounds as Mala keeps the towel
pressed to Shanta's mouth to prevent the bleeding.*

MALA. No. Don't speak. Don't say anything. Not now. Not
now.

Deepak is on the phone trying to call the ambulance.

DEEPAK *(since he can't get through).* Damn! *(Picking up Shanta.)*
Quick. Let's take her in the taxi. *(To the Man.)* Help me.

The Man goes to pick up Shanta. Mala stops him.

MALA. Don't you dare touch my mother!

*The Man steps back. Deepak and Mala help Shanta up
on her feet and take her out of the door to the waiting
taxi. The Man looks at them and stays frozen on stage.*

Cross-fade to:

*The counsellor's office as in the first scene. Mala is
seated in exactly the same spot. Mala walks across the
stage as the lights cross fade. The Man continues to
stand, fixed by a spotlight on him.*

MALA *(sighing, thinking about it almost as if it were a pleasant
memory).* I wish he were here now, so I could see his face
when I tell him I have nothing to hide. Because I know it
wasn't my fault . . . Now. I know now.

Pause.

MALA *(saying it with a growing sense of joy).* But what is the
point? He is dead. Today. February the 29th 2004. He is dead.
Today. I have made February 29th my Freedom Day. I will
celebrate it with my husband. We are going to have a
champagne dinner. He is waiting for me this very moment at
the restaurant.

*The Man remains in his spot. He speaks as a voice in
her head and not as the counsellor.*

MAN. You look very happy.

MALA. I am.

MAN. And what about your mother?

MALA. What about her?

MAN. Do you still carry any anger against her?

MALA *(thinking about it)*. Maybe. But I do see what she has been through. It's been more difficult for her I guess. *(Pause, a little troubled.)* He comes back. He ruined my mother's life too. No matter what I try to do, it all seems to come back to him. I want to forget! I just want to . . .

> *Mala stares at the doll which is now facing her. The Man walks to the doll and picks it up, holding the doll by its skirt so that the skirt covers the dolls face. He rocks the doll while he speaks. Mala looks at the Man.*
>
> *Silence. Music.*

MAN. Touch me here. Quickly before someone sees you. Touch.

> *Mala rises, looking at the Man and the doll.*

MAN. You said in front of mummy and daddy you loved me. Come on! Show it!

> *Mala hits out at him with her fist. The Man doesn't flinch.*

MAN. Don't cry!

MALA *(hitting him hard)*. Aaah!

MAN. I said, don't cry!

> *Mala continues to hit at him each time with more anger as the Man speaks, unaffected by the blows.*

MAN. This is our secret! . . . Ready for a real birthday present? . . . What did you learn in school? Come on sing it. Sing!

> *Mala grabs him by the throat and tries to strangle him, heaving with the effort.*

MAN. Thirty days has September. April, June and November. February has twenty-eight. All the rest have thirty-one! Once again. Keep on singing! Stop only when I stop.

MALA *(one last violent shove)*. You are dead! You deserve to be dead! Die!

The Man slumps in the chair as if dead. Mala heaves a sigh of relief. Mala picks up the doll, smoothens its dress and comforts it. Spot on Shanta in the temple, beatific. Praying with a sense of peace around her. Cross fade as Mala speaks. Moving in space. Music continues under Mala's voice. The spot on Shanta in the temple stays. Mala talks while looking at her. Shanta has lit some incense which makes her space appear sanctified somehow, by the smoke. There is a low spot on the Man still in the chair.

MALA. Dear mother. It just isn't easy to forget. Occasionally I catch his reflection in the glass of a subway, hiding behind a newspaper or pretending to be asleep. But it doesn't matter. I can live with it now. He as a person is not important to me any more.

The spotlight on the Man fades out.

While I accused you of not recognizing my pain, you never felt any anger at me for not recognizing yours. We were both struggling to survive but–I never acknowledged your struggle. Ma, no matter where I am, I always think of you. I want you to know that I am listening. Waiting for you to speak. I promise you I will listen. I am waiting for a sign from you . . . to say that you have forgiven me. Say something. Even a whisper.

The scrim wall around the prayer room rises. Mala is overjoyed. Shanta continues with her prayer. Mala walks up to her and kneels.

I just want to . . . I want to ask you whether you need my help. Please let me be of help. (*Gently turning her mother's face towards her.*) It's not your fault, mother. Just as it wasn't my fault. Please, tell me that you've forgiven me for blaming you. Please tell me that.

Shanta turns back to her God and continues with her prayers. Mala slowly rests her head in Shanta's lap.

MALA. I know you will, mother. I know you have.

Shanta picks up the bell and begins to ring it even as the lights fade out.

CLEARING THE RUBBLE

A Radio Play for Three Voices

A Note on the Play

Following the earthquake in Bhuj in January 2001, Mahesh Dattani was commissioned by BBC Radio to write a play to be broadcast on the first anniversary of the tragedy.

Clearing the Rubble followed three people whose lives were affected by the earthquake. An English journalist in the region at the time of the catastrophe goes back to Bhuj a year later. He is trying to track a boy he had met when he was helping with the relief effort. We also hear the story of the boy's mother, herself trapped in the rubble.

Jeremy Mortimer
(Jeremy Mortimer is Executive Producer,
BBC Radio Drama.)

Clearing the Rubble was first broadcast on 17 January 2002 at 2.00 p.m. on BBC Radio 4 and repeated on 26 January 2002 on the BBC World Service. The play was directed by Jeremy Mortimer.

Cast for first production:

TOBY	Robert Glenister
SALIM	Adam Dean
FATIMA	Nina Wadia

Children at break time in school. (Track 8.)

SALIM *(thought)*. Rahul lost his left leg. Pasha lost his sight. Nilima lost her . . . I don't remember now, what she lost. Her teeth? Was it she with the bloody face? No, that was not her, that was . . . Who? And I lost my mother, my uncle, my aunts, my grandfather and my grandmothers . . . I have lost everyone now, except for Jeffrey. *(Pause.)* Poor Jeffrey. He tries so hard.

Fade out children. Bring in Kutch Express.
(Interior. Track 25.)

JEFFREY *(thought)*. First Nora left me . . . we both wanted it I know but, she could have tried . . . harder . . . Then Jennifer. I was never there for Jennifer . . . I try hard to be there for Salim. Of course he is his mother's child. He will be, always.

Fade out Kutch Express as the Azan prayers fade in.
(Track 2.39.)

FATIMA *(thought)*. Allah be merciful! It is time for my prayer. Forgive me, but I cannot face Mecca. I cannot move. My Allah, please forgive me! Please show compassion. Both my daughters are with you now. I am coming too. Take me away from this unjust world now. I will hold the bodies of my daughters till I follow them to your world. I have no more strength to call out to those people who help others but not us. I cry out for you now. Only in your world is there justice. I want to be in your world.

Fade out. Credits.

Interior. Kutch Express.

JEFFREY *(writing a letter)*. I haven't told you how I met Salim. I guess we haven't had a chance to really tell our stories to each other. If we had, we would still be together I suppose. Strange that I feel I want to clear a lot of things with you while on a train ride from to Kutch. I have to be honest and tell you that I am not going back just to meet Salim. I do want to help. Him or anyone else. It's been a year since I visited India. I want to share with you what I have been through last year. Why? You may ask. Well, because I want you to know that I have changed.

Kutchi songs on the train. Fade out.

(As narrator.) Let me start with my journey about a year ago. January 28th 2001. Two days after a massive earthquake devastated the land of Kutch, a region in the Indian state of Gujarat.

Fade in bus interior.

I am on a bus that will take me to Malliya. That is where I want to go. A man on the bus asks me why I am not with the official rescue workers all around Bhuj, the epicentre of the earthquake. I reply that I am not a rescue worker. I am a journalist. He questions. Did you come all the way from England to write about us? But why? He persists. I tell him that it means a lot to me, to write about the condition of humanity in other parts of the world. He asks me whether I am married and have children. I say 'no'. He looks at me with sympathy and turns away, as if he had got an answer to his first question . . . I look out of the window. I see what I have seen for miles and miles. No sign of any buildings. All of them reduced to heaps of rubble. People lining up outside relief camps. Waiting for some paperwork to be done before they can have access to meagre shelters and food packets. In front of us, the road is split open. A whole row of vans and trucks with equipment and rescue workers, waiting for somebody to give them a go-ahead . . . I speak to the man about his family.

He has a wife and four children, all safe by the mercy of God. His village needs bulldozers and cranes to clear the rubble. He was in Bhuj pleading with the government officials to send some help. They didn't have enough equipment. So they will have to wait their turn.

The bus comes to a halt.

No, it's not another tremor. It's as far as the bus can go. We will have to walk the rest of the way. It's not too far, I am told by the man. Only seventeen kilometres. I look around. There are some with crutches. An old woman with a bandage around her head. We get off, the man thanking his good fortune that we were so close to Malliya. Some of the men choose a shady spot under an uprooted tree. I look up at the sun. Thank God it's only January. The men by the tree light up bidis. The old woman begins to walk, as if her house were round the corner. I wonder what to do. The man on the bus, walking ahead, turns back and looks at me. I follow him . . .

Silence. A woman singing, heard faintly at first.

(*As narrator.*) I come to the outskirts of the village. It is night now and I can only see areas lit by oil lamps. I understand that there is no kerosene available. The man tells me that they are completely cut off from the world. Not a single telephone in the village is working. I see silhouettes of piles of rubble everywhere. There is not a whole building or hut to be seen anywhere. People are preparing to sleep out in the open. The man offers to take me to his home. I have my sleeping bag with me. I thank him, but I prefer to wander. I promise to meet him tomorrow. He insists I join him for dinner. He is the head of the village. I just want to look at things by myself. I decline his offer for dinner. I still have some biscuits with me. I arrange to meet up with him in the morning. He walks away. I look around and for the first time since my arrival in Gujarat, I feel a tightening in my chest. I haven't brought my medication with me . . . I realize that these people have lost their homes, their livelihood, their loved ones . . . Everyone here has lost something or someone. They are not crying. There are no wails. Only silence. Grief everywhere but I cannot see it. Only shadows of people going about their nightly routine as if they were still in their homes with all their loved ones. Having their dinner or singing to their infants. Preparing for the night, as if the piles of rubble are a part of their lives. I walk past them all. They do not stare at me as they did on the bus. They do not notice the colour of my skin in the dark. In the night, I am one of them. For indeed, I am. I have lost someone dear to me. Only I cannot carry on with my life the way I see people around me do. As if the weight of their grief has given them a new momentum.

The woman singing grows louder as Jeffrey approaches.

I want to take a picture of the woman singing to her child. I approach her to ask her for her permission, ready to point at my camera when I catch her eye. I am about to speak, when I notice there is no child in the crib. She rocks the crib, pulling at a string attached to it, in rhythm to her song. Her eyes are shut as she sings her song, putting her baby to sleep. It looks a perfect picture. The stars are out, the fire burning closeby throwing a strong light on her face. Her song makes a perfect lullaby. I cannot understand the words but the tone sounds right to comfort a restless baby. Except there is no baby, any more. I walk away from her.

The singing fades out.

I hear a sound of something falling. I turn to another street to find the ruins of what must have been a large building. Probably the largest building in the village. There are beams on top of the debris. Men are trying to pull down the beam but it is far too heavy. The debris seems to have collapsed further making their work more difficult. They look at it in despair— and walk away. Suddenly a voice cries out. 'Don't go!' 'Don't stop now!' The voice of an adolescent. The men don't seem to pay any attention to him. I can't see him in the dark but he can't be far from the men. They don't seem to respond. They disappear. The man on the bus is among them. He says something to me about the cranes not arriving till at least a

week. It will be too late by then. The young lad cries out again
'Don't go! Help me! Help, please!'. The lad is talking to me.
He is thin and wears a tattered white shirt. That is all I can tell.
I dig out my flashlight from my bag . . . I look at his face. It
is covered in grime. There are wounds on his skin that need to
be taken care of. I take out my first aid kit . . . I ask him his
name. Salim. He doesn't want me to dress his wounds. He
wants me to help him get his mother and sisters out. 'They
tried! Not enough!', he exclaims, talking about the men who
were working here a while ago. 'Not enough! Not enough!
. . . I calm him down and wash his wounds. He needs some
stitches for his cheek. 'Is there a hospital here?' I ask him. He
points to the heap we are sitting on. 'Is there a doctor here in
the village?' I ask. 'The doctors have all gone to Anjar and
Bhuj', he tells me as a matter of fact. 'They have to go.' They
could have stayed here just as well, I think. 'They called all
doctors . . .' 'Who called all doctors?' I ask him. 'They,' he
responds simply, pointing in a direction vaguely. 'They, who?'
I persist. He doesn't respond. He doesn't know, or doesn't
understand what I am asking. 'We are Muslims.' I stop putting
the bandage around his arm. He looks at me and repeats what
he said—'We are Muslims.' He is trying to explain to me as
best as I can understand. I do finally. I nod at him to let him
know that I understand. But he doesn't want me to tend to his
wounds. He breaks away and points a finger at me—'You will
help!' 'You!' He cries out. He wants my help . . . He needs my
help. What can I do? I can only do some first aid on him and
give him a mild sedative if he is in shock. But he wants me to
do something about his mother and sisters buried alive. 'They
are alive,' he keeps on repeating. He takes my hand and leads
me up the heap and on the other side, moving with such speed
for someone who is injured as he is, and I can barely see in the
dark . . . I am balancing or trying to balance on a large piece
of stone. He points down to a spot. I look at the spot with the
help of my flashlight. I can only see the rubble.

FATIMA. Help! Save my children!

JEFFREY. 'There they are!' he says. I look but I cannot see them, it would be impossible to know for sure whether there was any life down there. 'See!' he persists as I try to look away.

FATIMA. Salim! Salim!

JEFFREY. 'Look,' I say, 'I don't see anything. How do you know for sure they are there? You weren't there with them, were you?' 'Yes,' he says, nodding hard. 'I was there. We were there. In the hospital. Downstairs.'

FATIMA. A curse be upon the people who built this hospital!

JEFFREY. How did he escape I wonder. What do I do now? It would be impossible to move the debris without a crane. The hospital must have been at least three stories high. If his mother and sisters were in the basement, the chances are slim that they would be alive.

FATIMA. Saira! Mumtaz! Speak to me!

JEFFREY. But then . . . He wants me to help him. I want to help him. But I cannot. 'You!' He points his finger again at me. Maybe I can help him. I cannot unearth his mother and sisters with my bare hands, but I can help by showing him that I tried. Try. Try to show that I care. That would help somehow. I am sure. I roll up my sleeves and try to pick up a large piece of concrete. I can barely move it. He yells at me to stop. 'What are you doing?' looking at me as if I was stupid. 'Get crane from city.' What a splendid idea! But how am I to go to the city? Who do I speak to for a crane and how long will it take to get one here? I cannot ask him these questions. I am supposed to sort that out by myself. 'Get crane!' Those are Salim's orders, and I must obey them. But what can I do? I am only a journalist not a rescue operator. Maybe they could help. But how do I get there? 'How can I get to the city?' I ask. Salim has no answer to that. I will have to walk it like I did getting here with the man. The man! Wasn't he in town precisely for that purpose? I tell Salim that I will return with the crane. He must rest. I take out my sleeping bag and find a flat spot to lay it out. I tell Salim to get in and stay there till

I get back. I give him some of my energy biscuits and water. I tuck him in and leave, going in the direction of the man's house.

Silence.

I find the man with his family and some of the men whom I saw earlier. I tell them we can try and get a crane if we all go to the city. There are people buried under the rubble and we must save them. The man looks at me with respect, and acknowledges that I am on their side. 'If we move any of that, we will cause the debris to collapse further and might kill the people who are alive. That is why we stopped our work.' 'Yes but with a crane we could manage to save Salim's family. And who knows? Many others too!' They look at each other and talk for what seems like quite a while. Finally, the man says to me 'Yes, you can help. We can use you. We have a plan . . .' Six of us start our long walk to the nearest bus.

Silence.

We arrive in Bhuj in the morning. It is quite a different picture that greets me. There are vans full of relief material everywhere. There is enough activity going on to show that all efforts are being made to rescue people or rehabilitate displaced families. Or simply offer food and clothing. We go to the Red Cross and I speak to a German woman in charge of the operations. I explain to her what we are going to do. She doesn't say a word. Only nods at me and the other men. She hands me a key and tells me to take the pick-up truck parked nearby with a mini crane in it. Perfect. We drive off casually trying to avoid eye contact with anyone who looks like an official. But as predicted by the wise men of Malliya, we are stopped. Since the man is driving the truck, they interrogate him. The officer asks us to get off. I bring out my video camera and point it in his direction much to his annoyance. 'Who are you?' he thunders. 'We don't want foreign workers! Go home! We will send our rescue team soon to those villagers.' 'I am a journalist and I am writing on the communal and caste biased nature of your relief operations.' I continue to shoot him with my camera. 'Are you preventing equipment and supplies from reaching Muslim and Dalit populations?' I try to sound like Tim Sebastian in one of his attack modes. 'No. No!' That is not true. We are a very tolerant people.' Suddenly he yells to some people to grab my camera. That was a bit unexpected. But the men of Malliya are on top of them. 'Get in the truck and drive away!' the man yells at me. I am not going to leave them there. Now is the time to practise my taekwondo. The seven of us overpower them, and get in to the truck before more people begin to gather. We drive away even as we hear them shouting for us 'Terrorists! Stop them!' We are victorious.

Kutch guitar.

We arrive at Malliya to be received with cheers and dozens of children running after our truck. We head straight to the site where the hospital stood. To our amazement and delight, we find that the truck contains not only the crane but a whole lot of stuff. Blankets, vitamins, food, clothing, tents. But there is hardly any time for celebrations. We get to work. We set up the crane to lift the heavy beams. Salim is watching from afar. I hope that we can unite him with his mother and sisters. I hope.

Kutch guitar continues for a while. Fade out.

Finally. We do manage to save some lives. There are children and women mostly and some older men. We save some of them. I ask for Salim. I cannot find him anywhere. Surely he should be here, to unite with his mother and sisters, or identify them . . . I look for Salim. I cannot see him anywhere. My heart begins to pound once again. I wish I had brought my medication, then . . . I ask if anyone knows who Salim's mother is. The man points her out to me. She is there with her children . . .

Kutch Express interior.

We men did succeed in saving our village. We men of the village. I helped save the village. I am a man. I played my part well. I will soon return to Salim's village. One year later. Salim and I. Yours, Jeffrey.

Silence. The Azan prayer.

FATIMA *(thought)*. The mosque is all right. Oh! We are fortunate! Everything will be fine soon. Everything will be like before. God knows that we are living in this not so fine world. But it is His creation and He gives us problems and He gives us strength . . . Where are my children? *(Coughing.) (Thought.)* Where is she? I was holding Saira. She must be here with me. Saira! Oh, speak to me! Move. Move! *(Speaking.)* Saira! Say something my child! If you can't speak, then come closer to me! Please!

Silence.

Fatima cries. Her sobs continue as we hear her thoughts.

(Thought.) I hope you went without a struggle. You never could stand pain . . . A curse be upon those who built this hospital! If we were in our home, at least we would have all been alive. Saira! Your fever is gone now. I do not have to worry about typhoid or malaria for you. I don't have to bring you here and wait in line for a doctor to finally see us. Just to tell us that we have to go to Rajkot for medicines. Saira, you will be more happy in Paradise. There will be justice and peace for you in Allah's kingdom.

She stops crying.

(Calling.) Mumtaz! Mumtaz!

Silence.

(Thought.) I have no more tears for you Mumtaz. Forgive me. Please forgive me. As the middle child you have more to be angry for. But you never complained. Now all the accounts have to be cleared. At Allah's mercy, I must seek my pardon. Now I have to present my case before you all my children. First with you, Mumtaz, since you were the strongest and most hard-working. I always saw myself in you. I never asked you to do anything I would not do myself. Wash the vessels, buy vegetables, fetch the water, light the firewood. I do what every mother does with their daughters. I taught you to work. If you work hard you have a future. Everyone will respect you. That is the way to an honourable life. An honourable life. That is

what I could not give you Mumtaz. It was not my fault. What could I do? Maybe I should have told you before what our situation was. You did not know what I have gone through. And I did not think that you will be humiliated in such a way. Even when you came back, you never told me how they treated you. I know I should not have sent you back, but if only you had told me. No, that is not true. I never gave you a chance to say anything. Even if you had, I would not have listened. There were more important things than you to think of. Fighting to keep us all alive. Your father was a very poor man. He did not leave us any money. A cobbler, he could not even support us when he was alive. I was earning more than him as a labourer. I built this hospital. Yes. I carried the bricks and stone to make this building. What sin did I do that the same building should kill my daughters and bury me alive? As if my bricks and stones were not acceptable to Allah and He refused them and threw them back at me. Or He is angry with others and is calling us to His Paradise. I will know His plan soon enough . . . Your father when he was alive did not want me to work on this building. As it is a cobbler's is not a very respectable profession but he did not want his wife to be a labourer. But in this land where people do not have sandals on their feet, how will he find work mending them? Mumtaz, I am not putting the blame on your father, and I am not trying to say I sacrificed for you. I did not obey him because I wanted Salim to go to school. I did not want him to be a cobbler like his father. I thought it was a good sign from Allah when the government wanted to build a hospital here. They were looking for labour. At least there will be work. But if I was to work all day, I had to prepare you to look after the home. You were very naughty and playful. You were only seven I think. I had to break you. There I did wrong I know. But Mumtaz, again I will say that I was not telling you to do anything that I did not do at your age. So there, when I seek my Justice, my account will be clear. But you did not obey me and I had to make you obey me by doing what I did not like doing. If I did not think of the future, there would not have been any future.

Think, Mumtaz. Maybe you will be my Judge at the gates of Paradise. Think. If we had suffered a little to send Salim to school, when he grows up he could earn much, much more. We will be more wealthy, and you will find a husband who can support you well. That is the honour I was seeking. For that I had to make you work hard. You were very angry with me. I did not let you play. But your anger I was prepared for. I knew it. But when your father died in the drought, you felt that the only protector in your life was gone, and so you obeyed my every wish. For that I had many, many tears, Mumtaz. But after he died, did I have a choice? I had to work. I still remember what you said to me that time when I could only buy one set of clothes for Id. When I gave it to Salim, you said that if only father had starved his wife, and fed himself well instead, he would be alive. And I would be dead. Such is the Fate, that I am the only one alive now . . . But why am I getting angry with you for thinking like that? This is the time for me to plead my case with you. When the hospital people told me that they needed cleaners, I had no choice but to send you. It was a blessing from above. There was no more building work for me. And I was only a servant in the Patel house. What I could earn I could not put food in your mouths. If I had asked Salim to stop going to school and work, that will be the end of us. All that hard work and suffering will be of waste. It would all be the same for ever. We would not last another drought. I did not think that the earth will move under us and take it all away so soon. Fate. But the day you told me you did not want to work there anymore, I should have asked you why. That is my greatest sin that I will take with me. Forgive me for that. When somebody at the marketplace told me what happened, I wanted to kill those people. Mumtaz, they did not strip you naked because you are a thief. They did that because they are the children of pigs. You are not a thief I know. I know that you will never be one. They must have lost the money somewhere else. I wish I had taken stones and bashed their heads in. Allah has done that for me. I hope they are all dead in this building.

Silence.

(Calling.) Help! Help me! *(Thought.)* Saira. I do not know how to explain to you. You were too little to understand anything. All you understood was your cough and fever and diarrhoea. You lost your father even before you were born. I believe I have been fair to you so far. Allah has taken you away before any injustice could happen to you. But the gravest injustice of all is that you were born to me. I had nothing to give you. When you were born I had to leave you with your grandmother so I could go out and work again. That was the best thing to happen to you. At least your grandmother gave you some love and affection. When you meet your grandmother again, I hope you will thank her. And your sister Mumtaz. You were lucky to have a sister like her. You never saw your father. For you, I have only relief that you are gone without too much pain. At least you played with your rattle and you smiled when your grandmother sang for you. That is an ocean of happiness Saira. Very few people are fortunate like you. But please, please salute your sister when you meet her.

Silence.

(Thought.) Salim, I come to you last in this time of departure, because you have always come first otherwise. I do not know where you are. I hope you are alive and well. You may feel that I have no reason to beg your forgiveness. But I have a reason. I can tell you now, because it is the time to do it . . . I gave you the best of what we all could. You did not see the hard work that I had to do so that you could buy your books or take some sweets for the schoolmaster. You did not see that your sister was spending the whole day to fetch water for you to drink or wash your feet the next morning. You only had to worry about your father's decision to teach you his trade, and my decision to send you to school. Finally, I won, because I showed you a lot of affection, whereas your father only showed you his interest in teaching you how to make and mend sandals. I did not want it, because as a cobbler you would continue to be a low caste. It is true we are Muslims and we are all equal in the eyes of Allah, but in the eyes of

others, as a son of a cobbler I know you would be treated differently. If what your father told me is true then I need to beg for your forgiveness too. He told me that I made you feel ashamed of who you are. That you felt ashamed of being a Muslim and the son of a cobbler. Is this true? I will only get that answer in some other world where perhaps it will not matter anymore. Or by some miracle if we are both alive! . . . But somehow I know that is not to be true. I can only hope that I did not make you feel ashamed. You should be proud of your faith and your father. I never wanted you to feel otherwise. I only wanted a better life for us. Only you could provide that. I did not want to see you suffer the humility your father had to suffer, or your sister. That is my only reason behind all that I did. Maybe I was wrong. Maybe I should have been happy with what Allah wanted to give us. I do not know.

Silence.

(*Thought.*) Salim. I spent the whole night thinking. I could not sleep because of the pain. I may have broken my leg. I cannot move and my head hurts. I do not know now whether anyone will save me. Whether anyone is interested in saving me. But before we part. I wanted to say something to you which you may not like, but I have to if I am to be truthful. I thought you respected me, after you started to go to school and learnt a lot of things about the world. I felt so proud of you when you showed me your map and told me where our village is on the map. We are but a speck of dust in this world of humanity. I know you are proud of yourself. But you were not proud of us. You told your friend that your father was a farmer . . . You lied. You should have told them you were a cobbler's son and your father was an honest man. But you betrayed him. I have to say something, Salim. Somehow I know you will hear my thoughts. You were not my favourite child. Mumtaz was the one I loved the most. I say this to you now, not to hurt you. But to let Mumtaz be at peace. You were my dream, our future. I could dream because of you. I know you had your dream too, but it seems to me there was no room for us in your dream.

Fade in music. Kutch guitar.

SALIM. Mother. I hear you now. After a year I return to listen to your voice. I was away, travelling to distant lands, meeting strange people. I wish you could see me now, but you don't. You can't. But I see you. I know what you mean. I have changed mother. I have seen the world and I have come back to the world. I can show you where we are on the map and I can show you where I have been. But we can no longer talk to each other. We never did talk very much. I just wanted to tell you that you were right in dreaming. At least you had a dream. While father did not dream at all. I did. You gave me one. I want to share with you what I was going through. Yes, you are right. I never thought about Mumtaz and what she went through for me. She didn't have a choice in what she did. Mother, she did not sacrifice her life for me. She did it for you. I wish I had paid more attention to her. She told me once that as soon as I was married and brought home a wife, she will sing and dance every morning even if it meant bringing Allah's wrath on her. I was wrong in thinking she said that ever so often because she wanted to see me married. I know now what she meant. She wanted someone else to share the burden, or take it off her shoulders. I was a burden. To both of you. Because you wanted me to ease your burden when I grew up and earned enough money to support you . . . I did not know the responsibility that awaited me with manhood. I simply accepted whatever you gave me. You gave me a lot. I enjoyed the attention.

Fade in. Class in progress (Days of the week.)

I enjoyed school. At least I didn't have to work hard like father in the heat. The school had a fan. It was a different world you sent me to. I learnt a lot of useless things at first. I did not mind learning them. I was suddenly amongst boys and girls from different castes. I was too little then to realize it, but as the months and years went by, I began to feel inferior to them.

There were other Muslim boys too. But somehow they treated me differently. One day, there was a dead rat in the classroom. The smell was so strong that no one could enter the room. One of the children told the teacher that I should be sent in to pick up the rat and clean the room. I did not want to do it. The bigger boys called me a cobbler's son and said that it was my job to do these things. If I could touch the hide of a cow, I could pick up a dead rat. The teacher did not say a word. Every day after that, the boys would mock me, look at me with a smile, telling me that I didn't know my place. Nobody said anything or did anything to me. But they were thinking about it. A week before the earthquake, a new boy joined our school. He asked me what my father did when he was alive. I should have told him the truth, but for a while I wanted to be treated as an equal. I knew it wouldn't be long before he found out. But till then . . . I asked him what his father did. He told me he was in town to work on a farm. They were farmers. I told him my father was a farmer too. I just wanted to be his equal. Never did I think that it would come to you, mother. After the lunch break, the others came to know. They called me a farmer's son, and they smiled at each other. I did not hit them. I did not speak to them. The only way I could handle that was not to show that it bothered me. I ask you now mother whether what I did was insulting to you or to father. If you say that I was not your favourite child, I understand. I never did anything to make you proud of me. I never made any sacrifices. I made a terrible mistake of separating my pride and identity from my family's. But if you ask me now mother, who do I respect the most between you, my father, my sisters. Mother, I would say it is you. I only wish that I could have done something to make you proud of me. Maybe if we had a few more years together. Yes. If only we had a few more years, I might have . . . I might have . . .

Fade in birds at sunrise.

(Thought.) Jeffrey . . . This is not my village any more. It has withstood many calamities. Droughts, floods, caste wars. But the earthquake that brought you here, took my village some place else. In my mind it is a peaceful village. Nothing much happens here. We are born, we live, we die . . . No different from other places. But for those who live here, it is the centre of the universe. This is where I belong, with the ghost of my village. You cannot even speak my language and I can only tell you so much in yours. For those who lived here, we knew no other universe. This was our world. You may not understand my words as I speak them now. You can only comprehend the words that I learnt in my school. The few you taught me. But I can show you the ghosts of my village. Maybe some of them can speak with you.

Farmers talking in field.

(*Thought.*) These are my friends' fathers, on their fields. Not all of them own the fields. They have managed to start afresh with some help from the government. They work here all day and hope that the rains will arrive in time, if at all. If they don't, then they start all over again. They all have wives and children who give them food, love, respect, obedience. Some of them are ghosts and some are not. Osmanbhai over there died in the drought. He and my father went together. Oh look, there is a really old ghost. He died during the Partition when he tried to cross the border to Pakistan way back in 1947. That one there is my friend's father. He is alive. You can tell by the sweat on his brow.

A cricket game.

(*Thought.*) Come with me and see how we play cricket. A few tin boxes as wickets. A tennis ball and a cracked cricket bat held together by twine. The one chasing the ball is a ghost. There are others silently cheering. The rubble from the old school building still remains. They have yet to send the equipment to clear the rubble. It will remain so for years to come. Children and ghosts will continue to play around the rubble. Do you want to know why ghosts stay on?

Prayers inside mosque.

(Thought.) But first it is time for special school. Learning from the Holy Koran. The mosque survived the quake. Held up by the faith of thousands of people in the village. If there is one thing that cannot break down it is their faith in Allah. Can you tell the ghosts from the living? . . . They are all ghosts. Those girls that were outside the mosque were my sisters. They are waiting. For me to finish my prayers and join them. It's Friday. It's our day of rest. You understand that. But why stay on? What do ghosts want? Jeffrey?

Fruit market.

(Thought.) I have never seen the market so busy. That is because as the years go by, there are more ghosts. That rich woman there bargains with the fruit-seller. It is a ritual. The woman haggles, the seller comes down on his price, just stopping short at the price he really wants. Yes they are both ghosts. The sellers with the empty stalls are living, talking with each other about the good times to come. The shoppers with empty bags, counting their soiled notes are living. They tell the sellers to reserve the juiciest mangoes for them in the coming summer. There may be no juicy mangoes or the money to buy them with, but they don't know that. They are living, you see. That woman there buying potatoes, is my mother. She is a strong woman. You know her. You rescued her and my sisters. She will survive in spite of the lost limb. She makes a living by running a tea shop in the ruins of our home. She will make enough money and get herself some nice clothes and a proper shelter. She will fix her home as soon as she gets some money from the government. She has waited for a year. What's a few more months? Or years. But wait, look at what she has in her bag. Look . . . It's a piece of paper, from the government. It has come through! How did she manage it? At last it's all over! Yes, it's time to move on. After a year of struggle she has succeeded in doing what others have failed. She managed to get compensation! She can live now! Her dream has come true . . . I wish . . . Jeffrey, I wish I could touch her. I wish I could wipe the sweat off her face . . . I know what she is thinking. I used to visit her when she was working on the hospital site.

I would wipe the sweat off her upper lip with my handkerchief. That is what she is thinking about! She is thinking of me! She has forgiven me! Jeffrey! Quick, give her your handkerchief. Yes! Just give it to her. Take it mother! Take it.

The prayer call begins.

FATIMA. Oh! Thank you! Thank you a thousand times, Allah!

SALIM. Goodbye, Mother! Goodbye, Jeffrey!

JEFFREY *(thought)*. Salim! Don't leave me now!

SALIM. Mother, I am leaving you.

FATIMA *(thought)*. Salim! Go my child, go straight to paradise.

JEFFREY *(thought)*. Salim, wait! Tell me why did you stay on? Tell me, why? Wait Salim!

FATIMA. Give my love to your sisters! I think of them, I think of all of you, in my prayers! Go!

Prayer call fades out.

SALIM. Jeffrey. We stay on because our lives and deaths haven't been acknowledged. The government offers compensation to those who have lost their loved ones only if they can show proof that they lived and died. For those of us who were buried or cremated before a doctor could reach us, we have no proof that we did exist. It is not enough that my mother tells them 'I had three children, I lost them all.' It is not enough that our neighbours tell them 'Yes I knew her children, they did exist!' The whole village can scream at them saying 'We did exist! We did live!' That is not enough. Jeffrey, I am sorry. I followed you. Outside my village I existed only in your mind. All of us, want to leave our mark behind. Even if only on a piece of paper in a government office, if not an impression on some unknown person's mind. That the ones we leave behind can say, yes I had a son, here is the proof! I lost two of my daughters, here is the proof! Proof that we existed! . . . Now that my mother has proof that we did live, and you know that we did live, I need not stay on. Goodbye, Jeffrey . . . Jeffrey, please call Nora. I will speak to her once again before I leave.

Silence.

JEFFREY *(voice on answering machine).* Hi, Nora. This is Jeffrey returning your call. I just got back from India this morning . . . Salim said he spoke with you and . . . no, no. That's all done with. I am taking my medication now. No more voices. No more panic attacks. I am happy that you do want to meet and—possibly work something out. Someone I knew said that if you can't clear the rubble you have to live with it, around it and over it, because what you lost is buried in there somewhere and until you find it, you have to keep on living with the rubble. Here I am rambling on again I . . .

A beep from the machine suggesting that he is cut off. Time's up. Fade in Kutch song on guitar. Credits.

DANCE LIKE A MAN

■

A Screenplay co-written with Pamela Rooks

A Note on the Play

I have a chair that belonged to my father and, since his death, has now passed on to me. Through some unwritten rule, it is understood that this is my chair and nobody else will sit on it. I used this chair on stage for the play's Amritlal Parekh, the autocratic father, to use and nobody else sat on it—a metaphor of the unwritten rules of authority that so many of us come to accept as part of the Indian joint family. The younger Jairaj tries to go against this in the play that examines authority and prejudice socially and culturally and as we sit in the dark watching the story unfold between time past and time present, Mahesh Dattani forces us to examine our own individual and collective consciousness.

Are we the liberal-minded persons we would like to believe we are or do we blindly kowtow to unwritten laws of family conduct that is the easier path to take?

In a city like Chennai, where everyone knows a dancer or has a dancer in the family, *Dance Like a Man* was bound to strike a familiar chord. The challenge to both my actors and myself as director was not just to bring the issues that the play raises to the fore but also to bridge Dattani's verbal ingenuity with a strong visual element.

I used a minimalistic approach to set design, which gave me the freedom to choreograph movement and composition with broad strokes, sometimes sculptural in quality and often fluid like a dancer in full flow. It was a challenge at every level of production.

To me, this was a personal journey, knowing that my own life, like Jairaj in the play has not been easy in trying to march to the beat of a different drummer.

Mithran Devanesen
(Mithran Devanesen is a Chennai-based theatre director and
one of India's leading set and light designer.)

The film was released in India in September 2004.
Principal characters:

RATNA	Shobana
LATA	Anoushka Ravishankar
JAIRAJ	Arif Zakaria
VISHWAS	Samir Soni
AMRITLAL PAREKH	Mohan Agashe
CHANDRAKALA	Arundhati Nag

The screenplay was co-written with Pamela Rooks, based on the play of the same title by Mahesh Dattani. The film was directed by Pamela Rooks.

Camera	Sunny Joseph
Music	Ganesh/Kumaresh
Sound	Dileep Subramaniam
Art Direction	Shashidhar Adappa
Casting	Dolly Thakore
Costumes	Himani Dehilvi

We hear the sound of dancing bells and perhaps the mridangam.

Fade in. Black backdrop.

Close-up of two pairs of feet with dancing bells, eyes darkly kohled, or hands with henna in various dance expressions. The identity of the dancers is not revealed. The music is backed with strong vocal rhythmic syllables. The dancers keep pace with the music as their feet execute a technically complex rhythmic pattern. The music builds to a crescendo increasing the complexity of their footwork, till the male pair of feet cannot keep pace anymore. The male pair of feet give up and walk away out of frame. Intersperse these images that fade in and out with the main titles. Fade to black as music fades.

Interior/Exterior. Muthiah's modest living room. Late afternoon.

Ratna and Jairaj are seated on the floor. Muthiah is seated on a cushion next to them. Sreenivas is seated in front of them.

Ratna hands a bundle of notes to Sreenivas, who begins to count them.

SREENIVAS *(looking up)*. What, Madam? Times have changed.

RATNA. I really can't afford to—Seri! (Oh all right!). How much more do you want?

MUTHIAH. Give him another thousand.

RATNA *(taking out the money reluctantly)*. I hope you two are not going to disappear when I want you for rehearsals.

SREENIVAS *(taking the money).* Don't worry, madam. My blessings are always with you and your daughter.

Sreenivas gets up to leave. He steps out to wear his chappals.

RATNA *(to Jairaj).* I hope that Vanamala is not going to charge us double.

JAIRAJ. Don't worry, we will speak to her . . .

MUTHIAH. Don't worry amma, I will speak to her.

RATNA. Don't worry, don't worry these men say . . .

We hear a loud crash. They rush out.

Cut to:

Top of stairs.

Ratna, Jairaj and Muthiah look on at Sreenivas lying on the floor, his dhoti undone, clutching his arm in agony.

Close on Ratna. Horrified.

RATNA. Aiyo, Devere! (Oh God!)

Jairaj and Muthiah rush to help him. Sreenivas is howling in agony throughout.

(On top of stairs, hysterical.) Uchcha! (The madman!)

JAIRAJ *(helping Muthiah take Sreenivas down the stairs).* Ratna, go home. We will take him to the hospital.

RATNA *(yelling from top of the stairs).* Take back our money from that clumsy fool!

Jairaj looks at Ratna to shut her up.

The camera moves away from Ratna.

(Striking her forehead with her palm.) Karma! Karma! *(To Jairaj.)* It's your father's curse on us!

Cut to:

Interior. Living room. Parekh bungalow. Evening.

Camera pans slowly across an antique table holding several framed photographs. These are largely of a couple, together or separately, in various classical dance postures.

The camera comes to rest on a photograph of a middle-aged man, dressed in formal Indian clothes, gazing sternly at the camera. A hand comes into the frame and lifts the photograph as the camera travels to the face of a young man in his twenties. This is Vishwas, a pleasant-looking, slightly plump individual. He gazes quizzically at the photograph.

YOUNG WOMAN *(background).* That's him.

Vishwas turns sharply.

This house was built by my grandad.

Medium shot as Lata, an attractive young woman of about twenty, walks upto Vishwas.

LATA. He was a great social reformer. Used to hold political meetings in this very room.

LATA. Oh, a politician!

Lata takes the photograph from Vishwas and looks at it.

LATA. Not really. Well—he did stand for elections once but he lost. Amma says he blamed it all on dad. Of course that was all long before I was born so . . . I don't really know.

VISHWAS. They must have had some fights. What with your father being a dancer.

She puts the photograph down and looks around the room. We see it now: a large, high-ceilinged room with furniture that is at least half-a-century old.

LATA. They had their differences, but Daddy always respected him. He'll never sell this house—he's kept it just the way it was.

VISHWAS. That's it!

LATA. Huh?

VISHWAS. So that's what it is!

LATA. What?

VISHWAS. This room reminded me of something. Now I know what—an antique shop!

LATA. Well, everything here is at least forty or fifty years old.

Vishwas looks around a high-ceiling room with stain-glass windows.

VISHWAS. Wow, I've never seen a house like this! Old-fashioned wood, probably rotting—

LATA. Do you know how much this land is worth?

VISHWAS. Maybe, your dad should sell it. The contractors would pay a pile to get a multi-storey building up here.

LATA. Are you crazy? They've spent all their dancing lives here. Even before marriage, they practised with the same guru under this very roof.

Cut to:

Interior. Dance Hall. Parekh bungalow. Evening.

Empty hall. The door opens even as we hear Lata whisper to Vishwas 'Take off your shoes'.

Lata enters first followed by Vishwas. In silence Lata walks towards one side of the room which has old musical instruments and pictures of gurus.

Close-up. of Lata as she reverently hold a pair of dancing bells close to her face. Lata closes her eyes almost meditating.

Cut to:

Interior. Dance Hall. Parekh bungalow. Day. Flashback. Circa mid-seventies.

Note: This scene intercuts with the next as appropriate.

Close-up. of a young man executing a complex piece of nritta. This is Jairaj, Lata's father in his youth. He wears a plain cotton dhoti and dancing bells on his ankles. His bare chest is covered with a sheen of perspiration.

Close-up of the guru, an elderly man with long hair. He sits cross-legged on the floor, giving Jairaj vocal rhythmic patterns.

Camera revolves around the dancing figure.

Intercut with Close-up of the guru and a young, beautiful woman, Ratna, who watches Jairaj, her mouth partially-open.

Cut to:

Camera revolves around Lata.

LATA. Can you believe it? These are the same bells my father wore for his debut! Ooh! I get goosebumps every time I touch them. This room has something special in it.

Intercut with Close-up of Ratna looking at Jairaj.

We come back to Lata looking at Vishwas.

Can you feel it?

Medium shot as Vishwas walks slowly around the room which has a wooden floor and mirrors on one wall. An assortment of musical instruments lie in a corner.

VISHWAS. What? The goosebumps?

LATA. Atmosphere! Vibrations!

She shakes the bells. With the shaking bells we hear an echo of the music that was playing in the flashback.

VISHWAS. Yes, that too.

LATA. This floor has felt a million adavus (dance steps). Over and over again.

She stamps the floor several times in demonstration. Again an echo of Jairaj dancing.

Feel that?

VISHWAS. I hear it too.

LATA. Vishwas, when we are married, you will let me come here to practise, won't you?

VISHWAS. Of course Lata!

LATA. Oh, thank you!

She holds the bells to her eyes and replaces them near the instruments.

VISHWAS. Don't thank me. I don't think our floor can withstand a million adavus.

LATA. And we won't have children.

Close-up of the young Ratna's tearful face as she silently screams out 'Shankar!'

VISHWAS. And we won't have—what?

LATA. I mean not right away. We can have them later, can't we?

VISHWAS. My father almost died when I told him I was marrying outside the caste. Wait till he hears this!

LATA. There's plenty of time. We are still young. My parents had me when they were in their thirties.

She switches off the lights in the dance hall.

We stay in the darkened hall. It is transformed to daylight for a moment as we see Guruji walking away even as Ratna and Jairaj cross the frame wiping the sweat on their faces. Back to dark empty hall.

Cut to:

Interior. Living room. Parekh bungalow. Evening.

As Vishwas and Lata walk in

VISHWAS. Where are they, anyhow? I thought you said it was all arranged. Wait a minute! They said seven.

LATA. I know but they had to go out. Emergency.

VISHWAS. What emergency? Only doctors and firemen go out on emergencies. Dancers stay at home till it's show time.

Lata makes a face at him.

LATA. One of our musicians fell down the stairs and broke his arm.

VISHWAS. Did he trip on his dhoti or what?

Cut to:

Interior. Hallway. Parekh bungalow. Evening.

On Lata as she dials the last digit and holds the receiver to her ear.

LATA. Hello, Muthu Uncle? Lata here. Yes, I'm fine, fine . . . No, they are not back, that's what I'm calling to find out . . . Oh, that's too bad. Multiple fractures? How did it happen? What? How could he trip on his . . .? That's sad. Do you know when amma and daddy . . . Yes, of course, I'll visit him . . .

Cut to:

Interior. Car. Evening.

Jairaj is driving, while Ratna sits beside him. They appear to be quite tense.

RATNA. What are we going to do?

JAIRAJ. We'll think of something.

RATNA. That's what you always say, but, in the end, it's I who has to do everything. How could he do this to us?

JAIRAJ. Must have been drunk.

RATNA. You should know!

Jairaj purses his lips. After a beat.

JAIRAJ. Don't worry. I'm sure you'll think of something.

Cut to:

Interior. Living room. Parekh bungalow. Evening.

On Lata as she walks in and sees Vishwas observing the cupboard.

LATA. Beautiful isn't it? Solid rosewood. They don't make cupboards like this any more.

VISHWAS. What's inside?

LATA. Oh, more books.

Vishwas starts opening the cupboard.

Be careful. Most of the books have turned yellow. They'll crumble if you touch them.

VISHWAS. Oh, wow!

On Vishwas as he takes out a splendid brocade shawl.

LATA. It's gorgeous isn't it?

VISHWAS. I'm going to ask for this as dowry.

LATA. He won't give it to you.

VISHWAS. Why not?

LATA. Same reason why he won't sell the house. It belonged to my grandfather.

VISHWAS. Looks like I should be lucky if he parts with you.

Lata takes the shawl from Vishwas, folds it and starts putting it away in the cupboard.

LATA. It was a present to my grandfather from the Maharaja of Mysore. He got some special award or something.

Lata heads towards the kitchen.

VISHWAS. Where are you going?

LATA. I'll make some coffee. They should be coming soon.

On Vishwas as he removes a book from a bookshelf, puts it back and dusts his hand. He looks around, slightly bored.

Cut to:

Interior. Kitchen. Evening.

Deviah the old family retainer is trying to get a peek at Vishwas, when Lata enters.

DEVIAH *(in Kannada)*. Is he a dancer?

LATA. Have you made the decoction?

They move to the kitchen counter where Lata takes the coffee off the stove.

No. He is not a dancer. He is the son of a businessman.

DEVIAH *(in Kannada)*. Your grandfather would not have approved.

Lata looks at Deviah as the latter busies himself by getting out the best crockery.

Cut to:

Interior. Living room. Evening.

Vishwas looks at the cupboard, then in the direction of the kitchen where Lata has disappeared. Quickly he walks to the cupboard, removes the shawl and gingerly puts it around his shoulders. He starts strutting around.

VISHWAS. Maharajah of Mysore, huh!

Cut to:

Exterior. Parekh bungalow. Evening.

Overhead shot as a car, an obviously old model, pulls up in front of the bungalow.

Cut to:

Interior. Living room. Evening.

On Vishwas who is now in the midst of a mock father act.

VISHWAS. So you want to be a dancer. Hah! Hah! Hah! Son, you'll never amount to anything. Look at me. Look at what I have achieved. And you dare to say there is more to life than money!

Cut to:

Interior. Hallway. Evening.

On the couple we had seen in the car earlier. They look at each other as they hear Vishwas's raised voice from the living room.

Cut to:

Interior. Living room. Evening.

On Vishwas as he continues on dramatically, unaware of the presence of the couple who have entered the living room.

VISHWAS. Where will you go being a dancer? Nowhere!

On Ratna.

What will you get being a dancer? Nothing? People will point at you in the streets and laugh and ask, 'Who is he?' 'He is a dancer.'

On Jairaj.

'What does he do?' 'He is a dancer.' 'Yes. But what does he do?' 'He is . . .'

Suddenly Vishwas notices the couple and stops short. He grins stupidly. They are obviously Lata's parents, Jairaj and Ratna.

Sir! I—I was just waiting.

The couple do not respond.

(*Rambling.*) Actually, I love dancing. Not disco or anything like that. I mean dance, our dance. So much more in them; you know what I mean. Lata!

Frantically, he looks towards the kitchen.

JAIRAJ. Please put the shawl back.

VISHWAS. Oh I'm so sorry—it's such a beautiful shawl.

He folds it clumsily.

RATNA. Give it to me.

She folds it neatly and puts it back in the cupboard, then sits down and looks at Vishwas.

Sit down.

Then without looking at Jairaj.

Sit down.

Cut to:

Interior. Kitchen. Evening.

On Lata and Deviah as Lata arranges cups on a tray.

JAIRAJ (*background*). Lata!

She looks up with a start. Camera follows her as she leaves the kitchen.

Cut to:

Interior. Living room. Evening.

POV Lata as she sees Ratna, Jairaj and Vishwas sitting stiffly in an embarrassed silence.

Intercut between Lata and them as—

LATA. I didn't hear you come in. I spoke to Muthu Uncle and he said you had already left. What took you so long?

They look at her silently.

Did I interrupt something? Anyway Deviah's made some coffee. I'll bring it along.

As she quickly exists the room, the others stare at each other.

RATNA *(bursting out).* This is terrible! What are we going to do?

JAIRAJ. There is no use worrying . . .

The camera pans back and forth between them as Vishwas looks on completely foxed.

RATNA. This has never happened before. In all my life . . .

JAIRAJ. Our lives . . .

RATNA. All right—our lives, I can't remember having ever been in such a crisis!

JAIRAJ. It's not a crisis.

RATNA. Crisis, problem, whatever!

JAIRAJ. We've had problems before.

RATNA. But never one like this! Oh God! What will we do?

JAIRAJ. We'll think of something. First, shut up!

Ratna stops.

Vishwas looks dumbfounded.

VISHWAS. Look, I know I haven't made a very good first impression, but please don't think of me as a crisis or a problem—really!

RATNA. What are you talking about?

JAIRAJ. We weren't talking about you. We don't even know you.

VISHWAS. Oh, I'm Vishwas and . . .

JAIRAJ *(irritated)*. We know that. But we don't know you well enough to think of you as a problem or crisis or whatever!

VISHWAS *(visibly relieved)*. Oh thank you! I was just . . .

RATNA. Just ten days. That's all we have.

> *On Lata as she enters with a tray holding a pot of coffee and four cups.*

LATA. So what do you think of him?

RATNA. We aren't thinking of him.

> *Lata starts serving the coffee.*

LATA. Oh, then it's me you're thinking of. Vishwas I hope you haven't told them you don't have any money. Don't believe him. His father owns half the buildings on Commercial Street.

VISHWAS. Your parents seem to be in the middle of another problem.

RATNA. Srinivas broke his arm. Who will play the mridangam for your performance?

LATA. Oh my God! Of course he broke his arm!

RATNA. Why did it have to be him of all the people? I wouldn't have minded if Muthiah had broken his neck—

JAIRAJ *(to Vishwas)*. A flutist or a violinist one can do without, but a mridangist is another matter.

RATNA. The fool had to go and trip on his dhoti. Must have been drunk.

VISHWAS. It's a special art, of course . . .

LATA. Playing any instrument is a special art.

VISHWAS. No, I mean wearing a dhoti. You have to get the hang of it. You know, I tried it once. You've got to kick it out of your way, like a sari. Of course I've never worn a sari but . . .

He is standing now attempting to demonstrate. The others stare at him as if he has lost his mind.

LATA. Vishwas, please! We are in the middle of a crisis.

JAIRAJ. I suppose we could ask Seshadri.

RATNA. Certainly not.

She gets up abruptly.

JAIRAJ. Where are you going?

RATNA. To take an Aspirin. I've got a headache.

She starts to leave.

JAIRAJ. You're always taking Aspirin. You've got to stop.

He starts to follow her.

VISHWAS. Maybe I should go . . .?

JAIRAJ *(abruptly)*. Sit down.

Vishwas sits down obediently. Jairaj turns and leaves.

Cut to:

Interior. Bedroom. Evening.

On Ratna as she rummages through a drawer of a bedside table, looking for medication.

Medium shot as Jairaj walks in. Ratna pops a pill into her mouth and washes it down with a glass of water.

JAIRAJ. You're going to kill yourself. Stop taking those tablets.

RATNA. I have to! I can't take this tension.

JAIRAJ. What tension? There's plenty of time. You're worrying about nothing.

RATNA *(getting excited)*. Nothing? Our daughter is giving a performance that will make her career and she is not going to have a mridangam playing for her. How do you expect her to give her best? How do you expect her to dance? What will we announce to the President of India if he comes? There will be no dance tonight? Tell all those foreign diplomats to go home? In my life I've had problems . . .

JAIRAJ. Now don't start . . .

RATNA. Problems which you know about but conveniently forget!

JAIRAJ. Ratna no . . .

RATNA. I did not go through all that to see our daughter's career finished overnight!

JAIRAJ. It's not . . .

RATNA. Your father was right. Dance has brought us nowhere. It's his curse on us. Nothing seems worth it any more. You should have listened to him. He was right. We were never anything great, never will be, and nor will our daughter be anything but an average human being.

JAIRAJ. Lata is not average!

RATNA. If she can't dance what else can she be?

JAIRAJ. There were times when we didn't dance.

RATNA. And look where we are.

Cut to:

Interior. Hallway. Evening.

On Lata as she stands very still looking up the stairs leading to the bedrooms. She turns slowly and walks back to the living room.

Cut to:

Interior. Living room. Evening.

Vishwas stands up as Lata walks in.

VISHWAS. Maybe I should go. We could always do this another time.

Lata throws him a look. He sits down.

Maybe, I'll just wait. I'm sure everything's fine.

Cut to:

Interior. Bedroom. Evening.

JAIRAJ. We are fine! At least I am.

RATNA. You! You are fine because you never left your father's home and stood on your own two feet . . .

JAIRAJ. Ratna! Don't . . .

RATNA. You stopped being a man for me the day you came back to this house . . .

JAIRAJ. For thirty years you've been holding that against . . .

RATNA. You're right I'm worrying about nothing, because nothing is what we are!

JAIRAJ *(quietly)*. You're going mad.

He walks away. He stops and turns.

Maybe it's Shankar's curse on us.

Jairaj walks out and we stay on Ratna who closes her eyes in anguish.

Cut to:

Interior. Living room. Evening.

On Lata and Vishwas as they stand up. Jairaj enters looking preoccupied.

VISHWAS. Sir, maybe I should go. I'll come back some other time.

Jairaj looks at him, as if suddenly aware of his presence for the first time.

JAIRAJ. No. Don't go.

LATA. Daddy . . .

JAIRAJ. Please stay. I'm sorry. We're usually a little more hospitable to our guests than this.

VISHWAS. It's alright, Sir.

JAIRAJ. Lata, go see to your mother.

LATA. Oh, Daddy, not when she's in one of her moods. You know how she gets.

JAIRAJ. I know. Now go to her.

Lata looks at Vishwas, then reluctantly leaves. Jairaj goes to the cupboard and removes a bottle of whisky from behind some books.

Do you drink?

VISHWAS. Well . . . No . . . Yes . . . Sometimes with friends. But never in front of elders.

Jairaj looks at him, then replaces the bottle in its hiding place.

JAIRAJ. I'm not supposed to drink.

Vishwas looks on befuddled by Jairaj's actions.

I've got a better idea. Let's get out of here.

He starts to leave the room.

VISHWAS. But where? Where are we going?

JAIRAJ. Do you always ask so many questions?

He keeps walking as Vishwas hurries after him.

Cut to:

Interior. Bedroom. Night.

Ratna and Lata lie on the bed in the darkened room. Lata is gently massaging her mother's forehead.

RATNA. Where have they gone?

LATA. I don't know, Amma.

Lata slides closer to her mother and puts an arm on her.

Amma, don't worry. No matter what, I will dance at the festival. For you. I won't let you down, Amma. Ever.

Ratna turns and looks at Lata.

RATNA. You are very talented. I will make sure everybody knows that.

LATA *(softly)*. If I have half your talent, Amma, I know I will be a great dancer.

Ratna is happy to hear that and gives her daughter a hug.

RATNA. Liar. You know how to make your mother happy.

They embrace warmly.

Cut to:

Exterior. Bar. Street. Night.

Overhead shot of a street, almost deserted. Two men exit a seedy bar, obviously inebriated.

Cut to:

Interior. Bar. Night.

Camera pan across a crowded, smoke-filled room. Camera comes to rest on Vishwas and Jairaj. The former looks decidedly uncomfortable in these surroundings. Two glasses of whisky are placed on the small, wooden table they share.

VISHWAS. So this is how the other half lives.

Jairaj does not respond, but takes a huge gulp of his drink.

It's just that I didn't expect . . .

JAIRAJ. What? That someone of my standing would patronize a place like this?

VISHWAS. Well—

JAIRAJ. Go on. Drink up.

Vishwas gingerly takes a sip.

Cut to:

Interior. Bedroom. Night.

Ratna smiles at Lata.

LATA. Now go to sleep. You need all the rest.

Ratna turns around.

Lata turns off the bed lamp and gets up to leave.

On Ratna who is still wide awake. Lata is at the cupboard taking out a sheet.

RATNA. Lata . . .?

LATA *(turning around)*. Yes?

RATNA. Nothing. Go to your room.

Lata sighs and comes back in, sitting on the bed.

LATA. Tell me.

Cut to:

Interior. Bar. Night.

Vishwas is waiting for Jairaj to say something to him, but the latter simply continues to drink.

VISHWAS. Er—you were going to tell me what's worrying you.

JAIRAJ. Was I?

VISHWAS. Yes. That's why you asked me to stay, I think.

JAIRAJ. Oh, it's not worrying that's worrying me. It's . . .

VISHWAS. Yes?

An inebriated client lurches against their table, partially spilling their drinks. He smiles apologetically, and continues to weave his way towards the exit. Jairaj watches him.

JAIRAJ *(to himself)*. Stopping. And looking back. And seeing that you haven't gone very far. And won't go much further.

Cut to:

Interior. Bedroom. Night.

Ratna turns to look at Lata.

RATNA. You want to dance, don't you?

LATA. What a question to ask? Yes!

RATNA. I—I am not forcing my dreams on you, am I?

LATA *(holding her mother's hand)*. Amma, you are helping me see my dreams come true. My own dreams.

RATNA. Good. I—I wouldn't want to hurt you in any way.

Ratna turns away and closes her eyes.

LATA. Amma, what do you think of him?

RATNA. Who?

LATA. Vishal, Amma!

RATNA. Oh, Vishal! He seems to be a bit strange but I suppose he is all right. Why?

LATA. He's asked me to marry him.

RATNA. He's well off, isn't he?

LATA. Amma!

RATNA. And he will let you dance, no?

LATA. Yes.

RATNA. Then let the wedding be after Navratri.

Cut to:

Interior. Bar. Night.

Jairaj turns to Vishwas.

JAIRAJ. So your father is a paanwallah.

VISHWAS. Mithaiwalla. Sweets and things like that.

JAIRAJ. Makes a lot of money?

VISHWAS. It's the family business. It's okay. He's really made his money from his buildings.

JAIRAJ. Hmm. Black?

VISHWAS. Jet black.

JAIRAJ. Buildings, is it?

VISHWAS. Yes.

JAIRAJ. Strange. That's how my father made his money.

VISHWAS. Buildings?

JAIRAJ. Houses, bungalows. Bought them real cheap. Back in the sixties there was a real demand for these bungalows. He made a lot of money.

Cut to:

Interior. Living room. Parekh bungalow. Day. Flashback.

JAIRAJ. Amritlal Parekh. The sethji of the city. Spent it all in reconstructing India—building the temples of the future.

Cut to:

**Interior. Dance Hall. Parekh bungalow. Day. Flashback.
Circa mid-seventies**

> *On young Jairaj dancing while young Ratna and their
> guru give him vocal rhythmic patterns.*

The craft of a prostitute to show off her wares—what business
did a man have learning such a craft? Of what use could it be
to him? No use. So surely no man would want to learn such
a craft.

JAIRAJ *(voice-over).* Hence anyone who learnt such a craft could
not be a man.

> *Jairaj finishes a complex, technically demanding tillana.
> He goes off rhythm. The guru corrects him. Ratna gets
> up and begins to dance the same piece with greater
> skill. Jairaj smiles a little self-consciously as he watches
> Ratna. The guru asks for some water.*

> *Cut to:*

Interior. Living room. Day. Flashback.

> *On Amritlal Parekh, a robust man of about fifty years,
> deep in conversation with a group of men. Patel, his
> general dogsbody is seated on a stool next to Amritlal.
> Around Amritlal's shoulders we notice the brocade
> shawl.*

> *A younger Deviah is clearing the English tea cups on
> a silver tray. He exits towards the kitchen.*

MAN # 1. So, we all feel that you should be our candidate for
elections.

AMRITLAL. I am deeply honoured. But I know nothing about
politics.

MAN # 2. Don't worry Sethji. We will work out the election
plans. You are well respected in the city and with your
background in freedom fighting—

> *The sound of bells distracts them. They look up.*

> *POV Men as they watch Jairaj cross the main hall
> towards the kitchen, his dancing bells still on.*

On Amritlal. He purses his lips in obvious distaste.

(Clearing his throat.) You have the right image in society as a man of iron with progressive ideas.

Cut to:

Interior. Dance hall. Day. Flashback.

On Ratna performing a tillana.

MAN # 1 *(voice-over).* You even have a daughter-in-law who is from Mysore. All social reformers are encouraging inter-community marriages.

Cut to:

Interior. Living room. Parekh bungalow. Day. Flashback.

On Amritlal and his guests.

MAN # 2. You are a forward thinking man. You don't believe in blind tradition and superstition. Together we can build a modern Mysore state with industries, dams and mechanized farming!

Amritlal is rather pleased with his image in the eyes of these men, till he hears the bells again. He turns to see—

POV Amritlal as Jairaj returns with a clay pot of water, humming a Carnatic tune, oblivious to the effect on his father and his group of friends.

Deviah comes rushing out of the kitchen and tries to take the clay pot from Jairaj.

JAIRAJ *(resisting).* No. I will serve Guruji myself. You look after appa and his guests.

Jairaj exits grandly.

Deviah looks on helplessly at Amritlal.

Cut to:

Exterior. Parekh bungalow. Night.

Deviah is seated in the veranda on the floor leaning against a wall, waiting. He gets up when he hears car approaching.

Interior. Car. Night.

On Vishwas and Jairaj as they come to a halt in front of the Parekh bungalow. Neither make a move to get out. Vishwas looks at Jairaj.

VISHWAS. You must have hated him.

A cynical smile appears o Jairaj's face.

Lata told me you respected him a lot.

JAIRAJ. Did she say that?

VISHWAS. Yes. That's why you keep the house the way you do. Like a shrine in memory of him.

Deviah opens the car door and waits for Jairaj to get out of the car. Jairaj looks at Deviah.

JAIRAJ. Rubbish. This was my world. I have kept it the same because it's mine.

He struggles to get out. He's clearly inebriated. Deviah helps him out. Vishwas gets out too and offers support to Jairaj.

Cut to:

Interior. Hallway. Parekh bungalow. Night.

As the main door opens, Jairaj enters the hallway with Deviah assisting him. Vishwas has a hand gingerly placed at Jairaj's elbow to assist him. Jairaj looks at him and pushes away his hand. He walks unaided towards the living room.

Cut to:

Interior. Living room. Night.

Medium shot as Vishwas follows Jairaj into the room. Deviah hangs around to see if he is needed. Jairaj stops to look at the cupboard. Jairaj gestures to Vishwas to come to him. Vishwas walks up to him. Jairaj goes to the cupboard and removes the shawl. He clumsily wraps it around Vishwas.

VISHWAS. It's fantastic!

JAIRAJ. Do you like it?

VISHWAS. Oh yes!

JAIRAJ. You can have it then.

VISHWAS. Oh! I don't know how to thank you. It's so generous of you. I promise to take good care of it. *(To Deviah, in Kannada.)* Could you give me a bag please?

Deviah exits to get a bag. Jairaj takes the shawl back.

JAIRAJ. I didn't mean you could take it now. When you are married to Lata.

VISHWAS. Oh yes, yes of course.

He takes Jairaj's hand and shakes it vigorously.

Thank you. Thank you very much, Sir.

Jairaj removes his hand from Vishwas's clasp.

JAIRAJ. It's only a shawl. Most boys would ask for a car.

VISHWAS. No! I mean—thank you for agreeing to our marriage. You approve of me!

JAIRAJ. I approve of you?

VISHWAS. Yes!

JAIRAJ. And you approve of us?

VISHWAS. Yes!

JAIRAJ. Good. Then go home. And tell your father to call me some time.

VISHWAS. Yes, Sir! Yes–Appa! Certainly.

Vishwas rushes out excited as Deviah enters with a carry bag.

Cut to:

Exterior. Bungalow. Night.

On Vishwas's car, a Zen or an Alto, as it starts up. On Ratna. She stands by a darkened window looking down at the departing car.

Cut to:

Interior. Car. Night.

Vishwas drives out of the Parekh bungalow. As he leaves the house behind, he turns on the stereo. A heavy metal band is playing. He heaves a sigh of relief and shakes his head to the strong rhythm as he drives off.

Cut to:

Interior. Living room. Night.

On Jairaj taking a nip from the bottle. He puts it back behind the books and shuts the cupboard. He turns around and notices the shawl. He picks it up and looks at it.

JAIRAJ *(to himself).* Your last memory. Soon I'll be rid of you too. Then I won't see you wearing this shawl, walking about this room.

He starts to pace up and down.

I won't see you wearing this shawl walking about this room. Walking about—wearing this shawl.

We hear the flute and the violin, followed by the mridangam as dissolve to:

Interior. Living room. Day. Flashback.

On Amritlal

AMRITLAL. Jai! Jairaj!

Cut to:

Interior. Library/Dance hall. Day. Flashback.

On Jairaj as he stops dancing the jathiswaram. He motions the musicians to stop playing. He turns to the doorway where his father stands glowering.

JAIRAJ. What Bapu?

AMRITLAL. When I call for you, please show your face.

He turns and walks back into the living room.

Cut to:

Interior. Living room. Day. Flashback.

On Jairaj as he follows his father into the room.

JAIRAJ. What is it, Bapu? I'm in the middle of an item.

AMRITLAL. You've been at it the whole day. How long will it last?

JAIRAJ. I don't know. Ratna and I take turns. Guruji decides when to pack up.

AMRITLAL. I want this din to stop. I want your guruji out. I have some important people coming and I want those musicians out before they arrive.

JAIRAJ *(coldly).* They will leave when your guests come, I assure you.

AMRITLAL. I want them out now.

JAIRAJ. I can't just ask them to leave!

Ratna walks in from the veranda.

RATNA. Are you coming? Guruji is waiting. He wants you to do the jathiswaram with me.

AMRITLAL. Tell him he is occupied for the time being.

RATNA. Jai?

JAIRAJ. In a minute Ratna.

RATNA. You know what he's like when he gets annoyed.

She returns to the dance hall where we can see her explaining matters to Guruji.

AMRITLAL. Doesn't he have any other students, your guru?

JAIRAJ. He is the most sought after guru in India.

AMRITLAL. Then why is he spending his entire day in my house?

JAIRAJ. I'm not going to get into an argument with you on that. Why can't I even have a decent rehearsal in this house?

He turns to leave. Amritlal flares up.

AMRITLAL. You can't have a decent rehearsal in this house? I can't have some peace and quiet in my house! It's bad enough having to convert the library into a practice hall for you.

JAIRAJ. Why did you do it if you didn't want to?

AMRITLAL. I thought it was just a fancy of yours. I would have made a cricket pitch for you on our lawn if you were interested in cricket. Well, most boys are interested in cricket, my son is interested in dance, I thought. I didn't realize this interest of yours would turn into an . . . obsession.

JAIRAJ. Didn't you have your obsessions?

AMRITLAL. If you mean my involvement in fighting for your freedom when I was your age. Marching to Dandi along with the Mahatma, fighting for Swaraj—yes, it was my obsession.

JAIRAJ. You had yours. Now allow me to have mine.

He returns to the dance hall. After a pause, Amritlal goes to the telephone and dials quickly.

AMRITLAL. Patel? It is I . . . Now listen to me carefully.

Cut to:

Exterior. Shiva temple. Morning. Flashback.

Idol of Lord Shiva. The aarti is in progress. We pull back to see the poojaris performing the ritual. We move back further to see a crowd of devotees waiting with folded hands for the prasad. Ratna is among them.

As the crowds move closer to the shrine, Ratna moves away looking at the people surreptitiously to make sure no one notices her. Ratna half runs down the temple steps to a waiting rickshaw. She gets in and the rickshaw driver gets on the cycle and begins to pedal the rickshaw away, just as another rickshaw follows them.

Cut to:

Exterior. Street. Morning. Flashback.

Overheard shot of Ratna in a rickshaw. It comes to a halt in front of a ramshackled building. In fact the whole locality looks quite run-down. On Ratna as she quickly pays the driver and enters the gate to the building. Medium shot as Ratna's rickshaw pulls way, the other rickshaw that was following her arrives carrying Patel, the middle-aged, portly man we had seen with Amritlal. He tells the driver to wait and then cautiously approaches the house, Ratna has just entered.

Cut to:

Exterior. Courtyard. Morning. Flashback.

On Ratna: Having put on her dancing bells she positions herself in front of an ancient crone, Chenni Amma, who sits on a mat on the floor. As Chenni Amma begins to sing a padam beating out the rhythm with a stick, Ratna moves gracefully to the beat, interpreting the text on love with facial expressions. Chenni Amma stops to sing. Ratna looks on awaiting some feedback.

CHENNI AMMA *(speaking in an archaic form of Tamil).* You won't get the bhava if you do not experience love and devotion. Feel the love and devotion for Shiva. See him as the perfect man.

Chenni Amma sings and demonstrates, her face transformed to expressing sensual love making her seem younger. Ratna watches her completely in awe. Chenni Amma gestures to Ratna to start. Ratna dances with renewed vigour and sensuality.

On Patel as he watches them half-hidden by a wall. Behind him the rickshaw driver comes up and tries to get a look.

On Ratna as she continues to dance, oblivious of Patel's presence.

On Chenni Amma as she observes Ratna and continues to sing. Chenni Amma stops as she notices Patel and the rickshaw driver. Patel feels a little embarrassed and shoos away the driver, slinking away to his rickshaw at the same time. Ratna notices Patel too and is disconcerted. Chenni Amma gestures Ratna to sit beside her. Ratna sits reverently by Chenni Amma's feet.

To master the art of abhinaya, you will have to find the woman and God inside you—and to dance, you must fight the demons outside you.

Ratna looks on waiting for an explanation.

To keep our tradition alive you have to be a rebel. Such is the irony of our times. There are people who do not see the beauty of what we do. They are the demons you must overcome. These people who do not understand the rhythm of life itself.

Cut to:

Interior. Dance hall. Evening. Flashback.

On Amritlal as he walks up to the entrance of the dance hall.

POV Amritlal. Jairaj, oblivious to his father's presence, is practising a complicated abhinaya while singing the text he is interpreting. As he turns and catches sight of Amritlal, he stops. They look at each other, the tension between them palpable.

AMRITLAL. All alone? Where is your wife?

JAIRAJ. I don't know. Now if you'll excuse me.

He starts to dance again, ignoring Amritlal but disconcerted all the same. After a pause, Amritlal enters the hall and slowly walks around the room.

AMRITLAL. I have always allowed you to do what you wanted to do. But there comes a time when you have to do what is expected of you. Why must you dance? It doesn't give you any income. Is it because of your wife? Is she forcing you to dance?

JAIRAJ. Nobody's forcing me.

AMRITLAL. Well, influencing you then, maybe. You know that's one thing I regret. Consenting to your marriage.

JAIRAJ. Don't pretend. It suited your image—that of a liberal-minded person, to have a daughter-in-law from outside your community.

AMRITLAL. And for that I repent.

Jairaj stops dancing and looks at his father.

JAIRAJ. What do you mean?

AMRITLAL. Where does she go every Monday?

Jairaj looks away.

You know and you don't tell me.

JAIRAJ. Where are your progressive ideas now?

He sits down and starts taking off his dancing bells.

AMRITLAL. This is different.

JAIRAJ. You have no knowledge of the subject. You are ignorant!

AMRITLAL. We are doing what we can for these unfortunate women. Educating them, reforming them—

JAIRAJ. Reforms? Don't talk about reform. If you really wanted any kind of reform in our society, you would let them practise their art.

AMRITLAL. Encourage open prostitution?

Jairaj gets up and starts to leave the dance hall.

JAIRAJ. Send them back to their temples! Give them awards for preserving our art.

Jairaj exits.

Cut to:

Interior. Living room. Night. Flashback.

Amritlal follows Jairaj into the living room.

AMRITLAL. I will not have our temples turned into brothels!

JAIRAJ. And I will not have my art run down by a a handful of narrow-minded individuals.

AMRITLAL. Nobody is running down your art. It is the people who perform it and for what reason, that we are trying to—

JAIRAJ. Alright then! You should be pleased that people from respectable families like yours are interested in reviving this dance.

AMRITLAL. I have no objection to your efforts in reviving the art, but I definitely do object to the people you are associating with.

JAIRAJ. What do you mean?

AMRITLAL. Your guru? What kind of family is he from?

JAIRAJ. His mother was not a devdasi, if that's what you want to know.

AMRITLAL. Why does he wear his hair so long? I have never seen a man with long hair.

JAIRAJ. All sadhus have long hair.

AMRITLAL. I don't mean them. I meant normal men.

JAIRAJ. What are you trying to say?

AMRITLAL. All I'm trying to say is that normal men do not keep their hair so long.

JAIRAJ *(appalled)*. Are you trying to say he's not—are you saying?

AMRITLAL. I've also noticed the way he walks.

JAIRAJ *(furious)*. This is disgusting! You're insane!

    Cut to:

Interior. Living room. Night.

    On Ratna as she walks into the dimly-lit living room. She stops. POV Ratna: Jairaj sits slumped in an armchair, the brocade shawl wrapped around him.

RATNA. Jairaj?

    He doesn't look up.

JAIRAJ. How are you feeling?

    Ratna walks up to him.

RATNA. Just awful.

    Jairaj hiccups.

(Sniffing.) You've been drinking, haven't you?

JAIRAJ. A little. The boy wanted a drink very badly. I just kept him company.

RATNA. I don't believe you. And where do you get the liquor from? If you send Deviah again to fetch you alcohol I will throw him out of the house.

JAIRAJ. Now who is pretending?

He looks at her slyly.

RATNA. What do you mean?

JAIRAJ. You know very well I keep it in the cupboard.

RATNA. If I had known, I would have thrown it away, no?

JAIRAJ. You did take it away. And you put it back. After diluting it with water . . . Sit down, Ratna devi, sit down . . .

RATNA *(disconcerted).* I–I have a little bit now and then to settle my nerves.

JAIRAJ. Can I get you a drink?

Jairaj gets a glass and pours Ratna a drink.

He hands Ratna the glass.

RATNA. All right. Just a little.

She takes a gulp.

JAIRAJ. You know we should drink together more often. At least then we can be more honest with each other.

RATNA. I have decided that we could ask Chandra Kala to lend us Seshadri, as a favour. She may need our help some day, so she is bound to oblige.

JAIRAJ. I'm sure she'll be happy to oblige you.

RATNA *(getting up to go).* So, I'll call her in the morning. As she makes to go.

JAIRAJ *(abruptly).* Do you think we would have been happier if we hadn't come back?

Ratna stops and slowly turns to look at Jairaj.

RATNA. Why bring it up after all these years?

JAIRAJ. Well, you did actually. What did you say? I stopped being a man for you because we couldn't survive on our own . . .

RATNA. You mustn't take notice of what I say when I'm upset.

JAIRAJ. That's the only time you make sense to me.

Ratna moves in the direction of the bedroom.

What did you want me to do? Carry on staying at your uncle's . . .

RATNA. Don't!

JAIRAJ. Stay with him after what he . . .

RATNA. Will you please . . .

JAIRAJ. Is that what you wanted me to do?

RATNA. Don't say it!

JAIRAJ. Look the other way while your uncle . . .

RATNA. Stop it!

She rushes out of the room.

Cut to:

Interior. Dance hall. Parekh bungalow. Day.

Close-up of Lata as she practises in front of a mirrored wall to taped music. Vishal comes into view behind her. Lata smiles but continues to dance. Vishal puts his arms around her.

LATA *(pretending shock)*. Vishal!

But she doesn't pull away. He kisses the nape of her neck.

VISHWAS. I don't know much about dance but when you move like that . . .

LATA. Someone will see . . .

VISHWAS. So what? Your father approves of me.

LATA. Oh yeah? What did you do? Drink him into submission?

VISHWAS. Pretty much.

She pulls away, goes to the tape deck and stops the music.

VISHWAS. What's the matter?

LATA. Nothing.

VISHWAS. I haven't done anything, have I?

LATA. It's not you—it's them! . . . The most important day of my life and they're at each other's throats.

VISHWAS. Oh don't worry about that! I don't mind. We just chose the wrong day to ask them.

LATA. What are you talking about?

VISHWAS. Well, our engagement of course.

LATA. My Arangetram is in a few days, I have to perform in front of hundreds of people and all you can think of is . . .

VISHWAS. The rest of our lives.

LATA. Oh Vishwas . . . do you know how important this is to my parents?

VISHWAS. I thought you were angry with them.

LATA. I don't know!

She flops on the floor.

LATA. It's just . . . I wish I didn't have to dance to please them. I want to dance to please me. All my life everything has been so . . . so cultivated. Sometimes I wish I could just breathe. Does that make sense?

VISHWAS. No . . . I guess.

LATA. Oh, Vishwas, maybe I'm lucky it doesn't matter so much to you.

VISHWAS. Where are they now?

LATA. In search of a musician.

VISHWAS *(pulling her to her feet)*. C'mon then, let's get out of here and let me show you what truly matters to me!

Cut to:

Exterior. Dance school. Day.

Overhead shot as Jairaj's car drives into the compound of a vast estate and comes to a halt.

Cut to:

Interior. Car. Day.

On Jairaj and Ratna.

RATNA. I wish you would come in with me.

JAIRAJ. I'd rather wait here. You are quite capable of handling her yourself.

RATNA. As usual . . . as usual . . .

She gets out of the car.

Cut to:

Exterior. Compound. Dance school. Day.

On Ratna as she starts walking up a path leading to a group of small, rustic looking buildings that give the impression of a small village.

Cut to:

Interior. Car. Day.

POV Jairaj. He sees Ratna asking directions from a young girl.

Cut to:

Interior. Dance studio. Day.

We hear the sound of music and dancing bells as Ratna walks through an enclosed courtyard which contains a dance hall.

POV Ratna. Chandra Kala, a woman of Ratna's age but not as well-preserved, is conducting a dance class with a group of young girls and boys. She catches sight of Ratna and smiles briefly.

On Ratna as she takes a seat on the floor and watches the lesson in progress.

On Seshadri playing the mridangam and watching the older girls lustfully.

On Ratna as she grimaces, observing Seshadri.

On the students as they finish their lesson, fold their hands then come and touch Chandra Kala's feet as a mark of respect.

On Chandra Kala as she dismisses her students. Seshadri packs his mridangam and leaves as Chandra Kala, beaming, walks upto Ratna.

CHANDRA KALA. Ratna Devi, you look as wonderful as ever.

RATNA. You too, Chandra Kala.

The two women smile insincerely at each other as they clasp hands.

I see you're doing very well with your dance school.

CHANDRA KALA. One tries to give back a little of God's merciful kindness. Now, tell me, what can I do for you?

RATNA. It's just a small favour. You see . . .

CHANDRA KALA. But where are my manners! You will have coffee, won't you?

RATNA. Well . . .

Chandra Kala summons a student.

CHANDRA KALA. Leela! Child, arrange for some coffee for our guest, please.

RATNA. It's just that Lata's show is only a few days away and—

CHANDRA KALA. Yes, Lata's show! Everyone is talking about it. Has she truly inherited her mother's talent? Oh, how jealous I used to be of you Ratna Devi.

Ratna laughs, a bit embarrassed.

RATNA. Come now, you never were Chandra Kala!

CHANDRA KALA. Of course, after Shankar you never were the same, so I got my chance.

Ratna stands very still.

(*Eyes narrowing.*) You are not still upset about that, are you?

RATNA. Please. I don't want to talk . . .

*Leela enters with the coffee interrupting their
conversation.*

CHANDRA KALA *(quickly)*. Ah, here's our coffee. Come sit down,
Ratna, and tell me what the trouble is.

*She takes Ratna's arm and they sit on low stools with
the coffee.*

RATNA. It's Sreenivas, our mridangist. He's broken his arm.

CHANDRA KALA. Broken his arm? What did he do?

RATNA. He tripped on his dhoti.

CHANDRA KALA. Sreenu has been wearing a dhoti ever since he
grew out of half-pants. He must have been drunk.

RATNA. Well, he . . .

CHANDRA KALA. This is a crisis. I mean a flutist or a violinist you
can do without . . .

RATNA *(quickly)*. So I was wondering if you could lend us
Seshadri?

CHANDRA KALA. Seshadri?

RATNA. Well, we do need someone to play the mridangam, and
everyone else is booked. Please . . . It–it will save us . . .

CHANDRA KALA. Seshadri! But of course Ratna—how clever you
are.

She stands up.

Sesha! Come and see who is here!

A pot-bellied man emerges from behind a door.

Look who's come to see us—Ratna Devi! She needs to beg a
big favour of you.

Cut to:

Exterior. Public garden. Day.

On Vishwas and Lata as they walk through the gardens.

LATA. It's like I've got to be everything they couldn't be.

VISHWAS. I thought they were really famous.

LATA. They were. But then everything came to a halt and I don't quite know why.

VISHWAS. Did you ask them about it?

LATA. Some things you don't talk about—especially with my mother . . . Oh Vishwas, I don't know what must you think of us!

VISHWAS. Wait till you see my parents!

She laughs. They walk away.

LATA. So what did you and my dad talk about?

VISHWAS. Oh, you don't want to know about that.

Cut to:

Interior. Car. Road. Day.

On Jairaj and Ratna as they drive away from the dance school.

JAIRAJ. What do you mean he'll only give us a day's rehearsal? He can't be rehearsing with Chandra Kala all the day for the rest of the days.

RATNA. When he's not rehearsing with her, he's sleeping with her.

JAIRAJ. That's just gossip.

RATNA. It's not gossip. I've seen it with my own eyes.

JAIRAJ. When?

RATNA. When we were in Moscow, at the hotel. At three in the morning, I saw him sneak down the corridor and into her room.

JAIRAJ. What were you doing in the corridor at three in the morning?

RATNA. Watching to see whose room you had sneaked into.

JAIRAJ. I was downstairs drinking vodka with the Yakshagana troupe.

RATNA. How do you know?

JAIRAJ. How do I know what?

RATNA. That was too quick an answer. How do you know which night I'm talking about?

JAIRAJ. There was only one night I stayed up late drinking vodka . . .

RATNA. That was twenty-five years ago. How can you remember so clearly?

JAIRAJ *(grinning)*. If you remember Seshadri sneaking down a hotel corridor twenty-five years ago, I can remember getting drunk with a gang of Yakshagana men with plucked eyebrows and bad make-up.

Ratna smiles reluctantly.

RATNA. Now, that's taken care of. What's next on our list? Oh—we have to pick up Lata's costume, we missed the turn. Go back . . .

JAIRAJ. No. We have another appointment.

RATNA. With whom?

JAIRAJ *(smiling)*. Trust you to forget that.

Cut to:

Interior. A restaurant that has seen better days. Day.

Vishwas is seated on one side of his father. On the other side of him is mother. Jairaj is on the other side of Vishwas's father. Ratna is next to Jairaj. On the other side of her is Lata. They are having a lavish lunch. The waiters are scurrying back and forth to serve them well.

FATHER *(to Jairaj)*. Eat. Eat fully.

Ratna looks around at the restaurant not very pleased with the surroundings.

RATNA. Do you come here often?

MOTHER. Oh yes! It's pretty expensive, but once a week we must come here. *(To Lata.)* Eat, eat fully.

RATNA. No. She can't eat this food—I mean she is training for her performance. *(To Lata, taking away a dish.)* Don't eat the fried stuff, Lata.

MOTHER. Nowadays, so many of our friends are also dancing. In fact we know Kumidiniben Lakhia. And Sonal Mansingh we know her family very well. Oh I forgot to tell you! I showed Lata and Vishwas's birth kundalis to our family astrologer. He said both their manglis are in the right house. There is just one thing.

Ratna looks up. So does Jairaj.

Nothing serious but . . . I hope Lata is not planning to join films or anything? *(Quickly adding.)* Not that we mind, but— the astrologer says—

VISHWAS. Mummy!

RATNA. No. We have no plans for her to do films.

MOTHER. Good. Very good. Then there is nothing to worry about. Only because of the astrologer. We have no problems with it . . . After all even the Ambanis and Madhwanis have film stars as bahus!

RATNA. Lata is an artiste.

MOTHER. Yes, yes, but nowadays even artistes are joining films also, no.

RATNA. Not all artistes are interested in movies. Even we are artistes, we never thought of doing films.

MOTHER. Oh yes. Lata told me you were a classical dancer also. I have heard of Rukmini Devi, Chandrakaladevi and all. But . . .

Jairaj looks at Ratna who is focusing on her plate, trying not to be provoked.

JAIRAJ. We . . . stopped dancing after . . .

MOTHER. After Lata was born? Very good of you to sacrifice your career for your daughter.

Ratna forces a smile and gets up.

RATNA. Excuse me.

Ratna exits to the washroom. Jairaj puts his fork down chewing on his food.

FATHER. I hope you don't mind Mr Jairaj, I checked your family background. Why didn't you tell me your father was Amritlal Parekh? My uncle knew him very well. What a great man he was. And so forward in his time, so culture-minded!

JAIRAJ *(slowing down his chewing, thoughtfully)*. Yes . . .

   Cut to:

Interior. Dining room. Parekh bungalow. Night. Flashback.

   On Amritlal sitting at the head of the dining table, helping himself to food from a dish.

AMRITLAL. No! It's not enough that I have to deal with a bunch of half-clad, long-haired men in my house all day and pay for the honour, now you want to go prancing on a stage with them in foreign lands!

   Pull back. Jairaj sits to the right of his father.

JAIRAJ. It is considered an honour. All we need is a few thousand rupees so that the musicians can accompany us. Is that so much to ask?

AMRITLAL. I said no. The matter is over. And tomorrow get your hair cut. It's getting too long.

   Jairaj pushes back his chair and storms out of the room, as Ratna enters with another dish from the kitchen.

RATNA. What happened?

   She puts the dish on the table.

AMRITLAL. Hmm?

   He starts to serve himself.

RATNA. What happened between you two? He looked upset.

AMRITLAL. Nothing happened. We were just talking I mentioned something about long hair and . . .

   Ratna starts laughing.

What's so funny?

RATNA. Oh, he told you?

AMRITLAL. What?

RATNA. That he's planning to grow his hair long? It would enhance his abhinaya.

AMRITLAL. I see. And was it his idea, or maybe yours?

RATNA. Actually, it was guruji's suggestion.

AMRITLAL. Tell him if he grows his hair even an inch longer, I will shave his head and throw him on the road.

Ratna falls silent, quite obviously intimidated.

RATNA. Let me go see if . . .

AMRITLAL. Where were you yesterday?

Ratna turns to look at him.

RATNA. Why do you ask? I told you where I was going.

AMRITLAL. But where did you go instead?

RATNA. I don't know what you mean.

AMRITLAL. You told me you were going to the Shiva temple.

RATNA. Like I do every Monday.

AMRITLAL. Every Monday, is it?

RATNA. Yes.

AMRITLAL. Times have changed. When we were newly married, Jai's mother and I were not allowed to go anywhere on our own, especially not to the movies. But we were allowed to go to the temple. So every time we wanted to go to the movies, we would tell everyone we were going to the temple.

Ratna looks away.

It was fortunate for me that it was Patel who saw you going there. I can trust him to keep his mouth shut. He called me out of concern for our family name.

RATNA. I haven't done anything to spoil the family name.

AMRITLAL. But people assume the worst.

RATNA. Well, you could start by reforming such people instead of . . .

Amritlal stands up enraged.

AMRITLAL. Don't preach to me!

They glare at each other.

RATNA *(quietly)*. Chenni Amma is the oldest living exponent of the Thanjavur school. I consider myself lucky to learn from her. So, yes, instead of going to the temple every Monday, I go to her house.

AMRITLAL. And practise in the courtyard of a prostitute for all passersby to see.

RATNA. She's a devdasi. People would naturally be curious to see where the sound of dancing bells are coming from. She is seventy-five years old.

AMRITLAL. And that makes it all right?

RATNA. You can't stop me from learning an art!

AMRITLAL. I don't want you seeing that woman again, that's final.

Ratna looks at him and starts to laugh.

What's so funny? Why?

RATNA. Tomorrow, Jairaj starts learning another dance form—Kuchipudi.

AMRITLAL. So?

RATNA *(triumphantly)*. In Kuchipudi, the men dress up as women!

Amritlal looks horrified.

JAIRAJ *(background)*. And what I wonder will you do about that, Bapu?

*Ratna and Amritlal turn to see Jairaj at the entrance.
In his arms he carries a small bundle.*

AMRITLAL. For God's sake, grow up Jairaj!

JAIRAJ. You can't stop me from doing what I want.

AMRITLAL. As long as you are under my care . . .

He smiles sardonically.

JAIRAJ. We are no longer under your care. We are leaving you bapu. You can't harm us any more.

AMRITLAL. Don't be a fool Jairaj. Where will you go?

JAIRAJ. That is no longer your concern. Come Ratna.

AMRITLAL. It is my concern! Jairaj! I lost your mother when you were born . . .

JAIRAJ. That's my fault too I suppose.

AMRITLAL. You misunderstand me Jairaj. We prayed to have you. After many years you were born to us. Don't go. You are all that I have.

JAIRAJ. Then I am sorry to say, Bapu, that you are left with nothing.

Jairaj exits grandly, taking Ratna by the arm.

Cut to:

Interior. Dance hall. Day.

On Lata as she practises her dance steps accompanied by musicians and supervised by Ratna.

On Jai as he sits by the door watching.

On Ratna as she looks in his direction and indicates that he make a call.

Cut to:

Interior. Hallway. Day.

On Jairaj as he speaks into the phone.

JAIRAJ. Chandra Kala? . . . It's I, Jairaj . . . Very well. How are you? . . . Good, good. It's just that we were wondering where Seshadri was? He was supposed to be at rehearsals two hours ago and . . . yes, yes . . . so he should be here soon. I'll tell Ratna . . . Thank you.

Cut to:

Interior. Dance hall. Night.

Ratna and Lata alone. Chenni Amma's photograph is in Lata's hands.

RATNA. Chenni Amma always said—'Let the Divine in you be possessed by the spirit of dance. And if the two meet, you will be transported to another world, taking your audience with you.'

Cut to:

Interior. Dance hall. Day.

On Vishwas watching mesmerized.

On Lata as she performs the varnam, accompanied with musicians and singer.

On Seshadri playing the mridangam and watching Lata appreciatively.

Cut to:

Interior. Hallway. Day.

On Ratna talking into the phone.

RATNA. You know C.V., how highly I regard your opinion. I don't care what other critics say, but your opinion is what counts . . . That's very kind of you, but it's what you write that matters.

On Jairaj as he enters with a newspaper in his hand.

Yes, it's very sad the President can't make it, but the Chief Minister will definitely be there . . . of course you will have a VIP seat . . . Yes, yes. Goodbye then.

She hangs up and looks at Jairaj.

RATNA. The old fogey loves to be garlanded on stage—it's a small price. But if he gives Lata a rave review, the others wouldn't dream of doing differently.

Vishwas enters hurriedly. He looks at Ratna.

VISHWAS. Oh, there you are! Lata is asking after you.

RATNA. It must be Seshadri again. He keeps giving her the wrong taal. I think it's deliberate. I wish Sreenu hadn't broken his arm.

As she starts to leave she looks at Jairaj.

I wish you would call Arundhati about the flowers. I can't do everything myself!

She sails out. Jairaj looks at Vishwas.

JAIRAJ. What do you say, should we go to our favourite watering-hole?

VISHWAS. Isn't it a bit early? Anyway, don't you have to make some calls?

JAIRAJ. Later, later.

He starts for the main door, but Vishwas hesitates.

What is it, boy? You don't always have to follow the dictates of women. Just pretend you do.

Vishwas nods and follows Jairaj out.

Fade out.

Exterior. Open amphitheatre. Night.

We hear an enthusiastic round of applause from an audience we do not see as lights dramatically fade on to the stage and Lata walks into a spotlight, resplendent in a brocade sari and heavy gold jewellery. She folds her hands to greet the audience, then salutes the musicians and comes to Ratna and Jairaj who are seated along with the musicians. She touches her father's feet. Jairaj smiles at her and blesses her. Lata touches her mother's feet. Ratna smiles at her with moist eyes. She looks at Lata before blessing her. Lata salutes the idol of Nataraja and takes centrestage. Ratna takes the cymbals in her hands and begins the first rhythmic syllables, glaring at Seshadri to make sure he will pick up the right taala. Lata begins her invocation dance to Lord Ganesha, projecting the splendoured personality of the Lord, with immaculate body movements and apt facial expressions. On Ratna who watches her daughter with intense concentration making sure Seshadri stays on the right taala, emphasizing each rhythmic cycle strongly with her hand cymbals. The

*camera pans the faces of the musicians travelling to
Jairaj who is beating out the rhythm with his palm on
his knee.*

*POV Jairaj: Lata continues her performance. Camera
tilts down Lata's form coming to rest on her ankles
ensconced in heavy dancing bells.*

Dissolve to:

Exterior. Veranda. Uncle's bungalow. Day. Flashback.

*On dancing bells. Camera travels up Ratna's body. She
is practising similar movements to what we have just
seen Lata enacting.*

Cut to:

Interior. Room. Day. Flashback.

*From a room which opens on to the veranda where
Ratna is practising the figure of a man moves into
frame. He lowers himself into a chair from where he
has a good view of Ratna.*

*On Ratna, who continues to dance oblivious of the
man's presence. On the man, who appears to be in his
forties. He watches her intently. On Ratna as she stops
and wipes the perspiration from her forehead with one
end of her sari. She turns sharply, as she hears the
sound of applause. On the man as he walks onto the
veranda.*

Cut to:

Exterior. Veranda. Day. Flashback.

*Medium shot of Ratna and the man. Ratna breaks into
a hesitant smile as the man approaches her.*

RATNA. I didn't see you, Uncle. Were you watching for long?

UNCLE. Long enough to know you are wonderful. Truly star
material.

RATNA. I was just practising. Have you seen Jairaj? He's been
gone all morning. He hasn't practised since we arrived here.

UNCLE. All the practice in the world won't make him as good as you.

RATNA. Oh, no, it's just that he's . . .

UNCLE. Sssh!

He puts a finger to her lips. She looks up at him wide-eyed.

Listen to me, Ratna. It's you that matters. Forget Jairaj! He doesn't have it in him. He is just the spoilt son of a rich father, who probably . . .

RATNA. Uncle!

UNCLE. All right, I'll grant he's devoted to dance, but can he match your grace and beauty?

Ratna doesn't respond.

Look, I haven't seen enough of you since you married, but I'm glad you sought refuge in my house.

RATNA. You've been very kind to us. I'm sure it won't be long . . .

UNCLE. Stay here, Ratna, . . . as long as you wish. I'm not Amritlal Parekh, but I can look after your needs. Get your musicians. I'll pay for it. Let me look after you the way you deserve.

RATNA. I don't think Jairaj would . . .

UNCLE. You need a man, not a boy, Ratna.

He puts his arms around her and draws her close. On Jairaj as he steps into the garden, looks up at the veranda and stops short. POV Jairaj: Ratna stands very still in the embrace of her Uncle. On Jairaj as he steps back, his face stricken.

Cut to:

Interior. Bedroom. Uncle's house. Night. Flashback.

On Jairaj and Ratna making love under a sheet. Suddenly he pulls away and throws himself to one side, with his back to his wife.

RATNA. What is it? Jai?

There is no response. She leans over.

What's the matter?

JAIRAJ. I don't want you practising in this house any more. Go to Chenni Amma, if you must—but not here!

RATNA. I don't understand.

JAIRAJ. Don't you?

Ratna draws away and lies back on the bed.

RATNA. He offered to pay for the musicians.

JAIRAJ. We don't need his charity.

RATNA. Don't we?

After a pause.

It would make life simpler . . .

JAIRAJ. For whom?

RATNA. He's my uncle.

JAIRAJ. An uncle who covets my wife!

Fade to black.

Exterior. Street. Chenni Amma's house. Day. Flashback.

On Amritlal's car as it edges to a halt.

Cut to:

Interior. Car. Day. Flashback.

On Amritlal as he gazes out of the window looking pensive. On Patel who sits in the front of the car next to the driver. He turns around to look at Amritlal. On Amritlal. He shakes his head.

Cut to:

Exterior. Courtyard. Chenni Amma's house. Day. Flashback.

On Ratna as she removes her dancing bells and puts them in a bag. She gets up and touches Chenni Amma's feet.

Cut to:

Exterior. Street. Day. Flashback.

Overhead shot as Ratna steps into the street, Patel approaches her. He points towards the car. Ratna looks startled.

Cut to:

Interior. Car. Day. Flashback.

On Amritlal.

AMRITLAL. I want to see you both happy.

Close medium shot on Amritlal and Ratna in the backseat of the car.

RATNA. We are.

AMRITLAL. Are you?

RATNA. Can't you tell?

POV Amritlal: Patel and the driver stand on the pavement away from the car. On Amritlal and Ratna.

AMRITLAL. Do you know where a man's happiness lies?

RATNA. No.

AMRITLAL. In being a man.

RATNA. That sounds profound. What does it mean?

AMRITLAL. I have seen the world. And I can recognize a clever woman when I see one.

Ratna looks at him, then shifts her glance.

How do you feel? How do you feel dancing with your husband? What do you think of him when you see him all dressed and . . . made-up?

RATNA. You seem to forget. I married him because he is a dancer.

AMRITLAL. That's what he believes. I'm a little harder to convince.

RATNA. It's the truth.

AMRITLAL. Is it?

RATNA. Yes.

AMRITLAL. Or did you marry him because he would let you dance?

Ratna looks ruffled.

A woman in a man's world may be considered being progressive. But a man in a woman's world is—pathetic.

RATNA. May be we aren't 'progressive' enough.

AMRITLAL. That isn't being progressive, that is—sick.

Ratna looks away.

Tell me, how good is he as a dancer?

RATNA. He's good.

AMRITLAL. Good? Not brilliant? And you?

RATNA. Well, if I practise hard then . . .

AMRITLAL. Then you might become famous?

RATNA. I might.

AMRITLAL. Just as I thought. He is wasting his time. Poor boy.

RATNA. He isn't . . .

AMRITLAL. It's up to you now.

RATNA. What?

AMRITLAL. Help me make him an adult. Help me to help him grow up.

RATNA. How?

AMRITLAL. That I'll leave to you. Help me and I'll never prevent you from dancing. I know it will take time but it must be done.

RATNA *(softly)*. I'll think about it.

AMRITLAL. You have to do better than that.

She opens the car door to leave, then stops and turns back to Amritlal.

RATNA. And once he stops dancing—what will you do with him then?

AMRITLAL. Make him worthy of you.

He turns to the window and calls to Patel who hurries up to the car.

Give the old woman Rs 500 on my behalf.

RATNA. That's very generous of you.

AMRITLAL. That is in compensation for depriving her of her only student.

Cut to:

Exterior. Amphitheatre. Night.

Lata is performing the tillana, the last item for the evening. The music builds up and so does Lata's technical skills. She finishes with a flourish. We hear tremendous applause as Lata finishes her recital.

On Ratna's face. There are tears in her eyes. On Lata as she glances at her mother and smiles, then leaves centre stage and walks up to her mother and touches her feet in respect and acknowledgement. Flashbulbs go off. On Jairaj as he smiles, a little sadly. On Vishwas, seated between his parents, as he looks at Jairaj, then towards Lata and Ratna who are embracing on stage.

Cut to:

Interior. Green room. Night.

People mill around Lata who is removing various garlands from around her neck. We notice Chandra Kala and Seshadri amongst others, as well as Vishwas' parents. The latter are obviously not at home with the company present but are impressed with the enthusiastic reception Lata is receiving.

MOTHER *(to Vishwas's father)*. Look! Over there! Isn't that Mr Sathyu?

FATHER. Who?

MOTHER. Arre. That MLA. Damyantiben always brags about how well her husband knows him. We will ask Ratna Devi to introduce us.

Camera travels through the crowds. We see Ratna talking to an important looking bureaucrat, Sathyu. Jairaj and Vishwas stand to one side, a little ignored.

SATHYU. A shining light! Ratna Deviji, you have outdone yourself.

RATNA. You are too kind, Sathyu Sahib. Being such a senior government official, you are also so knowledgeable about dance—and I know you can be so critical. If people like you praise her, she has every reason to be thrilled.

Jairaj exchanges a look with Vishwas.

And the Chief Minister himself gave her a standing ovation. Did you see? As soon as Lata finished her tillana, he stood up and applauded.

JAIRAJ *(to Vishwas)*. He was in a hurry to go to the toilet.

RATNA. I was just thinking—this festival you are organizing in Canada, if you need any help from us, Jairaj and I would be delighted to assist. Isn't that so, Jairaj?

JAIRAJ. What?

RATNA *(to Sathyu)*. You must have more dancers this time. Not like the French fiasco.

She laughs.

Have you decided on your selection committee?

JAIRAJ *(to Vishwas)*. She's overdoing it.

SATHYU. Chandra Kala and of course, her daughter, Mala, will be part of the troupe, and then . . .

RATNA. Chandra Kala? Oh, a very good dancer twenty years ago. And Mala shows so much potential. It helps if your mother is on the selection committee—not that she would be partial. There is such a thing as ethics . . .

JAIRAJ *(to Vishwas)*. Is there?

Vishwas's parents come to Ratna obviously wanting an introduction. Vishwas shakes his head, smiling. POV Vishwas we see Ratna introducing them to Sathyu.

VISHWAS. Mom and Dad will be inviting him home next.

While Sathyu is chatting with Vishwas' parents, Chandra Kala descends on Ratna. Chandra Kala drags Ratna aside. We can see Sathyu and company in the background.

CHANDRA KALA. I was just telling Lata I'm watching her very closely . . . very, very, closely.

She looks around, and lowers her voice.

You know it hasn't been announced, but they've put me on the selection committee for the festival for Canada. What do you say to that?

RATNA. Chandra Kala, what wonderful news! Congratulations! I am so happy for you. And your daughter, Mala.

She embraces her. On Jairaj as he turns away shaking his head, in disbelief.

Cut to:

Interior. Bedroom. Night.

On Ratna as she sits in front of the dressing table, undoing her hair. On Jairaj as he enters the room, with a drink in his hand. He looks at her, then walks across, puts his drink on the table and starts clapping.

JAIRAJ. Bravo, Ratna Devi! Bravo!

Ratna looks up and smiles.

RATNA. We did it, Jai. We did it!

JAIRAJ. We? You mean, you did it. All your doing . . . as usual. Of course, Lata's talent may have to some measures been appreciated but . . .

RATNA. Why must you be like that? Whenever you drink, you—

JAIRAJ. Whenever I drink?

He raises his glass.

To you Ratna Devi! To great . . . performances!

As he takes a big gulp, Ratna watches him, her eyes narrowing.

Won't you drink with me?

RATNA. I'm tired. Let's go to bed.

*Jairaj puts a hand on her shoulders as she starts to rise.
They look at their reflection in the mirror, as he runs
his hands through her hair.*

JAIRAJ. How beautiful you were. What I wouldn't have done for
you.

RATNA. And I for you . . .

JAIRAJ. Really?

*He runs his fingers over her face. Then turns abruptly
and starts to leave.*

RATNA. Jai? What is it Jai?

JAIRAJ. Go to bed. You're tired.

He walks out. On Ratna. She looks stricken.

RATNA *(softly)*. Jai . . .

Dissolve to:

Interior. Living room. Parekh bungalow. Day. Flashback.

On Amritlal.

AMRITLAL. All right. I will allow it. I realize of course, that you
have come back more out of necessity than any real intention
of patching up what you have undone.

*Pull back as we see Ratna and Jairaj standing in front
of him while he censures them.*

I don't mind. It doesn't give me much pleasure to know that
but—I don't mind. I don't gain much pleasure by reminding
you that you had vowed never to come back to this house. No,
I won't remind you of that. I am above it.

*They do not respond. Jairaj stares stoically ahead, not
meeting his father's eyes.*

AMRITLAL. But I do mind your silence. It carries too much hate.
It was never my intention to get you to hate me. Which parent
would want that from his children? So . . . I have changed my
mind. I will allow you to dance.

Jairaj looks at his father, a little startled.

AMRITLAL. Of course, I shall be very happy if you can earn your livelihood from it. If you ask me for money, I shall not refuse it, but I will be disappointed. You may carry on using my library as your practice hall and your guru may come here twice a week in the mornings. I hope I have made myself clear.

There is no response.

Have I made myself clear?

JAIRAJ. Yes. Very clear.

He turns and starts to leave the room.

AMRITLAL. And Jairaj.

Jairaj stops and looks back.

Don't grow your hair any longer.

Jairaj leaves. Amritlal turns to Ratna.

And you need not learn from anyone else. You understand?

Ratna looks at him slightly resentful.

You are intelligent enough to realize that the decision to let you dance is in my hands, not his.

RATNA. You have made that very clear.

AMRITLAL. Don't worry. I have no intention of stopping you. I will let you dance.

RATNA. And Jairaj?

AMRITLAL. I thought we had an understanding, Ratna.

Fade to black. Fade in.

Interior. Dance hall. Day. Flashback.

On the guru as he gives vocal rhythmic patterns. Pull back we see Ratna executing a technically demanding tillana. On Jairaj sitting to one side watching Ratna. Abruptly he undoes his dancing bells and walks out of the room. On Ratna. She stops. On the guru. He looks irritated. He clears his throat. On Ratna as she restarts her exercise.

Cut to:

Exterior. Garden. Day. Flashback.

On Jairaj. He sits on a bench stiffly, staring ahead.

Exterior. Veranda. Day. Flashback.

On Amritlal as he walks into frame. He stops. POV Amritlal: Jairaj turns and looks at him. On Amritlal as he turns and walks back into the house.

Cut to:

Interior. Stage. Auditorium. Night. Flashback.

We hear music as spotlight comes on Ratna attired in brocade and jewellery. In her background stands Jairaj. We can just about discern his form in the shadows. As Ratna begins to dance, Jairaj moves in tandem, but throughout the light and the focus is on Ratna, with Jairaj personifying just a shadow of her shining presence.

Fade to black.

Interior. Bedroom. Parekh bungalow. Night. Flashback.

On Jairaj. In the darkness we can make out tears glistening in his eyes.

Close overhead shot as Ratna reaches for him across the bed. He has his back to her and does not respond.

RATNA. Jai? Jairaj?

Her fingers caress his face and suddenly stop.

You're crying . . . Jai!

JAIRAJ. I'm suffocating.

She turns him over and looks at his face.

RATNA. Don't. Please don't. We'll find a way.

She kisses him gently on the forehead. He breaks into silent sobs as Ratna brings his head to her breasts. She rocks him gently as she murmurs words of comfort.

Fade to black. Fade in.

Exterior. Newsstand. Street. Day.

On Vishwas as he grabs a couple of newspapers off the stand, pays quickly and hurries to his car.

Cut to:

Interior. Hallway. Parekh house. Day.

We hear the telephone ringing. On Ratna as she comes out of the kitchen wiping her hands on her sari, and picks up the phone.

RATNA. Yes, hello . . . Seshadri! How are you? Did you sleep well? . . . Yes, yes, we read the *Express*. That C.V. Suri is such an intelligent critic, he really knows his subject . . . For what, Sesha? No really. I don't know why you are apologizing . . . No. No! Sesha . . . it is really nothing. So what if you gave her the wrong tala in the beginning? I immediately stopped you, didn't I?

The main door opens and Vishwas rushes in excitedly waving the newspapers. Ratna smiles at him and gestures him to go into the living room.

Cut to:

Interior. Living room. Day.

Medium shot: Jairaj sits in a chair reading a newspaper as Vishwas enters.

VISHWAS. Did you read them? *Herald* and *Times*! Rave reviews!

JAIRAJ. Did you read the *Express*?

VISHWAS. No. Let me see it!

They exchange newspapers and simultaneously turn the pages.

JAIRAJ. 'Lata Parekh-star of the festival'.

VISHWAS. 'Lata excels!' Wow!

Jairaj flicks through another paper.

JAIRAJ. 'Lata leaves rest behind!' Wait till she reads this!

Cut to:

Interior. Hallway. Day.

On Ratna as she continues to speak to Seshadri on the phone.

RATNA. Don't worry, Sesha. Bye now. Very soon, you will be in Canada.

She puts the phone down.

Very soon I'm going to break his mridangam on his head!

Cut to:

Interior. Living room. Day.

On Jairaj as he reads from the paper to an intent Vishwas.

JAIRAJ. 'Her angashuddha and grip over rhythm stand head and shoulders above the rest, even surpassing veterans like Chandra Kala Devi. Truly, Lata Parekh, with perseverance and dedication will find her place among legendary artistes like Balasaraswati and Rukmini Devi.'

VISHWAS. That's great. That's really—I don't know what angashuddha and all that means, but it sounds simply wonderful!

Ratna enters with a tray of coffee.

RATNA. Of course, these critics get carried away now and then.

VISHWAS. Who cares? They liked her. They adored her!

Lata enters the room. Immediately both men stand up and applaud.

JAIRAJ. 'The discovery of the decade!'

VISHWAS. 'A shining star in the sky of Bharatnatyam!'

Lata makes a mock namaste. Ratna places the tray on the table. She has a forced smile.

LATA. Thank you. Thank you.

RATNA. Congratulations Lata! They embrace. Now drink your coffee.

JAIRAJ. And read your reviews.

He hands her the newspapers.

RATNA. Vishwas, I hope you're staying for breakfast. I'm making idlis.

VISHWAS. Well . . .

She doesn't wait for a response and leaves the room. Lata starts looking through the papers and starts to laugh.

LATA. I can't believe it!

JAIRAJ. You'd better. You are famous now.

LATA *(still reading)*. Amma's efforts—all of it.

JAIRAJ. Hmm, I wouldn't give her the credit entirely.

LATA. This one actually liked my tillana. 'Her sculpturesque poses and flourishes were truly delightful to view'—that's a laugh.

JAIRAJ. They were very good, even if you made them all up.

LATA *(giggling)*. I forgot the last jathi and simply posed till the music finished and then finished with a flourish.

VISHWAS. Oh, I liked those poses. They reminded me of sculptures, like the ones you see on postcards, you know, where the dancer is talking to the parrot or something.

JAIRAJ. In the tillana she wasn't supposed to be talking to a parrot.

VISHWAS. Anyway, it looked good.

JAIRAJ. How can it look good? She had no business talking to a parrot in the middle of a tillana.

VISHWAS. Ah, but we didn't know that. And I liked the way she finished with a flourish. We knew then it was time to clap.

JAIRAJ *(coldly)*. Drink your coffee.

LATA *(laughing)*. Oh, listen to this one! 'Her rendition of the ashtapadi from *Geeta Govindam* was tenderly intense and intensely tender. The audience was transported to Gokulam and witnessed Radha pining for the divine lover, who has failed to arrive. Lata's tearful expression and heaving bosom conveyed all that was humanly possible'.

She turns to Vishwas laughing.

My bosom was heaving because I was breathless from the varnam.

VISHWAS. I didn't quite like that one.

JAIRAJ. You didn't like Jayadev's *Geeta Govindam*?

VISHWAS. Oh no!

JAIRAJ. No? What is it you didn't like?

VISHWAS. Well, nothing . . . on second thought, I quite liked it.

Jairaj turns to Lata who is still immersed in the reviews.

JAIRAJ. Your friend didn't like the ashtapadi. Ask him what was wrong with it.

VISHWAS. I didn't say I didn't like the ashtapadi. How can I not like something, when I don't know what it means!

Lata and Jairaj are staring at him.

It was just . . . you know . . . too erotic.

There is no response.

Look, I know I'm not very knowledgeable on the subject. I merely said that because it was Lata who was dancing and . . .

JAIRAJ. You don't want Lata dancing erotic numbers.

LATA. Daddy!

JAIRAJ. I danced the same item. 1978. For the Army. Your mother was too scared to dance for the Army, and we needed the money.

Lata looks at Vishwas.

LATA. It was choreographed by Daddy thirty years ago for mummy. They won critical acclaim abroad for pieces like the ashtapadi. I don't see why I can't perform the same piece today.

VISHWAS *(flustered)*. Yes of course. If that's what you really want, nobody can stop you.

JAIRAJ. Lucky for her. In the old days . . .

LATA *(to Vishwas)*. Do you want to stop me? Because you can't. But do you . . .?

VISHWAS. Remember what you told me? In this very room? One right away, and another let us see.

Lata smiles and nods.

Does that still hold good?

LATA. Yes.

VISHWAS. Thank you. Then I hope your father will teach you some more . . . ashtapadis. I really should be going. I have to get to the shop. My father is busy chasing government officials to sanction a plan for a multi-storeyed mithai complex.

JAIRAJ. Just what Bangalore needs . . .

Cut to:

Exterior. Bungalow. Day.

Medium shot as Vishwas starts up his car as rock music emanates from his stereo. He waves to Lata who is standing on the stairs leading to the entrance of the house. She waves back as the car moves away.

Cut to:

Interior. Hallway. Day.

As Lata re-enters the house Jairaj comes in from the living room.

LATA. What do you think of him?

JAIRAJ. A bit strange, isn't he?

LATA. He has his quirks. Like the rest of us.

She starts going up the stairs.

JAIRAJ. What's taking your mother so long with the idlis?

LATA. I don't know. I'm not hungry. I'm going to get ready and meet Vishwas for lunch.

She disappears up the stairs as Jairaj heads for the kitchen.

Cut to:

Interior. Kitchen. Day.

Deviah is in the backyard grinding chutney for breakfast on an old-fashioned grinding stone. The grinding noise underlines the scene.

On Jairaj as he enters the kitchen and stops short. POV Jairaj: Ratna sits on a stool, her face cradled in her hands.

JAIRAJ. What is it? One of your headaches?

She looks up. Tears glisten in her eyes. On Jairaj he sighs and approaches her.

What's the matter?

Ratna stands up and wipes her tears.

RATNA. Nothing.

JAIRAJ. Then why are you sitting in the kitchen crying.

RATNA. Where's Lata?

JAIRAJ. Gone to her room.

Ratna exits the kitchen.

On Jairaj looking in the direction of Ratna. The grinding stops.

Cut to:

Interior. Living room. Day.

Jairaj enters the living room. Ratna is heading towards Lata's room.

JAIRAJ. Have you read the reviews?

RATNA. Not all of them, not yet.

JAIRAJ. Don't you want to read them?

RATNA. Yes, I was meaning to—

JAIRAJ. Why didn't you read them earlier?

Ratna picks up the papers.

RATNA. Well, I'll read them now. I was busy earlier with Vishwas dropping in and . . .

JAIRAJ. He brought the papers.

Ratna searches the papers nervously.

RATNA. Yes, but I was in the kitchen . . .

JAIRAJ. Weren't you interested in knowing what kind of reviews . . .

RATNA. I know what kind of reviews she got . . .

JAIRAJ. You haven't even looked . . .

RATNA *(shouting)*. I heard. Rave reviews! The star of the festival! The dancer of the decade! And why shouldn't she get reviews like these? I deserved it. Spending sleepless nights arranging things. Sweet-talking the critics. My hard work has paid off, hasn't it? Hasn't it?

She takes the papers and makes to leave.

JAIRAJ. Where are you going?

RATNA. I have to paste these reviews in our album.

JAIRAJ. Our album?

RATNA. Yes.

She leaves the room.

Cut to:

Interior. Bedroom. Day.

Close-up of album as Ratna's hand flicks the pages filled with newspaper cuttings of her past performances. Close-up of Ratna. She sits on the bed gazing at the cuttings.

JAIRAJ *(background)*. You're going to paste her reviews in our album?

Ratna looks up. Jairaj walk up to the bed.

RATNA. Why not? There's plenty of space!

JAIRAJ. She deserves an album of her own.

RATNA. We don't have another album in the house.

JAIRAJ. Well, it's time we did.

RATNA. All right. You go and buy one. But these I'm pasting in my album.

JAIRAJ. Our album.

RATNA. Yes!

JAIRAJ. You are not pasting these reviews in our album.

She gathers up the newspapers and album.

They don't belong there. Those critics gave her good reviews because she deserved them. They weren't doing you any favours. Face it, woman!

Ratna glares at him and moves to leave the room.

Well, at least you have a daughter to be jealous of, Ratna Devi.

She storms out. Jairaj sinks slowly onto the bed.

Dissolve to:

Interior. Bedroom. Night. Flashback.

Ratna is putting on her dance costume. Jairaj is rocking their baby in his arms who is crying. Ratna takes out a silk kurta from the cupboard and flings it at Jairaj.

RATNA. Don't waste time. Give Shankar to me, I will make sure he sleeps. Come on, hurry up.

Ratna almost snatches the baby from Jairaj.

JAIRAJ. So now I am not even good enough for the baby.

RATNA. Don't be childish and get ready. *(Calling out)* Shantamma! *(To Jairaj.)* Go call the ayah.

JAIRAJ *(going out mumbling).* Get ready, call the ayah, get ready, call the . . .

After Jairaj leaves, Ratna takes the baby rocking it gently to the cupboard. We see her remove a jewellery box and take out something . . .

Cut to:

Interior. Bedroom. Night.

Wide angle. We see Ratna in the background cooing to the baby and feeding him some medicine with a dropper.

Cut to:

Interior. Corridor. Night. Flashback.

A sleepy elderly maid hurries into the bedroom.

Cut to:

Interior. Bedroom. Night. Flashback.

The baby is quiet in Ratna's arms. The maid enters. Ratna hands over the baby to the maid.

RATNA. The baby is gone to sleep. Sleep near him and keep the mosquitoes away.

MAID. Amma, the baby's feeding time is at nine. Will you be back by then?

RATNA. I am trying, Shantamma. I am trying very hard. Don't worry, he won't wake up before my return.

Ratna takes her shawl and exits from the bedroom. Maid yawns a little. She opens the cupboard and fishes out the same box . . .

Cut to:

Interior. Living room. Evening. Flashback.

On Ratna as she enters room, dressed in a beautiful sari, with flowers in her hair.

RATNA. Jai, we really should be off. We're running late and—

Jairaj sits on a chair, glancing through a book.

You're not even ready!

JAIRAJ. I'm not going.

RATNA. What do you mean you're not going?

JAIRAJ. I want to stay home with Shanker. He needs looking after.

RATNA. We have a maid.

JAIRAJ. I don't trust her.

RATNA. And who will play the flute? I cannot dance without the flute.

Jairaj doesn't respond.

RATNA. Stop being childish, Jairaj. You know I can't possibly go alone.

JAIRAJ. Take my father. He's become quite a fan of yours.

RATNA. We need a flutist. Your father doesn't play the flute.

JAIRAJ. He'll learn.

Deviah comes in through the main door.

DEVIAH. Amma, Sahib has asked me to take you in his car.

JAIRAJ. Oh! Now madam has been given the family car to go out.

RATNA. Please, Jairaj—don't start. Not now. We have a full house tonight. And Mr Gowda is coming. He's on the selection committee for the Moscow Festival.

AMRITLAL *(background)*. What is going on?

They both look up as Amritlal enters the room.

RATNA. Nothing. We're late. Jairaj isn't ready.

AMRITLAL. Don't be late. I especially requested Gowda to attend the performance tonight.

JAIRAJ. You requested Gowda to attend? Wonders will never cease. Congratulations, Ratna! You've made dance respectable in this house.

AMRITLAL. That's enough, Jairaj. You have a talented wife. At least have the decency to support her.

JAIRAJ *(getting up)*. Oh, I do. I do. Very well, what Ratna Devi wants, Ratna Devi shall get.

He leaves the room, a sardonic smile on his face.

AMRITLAL. What's the matter with him?

RATNA. You should know. You've finally made a man of him.

Cut to:

Interior. Bedroom. Day.

On Jairaj. He still sits on the bed, staring blankly ahead.

RATNA *(background)*. The idlis are ready. Come and eat.

JAIRAJ. I'm not hungry.

Medium shot: Ratna stands at the doorway. Jairaj turns to look at her.

Come here.

Ratna hesitates.

RATNA. What is it?

JAIRAJ. I just want to talk.

RATNA. You don't talk. You attack.

Jairaj stretches out his hand. Ratna walks to the bed and sits by his side.

JAIRAJ. Did you put the cuttings in your album?

Ratna looks away. Jairaj sighs.

Do you ever think about that night, Ratna?

RATNA *(suspiciously)*. What night?

Jairaj smiles sadly.

I don't want to talk about it. She gets up to leave.

He grabs her arm.

JAIRAJ. All right. Let's talk about Shankar.

RATNA. No—you promised!

JAIRAJ. Remember that night . . .?

RATNA. It wasn't my fault!

JAIRAJ *(softly)*. No, Ratna. It's never your fault.

Cut to:

Exterior. Garden. Parekh bungalow. Night. Flashback.

Overhead shot as Ratna, a shawl covering her performance attire, and Jairaj cut across the garden. Jairaj is evidently drunk and Ratna holds him by the arm to guide him.

Cut to:

Interior. Hallway. Night. Flashback.

As Ratna and Jairaj enter the house.

JAIRAJ. Walk in! The doors of hell are wide open.

RATNA. Sssh!

JAIRAJ. Come in, Ratna Devi. Into the house of Amritlal Parekh.

RATNA. Quiet! You'll wake . . .

JAIRAJ. The seth of the house is not in! He is away receiving awards for serving the nation—while his Lakshmi-of-the-house has been away receiving—acclaims for her . . . talents.

He starts to clap.

RATNA. Shut up, Jai! You'll wake the baby.

JAIRAJ *(mocking)*. Oh! The baby! I forgot about him. Our little baby is fast asleep. We mustn't disturb him. Where are you going?

RATNA. Up. To see if he's all right.

JAIRAJ. Yes. Let's go up. Up. To see if . . .

RATNA *(sternly)*. You stay right here. Till you learn to be quiet.

He hiccups loudly. She looks at him disgusted and goes up the stairs. Jairaj heads slowly for the living room.

JAIRAJ *(whispering)*. Oh, I will be quiet! Real quiet.

Cut to:

Interior. Living room. Night. Flashback.

As Jairaj walks in, he continues to talk to himself.

JAIRAJ. I'll stay here and you go and see how our little Shankar is sleeping. Make sure his nose is dry and his bed isn't wet. His grandfather checks his mattress every morning. He even turns him over and checks his backside. Then grandfather sticks his finger in his mouth and checks his gums. Once his teeth are fully grown, I hope he bites him!

He makes a snapping motion.

Cut to:

Interior. Nursery. Night. Flashback.

On Ratna as she enters the darkened room and walks towards the cot, throwing a cursory look at the maid asleep on the floor. POV Ratna: The baby lies very still on the mattress. On Ratna: She frowns slightly, then reaches out to touch the baby. Mid-way she stops, smiles slightly, then turns away.

Cut to:

Interior. Living room. Night. Flashback.

JAIRAJ *(to himself).* And then . . . and then when he grows up, I'll teach him how to dance—the dance of Shiva. The dance of a man. And when he's ready, I'll bring him to his grandfather and make him dance on his head—the tandav nritya.

He strikes the Nataraja pose and hops about widely.

The lord of dance, beating his drum and trampling on the demon.

He loses his balance and crashes as Ratna enters. She helps him to his feet.

How is our little lord of dance?

RATNA. Asleep.

JAIRAJ. Good. He's in dreamland. Let him be there. It's a far better place than this. Tomorrow I'm going to hang a board outside this house saying, 'If ever there is a paradise—it isn't this, isn't this, it isn't this, . . .'

RATNA. I'm going to bed. I think you better sleep here.

JAIRAJ. Oh, you don't want to sleep with me? Never again?

RATNA. You are in no condition to sleep next to. You . . . you stink.

JAIRAJ. And you? You with your smell of jasmine and cheap attar?

Ratna removes her shawl and throws it at him.

RATNA. Here, don't bother coming up.

Resplendent in her performance attire, Jairaj looks at her admiringly.

JAIRAJ. God, what a beauty you are! Is that why you like to dance? To have men admire your assets?

RATNA *(scornfully)*. Why do you dance?

JAIRAJ *(mocking)*. Oh, but I don't. I'm not good enough.

RATNA. How can you be, when you are drunk half the time? Oh, for God's sake, Jairaj, I wish you would do something useful before it's too late.

JAIRAJ. Do something that's useful to you, you mean.

RATNA. Do something. Do anything . . .

JAIRAJ. Do anything but be a dancer. Do something useful like choreographing items for you, or playing the flute.

RATNA. You're not even good at that any more.

JAIRAJ. Whose fault is that? Whose fault is that only you get invitations to dance?

RATNA. Not mine.

JAIRAJ. For one whole year I didn't dance—turning down offers because I didn't want to dance alone.

RATNA. I didn't ask for such a sacrifice. Tell me what you want. I'll do anything . . .

JAIRAJ. I want you to give me back . . . give me back my self-esteem!

RATNA. When did I ever take it?

JAIRAJ. Bit by bit. Insisting on top billing in all our programmes. Making me dance my weakest items. Focusing the entire show . . .

RATNA. Face it, Jairaj, it's me they want to see dancing.

JAIRAJ. A young, beautiful woman, yes.

RATNA. And you are jealous? What kind of man are you?

JAIRAJ. Oh, you are clever. No wonder you get along well with him.

RATNA. Get along well with whom?

JAIRAJ. My father. It was him, wasn't it?

RATNA. I don't know what you . . .

JAIRAJ. Don't pretend. I'm not blind. Why did he allow us to dance? He knew he had us in his hands when we came back to him. We would have listened to anything he said.

RATNA. You would have listened. Not me.

He looks at her, and his expression changes as he suddenly realizes the implication of her words.

JAIRAJ. But, of course! That's when you struck the deal. He lets you do what you want and you have me out of your way. He in turn is grateful to you. Oh, you are brilliant! Well, this evening has been very illuminating. Thank you. Good night.

He lies down on the sofa and covers himself with the shawl.

RATNA. Oh, how easily you fool yourself. I'm not going to let you off so easily.

She pulls the shawl off him.

Don't blame us for the state you are in! When you had your freedom, why did you come back? What did you truly want?

He covers himself with the shawl again.

Did you really want to dance?

She pulls the shawl away. Jairaj shuts his eyes pretending sleep.

Why didn't you accept those invitations to dance? Was it
because of me, or were you afraid that if you danced alone,
your mediocrity would be exposed? No one destroyed you.
They didn't have to. You did it all by yourself.

Jairaj continues to ignore her.

And don't expect me to feel sorry for you. I'm too busy feeling
sorry for myself and Shankar. When he gets older and really
needs a father, it won't take him long to realize that there's
nobody home!

*She points at his head. As she moves to leave, Jairaj
opens his eyes.*

JAIRAJ. If you take the trouble to knock, you'll find someone
home.

He gets up and looks at her.

Are you all there for Shankar? When he needs you, where are
you?

RATNA. I know my duties and my capabilities.

JAIRAJ. Oh, you're a clever actress but the role of a devoted
mother is beyond even your capabilities. You wouldn't know
where to start.

RATNA. I can start by ending this conversation and feeding the
baby. So good night.

JAIRAJ. Feeding the baby. That won't be necessary. He's fast
asleep. He won't miss his meal.

RATNA. How do you know? He usually wakes at this hour.

JAIRAJ. Not on the nights you perform.

RATNA. What do you mean?

JAIRAJ. The ayah.

Ratna suddenly looks very attentive.

RATNA. The ayah . . . Shantamma . . . what?

JAIRAJ. You wouldn't know. It's an old trick handed from one
generation of ayahs like her to the next. I know. I was raised
by one.

RATNA *(grimly)*. Opium?

Jairaj looks at her surprised.

JAIRAJ. Yes. It's very effective. He hasn't cried at all. Don't worry, they always give just the right amount.

RATNA *(panicking)*. She too?

JAIRAJ. Yes. She too. She wants to have a restful sleep on the floor, same as her mother, and her mother's mother.

RATNA. She too . . . she too has given Shankar?

Jairaj looks at her sharply.

JAIRAJ. What do you mean?

Ratna looks terror-stricken. Jairaj advances towards her.

What did you say? She too has given Shankar?

He grabs Ratna.

What did you say? She too has given Shankar?

He lets go off her.

You?

RATNA. No!

Jairaj pushes her aside and rushes out of the room.

Cut to:

Interior. Staircase. Night. Flashback.

Music has taken over as Jairaj takes the stairs in slow motion, his mouth silently screaming for Shankar.

Close-up: We intercut with a silent scream of Ratna as she collapses exiting the frame.

Fade to black. Fade in.

Exterior. Parekh bungalow. Day.

Crane shot as we see Vishwas and a contractor poring over architectural plans in front of the bungalow. Vishwas gesticulates extravagantly trying to convey the grand design he sees for a building to replace the house.

RATNA *(voice-over)*. The demolishers are arriving tomorrow. You should see Vishwas. He's as excited as a schoolboy . . .

   Cut to:

Interior. Room. Hospital. Day.

   On Ratna.

RATNA. Next year, this time, there'll be a multi-storey complex where our house stands.

   Camera slowly travels down to where her hands clasps Jairaj's motionless one on the bed.

(Background.) Sad about the gulmohur tree. They're planning to cut it down. It obstructs the traffic, they say . . .

   Camera travels to Jairaj's face. He is motionless with his eyes shut. Tubes and wires are attached to various life-supporting equipment to keep him alive.

(Background.) Oh, I went with Lata for her check-up.

   Dissolve to:

Exterior. Parekh bungalow. Day.

   Camera pans from the trees to where Lata and Ratna stand gazing at the bungalow. Lata is in an advanced stage of pregnancy.

RATNA *(voice-over)*. Lata says, if it's going to be a boy, she want to name him Shankar. Yes, I told her everything . . . finally.

   Lata and Ratna start to walk upto the main door of the bungalow.

   Dissolve to:

Interior. Hallway/Living room. Day.

   Camera pans from the staircase to the hallway as Lata and Ratna walk through the hallway towards the living room. The house now devoid of furniture, looks sombre and empty.

RATNA *(voice-over)*. She says she doesn't want to dance any more. May be she'll change her mind after the baby is born . . . just as I did.

In the living room the two women look around the empty room. Slowly, Ratna starts to walk towards the former library/dance hall.

(Voice-over). Do you remember how we once used to dance . . . you and I . . . so perfectly. In unison. Not missing a step or beat.

In Ratna's face as she stands at the doorway leading to the dance hall.

POV Ratna: Out of the darkness Fade in a spotlight on the younger Ratna and Jairaj, gloriously dressed, performing a duet of a pure dance sequence.

Then we had all the grace, all the brilliance, all the magic to dance like the gods.

As the music builds up, camera closes in on the dancing couple, as they move into an ecstatic embrace.

Fade to black.

MANGO SOUFFLÉ

—————————————————■—————————————————

A Screenplay

A Note on the Screenplay

Mango Soufflé is a product of two intense desires—my desire to make a film and Mahesh's to direct one.

The journey began when I approached Mahesh to write a script around an idea I had. He did. I lost interest in the idea and it was back to square one.

I asked Mahesh to suggest a modern and witty story that we could adapt for our film. After looking at some possibilities, his play *On a Muggy Night in Mumbai* struck a chord. It was modern, witty, limited in location (to suit our budget) belonged to Mahesh, and conveyed the virtue of being oneself regardless of consequences.

We made a gentlemen's agreement. Mahesh would write and direct the film. I would produce it.

With a script in hand, a director and finances, we were ready to roll after months of drifting.

Mahesh and I had several discussions on the script as he agonized to make the play more cinematic. The clincher was changing the setting of a muggy night in a Mumbai apartment into a summer day in Bangalore at a sprawling farmhouse (where I incidentally lived). This opened up many cinematic possibilities and suited our budget.

The process of casting, shooting and post-production was a marathon affair involving a large team, and large sums of money. After six months of hard work, particularly on the part of Mahesh and my wife Seema (who was art director), *Mango Soufflé* was created.

It was a labour of love and an enriching experience for all of us. The process of seeing the play becoming a screenplay was perhaps the most satisfying aspect of this whole endeavour for me, personally.

Having had the pleasure to work closely with Mahesh, I can say in my own voice that he is a gifted and hardworking writer. We are fortunate to be able to read his writings.

Sanjeev Shah
(Sanjeev Shah is the producer of Dattani's
film Mango Soufflé*.)*

The film was released in India on February 2002. It won the best motion picture award at the Barcelona Film Festival the same year.

Principal cast:

KAMLESH	Ankur Vikal
KIRAN	Rinke Khanna
ED	Atul Kulkarni
DEEPALI	Heeba Shah
SHARAD	Faredoon Dodo Bhujwala
RANJIT	Denzil Smith
MAQSOOD	Mahmood Farooqui
BUNNY	Sanjit Bedi

The film was directed by the author. The screenplay is based on his play *On a Muggy Night in Mumbai*.

Producer	Sanjeev Shah
Director of Photography	Sunny Joseph
Music	Amit Heri
Production Design	Seema Shah
Costumes	Nirmal and Sarita Mandoth (Ms Khanna's costumes designed by Ashley Rebello)
Editor	Harsha
Publicity Design	Deepa Shah

Interior. Day. Kamlesh and Kiran's parent's home.

A plain looking Kiran sits nervously in a single seater. Her father—on the phone—hangs up. He speaks to his wife.

KIRAN'S FATHER. They—don't want our daughter.

Kamlesh goes to his sister and puts his hand on her shoulder. Kiran fights her tears of humiliation and smiles at Kamlesh to say it is okay, when it is clearly not okay. Kiran leaves the room. Their parents look at Kamlesh.

Cut to:

Montage. All at Kamlesh's studio. Day/night.

Music. Kamlesh tries out different clothes on a reluctant Kiran. He changes her hairstyle. Deepali helps her with her make-up. End of music.

Kamlesh takes a picture of his creation. Flash.

White out.

Interior. Party.

A remix of some popular seventies tune. Chatter. We see people grouped informally, fashionably dressed. Kamlesh walks in with Kiran. Ed, who has his back on them, notices that the person he is talking to is looking over his shoulder. He turns around . . . Kiran and Kamlesh get to a corner. Kamlesh offers to get her a drink. Ed walks to Kiran. He asks her for a dance. Kamlesh comes back with a soft drink for Kiran. He smiles at Ed. Ed offers his arm to Kiran and leads her on to the dance area. Kamlesh's smile stays on his face, but leaves his eyes.

Cut to:

Dance sequence. Credits.

We see Ed dancing with Kiran. Kiran is a little clumsy at first but soon they are dancing very well. We see that they are conversing but the music drowns their conversation.

Cut to:

Exterior. Day. Car. Moving. Credits.

Outside Kamlesh's parents home, a concerned father and mother wave goodbye as Kamlesh drives off.

We see Kamlesh driving through the busy streets of Bangalore, till he comes to a quieter road, though a lot more bumpy.

He arrives at the family farmhouse. We see a sign Mango Grove on the gate.

The watchman does a salaam and lets him in. The watchman (Maqsood) looks at the car going up the driveway. End credit.

Black out. Six months later.

Exterior. Day. The mango grove.

The watchman is necking his girlfriend in the mango grove. We see the fruit on the trees. She bites his neck and laughs at the effect. She looks away. We follow her gaze.

Exterior. Day. Outside the farmhouse.

Kamlesh is standing at the door bare torso and batik sarong, looking towards the mango grove for the watchman.

KAMLESH *(calling)*. Maqsood!

Maqsood comes running out towards the house quickly buttoning up his shirt. Kamlesh goes in.

Cut to:

Interior. Bedroom. Day.

Kamlesh is taking out his wallet from his drawer. Maqsood enters.

KAMLESH. Suno.

MAQSOOD *(tucking the baton in his belt)*. Ji.

KAMLESH *(taking out some more money from his wallet)*. *Mere kuch dost ane wale hain. Tum unko aane dena. Tum to pehchante ho sub ko.* (I am expecting a few friends. Let them in. You know them all.)

MAQSOOD *(knowingly, after a pause)*. Ji. Sir.

Kamlesh looks at him sharply.

KAMLESH *(giving him the money)*. Do bottle Peter Scot. *Ek Peach Schnappes—woh safed bautal wala, malum hain?* (Two bottles of RC, one Old Monk and some Cola. Will that do?)

MAQSOOD. *Hahn, saab.*

KAMLESH. *Aurr . . . ek crate soda aur* Thums Up. *Baaki sab to hain. Ho jaayega na?* (And . . . Another crate of soda and Thums Up. Will this do?)

MAQSOOD *(counting the money quickly)*. *Chalega.* (It should do.)

KAMLESH. *Jaldi aana.* (Come soon.)

Kamlesh goes into the bathroom and slams the door.

Cut to:

Exterior. Day. Outside the farmhouse.

Sharad opens the door of his car. Sharad walks to the locked gate and peeps in.

SHARAD *(calling)*. Yoohoo! Maqsood! . . . Let me in you wanker!

The gates creak open by themselves. Sharad opens the gates and gets back near the car to find two boys staring at him.

Sharad smiles and waves at them to go away. They stare at him.

(*Waving.*) Shoo.

They continue to stare at him. Sharad makes a face. The two boys grin and move out of his way. Sharad gets in his car.

(*Slamming his car door.*) Infamy! Infamy! They've all got it in fo' me.

He drives in, leaving the two boys to stare at the farmhouse, looking to see who else is in there.
Fade out.

Interior. Day. Farmhouse kitchen and living room.

Close-up of stereo playing an FM station.

Kamlesh is in the kitchen, taking the place mats and runner and crockery. Sharad looks at Kamlesh's sketch book lying near the music system. He flips through it and finds a sketch of a bride and groom.

SHARAD. Oh my Gawd! Somebody's getting married in your frocks!

KAMLESH (*while passing him on the way out to the table*). Please don't mess around with my designs.

Kamlesh exits frame.

SHARAD (*placing it on the sofa*). I love your cool kitsch gold work. So who is the rich cow who will end up wearing it?

KAMLESH (*re-entering*). My sister, Kiran.

SHARAD. Oops. And who is the lucky guy?

KAMLESH (*moving back to kitchen*). Someone she is in love with . . .

SHARAD. Is he a prince or a frog?

KAMLESH. His name is Ed.

SHARAD. Ed? That's it? Your sister fell in love with an Ed? Is he sexy or just husband material?

KAMLESH. Why don't you go home and watch a blue film or something?

Kamlesh exits to dining table. Sharad wanders out.

SHARAD. Blue films are so boring—after six or seven hours. *(Going to him.)* So what's all this about?

KAMLESH. What do you mean?

SHARAD. You know—this sudden inviting people over. Especially me.

Kamlesh continues to lay the table.

Is it good news or bad news?

KAMLESH. I don't know.

SHARAD *(helping him).* Well, is it to do with your sister?

KAMLESH. No.

SHARAD. Prakash, then?

Kamlesh looks at him.

KAMLESH. How dare you bring that up?

SHARAD. I didn't. It just . . . *(Waving his arm in the air.)* You know, it just—came up.

As Kamlesh is going back in, Sharad stops him.

You know I still love you.

Kamlesh goes back in.

Exterior. Day. Outside the farmhouse.

Deepali drives to the side road leading to the farmhouse. She has to wait for the crowds to disperse. The bride is being taken to the shamiana. She looks at the bride, somehow connecting with her.

Cut to:

Exterior. Day. The farmhouse.

Kamlesh comes back in with more food stuff.

KAMLESH. I love you too.

SHARAD *(angry)*. Oh! Spare me the lies! You could never love anyone because you are still in love with Prakash!

Sharad goes back to humming a song as if the conversation never happened.

KAMLESH. Look, I am sorry. I know I hurt you.

SHARAD. The way Prakash hurt you.

KAMLESH. You mention his name one more time and I will throw you out of my house.

SHARAD. Again? I double dare you.

KAMLESH. Don't. I mean it.

Sharad looks at him with defiance. Then saunters over to the swimming pool, sprinkles some water on his face and dramatically—

SHARAD. Prakash! *(Rubbing off his 'sindoor'.)* Prakaash! *(Breaking his 'bangles' on the wall.)* Prakaaaaash!

KAMLESH *(giving up, fuming)*. Oh! You are just impossible.

SHARAD. So are you going to throw me out once again?

KAMLESH. No. I won't. I need you.

SHARAD. Ooh! Now we are on to 'I need you' mode, are we?

KAMLESH *(carrying on sincerely)*. I still need you to help me forget him.

SHARAD. Still? You mean that's all our relationship meant to you? A way to forget Prakash?

KAMLESH. Sorry.

SHARAD *(casual)*. It's okay. It's okay. No sweat off my pants, no nail cracked on my pinkie. Let's see how I can help you . . . Did you really get rid of all his photographs?

KAMLESH. Yes. I tore them all up.

SHARAD. That's what you told me earlier. Tell me the truth now, did you tear up all his pictures?

KAMLESH. Yes. Well—I did keep one.

SHARAD. I knew it!

KAMLESH. Sorry. I hid it from you. I'll get rid of it, soon.

SHARAD. Tell me something. Do you want to forget Prakash?

KAMLESH. Yes. I am trying. It would help if he didn't crop up in our conversations.

The sound of the car coming up on the driveway.

SHARAD *(shaking his head).* I don't think you will ever succeed. He will keep cropping up in your life—like herpes.

The car stops and we hear the door open and shut.

(Mock cheerful, clapping his hands.) Well, put on your party frock! The boys are here! *(Singing while Kamlesh goes to open the door.)* Life is a cabaret, old chum. Come to the cabaret . . .

Kamlesh opens the door. The driveway and portico.
Sharad is inside near the door while Kamlesh is out.
Deepali is walking up.

KAMLESH. Hi!

DEEPALI. Hi!

Deepali comes up to them.

Looks like someone is getting married.

KAMLESH. The Raos in the farm next door. Their daughter.

SHARAD *(dodging an imaginary insect).* This place is crawling with weddings!

DEEPALI. Intrusive. Very intrusive. Are you all right?

KAMLESH. I am fine.

DEEPALI. You just look a little . . .

Another angle.

SHARAD. Where's the significant other?

DEEPALI. Baby-sitting my niece.

KAMLESH. Come on in.

Cut to:

Interior. Day. The farmhouse.

As they enter. Sharad shuts the door after him.

KAMLESH. Sit down. I will be with you in a minute. Help yourself to a drink.

Kamlesh exits to dining table. Deepali joins Sharad outside.

DEEPALI. Is everything really okay with him?

SHARAD. Ya, sure . . . By the way, it might help if you bring up Prakash in the conversation somehow.

DEEPALI *(hopeful)*. Is he getting over him, then?

SHARAD. Oh, yes. So the more we talk about him, the better. Darling, if I were you I would burn those pants.

DEEPALI *(ignoring his insult)*. Are the two of you back together again?

SHARAD. Honey, if we were still together, would I be such a bitch?

DEEPALI. Don't—don't use that word. *(Showing him a fist.)* You can call yourself a dog, call yourself a pig, but never never insult a . . .

SHARAD. Insult! Insult!! Honey, it is with great pleasure and pride that I equate myself to a bitch! I may not have six tits but . . .

DEEPALI. Eight.

SHARAD. Hey—nobody's perfect.

KAMLESH *(from the dining table area)*. Is everything all right there? Deep?

SHARAD. Just buggery do, dear—as our coconut friend would say. You go ahead and do your stuff while Deeps and I have a little natter.

KAMLESH. Okay. Why don't you offer a drink to our guest?

Kamlesh goes out.

SHARAD. Your guest. Remember, I don't live here any more.

Maqsood walks by through the back of the house.

Oh, hello.

MAQSOOD. *Namaste saab.*

SHARAD. *Namaste. Kaise ho? Namaste.* (How are you?)

MAQSOOD. *Theek hu saab. Bohut dinon ke baad aaye hein?* (I am fine, Sir. It's been some time since you visited us.)

SHARAD. *Hmm. bolo. Kya le ayen hain hamare liye?* (Tell me. What have you brought for us?)

MAQSOOD. *Ji. Saab ne mangvai thi.* (Sir had ordered for these.)

SHARAD *(mock innocent). Kya?* (What?)

MAQSOOD. *Ji, botalein.* (Bottles.)

SHARAD. *Oooh! Daru ki botalein?* (Oh bottles of booze?)

MAQSOOD. *Ji.* Sir.

SHARAD. *To aise bolon na. Kya daru bolnein me sharam aati hein?* (Say that. Are you shy to say the word booze?)

Maqsood puts the bottles on the tables, removing the wrapping. Sharad observes him.

Arre. *Yeh kya?* (What's this?)

Sharad looks at the guard's neck.

MAQSOOD *(a little wary). Thodasa lag gaya. Salaam.* (Oh just a little bruise.)

SHARAD. *Kamlesh saab ke pas bahut si dawayian hain aise chot ke liye.* (Master Kamlesh has a lot of remedies for such bruises.)

MAQSOOD *(going to the door). Ji–ji nahin. Main theek hoon. Ye rahan saab ka bill. Aur ye chutta.* (Er–no Sir. I am fine. This is Master's bill and his change.)

Sharad is thinking about this when Kamlesh reappears.

KAMLESH *(to Sharad).* Why don't you get some serviettes? Second drawer from the bottom.

SHARAD. I know where they are.

KAMLESH. And the silverware is all in the—

SHARAD. I know where you keep the silverware!

KAMLESH. Then go get them.

SHARAD. Why should I? I never said I will.

KAMLESH. What's your problem?

SHARAD. What's *my* problem?

KAMLESH. You are being difficult. And you are not my lover!

SHARAD *(quieter)*. I wish you would acknowledge the fact, that I did live here not so long ago. I designed your kitchen cabinet, you pig! *(To Deepali.)* Notice I said pig, not bitch.

By the way, your lover came in while you were chopping your melons.

> *Deepali's cell phone starts to ring.*

KAMLESH. What are you talking about?

> *Deepali reaches for her phone.*

DEEPALI. Carry on guys . . . If you are doing this number for me, go on, I'm listening. *(Into phone.)* Hello.

KAMLESH. What do you mean by 'my lover'?

DEEPALI. Ya.

SHARAD. Whom do I mean, not what do I mean.

DEEPALI. Ya, sweetheart.

KAMLESH *(with great patience)*. Whom do you mean?

SHARAD *(fishing out the money he got from the guard)*. Aapka chutta saab. Salaam saab. Your change, Master. Salaam, Sir.

DEEPALI. Maybe she just needs a good burp.

(On phone.) Sugar, have you checked her diaper?

KAMLESH. I did not sleep with him. He is heterosexual.

SHARAD. Since when has that stopped you.

Kamlesh is upset at that remark. He looks at Sharad. Sharad mouths a 'sorry' while Deepali carries on over the phone.

DEEPALI *(still on phone)*. Oh nothing at all, just one of those things these boys do, you know—screwing anything that moves.

KAMLESH *(worked up)*. That's not true! Get off that damn cell phone!

DEEPALI *(on phone)*. Sweetheart, I'll talk to you later . . . But hey, don't be afraid to call if you need more help. Bye.

Deepali hangs up and puts her phone down on the coffee table.

I am sorry. I didn't mean that . . . I am concerned. You know Tinu and I love you very much.

KAMLESH. I appreciate that.

DEEPALI. So tell me. What's bothering you?

KAMLESH. Can we wait for the others to arrive?

SHARAD. Yes, hold on to that confession while I nip in to the loo. *(Rising and moving to bedroom.)* Mind if I do that? I hope there is no one hiding in the loo.

KAMLESH. Go ahead.

SHARAD *(going to his bedroom)*. Oh by the way, you never gave me any love bites. *(Inside but really for Kamlesh.)* Peek a boo! Is any hunk dunked in there? Ready or not I am coming!

    Cut to:

Interior. Day. Bedroom. (Intercut.)

Sharad pretends to exit into the bathroom but we see him actually looking around Kamlesh's bedroom.

    Cut to:

Exterior. Outside the farmhouse.

Bunny drives up the road. He stops because there are some children playing. Bunny rolls down the window and takes off his sunglasses. Ranjit is peeved.

RANJIT. Oh for goodness sake! They will recognize you! Or is that the idea?

Sure enough the children come running to Bunny. Ranjit gets off and walks to the farm, muttering under his breath, shooing away some of the children. Bunny is left with the children wanting to touch him. Bunny hands out his autographed photographs all ready for such an occasion. The marriage photographer leaves the bride and begins taking photos of Bunny. The bride and the groom join in as well and take pictures with Bunny.

Cut to:

Interior. Day. Bar.

DEEPALI *(looking at him for a while)*. Sharad tells me you hardly step out.

KAMLESH. I do most of my designing here. I like it here on the farm.

DEEPALI. It's been a while since you called us over.

KAMLESH. I–I just don't feel like throwing any more parties.

Sharad is now looking around the room. Kamlesh is fixing Deepali a drink. Deepali looks at him fondly.

DEEPALI. If you were straight we would be an item.

KAMLESH. If you were a man we would be an item.

DEEPALI. If we were both heterosexual we would be married.

Deepali looks at him with great affection as he makes her drink.

DEEPALI. We can love one another the way we want to.

Kamlesh leans over the bar table and kisses Deepali affectionately on the lips. Sharad rummages in Kamlesh's drawer and finds the photograph tucked in there. He smiles. Sharad slips the photograph inside his kurta. Sharad comes out into the living room. The doorbell rings.

SHARAD. Coming!

Sharad opens the door to let in Ranjit.

RANJIT *(ignoring Sharad)*. Buggery do! Such glorious weather! Oh! Thank God some people have air conditioning.

Ranjit moves to the air-conditioner.

SHARAD. Buggery do to you too. *(Peeping out.)* Where's Bunny?

RANJIT. Outside enjoying all that vulgar adulation from some dreadful children. There's a whole mob outside for some shaadi or something. They won't let Bunny go.

SHARAD. I will leave the door open in case he fancies joining us.

RANJIT. Just a crack dear. Don't want all this lovely cool air contaminated with all that muck outside, do we? *(Looking around.)* Well, how are you my dears? *(Moving to bar.)* Don't mind if I help myself. This is perfect Gin and tonic weather. Kamlesh, I hope you have oodles of ice. *(Pouring himself one.)* Kamlesh, tell me all about your new collection.

SHARAD. Collection? Is that what you call them?

Sharad stops right in his tracks as he spots something on the wall. We cut to a photograph of Kiran with Ed on the side table.

RANJIT. I mean his fashion portfolio.

KAMLESH. He knows perfectly well what you mean.

Intercut.

Bunny is posing with the bride and groom. Flash. Picture frame.

Cut to:

Exterior. The farmhouse. Day.

RANJIT. Hello Deeps. Kiss. Kiss. *(Sitting down.)* Well, tell me all about it. Have you been inspired by any of the European designers this year?

DEEPALI. You know, I wish you didn't think with your prick all the time.

RANJIT. I beg your pardon.

DEEPALI. Kamlesh hasn't called us here to discuss his portfolio.

> *Sharad enters and stares at Kamlesh who is putting the bowl of salad on the table.*

RANJIT. Oh, why not?

DEEPALI. You are a real dickhead.

RANJIT. Are you jealous?

DEEPALI. Why should I be jealous of you?

RANJIT. Because I have a dick. Would you want one? Of course you would.

> *Silence.*

KAMLESH. Brunch is served.

DEEPALI *(rising, with great dignity)*. I thank God. Every time I menstruate I thank God I am a woman.

SHARAD *(following her)*. Every time I menstruate I thank God I am not pregnant.

> *Deepali turns around and gives him a wink. Bunny enters pretending to be hounded by all his loyal fans.*

BUNNY. Sorry. Sorry to keep you all waiting. Hahn bhai! Kamlesh brother . . . *(Shaking his hand vigorously.)* Kaise ho, yaar? You sounded a bit thanda on the phone.

> *The others have moved to the dining table. Bunny joins them. Notices Deepali.*

Hi Deepali. *(Going to her.)* Sorry I didn't see you. How are you?

SHARAD. Don't mind me. I am just the doormat. Use me for all I care.

BUNNY *(seated next to him)*. Sharad sweetheart. How can I ignore you? How are you, baby?

SHARAD. I have come a long way and I am no baby.

BUNNY *(looking at the food)*. Only vegetarian? Maybe after this we can all drive down to Kabab Corner for some real food.

DEEPALI. I am going straight home.

BUNNY *(nibbling on the salad)*. Maybe we can all join the baraat. They were insisting that I come to the wedding. I think they are serving butter chicken. You guys want to join me—you are welcome.

SHARAD. Groovy. We can go as Bunny Singh groupies.

BUNNY. Sharad if you want to join me no problem. But behave yourself. No camp talk and flirting if you are going as my friend. This is all too bland yaar.

RANJIT. Kamlesh, why don't you tell us what you want to tell us while we are eating and be done with it? Hmm?

KAMLESH. Thanks. I think I'd rather wait.

BUNNY. Sorry boss. I have to catch my episode on TV.

DEEPALI. He will tell us when he is good and ready, okay . . . The salad looks delicious.

Deepali helps herself and passes it on.

SHARAD. Hmmm. Don't you like the crockery? I chose it.

BUNNY. Kamlesh, we should have a picnic in your mango grove when the fruit is ripe, what do you say? *(Slurping on his melon juice.)* Hmmm.

We start to pull back till the conversation fades.

RANJIT. Don't slurp. It's rude.

BUNNY. Relax yaar. Don't be such a coconut.

RANJIT. Don't you dare use that term on me!

BUNNY. Sorry, sorry.

Cut to:

Exterior. Car. Moving.

We don't see who is driving. The music builds up as the car hits a bumpy patch.

Cut to:

Exterior. Day. Maqsood's shelter by the gate.

Maqsood has his meal out of a box. He looks out at the mango grove.

Cut to:

Interior/Exterior. Day. The farmhouse.

Close-up of Ranjit sipping his coffee. He puts it down.
We pull back as he speaks. The table has been cleared.

RANJIT. Now, Kamlesh, are you going to be secretive any further or do we get it out of you now?

KAMLESH *(smiling, a bit embarassed)*. Perhaps I shouldn't really trouble you with my situation. Really I feel better already, just being with all of you.

SHARAD. You want to tell us, don't you?

BUNNY. Don't force him.

DEEPALI. Let him decide. *(To Kamlesh.)* Kamlesh? We are listening if you want to say something to us. I know you do.

Pause as all eyes are on Kamlesh.

KAMLESH. This is goodbye.

A slight commotion on that.

DEEPALI. What do you mean?

RANJIT. Come, come Kamlesh . . .

BUNNY. I hope you are not thinking of doing something to yourself . . .

KAMLESH *(explaining)*. No, no—I mean. I am leaving Bangalore. I am moving to Canada. But before I leave, I want something of you all.

Sharad is troubled by this.

DEEPALI. How can we help you Kamlesh?

KAMLESH. You can help by not telling anyone of my relationship with Prakash.

DEEPALI. How does that help you?

KAMLESH. It does, believe me . . . It's a promise I made to him. That I will never tell anyone about our relationship. But I broke that promise. I told you all.

RANJIT. I don't quite get the point of all this . . .

SHARAD. Is that truly the reason why you are leaving India?

KAMLESH. What do you mean?

SHARAD. Kamlesh. Are you leaving us because you can't forget Prakash?

KAMLESH. I just want to get on with my life.

RANJIT. Well, this is the price one pays for living in India.

BUNNY. Do you want to turn him into a coconut like you?

DEEPALI. I think this is ridiculous! We need to help Kamlesh . . .

SHARAD. Well, it's very simple isn't it?

DEEPALI. Is it?

SHARAD. Yes. It isn't something I haven't already told Kamlesh to do.

KAMLESH. It hasn't worked so far.

SHARAD. You haven't tried hard enough.

KAMLESH. You know I have.

SHARAD *(taking out the photograph from his pocket)*. I know you haven't.

KAMLESH. Give that back to me.

BUNNY. No. Give it to me.

KAMLESH. Don't.

BUNNY. I want to see what this Prakash chap looks like.

SHARAD. You want us to help you, right? *(To the others.)* We all want to help him out, right?

BUNNY. Give it to me, I'll tear it up.

RANJIT. Don't be silly. The whole point is that Kamlesh has to exorcise his spirit by destroying it himself. But first let me take a quick look at it.

SHARAD. It is an interesting picture. Cheek to cheek, pelvis to pelvis. Naked. *(To Kamlesh.)* May I show it to them?

KAMLESH. No.

SHARAD. Why not?

KAMLESH. I told you why. I promised him I wouldn't.

SHARAD. Liar! I know why! I know why you are doing this!

Kamlesh takes Sharad aside.

KAMLESH. Help me, Sharad.

SHARAD. Why should I?

KAMLESH. You very well know . . . It—it might work out between us, or maybe not . . . (*Backing away, louder.*) Or maybe it's better I just go away for good.

DEEPALI (*rising*). Kamlesh, you don't have to leave the country just to forget someone.

KAMLESH. I might reconsider that decision if you can help me forget him.

SHARAD. Right. As far as we are concerned, Prakash doesn't even exist.

KAMLESH. Thanks, Sharad. So do I have your word for it?

SHARAD. We need to seal it with a ritual.

RANJIT. A ritual?

SHARAD. A ritual to 'exorcise his spirit' as Ranjit put it. A break-up ritual—the opposite of a marriage—that he does not exist for you. Are you all with me?

DEEPALI (*to Kamlesh*). Do you want this?

BUNNY. Well, If it helps him . . . Why not?

RANJIT. A bit naff, but . . .

KAMLESH. I will do whatever you tell me to do.

SHARAD. Deepali?

DEEPALI. What have we got to lose?

SHARAD. So far, great. Now I want you to take this photo and stand by the pool.

Kamlesh goes to him. Bunny tries to take a look at the photograph. Sharad gives him a stare. Kamlesh takes the photograph and stands by the pool. There is a gentle breeze.

Good. Now let's have a little ritual.

RANJIT. Next we'll be chanting mantras!

SHARAD. We'll come to that shortly.

We can hear some nadaswaram music faintly.

Perfect.

RANJIT. Oh do get on with it. Might as well incite the ghost of Prakash.

SHARAD. He isn't dead, yet.

Cut to:

Exterior. Day. Outside the farmhouse.

Maqsood opens the gates quickly to let in a car. We don't see the driver. We move with the car up the driveway.

Cut To:

Exterior. Day. By the swimming pool.

As Kamlesh holds the picture up, the wind gets a little strong. The Brahmin priest's chants grow louder. Someone is coming up and towards the house.

SHARAD. Now take a look at the picture. And say it out loud— 'As my friends and this city are my witness, I break all ties with Prakash'. Then you will tear it up and throw it into the pool. Is that clear?

KAMLESH *(after a while)*. Yes. I will do it.

SHARAD. Go ahead. *(Prompting him.)* 'As my friends, this city and the trees are my witness . . .'

KAMLESH. And after I do it, none of you will ever acknowledge my relationship with Prakash.

SHARAD. Of course not. That's the whole point of it.

KAMLESH. Do I have your word for it?

SHARAD. On my honour as a Bangalore queen.

KAMLESH. What about the rest?

DEEPALI. If that's what you want—I promise.

BUNNY. *Bhagwan ki kasam.* (By God, I promise.)

RANJIT. You have my word.

> *Kamlesh looks at the photograph. He speaks the oath
> but we don't hear it as the music and the chants are
> too loud as the wedding union ritual is taking place.
> Kamlesh looks at the photograph. He wants to tear it
> up. He can't. Sharad gestures and shouts at him to go
> ahead. Kamlesh is about to do it, when he spots
> someone. Kiran is standing there looking quite
> embarrassed as she feels she has interrupted something
> important. Everyone turns around to see Kiran, who
> stands there looking very apologetic. Kamlesh puts the
> photograph face down on the lawn.*

KIRAN *(to Kamlesh)*. I am sorry. I–I couldn't wait till tomorrow
to see you.

> *Kamlesh moves to her.*

(Confused.) Am I disturbing something? I could go away . . .

KAMLESH. Kiran!

> *Kamlesh rushes to her and embraces her.*

KIRAN *(relieved at the embrace)*. Oh thank God you are all
right.

KAMLESH. I am fine! Don't worry about me. And you?

KIRAN. I haven't been so happy in years!

KAMLESH. Let me introduce you to my friends.

KIRAN *(laughing nervously)*. Oh, I really feel I shouldn't have
. . . I feel like–like an–*(Laughing)* intruder!

RANJIT. Such perfection! *(Going to Kiran.)* Such exquisite bone
structure. The right colours, the right fabric. That eye make-
up . . .

KIRAN. Well it is all Kamlesh's—I am his creation you could say.

RANJIT. Brilliant! God couldn't have done a better job. *(To Kamlesh.)* Now tell us—who is he?

KIRAN *(wringing her hands)*. I–I suppose I should take it as a compliment.

KAMLESH. God did it all. This is my sister Kiran.

RANJIT. Charmed!

KAMLESH *(to Kiran)*. This is Ranjit, visiting from UK. Working with HIV counsellors.

KIRAN. Pleased to meet you.

KAMLESH. And this is Sharad.

KIRAN. Oh Sharad! I have heard so much about you!

SHARAD. You have?

KAMLESH. I have been telling her about how good you have been to me.

Sharad looks a little puzzled.

KIRAN. I do hope that things are . . . all right between the two of you.

KAMLESH. Oh yes, they couldn't be better.

KIRAN. Oh Sharad! I am so happy that my brother has a wonderful person like you in his life!

SHARAD. He does?

KAMLESH *(to Sharad, quickly)*. It's all right darling, she knows about us.

SHARAD. What are you?

KAMLESH. And you remember Deepali.

KIRAN. Hello Deepali. How are you?

DEEPALI. Fine. And you?

KIRAN. In heaven! I am getting married next month!

DEEPALI. Congratulations!

KIRAN. I am really so happy! Ed and I will be moving to Bombay. *(To Kamlesh.)* We have just seen a flat in Andheri, you will like it.

Kiran recognizes Bunny.

Hello. Oh! You are the Bunny Singh! I can't believe it.

BUNNY *(switching on to star mode).* *Banda haazir hai.* (Your humble servant.)

KIRAN. I just wouldn't have guessed.

BUNNY. Guessed what?

KIRAN *(now unsure).* That you are—well—like my brother.

BUNNY. Oh no! I am not! I am not—like them. They are such intelligent people and good company. I am a very liberal minded person.

RANJIT *(moving indoors).* I need another drink.

KIRAN. This is very noble of you—to be their friend.

SHARAD. We can't stop singing his praises!

BUNNY. As long as they understand that I am not interested in such things, I have no problem.

KAMLESH. Where is your stuff? Aren't you spending the weekend here?

KIRAN. I am sorry, but Ed wants me to spend the weekend visiting his aunt in Whitefield. I really had to see you today. Mummy is concerned about your health.

Kamlesh looks at her.

We all are.

KAMLESH. Let me get you something to drink. Have you had lunch?

KIRAN. Yes. I am sorry, I didn't know you had friends over.

Kamlesh gives her a reassuring smile and goes in.

Exterior. Moving.

We are moving with a motorcycle at quite a fast speed.

Cut to:

The farmhouse.

Ranjit comes back with a drink.

KIRAN *(looking around).* Kamlesh looks after the farm so well
. . . We grew up on this farm. I will miss it. Of course it's good
that Kamlesh has moved in here . . . *(To Deepali.)* If you don't
mind me asking you, what is the matter with Kamlesh?

Silence as the group contemplate on Kiran's question.

KIRAN *(persisting).* What's wrong with him?

SHARAD. We don't know. Do we?

RANJIT. No.

BUNNY. Not a clue.

Cut to:

Exterior. Outside the farmhouse.

*Maqsood opens the gate in a hurry doing a quick
salaam as the motorcycle squeals into the compound.*

Cut to:

The farmhouse.

Kiran turns around as she hears the squeal of tyres.

DEEPALI. Look I think we should tell you the truth.

SHARAD. No, you can't. It is all over anyway. That is the whole
point.

DEEPALI. Kiran should know that her brother is being treated
for depression. Kiran is torn between the familiar motorcycle
and the revelation about her brother.

KIRAN. Oh! I didn't know! He never told me! Why?

Kamlesh enters setting down her drink by the poolside.

KAMLESH. Come on in.

Kiran is now looking at the figure approaching them.

Ed walks up to them. Kiran runs to him.

ED *(holding Kiran).* Sweetheart—I was waiting for you.

KIRAN *(clinging to him).* Oh Ed! I am sorry. *(Turning around.)* Oh—everybody. Meet my fiance, Prakash. Edwin Prakash Matthew.

Deepali looks at him and at Kamlesh. Kamlesh is frozen. Sharad looks at Kiran. Bunny and Ranjit look at Ed.

ED. Hi. Call me Ed. Everyone calls me Ed.

The photograph on the bench flies away in the wind. Everyone remains frozen. Music.

Slow fade out to black as party music takes over.

Interior. Party.

Fade in black of someone's dress at the party dancing. Kamlesh is staring at Ed and Kiran dancing, as before.

Extreme close-up of Kamlesh.

Dissolve into:

Exterior. Night. Park. Dark blue filter.

We see Ed sitting on a park bench looking around. He spots someone walking by. His eyes follow him. The person walking by, whom we don't see, turns around and walks past Ed. Ed smiles at him, again following him with his eyes as he walks by. Now the person walks by again and this time Ed gestures to him to sit next to him. The person sits down next to Ed. The person is Kamlesh.

Silence. Ed looks around furtively to see if anyone is watching.

ED. Yes?

KAMLESH. Yes?

ED. No. Did you say something? . . .

KAMLESH. No.

ED. Oh. Sorry . . . What time do they close the park?

KAMLESH. Eight thirty.

ED. You seem to be a regular. No?

Kamlesh shrugs his shoulders. Ed stares at him.

Ed.

KAMLESH. Huh?

ED. My name. Ed. Just call me Ed. Everyone calls me Ed . . . *(Claiming to read Kamlesh's mind.)* I am not a regular here. *(Looking him up.)* What's your name? I didn't get it the first time . . .

KAMLESH. I never gave you . . . Kamlesh.

ED. Kamlesh. *(Looks around.)* Why do you come here? . . .

KAMLESH *(smiling),* For the same reason—as you.

ED. No. It can't be for the same reason I come here . . . why did I come here? . . . You want to know the truth? *(Turning to him.)* I lost my job this morning . . . I went home, sat down . . . had a couple of large ones. And then thought to myself. Why don't I just jump off the balcony?

Ed stares at him. We see for the first time that Ed is quite drunk.

Are you scared?

KAMLESH. No. *Pause.*

ED. As you can see I didn't do that. I just thought to myself, let me check the park tonight. If I don't find someone who will listen to my story, I will go back to my flat and—do it. *(Looking at him closely.)* You did listen to everything I said, didn't you?

Kamlesh nods to show he understands.

ED. Let me hear your story.

KAMLESH. No. Not tonight.

Ed moves his hand so it could be holding Kamlesh's hand. They stare out at the trees holding hands, though we don't see their hands clasped together. We see people or cars on the main road.

They can't see us.

ED. No. They can't.

KAMLESH. They can't see us at all, although we can see them. They must be blind.

ED. Good.

KAMLESH. If only they could see how beautiful we are together.

ED. Are we?

KAMLESH. What?

ED. Beautiful?

KAMLESH. Yes.

ED. I don't know. *(Pointing to the people on the road.)* They wouldn't think so.

KAMLESH. They don't really see us. Close your eyes. Go on close your eyes . . .

Ed closes his eyes.

Now I want you to imagine that you are standing behind us.

Angle from behind.

Can you imagine you are standing behind us and watching us?

ED. I can.

Camera goes out even further.

KAMLESH. Now imagine that you kiss me.

They stay as they are.

ED. Kamlesh?

Camera back to where it was.

KAMLESH. Hmm?

ED *(opening his eyes).* You saved my life.

Kamlesh moves to kiss him. Ed is oblivious of his presence. Kamlesh looks at him slightly puzzled. He can't figure him out.

Dissolve into Kamlesh at the party with a similar expression.

Dissolve to:

Interior. Day. Kamlesh's studio.

Montage of Kamlesh styling Ed's hair. Kamlesh trying to trim Ed's moustache while Ed protests about his moustache being altered. Kamlesh tries on some clothes on Ed. Kamlesh takes pictures. Kamlesh taking pictures of both of them together after setting the camera on automatic.

Dissolve to:

Interior. The party.

Kamlesh arrives with Kiran as in the first scene. Kiran appears nervous.

KAMLESH. How are you feeling? You look terrific.

KIRAN. Oh Kamlesh, let's go. This is not my scene really.

Ed approaches them.

ED. Hello. Hi Kamlesh.

Kamlesh smiles at him.

Can I dance with your sister? . . . Would you care to have this dance with me?

Ed begins to dance with Kiran.

Intercut with swimming pool. Day.

Kamlesh and Ed swimming. Ed drops his cross in the pool. He dives underwater to get it. Kamlesh follows. Nude, underwater.

Cut to:

Interior. The party.

Ed smiling at Kiran. Kiran blushing, feeling the chemistry developing between them.

Cut to:

Swimming pool. Day.

Kamlesh and Ed pop up above the water. Kamlesh smiles at Ed. Ed turns away and swims to the steps.

*Kamlesh watches, disheartened, as Ed gets out, wraps
a towel around his waist.*

Cut to:

Interior. The party.

Ed and Kiran slow dancing.

Cut to:

Exterior. The mango grove. Day.

KIRAN. I quite like your friend.

Cut to:

Interior. The party.

ED. No problem, just follow my feet. Relax . . .

Cut to:

Exterior. The mango grove. Day.

KIRAN. He told me how he met you at Sushma's party.

Cut to:

Interior. The party.

ED. There you go. Once you relax, it's a lot easier.

Cut to:

Exterior. The mango grove. Day.

KIRAN. And he told me you thought he was gay! Whatever gave
you that idea?

Cut to:

Interior. The party.

ED. I love ballroom dancing. It is very difficult to find the
appropriate partner . . .

Cut to:

Exterior. The mango grove. Day.

KIRAN *(laughing)*. I mean he doesn't look gay.

Cut to:

Interior. The party.

KIRAN. I am afraid I am not very good at this . . .

Cut to:

Exterior. The mango grove. Night.

Ed is avoiding Kamlesh's gaze as they sit under a mango tree. There are raw mangoes on the trees.

KAMLESH. Prakash, can I tell my sister about you?

Cut to:

Interior. The party.

KIRAN. How do you know my brother?

Cut to:

Exterior. The mango grove. Night.

KAMLESH. She is very understanding, and I think you need to get used to the idea of coming out to people!

Cut to:

Exterior. The mango grove. Day.

KIRAN. At first I was afraid. I–don't think I can face one more rejection.

Cut to:

Interior. The party. Night.

ED. I really admire Kamlesh. He is so open about himself . . . Oh I have no problems with it at all. None whatsoever.

Cut to:

Exterior. The mango grove. Day.

KIRAN. One has to be so careful about these things.

Cut to:

Interior. The party. Night.

ED. So . . . do you have anyone special in your life?

Cut to:

Exterior. The mango grove. Night.

KAMLESH. People will know anyway, sooner or later. If you are seen with me . . .

Cut to:

Exterior. The mango grove. Day.

KIRAN. People talk. It is difficult for me. You are a man, I know you have it hard too but, it is easy for you to be—invisible.

Cut to:

Exterior. The mango grove. Night. Fishbowl.

KAMLESH. How long shall we continue to hide? We can't hide for ever!

Cut to:

Interior. The party.

KIRAN. Look, this is not really me.

Cut to:

Exterior. The mango grove. Night.

KAMLESH. Are you embarrassed to be seen with me?

Cut to:

Interior. The party.

ED. Relax. Don't be so afraid of what people think of you. But if you are really embarrassed, we could stop.

They continue to dance.

Cut to:

Exterior. Day. The mango grove.

KIRAN. Ed doesn't seem to care about what people think or say. He is so open!

Cut to:

Exterior. The mango grove. Night.

KAMLESH. We live in a small town, that's why. We could move to Bombay.

Cut to:

Exterior. Day. The mango grove.

KIRAN. I would never have survived if it wasn't for your help.

Cut to:

Interior. The party.

ED. It is a nice tune.

KIRAN. I can hardly listen to it. I–I am too nervous.

Cut to:

Exterior. The mango grove. Night.

ED. Look, I don't know how to tell you this . . . but this just isn't working out.

Cut to:

Exterior. The mango grove. Day.

KAMLESH. Kiran, I want you to be happy.

Cut to:

Interior. The party.

KIRAN. Oh! I feel a little dizzy.

Kiran rests her head on Ed's shoulder even as he continues to lead round and round, enjoying Kiran's dependence on him.

Dissolve to:

Exterior. The mango grove. Night.

Kamlesh fights his tears as he looks at Ed pleading.

Dissolve to:

Interior. The party.

KIRAN. Please Ed, let's stop. I–I don't feel too well.

Kiran stops dancing, and sits down. Ed comforts her. Some other people at the party are concerned.

Dissolve to:

Exterior. The mango grove. Night.

ED. Let's not get too emotional. Think for yourself. There is no real future for us.

Ed walks towards the farmhouse.

Dissolve to:

Interior. The party.

KIRAN (*accepting a glass of water from Ed*). Oh, thank you! Don't worry about me. God! Everyone's looking.

Ed nods at the people around to say its all right, he will look after her.

Dissolve to:

Exterior. The mango grove. Day.

KAMLESH (*finding it difficult to answer the question*). Well, yes there is someone special I am seeing.

Dissolve to:

Exterior. The mango grove. Night.

Kamlesh stops Ed from going away.

ED. Kamlesh, I can never forget what you did for me. You were there for me when I needed someone. But . . . Kamlesh I am not gay!

Dissolve to:

Interior. The party.

Kiran is leaving with Kamlesh.

KIRAN (*slowly getting up*). Thank you. I really needed it to . . . face the world again. Thank you Ed.

Cut to:

Exterior. The mango grove. Day.

KAMLESH. His name is—Sharad . . . I am so happy for you Kiran.

Dissolve to:

Interior. The farmhouse. Night.

ED (*presumably looking at the photographs*). When did you take these?

Cut to:

Exterior. The mango grove. Day.

KAMLESH. Sure . . . You will meet him some day.

Cut to:

Interior. The party.

The MC makes an announcement.

MC. And the best couple on the floor are . . .

Roll of drums.

Edwin and Kiran!

Loud cheers and flashbulbs as Kiran looks on dazed.

KIRAN. What? What did he say?

Cut to:

Interior. The farmhouse.

ED *(horrified).* No! You are a cheat. So that's why you got me drunk! I don't want to look at this filth!

Ed begins to tear the pictures.

Cut to:

Interior. The party.

KIRAN *(laughing nervously).* Best couple?

Ed beams with pride and is ready to pose with Kiran for more pictures.

Cut to:

Interior. The farmhouse. Night.

ED. This is ugly!!

Cut to:

Exterior. The mango grove. Day.

KAMLESH. He loves me a great deal.

Cut to:

Interior. The farmhouse.

ED *(tearing up the photographs).* Filth! Rubbish!

Cut to:

Exterior. The mango grove. Day.

KAMLESH. He is witty, charming and—gay.

Cut to:

Interior. The farmhouse. Night.

Ed gets a little aggressive with Kamlesh.

ED. The negatives! I want them all! Promise me you won't tell a soul about this filth!

Cut to:

Interior. The party.

A smiling Ed leads a reluctant Kiran up to the dais.

Cut to:

Interior. The farmhouse. Night.

Ed picks up his helmet and storms out. Kamlesh follows him.

Cut to:

Interior. The party.

Kiran stops.

KIRAN. Ed, you go.

Cut to:

Interior. The farmhouse. Night.

Kamlesh is at the door and calls out to Ed who is starting his motorbike.

KAMLESH. Ed! You led me on! You made me believe you were gay! I need you, Ed. I love you!

Cut to:

Interior. The party.

Kamlesh looks on as the crowds whistle and clap for Ed and Kiran. Music builds up. Slow motion. Kiran and Ed together moving to the dais. Slow motion. Ed driving away from Kamlesh.

Exterior. The night. The gate.

Maqsood opens the gate for Ed to leave. Maqsood looks at an anguished Kamlesh. Fade out.

Exterior. The gate. Day.

Maqsood looks on and tries to see what's going on in the garden. Completely puzzled.

Cut to:

Exterior. The farmhouse. Day.

They are frozen for a moment as they digest Ed's presence.

SHARAD *(almost a question).* So here we are!

DEEPALI. Pleased to meet you—finally.

RANJIT. These damn weddings!

ED. I beg your pardon?

RANJIT. Oh I didn't mean yours. I meant the one next door. Congratulations, by the way.

KIRAN. Thank you. *(To Ed.)* Darling I have invited them all to our wedding.

RANJIT. That does it. I can't take it any more!

ED *(to Kiran).* Let's go.

KIRAN. Don't you want to see our farm? You've never been here before.

ED. Later. Why didn't you tell me you were coming here?

KIRAN. I–I just came on an impulse. I . . .

ED. We are leaving now.

KIRAN. Yes–of course.

DEEPALI. No. Do stay.

KIRAN. I wish we could . . .

Ed looks at Deepali, who feigns innocence. Ed looks at Kamlesh.

KAMLESH. If you want to . . .

ED *(turning on his charm).* Well, I don't want to be the villain of the piece. If you want to have a chat . . . we might as well do it now since we are all here.

Ed looks at Deepali, smiling but slightly guarded now.

KAMLESH. Oh thank you, Ed. Maybe you can help.

KIRAN. I don't see how. *(Looking at Kamlesh.)* I would like to, but . . .

RANJIT. It's too hot out here.

ED. Well, let's go in for a bit.

Ranjit leads the way back indoors. Sharad goes over to Ed and Kiran while they move in.

KIRAN. Oh Ed, this is Sharad. Kamlesh's special . . .

SHARAD *(offering a limp hand to Ed)*. So pleased to meet you.

Ed takes his hand and smiles back, again slightly guarded.

Cut to:

Interior. The farmhouse. Day.

Ed and Kiran are seated so that they have their back to the swimming pool.

KAMLESH. Can I get you something? There is some dessert going.

KIRAN. Oh I need to watch my weight. Ed?

ED *(to Kiran)*. I am fine thanks.

KIRAN. Ed, you haven't said a word to Kamlesh! Why?

ED. Sorry. It's just that we are obviously uninvited. *(To Kiran.)* You shouldn't come barging into your brother's party like this.

KIRAN *(to all)*. I am sorry. I really am.

DEEPALI. Maybe you ought to know something . . .

KAMLESH. There's nothing to tell! You promised all of you!
Silence.

KIRAN. What is it?

KAMLESH. Nothing. Nothing at all. They are simply . . .
Kamlesh stares outside.
Cut.

A gust of wind. The picture blows and stays on the French window for just a moment. Ed and Kiran can't see it. Kamlesh is about to say something. The others notice it too except Kiran and Ed. The wind blows it away.

Cut to:

Kamlesh moves towards the French windows.

Excuse me, I–I need to get something . . . out of the way.

Kamlesh rushes out. Deepali gets up.

DEEPALI. Excuse me. I think I need to get something too.

Deepali rushes out. Ranjit and Bunny get up.

RANJIT. I think I will take a walk.

BUNNY. Funny I feel like a walk too. Won't be long.

Both Ranjit and Bunny rush out, leaving a befuddled Ed and Kiran. Sharad stares at Ed.

Cut to:

Exterior. The mango grove. Day. Moving.

Kamlesh is running after the photograph. Deepali is chasing him followed by Ranjit and Bunny.

DEEPALI *(catching up with him)*. You have to tell her for God's sake!

KAMLESH. No!

RANJIT. I will tell her.

KAMLESH *(stopping to look for the picture)*. Tell her what? You cannot acknowledge anything. You are all under oath. Where the hell is it?

BUNNY. Don't tell her. It will ruin their lives. If both of them want it then what is the problem? I think it went that way!

They all head towards the mango grove.

Cut to:

Interior. The farmhouse. Day.

Ed stares outside.

ED *(suspicious)*. What was that all about?

SHARAD. Oh that—you know—boys will be boys. They will chase anything.

Cut to:

Exterior. The mango grove. Day. Moving.

They are looking for the picture.

DEEPALI. At least tell her about him and you.

RANJIT. I know what! I think we should make Ed tell her.

KAMLESH. He won't—and neither will you.

BUNNY. There it is!

They rush to a spot.

Cut to:

Interior. The farmhouse. Day.

Kiran is perplexed. Ed goes to the door and opens it. He tries to see what's going on.

KIRAN. There is something strange going on and I want to know.

SHARAD *(going to the kitchen)*. Nothing strange. Would you like some more juice?

Kiran follows him.

KIRAN. Sharad. I want to know. I insist.

Ed is still at the door. Sharad looks at her, wondering what to tell her.

SHARAD. Well—Kamlesh hasn't been entirely honest with you.

Cut to:

Exterior. The gate. Day.

Maqsood sees that there is a commotion in the mango grove and rushes there.

Exterior. The mango grove. Day. Moving.

Bunny picks up a magazine hidden in a corner.

KAMLESH. Give it to me!

The magazine has a picture of a semi-naked woman.
Let it go! It doesn't concern you!

BUNNY. It's a dirty magazine!

RANJIT *(looking at it)*. Oh dear.

KAMLESH. It's Maqsood's.

Maqsood rushes to the spot. He takes the magazine and hides it behind his back looking embarrassed.

BUNNY *(to Maqsood)*. *Hamein doosri photo ki talaash hein. Nange mardon ki.* (We are looking for another kind of picture. Of naked men.)

MAQSOOD. *Ji saab. Mujhe maloom hain.* (Yes, Sir. I know.)

RANJIT. Has he got it? Get it from him, show it to Kiran and have this Ed person all for yourself!

BUNNY. Don't be mad. Let them get married. *(To Kamlesh.)* You too find yourself a nice wife and have sex on the side.

KAMLESH. Don't be silly! We have to let her know.

RANJIT. She loves him!

DEEPALI. You love him!

KAMLESH. He loves her!

RANJIT. He can't possibly!

BUNNY. He can! Let's get the picture first.

KAMLESH *(to Maqsood)*. *Le aao woh photo.* (Bring me the photo.)

MAQSOOD. *Abhi?* (Right now?)

KAMLESH. *Hahn. Kahan rakhi hain tumne?* (Yes. Where have you kept it?)

MAQSOOD. *Main aisi photo nahin rakhta hoon!* (I don't keep such pictures!)

KAMLESH. *To abhi bola tha tum leke aaonge?* (You just said you will bring it now.)

MAQSOOD. *Hahn. Aap logon ke liye. Woh magazine wale ke pass zaroor milega saab. Sab kisam ki photo hain unke pass.* (Yes. For you all. I can get it from the magazine store. They have all kinds of photos.)

Kamlesh lets him go and moves away.

KAMLESH. He doesn't know. *(Back to Maqsood.) Dhoondon. Poori farm dhoondon. Ek photo hain. Meri aur Ed ki.* (Search the whole farm for it. A photo. Of me and Ed.)

Maqsood looks at him and at the farmhouse.

MAQSOOD. *Yeh toh bahut galat hua, saab.* (That's a big blunder, Sir.)

KAMLESH. *Pata hain. Jaao. Jaldi karo.* (I know. Go! Be quick!)

MAQSOOD. *Ji. Sir.*

Maqsood runs to the centre of the grove, undecided, he changes direction and disappears.

KAMLESH. It could be anywhere.

Kamlesh walks towards the house.

DEEPALI. There's got to be a way out for her. And Kamlesh.

Cut to:

Exterior. Another part of the grove. Day.

Maqsood is looking for the photograph not expecting to find it. He stops and scratches his head.

Intercut with:

Exterior. The gate/mango grove. Day.

The two kids see that Maqsood is not guarding the entrance. They slip in. They run to the mango grove. One of them climbs up a tree and throws down some mangoes. He notices the photograph stuck in the tree. He looks at the picture, gasps, and falls off the tree.

Cut to:

Interior. The farmhouse. Day.

Kamlesh enters through the main door. Ed and Kiran are seated separately now. Sharad is in the kitchen making more watermelon juice.

KAMLESH. Sorry about that. I remembered I had left the sprinkler on. Too much water everywhere . . .

Deepali, Bunny and Ranjit enter.

BUNNY. Sorry about that. We were helping Kamlesh put the sprinkler on. Too much heat.

SHARAD. More juice for you boys? Deeps?

DEEPALI. No thanks. *(To Kiran and Ed.)* Sorry to leave like that.

KIRAN. Kamlesh, I don't know what you were doing outside, but there's no need to hide anything. I know.

KAMLESH. You know?

KIRAN. Sharad told me. I feel awful.

Kamlesh turns to Sharad, angry.

KAMLESH. How could you? You . . .

KIRAN. Kamlesh, don't take it out on him. I insisted.

SHARAD. I had to tell her that you . . .

KAMLESH. Get out of my house.

KIRAN. Kamlesh!

KAMLESH. Out!

SHARAD. You say that one more time and I will wave my wand and turn you from a selfish bitch to an insensitive pig.

Kamlesh physically pushes him out, shouting 'Out'.

KAMLESH. You are jealous! I shouldn't have allowed you to . . .

Ed gets up and physically restrains Kamlesh.

ED. Just relax, okay . . . Calm down.

Kamlesh is still for a moment because of Ed's proximity.

Sharad told us that the two of you are no longer together.

Kamlesh visibly relaxes. Kiran goes to him, concerned. Ed looks at Kamlesh. He looks away when Kiran comes close to them.

Pause.

Kamlesh looks at Ed.

KAMLESH. Oh, is that all?

Sharad is hurt at this remark.

SHARAD. Yes. That is all. Goodbye pal.

Sharad makes a grand exit, slamming the door behind him.

KAMLESH. Wait! Sharad!

Kamlesh rushes out, leaving the door wide open. Through the door we can see Kamlesh running after Sharad. During Kiran and Ed's exchange we can see Kamlesh pleading with Sharad.

KIRAN. Oh Ed, I really feel awful. To think I am here to boast of my happiness. Thinking only of us and our wedding.

ED. Stop worrying. Kamlesh will find someone else.

KIRAN. How can you say that? If that were to happen to us . . . I–I–it's not a question of finding somebody else!

ED. Sweetheart, what can I do? I can't find him a lover, can I? Is it my fault? Huh?

KIRAN *(clinging on to Ed).* I wish we could help him, somehow. I wish he could be as happy as we are.

Silence.

The wedding music is heard again.

RANJIT. Why do people get married?

ED. I beg your pardon?

RANJIT. It is so bloody unnatural.

ED *(defensive).* What do you mean?

RANJIT. Oh, I was talking about marriage. The one outside I mean. Am I the only one sweating in here or what?

Ranjit goes to the air conditioner. Ed recognizes Bunny.

ED. Aren't you Bunny Singh? Of course. I have seen you on TV.

BUNNY. A pleasure to meet you Ed. Oh I am just a friend of theirs. I am a very liberal-minded person.

DEEPALI. Of course. The same as Ed.

Ed looks at Bunny trying to suss him out.

ED. Yes.

RANJIT. Oh for crying out loud!

Ed looks at Ranjit.

The air con isn't working. Oh no! Those–those wedding people must have tampered with the junction box, to get more power for their lights!

Ranjit goes to the window.

We must do something! We are going to drown in our sweat at this rate.

ED. It's only for a day or so.

RANJIT. People can get a heart attack, you know.

BUNNY. Relax.

RANJIT. They are using our electricity to light up their silly marriage lights.

Sharad enters, followed by Kamlesh.

SHARAD. Sorry if I took so long. The shaadi is great fun. The dulha is especially cute. Right, now where were we?

Ed has his hand around Kiran's waist.

Oh, don't mind me. I am just pretending to be visible.

KIRAN. Kamlesh, I know this doesn't concern me but . . .

SHARAD *(to Kiran)*. Why don't you sit down and entertain your guest while I make you some melon juice?

KIRAN. Why have you two broken up and why haven't you told me?

SHARAD. Kamlesh, I'll get the juice and you get the question.

Sharad exits to kitchen with a flourish.

KIRAN. Kamlesh, what happened?

KAMLESH. It just didn't work out, that's all. Don't worry, I am fine.

KIRAN. But why?

Sharad enters with the juice. Deepali gets a brainwave.

DEEPALI *(to Kiran and also Ed)*. It didn't work out because Kamlesh's lover wants to be straight. *(To Sharad.)* Sharad wants to be straight!

Sharad almost spills the juice.

It's all right dear. You might as well come out with it. *(Looking at him directly.)* The reason why you broke up with Kamlesh is because you want to be straight isn't that so?

SHARAD. Let me think about it. *(To Kiran.)* Your melon juice dear.

KIRAN. Thank you. But that's absurd.

SHARAD *(to Deepali)*. Yes, it's absurd!

Kamlesh just drops his face in his hand.

DEEPALI *(spelling it out)*. Precisely. That's the whole point. That some people don't see how absurd the idea is.

SHARAD *(catching on)*. Oh right. Yes, I want to be as straight as a stick. *(Immediately speaking more aggresively.)* I want to be straight. Like a rod.

KIRAN. But you can't!

ED. Of course he can. If he wants to then he can do anything.

KIRAN. What are you saying, Ed? I am trying to help out Kamlesh.

ED. It's too bad for Kamlesh. I think it is better he comes to terms with it now that Sharad wants to be a man.

RANJIT. A man? Did you say he wants to be a man?

ED. Of course he is a man. I mean he wants to be a real man.

RANJIT. And what in tradition is that supposed to mean?

ED. Look around you. Look outside. *(Going to the window and flinging it open.)* There are real men and women out there! You have to see them to know what I mean. But you don't want to. You don't want to look at the world outside this—

this den of yours. All of you want to live in your own little bubble.

The wedding band has stopped.

DEEPALI. And that's the reason why Sharad wants to be straight. So he can belong to that world. Right Sharad?

SHARAD. Right.

KIRAN. But is it possible? How will he go around doing it?

ED. Of course it's possible.

DEEPALI. Really? Do you know of anyone who has done that?

ED. I mean—No! I don't know of anyone. It's common knowledge. Maybe he is bisexual.

SHARAD. No I am not bisexual, I am as gay as a goose.

KIRAN. Then why? Just tell me why?

SHARAD. Weeell, let me see how I can put it. You see, being a heterosexual man—a real man as Ed put it—I get everything. I get to be accepted–accepted by whom? . . . Well that marriage lot down there for instance. I can have a wife, I can have children who will all adore me simply because I am a hetero . . . I beg your pardon—a real man. Now why would I want to give it all up? So what if I have to change a little? If I can be a real man I can be king. Look at all the kings around you, look at all the male power they enjoy, thrusting themselves on to the world, all that penis power! Power with sex, power with muscle, power with size. Firing rockets, exploding nuclear bombs, if you can do it five times I can do it six times and all that stuff. *(Thrusting his pelvis in an obscene macho fashion.)* Power, man! Power!

ED. You are mad!

SHARAD. Why not? All it needs is a bit of practise. I have begun my lessons. *(Demonstrating.)* Don't sit with your legs crossed. Keep them wide apart. And make sure you occupy lots of room. It's all about occupying space, baby. The walk. Walk as if you have a cricket bat between your legs. And thrust your hand forward when you meet people. *(Speaking in a base voice, an imitation of Ed.)* Hi! Call me Sharad! Everyone calls me Sharad! *(Squeezing an imaginary hand.)* And the speech. Watch the speech. No fluttery vowels. Not 'It's soooo hot in here!'—but—'It's HOT! It's fucking HOT!'

RANJIT. As a matter of fact it is—soooo hot.

BUNNY. I am feeling the heat too.

Kamlesh has got his back to the group. His shoulders are shaking.

KIRAN. It's all wrong, Sharad. Somehow it is all so . . .

Kamlesh turns around. He has been trying hard to control his laughter. Now he lets out a big laugh.

KAMLESH. You are funny! Sharad you are wonderful. I love you.

SHARAD. Don't be silly my dear.

KIRAN. He loves you, Sharad. What more do you want?

Silence.

SHARAD *(to Kamlesh)*. Could you just repeat what you said? I think I have missed out on something.

KAMLESH. I said you are wonderful and I said—I love you.

SHARAD. And I said 'don't be silly my dear.'

KAMLESH. No. It's true. It took me this moment to realize it. *(Looking at Ed.)* I know now that I have been chasing an illusion. Perhaps the man I loved does not exist. *(To Sharad.)* But you do. And I love you.

SHARAD. Just because you find me good looking, witty, charming, bold and truly wonderful doesn't mean you love me.

KAMLESH. But I do, really.

Kamlesh kisses Sharad.

ED *(turning visibly upset)*. Excuse me, but I think I will like to use the bathroom. Could someone show me where the bathroom is?

KAMLESH. In there.

ED. Thanks. *(Moving to the bedroom.)* Er–Actually I have a headache. Would you have something?

KAMLESH. I could get you some Imol.

Kamlesh exits to the bedroom. Ed follows him.

KIRAN. Who did he mean by that?

DEEPALI. Sorry?

KIRAN. He said the man he loved does not exist.

SHARAD. Oh, that! He was speaking metaphorically I am sure. *(Looking at the others.)* Right?

DEEPALI. He does not exist.

RANJIT. No he does not.

BUNNY. You are right. He does not exist.

RANJIT. You agree?

BUNNY. I know. Just as the man whom my wife loves does not exist. I have denied a lot of things. The only people who know me—the real me—are present here in this room. I have tried to survive. In both worlds. Everyone believes me to be the model middle class Indian man. I was chosen for the part . . . I believed in it myself. I lied—to myself first. And I continue to lie to millions of people every weekday on prime time. There's no such person . . .

DEEPALI. You have a lot to undo. But you will be all right . . . I know.

Bunny smiles at her weakly.

KIRAN. I would never have imagined—Bunny Singh!

BUNNY. Yes. Precisely.

Fade in bedroom interior.

Interior. Day. Bedroom.

ED. Tell me, is it true?

KAMLESH. What?

ED. That you love Sharad.

Cut to:

Interior. Day. The farmhouse.

KIRAN. I think we should be leaving.

Kiran goes to the bedroom door and hesitates to knock.

Cut to:

Interior. Day. Bedroom.

ED. Answer me.

KAMLESH. Yes. I do love him.

Cut to:

Interior. Day. The farmhouse.

Kiran moves away, feeling a little faint, shaken by Bunny's disclosure.

DEEPALI *(moving to Kiran)*. Are you all right?

Cut to:

Interior. Day. Bedroom.

KAMLESH. What's more—he loves me . . . I want to be loved.

Cut to:

Interior. Day. The farmhouse.

Kiran sits down on the sofa. Deepali sits next to her.

KIRAN. It's all this stress with wedding details.

RANJIT. Yes. I am sure that must be quite stressful.

Intercut with.

Interior. Day. Bedroom.

Ed moves closer to Kamlesh.

ED. You don't really love Sharad. You love me.

Cut to:

Interior. Day. The farmhouse.

Maqsood enters quite agitated.

MAQSOOD. Saab!

BUNNY. *Kya hua?* (What is the matter?)

MAQSOOD. *Aap log apna kam sari duniya ko batana chahte hain kya?* (Why do you want to show the whole world your affairs?) *Aapka yeh photo!* (Your photo!)

ED. You don't love Sharad.

MAQSOOD. *Sab bache dekh rahe the! Sab hans rahe the.* (All the children were looking at it. Laughing.) *Aur phir badon ne bhi dekh liya. Sab ne dekh liya! Mujhe pooch rahe the, yahan kaun kaun aate hain.* (And then the adults saw it. They questioned about everyone who visits this place.)

ED. Nobody would know. Nobody would care.

Kamlesh is frozen.

I'll take care of Kiran. And you.

Ed begins to caress Kamlesh.

MAQSOOD. *Abhi aap logon ka kya hoga? Aap yeh sab khullam khulla kyo karte hain?* (What will become of you all? Why do you do these things so openly?)

SHARAD. They can't do us harm—any more than the harm we do each other.

Maqsood fishes out the photograph from his pocket and hands it over to Bunny. Maqsood gives a sarcastic salaam to all in the room and exits.

Cut to:

Interior. Day. Bedroom.

Ed puts Kamlesh's hand on his shoulder. Sharad looks at Deepali. Deepali nods. Sharad offers the photograph to Kiran. Kiran takes the photograph and looks at it. Ed moves to kiss Kamlesh. Kiran continues to look at the photograph, almost frozen.

ED. No one will ever know. Not even Kiran.

Kiran cries out. Kamlesh grabs Ed by the throat.

KAMLESH. Liar!

There is a struggle as Ed slowly gains power to defend himself.

Cut to:

Interior. Day. The farmhouse.

Deepali goes to Kiran and helps her settle down, just as Ed comes rushing out, followed by Kamlesh. Kiran looks at Ed.

ED *(to Kiran)*. Look. Can we just get out of here? I don't think I like it here.

KAMLESH. Kiran, don't marry him! He is not good enough for you.

ED *(to Kiran)*. Listen to me.

KAMLESH. Kiran please believe me. You deserve better.

ED. No offense meant but we don't have very much in common with these people here. I sympathise and understand that Kamlesh is your brother and that you love him very much I am sure. But we have our own lives to lead.

Silence.

(Nervous now.) I mean—we can always come back later . . . But now, I just want to be alone with you! . . . I love you sweetheart.

KIRAN. What do you love about me?

ED. Kiran, that is such a—pardon me—but you are behaving like a typical woman again.

KIRAN. Exactly! Isn't that what you want?

ED. No! I want you to be yourself.

KIRAN. You want me to be a woman.

ED. But that's who you are! What's wrong with that?

KIRAN. A woman.

ED. Yes! Now let's get out of here!

KIRAN. That's why you want to marry me. Typical, you said. You are right. If there are any stereotypes around here, they are you and me. Because we don't know any better, do we? We just don't know what else to be!

ED. We can be whatever we want to be!

KIRAN. We can?

ED. I will love you in whatever way you want me to love you.

KIRAN. You tried. But no thank you.

Kiran puts the photograph on the table and sits down looking away. Ed looks at the photograph and moves away. Kamlesh moves to Kiran and holds her. Ed looks at Kamlesh.

ED *(to Kamlesh).* You promised.

KAMLESH. I did keep my promise, Ed. Now get out of our house.

Ed looks around at everyone.

KIRAN. You heard my brother, Ed. Get out.

Ed goes to the front door.

Before you leave, Ed. I think you ought to know . . . the photograph . . . was found by the watchman. The children found it first . . . One of them showed it to their father. The father showed it to other men—and women. They are talking about it.

ED. They don't know me.

KIRAN. But I know who you are. I may meet you somewhere. At a wedding. Not ours of course. You may have another woman with you. What will you say to me?

ED. You need me Kiran. I am good for you. Think about it. You know I can love you.

KIRAN. You can. But do you?

ED. I do.

KIRAN. Well, if that is true, you have to do one thing for me.

Ed looks on.

I want you to go outside, meet those people at the wedding. They know you. You met them at my parents'. They know you, they know your parents . . . look at them in the eye and come back in here.

ED. I can't.

KAMLESH. Do it Ed and get it over with.

DEEPALI. You can. You will get over it.

RANJIT. It doesn't matter what they think of you.

ED. It does. It does matter what they think of me.

BUNNY. I know it's tough, Ed. I know. Maybe we can all go with you.

KIRAN. No. He must do it alone. We will watch him from the gate.

Ed moves slowly to the bar instead of the door.

ED. I–I . . .

Ed goes quickly to the bar and pours himself a large rum. He gulps most of it down.

KAMLESH (*observing his every move*). Something doesn't seem right. Ed, don't drink . . .

ED. I am sorry Kamlesh. For all the harm I did to you.

Ed puts down his glass.

Do you remember, Kamlesh, the night we first met? If I hadn't met you . . . If I hadn't met you . . .

Ed goes to the door. And in a flash he is gone.

Cut to:

Exterior. The farmhouse. Day.

Ed runs out to his bike. Kamlesh follows.

KAMLESH. Ed! Don't! (*Yelling out to Maqsood.*) Stop him!

Ed jumps on to his motorbike, kick starts it and he races down towards the gate at breakneck speed. Maqsood tries to stop him. Ed kicks him in the shin and kicks the gate open.

Cut to:

Exterior. The Gate. Day.

There is an explosion of fireworks. The children scream as the crackers continue to explode.

Cut to:

Exterior. The farmhouse. Day.

Kamlesh rushes out. Followed by Kiran and Sharad. Bunny is behind them. Ranjit at the end.

Cut to:

Exterior. Near the gate. Day.

Maqsood sees Ed speeding towards him and hurriedly opens the gate. There is hardly enough room for Ed to pass. He takes a quick turn and speeds out. He gets into a loud skid and topples over even as the firecrackers continue.

Cut to:

Exterior. The farmhouse. Day.

Both Kamlesh and Kiran are concerned. They both let out 'Ed'. They run towards the gate.

Cut to:

Exterior. Outside the farmhouse.

Ed is lying on the road. He crawls out from under the bike and looks around in a panic.

Cut to:

Montage. Surreal.

Faces of people at the wedding laughing grotesquely at Ed. The children are laughing too. Maqsood is laughing too.

Cut to:

Exterior. Outside the farmhouse.

The firecrackers stop. Smoke covers the background. Silence.

Ed looks up. Maqsood is standing there quietly concerned about Ed. Ed looks around. The smoke from the fireworks clears. There are men and women looking on concerned. Some of the people go to him to help him up. Ed looks at each one in the eye. Ed finds it difficult to stand up. Maqsood goes to him. Maqsood helps him up. Ed has hurt his leg. He looks at the farmhouse. Kamlesh makes to go to him, Kiran restrains him. Ed hobbles in through the gateway. The crowds stare at him. Ed goes right up to Kiran and Kamlesh.

ED. I love you.

He walks to Kamlesh. Kamlesh looks at Ed, digesting this. Even as Kamlesh is about to say something, Ed turns around to Kiran.

I love you . . .

Ed slowly walks away from the group and towards his motorbike held by Maqsood.

Fade out.

Exterior. Day. By the swimming pool.

Kamlesh looks at the pool and throws the torn bits of the photograph into the pool. Sharad applauds. Kiran too stands by the pool and throws the torn bits of her picture into the pool. Sharad and Kamlesh applaud. Kiran looks at the pool. Kamlesh walks towards the house, puts his arm on Sharad's shoulder as they walk in. Kiran walks toward the house. She throws one glance at the pool and runs inside.

Music.

Close-up of the torn bits of photographs floating in the water as credits appear.

SEVEN STEPS AROUND THE FIRE

A Stage Play

A Synopsis of the Play

Uma Rao, daughter of the Vice-Chancellor of Bangalore University, is married to Chief Superintendent Suresh Rao, who has high expectations of succeeding his father as Police Commissioner. But it is Uma, a postgraduate student of sociology, who is the sleuth in this relationship, and using rather unconventional means she uncovers the truth behind a brutal murder in the city's hijra community.

When Kamla, one of the hijra sisterhood, is murdered, the police assume that Anarkali (another hijra) is the murderer.

But with the tentative help of Constable Munswamy (briefed by her husband to keep her out of trouble) Uma infiltrates the hijra community and unravels a thread of corruption and cover-up that leads right back to the cream of Bangalore society.

Jeremy Mortimer
(Jeremy Mortimer is Executive Producer,
BBC Radio Drama.)

The stage version of *Seven Steps around the Fire*, adapted from the radio play of the same title by the author, was first performed at the Stein Auditorium, India Habitat Centre, New Delhi on 10 July 2004. The production was directed by the author and produced by Vivek Mansukhani for Scene Stealers.

Cast for production:

UMA RAO	Tillotama Shome
SURESH RAO	Dhruv Jagasia
CONSTABLE MUNSWAMY	Vijay Singh
ANARKALI	Daman
CHAMPA	Danish Iqbal
SALIM	Ankur Bhardwaj
MR SHARMA	Jagmohan Bhasin
SUBBU SHARMA	Imran Khan
KAMLA	Sheena Bhalla
SUBBU'S BRIDE	Rahya Kardam
HIJRA ENSEMBLE	Lohit Jagwani
	Sundeep Sharma
	Rohit Kaul
	Gobind Bhoot
Company	Siddhartha Mishra
	Kunal Pruthi
	Anant Dwivedi
Understudy for Uma Rao	Vandana Mohindra
Director	Mahesh Dattani
Producer	Vivek Mansukhani
Sets Design	Lucia King
	Aditee Biswas
	Smita Bharti
Sets Fabrication	Bunty
Lighting Design	Jaspreet Uppal
Sound Design	Kabir Singh
Choreography	Gilles Chuyen
Assistant to Director	Shalini Singh
Assistant to Producer	Jigar Mehta

Production Team	Revathy Venkataraman
	Anant Dwivedi
	Rahya Kardam
	Siddhartha Mishra
	Kunal Pruthi
Costumes	Varun Narain
Assisted by	Amritha Venkataraman
	Malavika Talukder
	Vandana Mohindra
Make-up and Hair	Deepak Johri
Poster Design	Siddhartha Das
Photography	Serena Chopra
	Vandana Sood
Publicity	Krishna Omkar
Acknowledgements	Parul Sehgal
	Nicholas Kharkongor
	Vidyun Singh
	Srilata Prabhakar
	Renu Oberoi
	Shahdab
	Sunil Rawat
	Neha Hora
	Pramuch Goel
	HT City
	Indian Express
	Outlook
	India Today
	The *Financial Express*
	The *Asian Age*
	First City
	The *Hindu*
	Madhureeta Anand Negi
	Old World Culture
	India Habitat Centre
	Hutch

ACT I

A composite set comprising levels and gauze curtains which could be back lit to reveal interiors or drawn aside when needed. Props should be minimal and scenes need to move without too many black outs.

Sanskrit mantras fade in, the ones chanted during a Hindu wedding. The crackle of fire. We see a beautiful woman in a bridal outfit enter. The crackle from the fire grows louder. She screams and tries to run but is now on fire. She rolls on the ground. Her screams turn silent as sounds of the mantras and flames take over.

Black out.

Interior. The office of the Superintendent of Police.

We see Uma Rao, a young woman in her mid-twenties looking around, waiting for someone to come in. She looks at some files on the table. She hears footsteps approaching and quickly shuts the file and sits down.

A young police constable Munswamy enters.

MUNSWAMY. You may see the hijra now if you wish, Madam.

UMA. Will she talk to me?

MUNSWAMY *(chuckling).* She! Of course it will talk to you. We will beat it up if it doesn't.

UMA. Please don't. If she doesn't wish to talk to me, I will—it's okay. Don't force her.

MUNSWAMY. Madam, if you don't mind me saying, why is a lady from a respectable family like yourself . . .?

UMA. What? Wish to see someone like her?

Munswamy feels a little awkward. He speaks after a while.

MUNSWAMY. There are so many other cases. All murder cases. Man killing wife, wife killing man's lover, brother killing brother. And that shelf is full of dowry death cases. Shall I ask the peon to dust all these files?

UMA. No. Maybe some other time. I think this particular one is of interest to me right now.

MUNSWAMY. If you don't mind me saying, what is the use of talking with it?

UMA. Why not?

MUNSWAMY. It will only tell you lies.

UMA. How do you know?

MUNSWAMY. I know.

UMA. How?

MUNSWAMY. I am telling you I know.

UMA. You don't. You don't know for sure.

MUNSWAMY *(resigning)*. I will bring her.

UMA *(stopping him)*. No!

MUNSWAMY *(turning around)*. You don't want to meet her? Very good Madam. I . . .

UMA. Can I meet her in there?

MUNSWAMY *(shocked)*. Madam!

UMA. I would like to meet her where you have kept her.

MUNSWAMY. But Sir will not like it if you go there!

UMA. I will handle that.

Fade out. Quick fade in.

A prison cell. A whole group of inmates banging plates. Some are pulling down one person whom we don't see. Another stands in front and begins to undo

*his pants to get a blow job done from the one who is
down. He yells in pain.*

INMATE 1. Owwwww! It bit me! . . . I will teach you! Down!

*He begins to hit the person. Banging of metal plates on
the floor. Quite a din. Munswamy enters with a
hesitant Uma behind him. Munswamy runs his stick on
the bars of the prison.*

MUNSWAMY. Quiet! Quiet! Quiet I say! You sons of . . . loafers.
Do you know who this madam is? She is the daughter-in-law
of the Deputy Commissioner and the wife of our Superintendent!

Silence.

(Tapping on bars with his stick.) Now come on, come on. Do
namaskara to madam.

Silence.

UMA. Er—namaskara.

A chorus of meek namaskars.

MUNSWAMY. Madam, once again I request you to take up some
other case. Look at this man. He cut off his wife's nose. He
will give you an interesting story.

UMA. I would like to meet Anarkali.

Titters from the prisoners.

Where is she?

MUNSWAMY. Ai! Anarkali! Come here.

ANARKALI *(from far)*. No! I don't want to meet any journalist.

MUNSWAMY. I will come inside and beat you up, you worthless
pig!

ANARKALI. I am not in the mood.

UMA. I am not a journalist.

ANARKALI. I don't care if you are the mother of all the whores
in Bangalore, I said I am not in the mood!

MUNSWAMY. Why do you want to bring this shame on your
family Madam? I beg of you go home.

UMA. Anarkali! Please, help me.

ANARKALI. Go away. After servicing all these sons of whores, my mouth is too tired to talk.

UMA. God!

MUNSWAMY *(in tears).* Madam! I beg of you! If Sir finds out I let you in here, he will have me transferred!

Silence.

UMA. All right. Perhaps I better look at some other . . . case.

MUNSWAMY. Yes! Come Madam, you can sit comfortably in the office. Will you like some tea or Pepsi?

ANARKALI. Wait! *(Approaching.)* Are you really the wife of the big police officer? Or is this man lying so I will talk to you?

MUNSWAMY. Go away. Madam is no longer interested in your filthy lies.

ANARKALI. I didn't kill her. She was my sister!

MUNSWAMY *(hitting the bars with his stick).* Ai! Go back! *(Hitting harder.)* Back!

ANARKALI. Would you kill your sister?

MUNSWAMY *(hitting the bars).* Back! Beat it! Kick the hijra!

The other inmates begin to beat Anarkali up.

ANARKALI *(hitting back at first).* Ai! Don't touch me!

The other inmates scream with pleasure as they beat up Anarkali.

Aaagh! Aaaagh!

UMA *(her voice almost drowned by the anarchy).* Stop! Stop it!

Uma runs out. Munswamy watches as Anarkali gets beaten up.

Fade out.

Interior. The bedroom of Suresh and Uma.

Suresh is in his night clothes, a lungi and T-shirt. He is on the bed, cleaning his gun. Uma is folding his uniform. Her nightie is on a chair.

UMA. Why did they put her in a male prison?

SURESH. Who?

UMA. Anarkali.

SURESH. That is just the sort of name a hijra would fancy. *(Chuckling.)* Anarkali!

UMA. Suresh, why is she in a cell with men?

SURESH. They are as strong as horses.

Uma picks up the nightie.

Wear the purple one.

UMA. I wore that last night.

SURESH. Again.

Uma takes the nightie to the cupboard. She turns around.

UMA. She is being beaten up by all the male prisoners.

SURESH. How do you know?

UMA *(not wanting to say the truth).* She told me.

SURESH. Don't worry about all that. Wear it in front of me.

Uma remains where she is.

What's the matter? *(Sitting up.)* Are you all right? Did that creature upset you?

UMA. Munswamy brought her into your office, just as you instructed.

SURESH *(getting up).* Good. *(Exiting to the bathroom.)* Don't believe a word of anything it says. They are all liars.

Uma sits down on the bed. She picks up the gun.

UMA. Yes.

Suresh comes back in throwing the purple nightie at her.

SURESH. Wear it in front of me.

Suresh exits.

UMA. Why did you arrest her?

SURESH *(off)*. Didn't you go through the file?

Sound of gargling.

UMA. Yes. I know she is arrested for the murder of her sister, but . . .

Choking on the mouthwash with laughter. Coughing.

SURESH *(off)*. What's that you said? Sister? *(Approaching.)* There is no such thing for them. More lies. They are all just castrated degenerate men. They fought like dogs every day, that Anarkali and . . .

UMA. Kamla.

Suresh goes to her and sits beside her.

SURESH. Look, it is one thing that I am allowing you to go through these cases for your thesis, but don't feel any compassion for them. They will take advantage . . . *(Holding the nightie out for her to wear.)* Keep your soft heart for me.

Suresh tries to take the gun from her. She resists a little, then gives it to him with a smile. Uma takes the negligee and gets up.

UMA. What is the evidence against Anarkali?

SURESH *(pulling her back)*. Come here.

Uma goes to the bed and lies down. Suresh takes the negligee and covers her body with it. He looks at her, slowly lifting the negligee.

Hmmm. Uma, I really love you. You know that.

UMA. Yes.

Uma starts to say something but Suresh is kissing her. He immediately jumps up.

SURESH. Ow! You bit me! You bit me!

Uma apologizes while he checks his tongue.

Hmmm. It's okay, sweetheart. I know you didn't mean to.

UMA *(quietly).* No, Suresh. It's just that you put your tongue in my mouth while I was trying to talk to you.

Suresh looks at her trying to figure out if she means more than what she said. Uma gives him an innocent smile.

SURESH *(checking his tongue).* Excuse me.

Suresh exits. Uma stares after him. The voice over begins as the lights fade.

Uma's voice-over:

UMA *(voice-over).* Case 7. A brief note on the popular myths on the origin of the hijras will be in order, before looking at the class-gender-based power implications. The term hijra, of course, is of Urdu origin, a combination of Hindi, Persian and Arabic, literally meaning 'neither male nor female.'

The lights come on again to show Uma at her laptop.

Another legend traces their ancestry to the Ramayana. The legend has it that God Rama was in the forest to cross the river and go into exile. All the poeple of the city wanted to follow him. He said, 'Men and Women, turn back'. Some of his male followers did not know what to do. They could not disobey him. So they sacrificed their masculinity, to become neither men nor women and followed him to the forest. Rama was pleased with their devotion and blessed them. There are transsexuals all over the world, and India is no exception. The purpose of this case study is to show their position in society. Perceived as the lowest of the low, they yearn for family and love.

Fade out on Uma even as the voice-over continues. The lights come on in the office. Uma and Anarkali are together.

The two events in mainstream Hindu culture where their presence is acceptable—marriage and birth—ironically, are the very same previleges denied to them by man and nature. Not for them the seven rounds witnessed by the Fire God, eternally binding man and woman in matrimony, or the blessings of 'May you be the mother of a hundred sons.'

Fade in Anarkali. Whirring of fan.

Interior. The office of the Superintendent of Police.

ANARKALI. We make our relations with our eyes. With our love. I look at him, he looks at me, and he is my brother. *(Munswamy looks away.)* I look at you, you look at me, and we are mother and daughter. *(To Munswamy.)* Oh, brother, give me a cigarette, na.

MUNSWAMY. Shut up. And don't call me brother.

ANARKALI. Just one, na. *(Very sexual, going to him and lifting her sari.)* I will do anything for you, brother. Give, na.

MUNSWAMY. Chee! Who would want to . . . *(Flustered, he looks to Uma for help who is busy observing and taking notes.)* I–I don't smoke.

ANARKALI. If you had a beautiful sister, you will give her a cigarette for a fuck, no?

MUNSWAMY. Just because madam is here . . .

ANARKALI. You are not a sister-fucker?

MUNSWAMY. Just talk to madam and then I will see to you.

ANARKALI. I don't want to talk to madam! I want a cigarette!!

UMA. I think there are some here. My husband must be keeping his Gold Flakes here somewhere . . . *(Opening a drawer.)* Aha!

ANARKALI *(delighted)*. Oh!!

UMA. Here.

ANARKALI. One for the night. One for the morning.

UMA. Keep the whole pack.

MUNSWAMY. Madam!

ANARKALI *(snapping her fingers at Munswamy)*. Maachis. Maachis.

MUNSWAMY. What will Sir say?

UMA. Nothing. You will replace the pack.

Munswamy gives a box of matches reluctantly.

MUNSWAMY. If Sir finds out . . .

UMA. How will he know? Unless you tell him. *(Smiling at Anarkali, winning her over.)* And if you do, I'll just tell him I caught you stealing his cigarettes.

MUNSWAMY. Madam!

Anarkali laughs loudly.

UMA. Here. Buy a pack for Sir, and one for yourself.

MUNSWAMY. M–Madam . . .

UMA. Quickly before Sir comes back.

Anarkali inhales enjoying her cigarette.

MUNSWAMY. Yes, Sir.

Munswamy exits. Anarkali blows smoke. Uma coughs a little.

ANARKALI. So you are really the wife of Superintendent.

UMA. Yes. I teach at Bangalore University.

ANARKALI *(more focussed on the cigarette).* Oh.

UMA. I teach Sociology.

ANARKALI *(smoking).* Very good.

UMA. I am doing my paper on class gender related violence.

ANARKALI. What do you want me to do? Shall I come to sing and dance when you pass exam?

UMA. I have told you a little bit about myself. Now tell me something about you.

ANARKALI. What is there to tell? I sing with other hijras at weddings and when a child is born. People give us money otherwise I will put a curse on them. *(Laughing.)* As if God is on our side. *(Smoking.)* I did not do anything to Kamla. She was my sister.

UMA *(still making notes).* Why did you fight with your sister?

ANARKALI. You never fought with your sister?

UMA *(looks at him briefly, then back to her notes)*. I . . . don't have a sister.

ANARKALI. Not even one?

UMA. I have cousins, but we didn't grow up together.

ANARKALI *(offering sympathy)*. Oh. *(Smoking.)* If you were a hijra I would have made you my sister.

UMA. Oh. Thank you.

Anarkali studies her while she is busy writing.

ANARKALI. But you are not a hijra, no?

UMA. No.

ANARKALI. So you will not be my sister.

Pause.

UMA *(looking up at Anarkali)*. Of course we can be sisters!

ANARKALI. Where are you, and where am I?

UMA. But . . . I wish you could understand . . . This is just what I am trying to do with my paper!

ANARKALI. What paper?

UMA. One day you will understand. Anarkali, I would love to be your sister, if you will be mine.

ANARKALI. Oh! You are only being kind. Don't hurt my heart.

UMA. No, I mean it.

Uma is putting away her note pad.

ANARKALI. Look at me.

Pause.

Oh! My sister! You are my sister, no?

Uma looks at Anarkali for a while, then puts her hand on her arm.

UMA. Yes.

ANARKALI. Get me out of here.

Pause. Uma withdraws.

Sister, I did not kill Kamla. You believe me, no?

(Pause.) You don't believe me? You doubt your own sister?

UMA *(putting away her stuff in her bag)*. Er—no. I don't . . . But what can I do?

ANARKALI. You are the daughter-in-law of the DCP and you ask me what you can do to save your sister?

UMA. Look, I am here to gather some information for my thesis—

ANARKALI. Then say that. Don't pretend to be my sister.

UMA. I don't have any power!

ANARKALI. I will tell you who killed her.

UMA. You mean—you know?

ANARKALI. But don't tell your husband.

UMA. Why not?

ANARKALI. They will kill me. But I will tell you because you are my sister.

UMA. Look, I—I don't think I want to get involved . . .

ANARKALI. Go away! You are worse than all those journalists!

UMA. Maybe you should tell my husband. They will protect you.

ANARKALI. You are innocent fool.

UMA. Look . . .

ANARKALI. But you are my sister. If you do not want to help me it is all right.

UMA. I do . . .

ANARKALI. Maybe you are more unhappy than I am.

UMA. Look, I want to help you but I don't know how.

ANARKALI. If you give them money they will release me.

UMA. But I can't bail you out!

ANARKALI. Please, sister! I will die here. Help me get out, then I will run away.

UMA. You can't do that! You have to report to the police station.

ANARKALI. They will kill me also if I tell the truth. If I don't tell the truth, I will die in jail.

Pause.

UMA. My husband won't let me.

ANARKALI. You don't have any money?

UMA. No . . .

ANARKALI. Get it from your father. Say it is for your baby.

UMA. I don't have any children.

ANARKALI. Oh, sister! Make up some excuse!

Munswamy enters.

MUNSWAMY. Madam! Sir is coming. Please, put this packet where you found it.

Uma takes the pack and is putting it where it belongs.

UMA. Wait. There were three short of a full pack. Anarkali, here take these—one, two and . . .

Anarkali quickly takes the extra cigarettes.

MUNSWAMY. And you! Stand up and stop smoking!

Anarkali stands up.

Madam, I hope you are finished with this . . .

UMA. Leave us alone for a few minutes.

Munswamy leaves reluctantly and stands outside the office.

ANARKALI. Give me a hundred rupees, sister. Quickly.

Uma fumbling in her bag.

You will help me go away?

UMA. Here. That is all the money I have. Even if I wanted to I couldn't explain to my husband why I am paying for your bail.

ANARKALI. Go to Champa. Go behind Russel Market in Shivajinagar and ask for the hijra Champa. Give her the money.

UMA. Anarkali. If you loved your sister Kamla. Why did you scar her face with a butcher's knife?

Pause.

ANARKALI. I would do it to you also. If it will save your life.

UMA. What do you mean?

Pause.

ANARKALI. She was beautiful. Very beautiful.

Footsteps.

That is why Salim's wife put fire to her beautiful skin and burned her to the other world.

Suresh enters followed by Munswamy. He is in his uniform now.

Salaam, Saab.

SURESH. I hope this thing didn't give you any trouble.

UMA. No. She is very well behaved.

SURESH. Are you through with it?

UMA. Yes, I am for now.

SURESH *(snapping his fingers)*. Take it away.

MUNSWAMY *(clicking his heels)*. Sir! *(Snapping his fingers.)* Come!

ANARKALI. Salaam, Saab . . . Salaam, Memsaab.

Anarkali and Munswamy exit. Uma tries to catch Anarkali's eye but Anarkali avoids it.

SURESH. Did you get what you want?

UMA *(trying to be casual)*. Not really.

SURESH. You look tired. I will have Munswamy take you home.

UMA. Yes. I am a bit tired. But if you don't mind, could you ask him to take me to my dad's home.

SURESH. Why not? It has been a long time. I hope that bud of a pomegranate didn't frighten you. What did it tell you?

UMA. She is a real liar as you said. The usual stuff. Hard luck stories.

SURESH. That is the sort of crap that finds its way into your academic papers.

UMA. Well . . . Mine is going to be different.

A spotlight on Uma as we hear her inner thoughts.

UMA (*voice-over*). (*Thoughts.*) If only I could tell Suresh how wrong he is. About many things. But he loves me—I guess that matters. If I do help him out with this one case, it might even help him. He mustn't know, though. He would disapprove. He will see it as interference . . . One day he will listen to me. He will have to. Until then—

Black out. Lights come on Uma and Munswamy in a car. Munswamy is driving and Uma is seated at the back, deeply involved with her thoughts.

(*Pause in her thoughts but the traffic noise continues.*) Nobody seems to know anything about them. Neither do they. Did they come to this country with Islam, or are they a part of our glorious Hindu tradition? Why are they so obsessed with weddings and ceremonies of childbirth? How do they come to know of these weddings? Why do they just show up without being invited? Are they just extortionists? And why do they not take singing lessons?

(*Pause.*) Is it true? Could it be true what my mother used to say about them? Did they really put a curse on her because my parents did not allow them to sing and dance at their wedding? Or was that my father's explanation for not being able to have children of their own? Or—a reason to give to people for wanting to adopt me?

MUNSWAMY. Madam, close your window. At this traffic light, there are too many of them.

UMA. Oh don't worry. I can handle them. I always carry coins.

MUNSWAMY *(disapproving).* You are too kind, Madam.

UMA. No. I don't think so.

(Pause.) Who found the body?

MUNSWAMY. What? Oh, you are still thinking of . . . the body was found by some passerby, after four days. The temple priest complained about the stench. It was thrown into the pond after being burned.

UMA. Didn't the hijras report Kamla missing to the police?

MUNSWAMY. Hah! As if they care! After we found out the body was a man's without . . . that the body was a hijra's, we called them. Then they came. They were more interested in the jewellery.

UMA. Jewellery?

MUNSWAMY. So much jewellery she was wearing when she died! Even a bride will not wear so much. That too gold. All stolen, I am sure. How will hijras get so much gold if they can only beg for a few rupees?

A labourer carrying a construction work basket crosses the road. Munswamy brakes and gives him a stare, muttering to himself. The labourer jumps through the traffic.

UMA. Things haven't changed much have they? Look at those pavement dwellers there. They have been around as long as I can remember.

MUNSWAMY. Madam, there are a lot of changes. My father was also a constable. Let me tell you that I am seeing more in today's world than my father.

UMA. Really? Such as?

MUNSWAMY. More crime. So much crime and the police cannot do anything.

UMA. Why? Because they don't know who the criminals are?

MUNSWAMY. Everyone knows . . . *(Pause.)* And beggars. More and more beggars. God knows what all they do. They are spies all of them. How else do the thieves know where to loot and when? Madam, don't pity any of them. They are not worth it.

Silence.

UMA. When I was small . . . my mother always carried small change. When we stopped at the traffic lights . . . she would throw the coins as far as she could on the pavement . . . I would watch, while they fought with each other for the coins. The lights would change, and we would drive away. When she died, I took her jars of coins—there were four pickle jars filled with worthless paises—I stood on the veranda and threw them over the walls.

MUNSWAMY. Madam, be careful. The hijras will come running now.

UMA. There are no hijras. Children! Just children.

MUNSWAMY *(rolling up the window on his side)*. Same thing. Beggars only, no?

> *The lights change to suggest a more surreal mood. The ensemble, wearing hessian robes come to the car and start tapping on the window, asking for some money, their hands outstreched. We do not see their faces. They are persistent. Uma smiles at them and says a firm 'no' with her finger. Munswamy yells at them and they withdraw. They drop their robes and we see the hijra ensemble. They surround the car, clapping loudly. 'Money, madam. Give me money!' They bang on the car. Uma is terrified. Uma fumbles in her bag and throws some money out of the window. The ensemble hurries to pick up the coins and notes.*

Good idea! Very good idea.

> *One persistent hijra comes to her side and continues to pound.*

HIJRA. Give me fifty rupees, Madam. I will bless you. Madam! Fifty rupees only and you will have a son! If you don't give me money I will put a curse on you! Madam! Madam.

Uma stares at the hijra. She rolls up her window in fear, the ominous words of the hijra resonate in her mind.

Fade out.

Interior. Ramaswamy's home.

MUNSWAMY. What shall we do? Shall I take you to your home?

UMA. Maybe he is still at the university. Er—I think I will wait for him.

MUNSWAMY *(clearing his throat)*. Madam, I have received instructions to wait for you and take you back. Your father-in-law is expecting some guests . . .

UMA. Let me call to see if he has left.

Uma picks up a phone and begins to dial. Munswamy lingers on obviously wanting to listen in on her conversation.

(To Munswamy.) Would you like an ice cream? Go into the kitchen and ask the maid for some.

MUNSWAMY. No, no. It is okay.

UMA *(on the phone)*. Could you put me through to the Vice Chancellor's office? . . . This is his daughter Uma Rao . . . Tell him it's urgent . . . *(To Munswamy.)* Try the ice cream. It is really good.

MUNSWAMY. No. It's okay.

UMA. Why don't you get some for me? In there. Almond and pistachio. Just tell Mary.

MUNSWAMY. Er—okay.

Musnwamy leaves reluctantly.

UMA. Hello? Dad? How are you? . . . At home, your home . . . Things are fine, don't worry. I was just passing by and . . . oh, nowhere in particular. I have Suresh's car and one of his constables, so I thought I might drop in and surprise you. How are you? . . . Oh. I hope you are taking your medication . . . I wish I could come back and live here with you . . . I just might . . . Well, you taught me to do exactly what I want to do, and one day I just might . . . He is doing well . . . I did go. There is nothing wrong with me. He needs to go for a check-up. In many ways I am quite glad. I–I don't think I want any . . . I don't know. Look, I have to get back . . . I was wondering . . . could I borrow some cash from you? Suresh is busy right now and I don't want to disturb my father-in-law for these things . . . Good question. About 20,000? . . . It's to buy a present for Mr Sharma's son's wedding. Subramanyam— Subbu. You do remember him don't you? I–I just thought it might be good idea to buy him something different . . . I haven't decided yet. Since I am free now I thought I will go to the old bazaar and get it over with . . . Can I have it right away? I know where you keep the key . . .

MUNSWAMY *(entering)*. Madam, your ice cream.

UMA *(still on phone)*. Thank you! . . . No I better rush. I will see you some other time. Bye.

    She hangs up.

MUNSWAMY. It is very nice. Mary gave me a little bit to taste.

UMA. If you like it, you may have it. I will be right down. Just freshen up a little.

MUNSWAMY. Then are we leaving?

UMA. Yes. But we won't be going home.

MUNSWAMY. Then where?

    Pause.

UMA. Constable Munswamy.

MUNSWAMY. Sir!

UMA. I had a very very long meeting with my father right now. Understand?

MUNSWAMY. But he is not here.

    Uma gives him a stern look.

Y–yes, Madam.

UMA. Good. Wait here for me.

MUNSWAMY. And then? Where are we going?

UMA. You will know in good time. In the meantime, have your ice cream while I . . . freshen up.

> *Munswamy looks at the ice cream as Uma exits. He tastes the ice cream tentatively at first and then begins gobbling it up.*
>
> *Fade out.*

Exterior. In the car.

> *They get into the car. Uma clutches her handbag close to her.*

MUNSWAMY. Where are we going Madam?

UMA. Take me to Shivajinagar.

MUNSWAMY. Why?

UMA. We are going to visit Anarkali's friend Champa.

> *Munswamy switches off the engine.*

MUNSWAMY. No. No . . . Madam.

UMA. But we must! Don't you want to help Anarkali?

MUNSWAMY. No. My duty is to protect you Madam.

UMA. Then you must go where I go.

MUNSWAMY. Yes but . . .

UMA. So what are we waiting for. Hurry up, I have to be back home soon.

MUNSWAMY. I don't know what Sir will say.

UMA. Who is going to tell him? You?

MUNSWAMY. It is my duty Madam. If he finds out, he will suspend me.

UMA. Take off your cap . . . *(Before he can say anything she takes his cap off.)* Now you are not on duty. Let's go.

MUNSWAMY. N–no, Madam . . .

> *Pause.*

UMA. Very well, I will go on my own.

MUNSWAMY. It is dangerous for you to go there. Please understand! If something happens to you, then I am responsible.

UMA. Constable Munswamy!

MUNSWAMY. Sir!

UMA. To Shivajinagar.

Pause.

MUNSWAMY. Madam, I will take you to your residence. Those are my orders.

UMA. You will take the car to my residence.

Uma opens the car door, gets out and slams the door shut.

MUNSWAMY. Madam! Wait.

He opens the car door, gets out and slams the door shut. Traffic noises increase as we have exterior acoustics.

UMA *(yelling).* Rickshaw!

MUNSWAMY. Please! Madam, what will I say to Sir?

UMA. Get your car out of the way. You are blocking the traffic. *(Waving at a rickshaw.)* Rickshaw!

Uma runs offstage to get into the rickshaw after dodging some traffic. Munswamy looks on helplessly.

MUNSWAMY *(shouting at beggars).* Ai! If you touch the car I will put you in jail! Get away you beggars!

He opens the car door, gets inside, shuts the door and starts up the car. Music. Traffic noises. Cross-fade to the bazaar. We see Uma walking down the street. Looking at the marketplace. Uma spots a beggar.

UMA. Do you know where Champa lives?

BEGGAR. Who Champa?

UMA. Where do the hijras live?

BEGGAR *(laughing)*. Oh! You are a journalist no? Give me money. *(Pointing.)* There.

Uma opens her bag to give some change to the beggar.

MUNSWAMY *(approaching Uma)*. Madam!

The beggar runs away on seeing Munswamy.

UMA. What are you doing here?

MUNSWAMY. Why are you . . .?

He notices the money in her bag.

Why do you have so much money in your bag? Oh—why are you inviting so much trouble?

UMA. Go home. I don't need you.

MUNSWAMY. No. I will not leave you now.

UMA. Oh all right. But stay about a hundred yards away from me. I don't want you scaring all the hijras away.

MUNSWAMY *(sighing)*. Yes, Sir.

Uma arrives at a section where the hijras are. They are combing each other's hair and going about their routine. The camaraderie is very much evident. After a while they notice her presence and eye her warily at first.

UMA. Er—I was wondering if any of you could tell me where I can find Champa.

HIJRA. Oh! She is our guru!

They look at her and point in the direction of Champa's house. They follow her to the house, smiling at her. She smiles back a little nervous.

Cross-fade.

Interior. Living room of Champa.

Champa, an elderly hijra is fanning herself with a delicate punkah and reading Femina. *Uma coughs a bit at the door.*

CHAMPA. Come in.

Uma enters and looks around, clutching her bag tightly towards her body. The other hijras stand at the door looking in, curious to know what Uma wants from their guru.

UMA. Namaskar.

CHAMPA. Sit down.

UMA. Thank you . . . So, you are Madam Champa.

Champa guffaws.

I am sorry if I said something . . .

CHAMPA *(booming).* Don't say sorry!

UMA. I–I'm . . . confused.

CHAMPA. Who are you? And why do you visit us?

UMA *(looking at the other hijras).* I want this meeting of ours to be kept a secret.

Champa gestures grandly with her fan. The other hijras quickly disappear.

CHAMPA. Hah! . . . So, you are not a journalist.

UMA. No.

CHAMPA. We did not kidnap your son. Ramu came to us of his own free will. If you want you can take your son away.

UMA. I don't have any children.

CHAMPA *(showing sympathy but only for a moment).* Oh! Poor woman . . . How did you come to know of our meeting? Did the police send you?

UMA. Er—no. Anarkali sent me.

CHAMPA. Anarkali? But she is–she is not in town.

UMA. I know where she is. I met her there.

Champa's attitude changes.

CHAMPA. Oh. So you are a social worker. Say that.

UMA. Yes . . . I am a social worker.

CHAMPA. Please excuse me, Madam. I did not know that . . . you see us also as society, no?

UMA. Of course. I mean—you are.

CHAMPA. Good. But don't do any good work for that bitch Anarkali!

UMA. Oh.

CHAMPA. She deserves to be where she is! I hope she dies.

UMA. Oh . . . Why?

CHAMPA. I am the head hijra, and I will decide who the guru will be after me.

Champa yells out in the direction of the other hijras.

Anarkali will never be the guru! I will burn this place down before she sits here.

UMA. Oh.

Uma clutches her bag tightly and makes to go. Champa blocks her way.

CHAMPA. But first, you tell me. Why are you here?

UMA. Well, er . . . Well . . . Just to let you know that Anarkali is well. And I hope she will be released shortly.

CHAMPA. Hmm. You are hiding something from me.

UMA. No. Why should I?

CHAMPA. What is in that bag?

UMA. Why? Why do you ask?

CHAMPA. Why are you holding it so tightly?

UMA. I–I didn't notice that I was. *(Letting the bag hang loose.)* There.

CHAMPA. You have a lot of money in that?

UMA *(laughing with embarassment)*. . . . Yes, but . . .

CHAMPA. Are you mad? Hold the bag tightly. You should not bring so much money in to such places.

UMA. I–I thought it would be safe.

CHAMPA. You said Anarkali sent you.

UMA. Yes.

CHAMPA. Why?

UMA. Actually, she said you will help her, but . . .

CHAMPA. Of course, I will help her. Did I say I won't help her?

UMA. No . . .

CHAMPA. If I had the money I would throw it on that Superintendent's face and get her back. Sons of whores, all of them.

UMA. Oh . . . Some of them are not that bad you know.

CHAMPA. I know I said she should die in jail. But after all I am the head hijra and she is my daughter.

UMA. Yes. Then I guess . . . Well . . .

CHAMPA. Have you brought money for her bail?

UMA. Yes.

CHAMPA. Oh, may you have a hundred children! I knew that you are really a social worker.

UMA. You will bail her out?

CHAMPA. What a question to ask!

UMA. She—she didn't really kill Kamla, did she?

CHAMPA. What difference does it make whether she did or not?

UMA. I certainly don't want to help anyone who is a murderer!

CHAMPA. Yes, yes. That won't suit you. No. She did not kill Kamla. They were sisters.

UMA. If I gave you the money, will you go to the court and get her release orders?

CHAMPA. Did I come begging to you—'please give me money to save my daughter'? Huh?

UMA *(opening her bag)*. Here.

CHAMPA *(leaning over)*. Aah, these old bones! How much is it?

UMA. Enough for the bail amount and some more for your trouble.

CHAMPA. Oh! May you have a hundred sons! As soon as that bitch is out I will make her the head. Now that Kamla is gone who else do I have?

UMA. Wait a minute. You mean—Kamla was your first choice?

CHAMPA. Kamla was everyone's first choice.

UMA. And Anarkali, your second? I mean, now that Kamla is dead, Anarkali stands to gain from Kamla's death?

CHAMPA. Yes. But what can I do? There is nobody else who I can . . .

UMA. Can I have my money back?

CHAMPA. Why? What is your problem now? Anarkali did not kill Kamla, I am telling you!

UMA. But it seems like she may have.

CHAMPA *(fiercely)*. I know she did not kill her! Why can't you understand?

> *A commotion outside. A man's voice (Salim) rising above the commotion of protests.*

Quickly! *(Throwing the bundle of money near her.)* Put it in your bag.

> *Uma putting money in her bag in a hurry.*

UMA. Maybe I should leave. Thank you for your hospitality.

> *Salim storms in, sending the bells tinkling wildly.*

CHAMPA. I told you not to show your face here!

SALIM. Shut up you old bag! I told you to send me her things. Where is her trunk?

CHAMPA. Quiet you fool! I have a guest here. A memsaab. Madam this is Salim. Do salaam to madam.

SALIM. Salaam.

CHAMPA. Now go away.

SALIM. First give me her trunk.

CHAMPA. I have the right to her clothes and jewellery even if you gave them to her!

SALIM. You can keep all that. Let me first go through her trunk. And I didn't give her anything.

CHAMPA. Then who gave her all that? The Prince of England?

   Pause.

Now don't make a noise in front of my guest. Do you know who she is?

SALIM. No.

CHAMPA. She is . . . she is. Tell him, Madam. Tell him who you are.

UMA. Er . . . I am the daughter-in-law of the Deputy Comissioner of Police.

   Pause.

CHAMPA. Madam!

SALIM. I am sorry to disturb you Madam. I–I will . . .

CHAMPA. And don't come to my house like this. Don't you know we have important guests like this all the time?

SALIM. I am very sorry.

UMA. What do you want from them?

SALIM *(backing off)*. It is okay. I will leave now.

UMA. No. Wait!

   Salim leaves in a hurry.

Who is he?

CHAMPA. Please don't mind him Madam. Now, Madam, before anyone comes, give me the money for poor Anarkali quickly. I will hide it in my room.

UMA. What was he looking for? Unless you answer that question I am not giving you the money.

CHAMPA. Why? Why should I tell you?

UMA. It's to do with Kamla, right?

CHAMPA. Madam, please. Don't ask so many questions!

UMA. Unless you help me, I am not going to help you.

CHAMPA. I—I cannot say all that. You are the police and . . .

UMA. And?

CHAMPA. We cannot speak . . . When we want to speak nobody listens. When we cannot speak . . .

Uma goes to Champa.

UMA. I am listening.

Pause.

CHAMPA. That man used to come . . . for Kamla.

UMA. Oh, I see . . . What is he looking for now?

CHAMPA. A photograph.

UMA. What kind? Of whom?

CHAMPA. He says he wants a photograph that Kamla has . . . of Kamla and him together.

UMA. Where does Salim live?

CHAMPA. I don't know.

UMA. You are lying.

CHAMPA. I don't know.

UMA. Well, I can't help you then. I was hoping that in some way I could find justice for Anarkali . . . and for Kamla, but . . . If you, their guru do not want to help . . .

Uma gets up to leave.

CHAMPA. In Palace Orchards . . . He is from there.

UMA. Where exactly in Palace Orchards?

CHAMPA. I don't know.

Uma does not believe that.

UMA. In Palace Orchards? He lives in one of the poshest part of town?

CHAMPA. That is all I can tell you. I beg of you not to ask any more questions about him.

UMA. All right . . .

Uma gives Champa the money. Champa takes it slowly, not really interested in it now.

Champa, it is very important for me to look through Kamla's things.

Pause.

CHAMPA. Come with me.

Cross-fade to the group of hijras practising for the wedding.

Interior. Cramped quarters. Kamla's room.

CHAMPA. Ai! Get out! All of you.

Grumbles as the occupants leave, taking the tape player with them.

This is her trunk. I don't give the key to anyone. All the jewellery belongs to me.

Unlocking and opening a rusty tin case.

Everything that she owned is in here Madam. I myself put it all there.

UMA. Then you must have seen the photograph.

CHAMPA. There are some photos in this.

Uma opens a tin box.

UMA. Who is this beautiful young man?

CHAMPA. Kamla. Before she became Kamla. *(Going through the pictures.)* These were his first father and mother. Afterwards I am her father and mother . . . This one we took together after she became my daughter . . .

UMA. But where is the one with Salim?

CHAMPA. There is no picture there Madam.

Uma empties the contents out. She notices the box is lined with a paper. She slowly pulls the paper out. She unfolds it. Champa looks over her shoulder. She quickly snatches it away.

This is just some old paper Madam.

UMA. That was Salim in the background of that picture. He is the Deputy Chief Minister's bodyguard . . . Show me the news cutting again, Champa. There is someone else in the picture.

Champa tears up the news cutting.

Give that to me!

CHAMPA. No. It is unimportant.

UMA. It is a newspaper. I can always find out the picture. That is not what Salim was after. And you know that. You are pretending this news cutting is important when it isn't. I know how deviously clever you can be!

Champa simply looks at Uma with dignity.

Was he planning to take Kamla away?

CHAMPA. Yes.

UMA. That would not have suited you at all. Kamla was young and attractive. You would lose an earning member of the family.

CHAMPA. That is true but that is not the reason why I did not want her to go.

UMA. What other reason could there be?

CHAMPA. She would not have been happy in the outside world.

UMA. Salim would have looked after her well.

CHAMPA. There is no world for a hijra other than the one we make for ourselves.

UMA. That maybe so. But the real reason you wanted her dead was to warn others who may wish to leave the fold, of the consequences.

CHAMPA. That is not true!

We had fights. But Anarkali and me—we are not killers.

UMA. Anarkali couldn't have killed her. Kamla was running away anyway, leaving the way clear for her. Oh no. One person who wanted her dead is yourself. She defied your authority.

CHAMPA. She was my only daughter!

UMA. Oh don't give me all that rubbish! Daughter indeed!

Champa throws the bundle of money at Uma.

CHAMPA. Take your money and get out of my house! Go! This is my house! In my house you respect me!

Pause.

You don't know! You don't know!

Pause.

You don't know how much we all loved her! You will not understand. I loved her more than you can love your daughter! You don't know!

Uma looks at Champa as she breaks down feeling unsure about her stance. Uma picks up the bundle of money and leaves. Champa takes out the photograph from the pages of the magazine she was reading and looks at Kamla's picture.

Fade out. End of Act One.

ACT II

Uma looks at her laptop while she is on the phone.

UMA. Professor, this is Uma Rao! Do you have some time to discuss my paper? . . . Well, I will be brief. I am wondering whether I could leave out the case study on the hijras . . . Well, it all seems a little too sordid and I find it more and more difficult to do a thorough research . . . I know there is very little written about them, and now I understand why . . . But there is no way I can win their trust! Maybe there is but I don't know. And I don't trust them either . . . How important is it? . . . Oh . . . I guess I will have to . . . If my family throws me out, I hope that doctorate will come in handy. Thank you for your time. Goodbye . . . I guess I will.

Uma hangs up. Uma goes out of her home to a waiting Munswamy.

Cross-fade.

Exterior. In a car.

Uma gets in the car.

MUNSWAMY. Where are we going?

UMA. To Salim's. I know where he lives.

MUNSWAMY. Where?

UMA. No. 12 Palace Road.

MUNSWAMY. Madam! We cannot go to the minister's house!

UMA. Oh, be quiet! We are not going to meet him. He is in America. Don't you read the newspapers? Remember to do exactly what I told you.

MUNSWAMY. B–but Madam. I am not on duty.

UMA. Who is to know?

MUNSWAMY. Still, if Sir finds out I am using the police car.

UMA. How will he know unless I tell him?

Uma removes his cap.

There. You are not on duty any more. You have applied for leave. Your father is unwell. Start the car. Let's go! I need to see him before he leaves town.

Munswamy reluctantly starts the car. They drive on.

Do you know his bodyguards well?

MUNSWAMY. No Madam.

UMA. But surely you have been to his place several times with my husband. Don't you have a chat with the staff there?

MUNSWAMY. Madam, no . . . I only have some coffee in the kitchen. What are you thinking Madam? What has this to do with those hijras?

UMA. I don't know yet. But my hunch is that Salim used to come for Kamla and . . . Maybe she came to know something . . . or he wanted to marry her . . .

MUNSWAMY. Marry? Who would want to marry . . .? Tchee! What kind of people are there in this world?

264   *Collected Plays Volume Two*

UMA. It's a strange world. There's a lot we don't know. About the world and ourselves . . . What do you know about me?

MUNSWAMY. You Madam? You are the wife of Sir.

UMA. Exactly . . . And you are my husband's subordinate. That is all we care to know . . . You don't know me and I don't know you . . .

UMA (voice-over). Champa and the others were hiding things from me. Why? Have they lied? Maybe they tried to tell me the truth but I wasn't listening. All I know is that if I win their trust, I might get them to talk to me about themselves . . .

Cross-fade.

Exterior. The gates of the minister's residence.

A watchman appears.

MUNSWAMY (commanding). Ai, Watchman! Open the gates! We are here on official work. To the servants' quarters.

The gates open. They are led to the servant's courtyard.
A group of people stand there.

Who is Salim amongst you?

Salim appears, a little frightened.

SALIM. I am Salim, Sir. Salaam, Madam.

UMA. I would like to have a word with your wife.

SALIM. My wife?

MUNSWAMY. Go on. Don't waste time. Call her here.

SALIM. But, she is not here sir.

MUNSWAMY. Don't lie.

SALIM. She has gone to her village.

UMA. Why did you send her away?

SALIM. I did not send her away. Her mother is not well, so she went to . . .

UMA. Salim, please do understand, we do not want to arrest her. We just want to ask her some questions.

SALIM. W–what questions?

UMA. You know perfectly well what about. You do not want us to talk about it in front of these people do you? . . . Now let me talk to your wife. I know she is hiding in there somewhere.

Pause.

SALIM. I am not married.

UMA. So Anarkali was lying. She said your wife killed Kamla because she was jealous of your affair with her.

SALIM. I–I–will confess Madam. I killed her.

The others are stunned.

UMA. Constable Munswamy. Please take down his statement.

Munswamy hesitates. Pause.

What's wrong? Why do you look so frightened?

MUNSWAMY. Madam, I–I am not on duty.

UMA. This man is about to confess to a crime and you do not want to take down his statement? Very well, I will bear witness to his confession. *(To Salim.)* Why did you do it Salim? Why did you burn her on the day you were getting married to her?

Salim breaks down.

SALIM. Madam, I beg of you! Do not bring so much shame to me and my family. I have two sisters to marry, and–and my parents . . . I–I cannot!

A voice booms from behind.

MR SHARMA. What do you want and who sent you here?

MUNSWAMY. S-sssir!

MR SHARMA. I will have you two arrested unless you have official permission to be here.

UMA *(hiding her nervousness)*. Mr Sharma, I am afraid that we may not have permission, but we are here in your own interest.

MR SHARMA. And who may you be?

UMA. I am Uma Rao.

MR SHARMA. So?

UMA. I am DCP Rao's daughter-in-law.

MR SHARMA. I will verify that right away.

UMA. Please don't call my father-in-law!

MR SHARMA. Oh. Why not?

UMA. I was meaning to call you, but I thought you were away in America. Look, can we talk in private?

MR SHARMA. What about?

UMA. It is about one of your employees. Salim.

Mr Sharma looks at Salim. He gestures for Uma to go in.

MR SHARMA. This better be important.

Uma goes in. Mr Sharma follows. The others look at Salim.

MUNSWAMY *(to Salim)*. Tchee!

MAN. I always knew there was something wrong with him.

WOMAN. Such a strong man, he can get a decent girl from his community.

They leave. Salim stares at Munswamy.

SALIM. My boss will get me out of this mess. Then I will get you and that woman for insulting me like this!

Munswamy softens.

MUNSWAMY. Please, Mr Salim. I have nothing against you. What do we know about each other. You don't know me I don't know you . . .

Cross-fade.

Interior. Living room of Mr Sharma.

Uma and Mr Sharma have finished with their tea.

MR SHARMA. Hmmm. You are doing all this for your thesis?

UMA *(sighing)*. I don't know. I think so.

MR SHARMA. So you feel that Salim was having an affair with this—person, and he killed her?

UMA. Yes. He confessed.

MR SHARMA. Has he given a statement? Did he say why he did it?

UMA. I am just checking out his story. You see it is important to take him to the station for questioning.

MR SHARMA. It is all very disgusting.

UMA. But why did he do it?

MR SHARMA. A pervert.

UMA. I meant, why did he kill her?

MR SHARMA. One of the hijras must have paid him to do it. They do fight amongst themselves a lot.

UMA. That is . . . probable. But somehow . . .

   A voice from the staircase.

SUBBU. Are you going to arrest Salim?

MR SHARMA. Go back to your room, Subbu. You are unwell.

SUBBU. Please don't arrest him. He is a good man.

MR SHARMA. Nobody is arresting anybody. *(To Uma.)* My son Subramaniyam. He is unwell. A bit tired with all the wedding preparations.

UMA. Hello, Subbu. You remember we met at my place some years ago?

SUBBU. Yes. I remember.

UMA. Congratulations.

SUBBU. I hate weddings. I don't want all this! I don't wish to go ahead with this.

MR SHARMA. Subbu please go back to your room.

UMA. I am sure your father has found a wonderful person for you Subbu. You must go ahead with it.

SUBBU. Do you think so? Everyone says I should.

UMA. Of course, you should.

MR SHARMA. Well, I must say goodbye now. I do hope you will make it to the wedding.

UMA. We are all looking forward to it. Thank you for your time. A pleasure to meet you, Subbu.

SUBBU. Please don't arrest Salim. He is a good man.

Subbu exits. Uma is a little unsure.

UMA. Why do you think he said that?

MR SHARMA. He is very fond of the man. May I make a request to you?

UMA. Certainly.

MR SHARMA. Let's keep this pending till after the wedding. You see . . . my son is not quite . . . all there. And something like this will upset him terribly.

UMA. Oh . . . I don't know. What if Salim runs away?

MR SHARMA. I will guarantee that. Soon after the wedding I will hand him over. I suggest you leave it to me.

UMA. I am not sure what to do.

MR SHARMA. Now if you will excuse me, I have some urgent work to attend to.

UMA. Oh why did I get involved?

Mr Sharma leaves. We stay on a troubled Uma.

Fade out. End of Act Two.

ACT III

Interior. The bedroom of Suresh and Uma.

Suresh is reading the newspaper. Uma is pouring tea.

UMA. Some more tea?

SURESH. Hmm? No.

Uma pours herself some tea.

UMA. What are we buying for Subbu?

SURESH. Who?

UMA. For Subbu on his wedding day.

SURESH. Oh. Sharma's son. I don't know. You decide. Does it have to be very expensive?

UMA. No. But I would prefer to give him something special.

SURESH. Your father called.

UMA *(stirring her cup)*. When?

SURESH. Yesterday sometime, I can't remember when. He said something about money.

Putting down paper.

Why do you need so much money?

UMA. I don't. It's for something else. I have it all with me right here in my bag.

She shows him the money.

See . . . I was a bit concerned about Subbu's wedding present. After all, my father knows the Sharmas quite well. And so do you and your parents.

Zipping up her bag.

So I thought they might appreciate a Persian rug.

SURESH. Fine. Buy whatever you think is best.

Pause.

UMA. I went to the doctor again. Your mother insisted she takes me.

SURESH. What did they say?

UMA. Nothing . . . They want to see you.

SURESH. I don't think so.

UMA. Just a test for your sperm count.

SURESH. I don't have to go . . .

UMA. Would you like to go shopping with me?

Pause.

SURESH. Why did you ask your father for the money?

UMA. Oh no particular reason. I was visiting him and . . .

SURESH. You should have asked me. Have I ever refused you any money?

UMA. We could go shopping together.

Rustle of newspaper.

SURESH. Are you through with your research?

UMA. Not yet. I think I would like to have some more time with Anarkali.

SURESH. That would be difficult.

UMA. Oh, please! It is important. My guide is very impressed with her case. He feels it will go a long way in making my paper relevant.

SURESH. No. What I mean is she . . . he is no longer in our custody.

UMA. Where is she?

SURESH. She left. Someone came and bailed her out.

UMA. Oh . . . When was this?

SURESH. A couple of days ago. Some old hijra. Made quite a scene. Said she had pawned her jewellery or some such thing . . . Are you feeling all right?

UMA. But she will report to the police?

SURESH. Maybe. Who knows. If she runs away to another town, who can trace these people? Anyway, we only arrested her because there was no one else. There is no real proof against her. These hijras . . . they cut off their balls . . . they kill. It could be any one of them.

UMA. I–I must go . . . shopping.

Uma hurriedly sips her tea and goes in. Suresh lowers his paper and looks at her.

Cross-fade.

Exterior. Bazaar.

Bazaar noises as Uma walks through the bazaar. The bazaar noises fade as she enters a narrow lane. Film music can be heard from a transistor. A dog barks. Uma knocks on a door. A window opens.

CHAMPA *(from window).* Go away!

UMA. Champa, let me in. I want to talk to you.

CHAMPA. Madam, you should not mix with people like us.

UMA. I am sorry if I offended you in any way. Please do let me in. I must speak to Anarkali.

Champa opens the door.

CHAMPA. What do you want now?

UMA. Help me in having the murderer of Kamla arrested.

CHAMPA. How can I help you?

UMA. Anarkali must have taken the photograph from Kamla's box!

CHAMPA. Shh! Come in.

Champa lets her in. They go in.

UMA. She was the only one close to Kamla. If you don't have it . . .

CHAMPA. What use is the photograph?

UMA. If Salim wants it so badly, it must be important. I have a feeling he is not going to confess. Mr Sharma wouldn't want to lose a trusted bodyguard and will use his influence. There is no real proof. Except maybe the photograph.

CHAMPA. Listen to me, Madam. Forget it.

UMA. No. I feel I owe it to you and Anarkali and . . . and . . . all of you!

CHAMPA. We don't know anything about any photo!

UMA. What about Anarkali? Where is she?

CHAMPA. She is not here. Now please go before anyone sees you here.

Pause.

UMA. Who are you scared of? Salim?

CHAMPA. No. Not Salim. There are others more dangerous than he.

UMA. Who?

CHAMPA. I don't know.

UMA. You do. But you don't trust me.

CHAMPA. Not even your father-in-law can put them in jail.

UMA. Please! Let me speak with . . .

CHAMPA. You want to meet Anarkali?

Champa calls out to Anarkali. Anarkali enters. Her face is bruised and her arm is in a sling.

UMA *(gasping)*. Anarkali.

ANARKALI *(in pain, barely audible)*. Hello, sister.

CHAMPA. They broke her nose.

Anarkali staggers and sits down.

ANARKALI. Come closer. *(Uma moves closer to Anarkali.)* Does your husband know you are here?

UMA. No.

ANARKALI. Why did you not tell him?

UMA *(after a while)*. He wouldn't allow me to visit you.

ANARKALI. Then what will you do knowing who killed Kamla?

UMA. Tell my husband to make an arrest.

ANARKALI. One hijra less in this world does not matter to your husband.

UMA. Trust me, and tell me. Who is it?

Pause.

ANARKALI. You will be there at the minister's son's wedding?

UMA. Yes.

ANARKALI. With your husband?

UMA. Yes.

CHAMPA. Anarkali!

Pause.

ANARKALI. Don't put your own position in danger. Go home.

CHAMPA. Madam, do as she says. Go home. To your—husband.

Pause. Uma leaves.

ANARKALI. She wants to help.

CHAMPA. Ignorant woman. She thinks she knows her husband.

ANARKALI. Aah!

CHAMPA. It hurts?

ANARKALI. Yes . . . Do you think the doctor will see me?

CHAMPA. I tried.

ANARKALI. If we gave him more money?

CHAMPA. Stupid woman. As if they want our money.

ANARKALI. What about the other doctor? Gulab's customer?

Champa shakes her head. Anarkali winces.

CHAMPA. It will go away. Let me give you some more brandy.

She gets up. Anarkali pulls her back.

ANARKALI. I drank it. It is not going away, the pain.

Champa holds her and puts Anarkali's head in her lap.

CHAMPA. What can I do? What can I do?

Champa rocks her like a baby.

ANARKALI. You know, for the minister's son's wedding, I want to wear the red ghagra.

CHAMPA. Yes.

ANARKALI. But you said yes to Gulab also. I want to wear that.

CHAMPA. I will tell Gulab. You wear the red ghagra. But first you have to get better.

ANARKALI. My mother used to sing me when I had fever.

CHAMPA. You shut up. I am your mother. Understand?

ANARKALI. Then sing.

CHAMPA. Say that, you bitch! . . . Now close your eyes. Close.

*Anarkali closes her eyes. Champa sings a lullaby from
a film. La lalla lori, doodh ki katori . . . Champa has
tears in her eyes as she continues to sing. Slow cross
fade even as the song continues to reveal Suresh and
Uma in the car. The spot on Champa and Anarkali
fades out.*

Exterior. In the car of Suresh and Uma.

*Fade in car in motion. Occasional honks from other
vehicles.*

SURESH. You look good in red.

*Uma is wearing a bright red shawl and has flowers in
her hair.*

UMA. It's the shawl you bought me for Diwali.

SURESH. You should have worn your diamonds.

UMA. This is only the wedding ceremony. I will wear them for
the reception.

SURESH. I think we have lost them.

UMA. No. There they are . . . At least, the car following them.

SURESH. One day, I too will have a five-car escort . . . There is
talk, that father will become the Comissioner soon . . . So what
did you buy for them?

UMA. A huge carpet. From us. Your parents are giving them a
chandelier for their new home.

SURESH. Do you think the carpet is flashy enough?

UMA. It takes three servants to carry it.

*A group of people run across in front of the car.
Suresh brakes.*

SURESH *(mutters).* Bloody beggars!

*Cut traffic. Fade in marriage music. Chatter of guests.
The bride and groom are brought to the sacred fire.*

The priest's chants can be heard. Suresh arrives at the house. A woman is sprinkling rose water. They get out and say hello to a few people.

Who was that waving to you?

UMA. That was Mrs Nair, the liquor baron's wife. And that's his brother with her, visiting from Canada. Do you want me to introduce them?

SURESH. No, no. Excuse me. I think I will say hello to Mr Birla.

Chatter of guests continues.

(Going off stage.) Hello Mr Birla . . .

Uma wanders around.

MR SHARMA. Looking for someone as usual?

UMA. Oh!

MR SHARMA. I am sorry, I didn't mean to startle you.

UMA. No, no. I wasn't . . .

MR SHARMA. You had that searching look again.

UMA. Did I? How can you tell?

MR SHARMA. I have seen it in many people. It is usually a spiritual search that I see.

UMA *(laughing)*. And is that what you see in me?

MR SHARMA. Yes. I see a search for the truth.

UMA. Do you think I will find it?

MR SHARMA. If you look in the right place.

UMA. Which would be?

MR SHARMA. You know the saying about the musk deer? He searches everywhere for the source of the heavenly fragrance, not realizing it is contained within his own body.

Uma laughs.

You don't believe it is true?

UMA. And yourself? Have you found what you have been searching for?

MR SHARMA. Yes. My son is getting a wife from a fine family. I am happy to see that he is entering the phase of the householder.

UMA. And you feel the truth lies in that?

MR SHARMA. For him yes. My truth is in ensuring he is on the right path . . . Come. The time is auspicious.

> *Cut chatter to fade in Sanskrit shlokas being chanted signifying the final ceremony. Occasionally the fire crackles as butter is thrown into it. Spot on Subbu in a silk veshti and traditional headdress. Beside him is a bride. The poojari is chanting. The smoke from the fire fills the space.*

Don't they look fine together? This is the happiest moment for any parent—watching their child perform these rites.

> *The crackle takes on an ominous proportion and so do the chants. As the chants are amplified, Uma wanders off on her own into another lit area. Salim appears from nowhere. Uma looks at him.*

SALIM. Madam, you should not be seen here near the servants' quarters.

UMA. I want to know why you killed her.

SALIM. It is not what you think it is.

UMA. You brought Kamla here night after night. There are enough witnesses. Tell me Salim. Did she betray you? Did she go out with another man?

SALIM. Go back to the wedding!

> *Uma goes back to the wedding. The bride and groom get up to take the seven steps. They touch Mr Sharma's feet. The guests throw rice to signify the end of the wedding. Munswamy comes running to Uma.*

MUNSWAMY. Madam, they are here!

> *The hijras approach from all over. They are brightly done up and now look very much like the hijras we see*

at weddings. They are led by Champa and Anarkali.
Anarkali looks fine now.

CHAMPA. May God bless this house with many children!

ANARKALI. May God always smile upon this house!

UMA. Look! That's Anarkali! And Champa!

SURESH. Ssh!

UMA. Oh! I can't be bothered!

CHAMPA. Salaam to all! We will bless this marriage with our singing and dancing.

One of the hijras begins to beat on a drum.

MR SHARMA. Stop! Stop it!

They stop beating the drum.

Who invited you here? Where are those security people!

SURESH. I will check.

Suresh walks away in a hurry.

CHAMPA. Do not be so angry, Sir. It is a happy occasion.

MR SHARMA. Shut up. Get rid of them, someone.

UMA. No. Wait! You can't do that.

MR SHARMA. Are you taking their side?

UMA. No. It is bad luck to turn away a hijra on a wedding or a birth.

CHAMPA. Thank you my daughter! May you have a hundred sons!

MR SHARMA. Do you really believe in that?

UMA. Mr Sharma, what have you got to lose? The marriage ceremonies are done. You should be happy. Just let them dance a little. Is that asking for too much?

Suresh approaches with security guards.

SURESH *(approaching)*. I will have you all suspended for this! Here they are. Throw them all out. *(To the hijras.)* Get out of here, or I will lock you all up in jail!

MR SHARMA. Er . . . maybe I overreacted. After all their presence is expected. I will just give them some money . . .

CHAMPA. Thank you Sir, but we must sing and dance to bless this house and the handsome couple.

MR SHARMA. Well, all right. Just one number and you will get your baksheesh.

ANARKALI. Where are the newly married? They must be here.

MR SHARMA. Oh!

UMA. Please! It is important!

MR SHARMA. Request the young couple to come here.

The bride and groom come forward. Champa goes to bless them. The bride is a little scared and takes Subbu away from Champa.

CHAMPA *(to the other hijras)*. Come on! Come on, start!

The hijras begin to dance. again we lose the singing as the drum beat and the dancing bells are unrealistically overpowering. It builds to a crescendo. While they dance, Subbu comes forward looking at them. He looks away to see a vision of Kamla dancing on another level. The music builds to a crescendo. Kamla opens her arms wide.

SUBBU. No!

Subbu reaches out for Suresh's gun.

SURESH. What the . . .?

A short scuffle in which Subbu manages to get the gun from Suresh.

MR SHARMA. Subbu!

SUBBU. Stay away!

SURESH. Subbu, give it back to me!

ANARKALI. Subbu, no!

MR SHARMA. You keep out of this!

Kamla calls out to him from her level, her arms beckoning him to join her.

KAMLA. Subbu!!

SUBBU. I–I am leaving you all! You can't keep me away from Kamla.

UMA. Subbu, forget what I said. Please, let us talk.

MR SHARMA. Son, please put that gun down. Let us talk.

SUBBU. No.

MR SHARMA. It was a mistake. I am sorry, son. *(Calling out.)* Salim!

UMA. Subbu, I am sorry. I did not know.

SALIM. Subbu. Sir. Please . . .

SUBBU. Salim, I trusted you. You promised.

ANARKALI. Subbu, I have a gift for you.

SALIM. You stay away from him!

MR SHARMA. It's okay, Salim. Anything, just . . .

ANARKALI. See. See, Subbu.

SUBBU. W–what is it?

ANARKALI. A photo . . . Take. These people cannot take this away from you.

SALIM. Give that to me.

SUBBU. No. It's mine. Only I shall have it. Give it to me.

CHAMPA. Give it to him. Take it my son.

Anarkali walks up to Subbu and gives him the photograph. Subbu looks at the photograph.

SUBBU. They killed you, Kamla!

KAMLA *(echoing)*. They killed me!

SUBBU. Why?

KAMLA. Because you loved me!

SUBBU. I still love you Kamla!

KAMLA. I love you, Subbu.

MR SHARMA. Subbu, your Kamla is gone. It's all over. You have a whole life ahead of you.

KAMLA *(echoing)*. I am gone!

MR SHARMA. Subbu you can do whatever you want. Give me the gun.

SURESH *(going towards him slowly)*. Come on now, give me the gun.

SUBBU. Stay away!

> *Subbu backs away. He begins to cry. He points the gun at his father.*

You killed her!

> *Silence except for Subbu's sobs. Mr Sharma backs away.*

MR SHARMA. Subbu, I did it for you! It was wrong. It was wrong. Forgive me!

SUBBU. You cannot bring back Kamla.

> *Mr Sharma falls at Champa's feet.*

MR SHARMA. Help me! Talk to my son! Tell him to forget Kamla. He will listen to you!

CHAMPA. Even God does not listen to us!

> *Subbu is about to shoot at his father. Instead he turns the gun on himself and fires. A gunshot. Some screams.*

MR SHARMA. Noooo!

> *They rush to Subbu. They take him away. Uma and Suresh remain on stage. A spot on Anarkali comforting Champa. Champa exits. Anarkali moves away but stays on stage. A surreal spot on Kamla. Music. Subbu joins her. Subbu embraces Kamla. They kiss as the music builds up. The light on them stays as they freeze as in a picture frame. Uma picks up the photograph.*

UMA *(to Suresh)*. The photograph was what Mr Sharma was after. A polaroid picture that Subbu and Kamla had taken soon after their private wedding in some remote temple. A picture of Kamla as a beautiful bride smiling at Subbu with the wedding garland around him. The poojari probably didn't know that Kamla was not a woman. Of course Mr Sharma couldn't have it, totally unacceptable. So he arranged to have Kamla burned to death. But Salim had to tell him about the picture. Mr Sharma simply had to have that picture. He sent Salim to threaten Anarkali and Champa . . . He did get the picture eventually . . . after losing his son. What a price to pay! And now he will be arrested and tried for murder.

SURESH *(taking the photograph from Uma).* That I don't know . . .

Pause.

Suresh tears up the picture. Spot on Suresh fades out. Uma walks in through the beaded curtains. Anarkali greets her.

ANARKALI. Madam!

UMA. I am so glad you are here.

ANARKALI. I am not going anywhere. I am now the head hijra. Champa has retired. She is leaving to spend the rest of her days in her sister's house in Bombay . . .

Anarkali trails off as Uma puts her hand on her arm.

UMA. Why didn't you tell me?

ANARKALI. Would you have believed me? Anyway what is the use of all that? What does it matter who killed Kamla? She is dead . . . So many times I warned her. First I thought Salim was taking her for his own pleasure. When she told me about Subbu, Madam, I tried to stop her. I fought with her. I scratched her face, hoping she will become ugly and Subbu will forget her. He wanted to marry her . . . I was there at their wedding . . . She gave me that picture to show to Champa. I saw the men coming for her. I told her to run . . .

Anarkali controls her tears and takes out a locket.

Here Madam, take this.

UMA. What is it?

ANARKALI. A special mantra is in the locket. Champa ga
to me for you.

Uma looks at it.

Wear it.

Anarkali puts the locket around Uma's neck.

You will be blessed with children.

Uma is moved by this. She embraces Anarkali.

Sister!

They look at each other.

May you and your family be happy! Now go away, and
come here again.

Uma wants to say something.

Please go, sister!

Silence. Uma leaves.

UMA *(voice-over).* They knew. Anarkali, Champa and
hijra people knew who was behind the killing of Kamla
have no voice. The case was hushed up and was no
reported in the newspapers. Champa was right. The
made no arrests. Subbu's suicide was written off as an ac
The photograph was destroyed. So were the lives of two
people . . . But Anarkali's blessings remain with me. *(To
the locket.)* I could not tell her I did not want her blessir
a child. All I want is—what they want . . . To move c
love. To live.

> *The hijras do their dance in slow motion, smilir
> clapping in slow motion. Uma remains fixed in
> spotlight in the centre while the hijras move in
> shadows on the periphery.*

THE SWAMI AND WINSTON

A Radio Play

A Note on the Play

Another case for the intrepid Uma, daughter-in-law of Bangalore's Deputy Commissioner of Police, and wife of the Superintendent.

Still researching her thesis on violence in India, and having one solved case to her credit, Uma comes into contact with religious fanaticism at its most extreme when investigating the death of a member of the English aristocracy.

An English Burberry raincoat and a mischievous dog provide the only clues as to the identity of the murderer. But why did Lady Montefiore visit the ashram in the first place when she had little interest in the Hindu religion, and what can be a possible motive for her murder?

Jeremy Mortimer
(Jeremy Mortimer is Executive Producer,
BBC Radio Drama.)

The Swami and Winston was first broadcast on 3 June 2000 at 3 p.m. on BBC Radio 4. The play was directed by Jeremy Mortimer.

Cast for first production:

UMA	Priyanga Elan
SURESH RAO	Ajay Chabra
MUNSWAMY	Shiv Grewal
SWAMI	Saeed Jaffrey
SITARAM TRIVEDI	Paul Bhattacharjee
CHARLES MONTEFIORE	Andrew Wincott
LADY MONTEFIORE	Richenda Carey
DRIVER	Amerjit Deu
FARMER	Nitin Chandra Ghanatra

Exterior. Lady Montefiore and the driver are negotiating in the car.

LADY MONTEFIORE. Surely this isn't the place! I know an ashram when I see one.

DRIVER. No Madam. This is the famous Bull Temple. All tourists come to this . . .

LADY MONTEFIORE. I am not a tourist!

DRIVER. It is very old. You can see the statue of the great big bull of Shiva. Very big.

LADY MONTEFIORE *(speaking slowly but raising her voice).* I want to go to the ashram. I am not here to waste my time looking at your bulls! Can you understand that?

Winston whines some more.

DRIVER *(hurt).* Not my bulls. I am a Muslim. This is a very sacred bull, the vehicle of God Shiva Himself.

LADY MONTEFIORE. Oh well . . . if it makes a difference to you. *(Getting out of the car.) (Firm.)* But after I see the bull, we go straight to the ashram. Is that clear?

DRIVER. Yes, Madam.

Shutting her door.

LADY MONTEFIORE. Cross your heart.

DRIVER. Huh?

LADY MONTEFIORE. Or swear by the big bull . . . no never mind. What do I do with Winston?

DRIVER. Leave the dog in the car.

LADY MONTEFIORE. Nonsense! I never go anywhere without Winston. Tell all these people to go away. Winston is very sensitive to . . .

DRIVER. They have never seen a dog like this before.

Winston barks.

Give the dog to me Madam.

LADY MONTEFIORE. No. He is not used to anyone else! Winston! Oh dear. Maybe it isn't such a good idea after all.

DRIVER. Don't worry Madam. I will take him for a walk. Give him to me.

LADY MONTEFIORE. No! Oh dear, oh dear! Here hold on to this—Now Winston, I know we don't like the leash but—the temple priest begins to blow on the conch, a loud steady note. Oh! *(Winston whines and yelps.)* Winston! Oh!

> *The bells at the temple begin to clang and continue to do so.*

Winston! No! Stay! Winston!!

Initial credits. Fade out.

Interior/Exterior/ Uma and Suresh Rao's home.

> *Steady fall of rain on a window pane. The whistle of a pressure cooker. Knock on a window pane.*

UMA. Come in! Through the kitchen door!

Boots on slush.

How are you, Constable Munswamy? Would you like some breakfast?

MUNSWAMY. Madam! Please help me Madam!

UMA. What is the matter? Are you unwell?

MUNSWAMY. I have to find a dog! Help me Madam.

UMA. I will pour you some coffee and you can explain it to me.

MUNSWAMY. I have to find her dog in twenty-four hours or else Sir will get me transferred to some village! I tell you her driver only must have done some mischief! What am I to do?

UMA. Munswamy!

MUNSWAMY. Sir!

UMA. Have some idlis. Drink your coffee. Then explain everything to me properly. And remember—you are not to tell my husband I am helping you out.

Fade out on rain.

Exterior. Car driving on a busy road.

They drive slowly because of the rains.

MUNSWAMY. If it continues to rain like this, the roads will be flooded again.

UMA. Lady Caroline Montefiore. Quite an impressive background.

MUNSWAMY. You know who she is?

UMA. A wealthy woman even by European standards. I spent some time after class searching the web for information on her. There are quite a few news articles on her.

MUNSWAMY. If I had more time to find the dog . . .

UMA. Munswamy, you really are capable of handling this by yourself. You don't need me to find her dog.

MUNSWAMY. I cannot understand what she is saying. She cries as if she has lost her child.

UMA. Indeed, she has . . .

Fade out traffic.

Interior. Hotel lobby.

LADY MONTEFIORE. What am I to do? I shall never see my Winston again!

UMA. I am sure Winston wouldn't want to be separated from you for very long.

LADY MONTEFIORE. You do see that, don't you? If it weren't for those temple bells and those crowds making my poor Winston nervous. It was all a big mistake! Coming here was a big mistake. I should have sent my secretary instead!

UMA. I take it this is not a pleasure trip you are on.

LADY MONTEFIORE. I am not leaving this country without my Winston. That's certain. What did you say your name is?

UMA. Uma. Uma. My husband is the Superintendent at the police station where you made your complaint.

LADY MONTEFIORE. Oh. Tell me something, what do you think of this . . . person or Swami or whatever they are called Jeevananda?

UMA. I believe he is a great spiritual leader. Why do you ask?

LADY MONTEFIORE. How long does it take to find a King Charles Spaniel in this city? Do you think it will help to offer some money?

UMA. I don't think that will be necessary. You don't want people thinking the dog is valuable do you?

LADY MONTEFIORE. He is! He is priceless!

UMA. Yes. But you don't want people to know that do you?

LADY MONTEFIORE. I don't trust your police. I have made my own arrangements, thank you. I instructed the hotel manager to advertise in the local papers. I am offering a reward of five thousand pounds.

UMA. I would strongly advise you not to do such a thing. By all means give your money to whoever finds him, but don't announce a reward.

LADY MONTEFIORE. Nonsense. Nobody will do anything unless there is some money in it for them. And Charles is too silly to realize that . . .

UMA. Charles?

LADY MONTEFIORE. Young lady, I am off to the Bull Temple. Not that I believe in praying to bulls but that's where I lost my Winston. Oh, there is the driver person! (*Clapping her hands.*) Hellooo. Let's go!

DRIVER. Oh, Madam. Shall I take you to the ashram? Big ashram?

LADY MONTEFIORE. Not the ashram. *(Spelling it out)* To the Bull temple. Take me to the Bull Temple.

Fade out.

DRIVER. But first we go to the ashram, yes?

LADY MONTEFIORE. To the Bull Temple . . .

Fade out.

Interior. Uma's kitchen.

Rustle of paper.

MUNSWAMY. Five thousand pounds!! How much is that in rupees?

UMA. Multiply that by seventy-two.

MUNSWAMY *(doing some mental calculations)*. Seven into five . . . Over three and a half lakhs to find a dog!!

UMA. Well, if you find it, the money is yours.

MUNSWAMY. Then I don't have to worry about my daughter's marriage.

UMA. You don't have a daughter, Munswamy.

MUNSWAMY. But still . . .

Distant thunder. Fade out.

A long drawn out chorus of 'Om'. the 'Om' blends in with the thunder and downpour. Sound of a car driving in the rain.

Interior. Car driving on a lonely stretch.

LADY MONTEFIORE *(to Winston)*. There! there . . . we shall soon be out of all this mess. Did you miss me? Oh! *(After a while.)* I can't see a thing. *(To driver.)* How long do you think this dreadful rain will last?

DRIVER. We should not have gone to the ashram today itself, Madam.

LADY MONTEFIORE. I simply had to sort out this business. Thank God we found Winston in time. *(To Winston.)* Oh Winston! Don't you ever run away like that!

DRIVER. The road is like a river.

LADY MONTEFIORE. Well we'll just drive slowly and surely back to the hotel, and there's a nice tip waiting for you, young man.

DRIVER. Did we turn this way or this way?

LADY MONTEFIORE. Are you asking me for directions?

DRIVER. No, no Madam. I am only asking which way to go.

LADY MONTEFIORE. Why don't you just stop and ask some nice people somewhere out there?

DRIVER. Who is there to ask in this rain?

LADY MONTEFIORE. I thought there was a car behind us. Why don't you stop for a while so they can catch up with us?

DRIVER. Don't worry Madam, the Bull Temple is not far. We will ask there.

LADY MONTEFIORE. Just the place I want to be in this weather.

DRIVER. Don't worry Madam, I will take you to the Bull Temple tomorrow also.

LADY MONTEFIORE. Hah! That's what you think!

The car coughs a little and comes to a halt.

Now what?

DRIVER *(opening his door)*. The engine is overheated.

LADY MONTEFIORE. Never heard of such a thing. In this rain?

Driver steps outside and opens bonnet. We are outside the car now.

DRIVER *(shouting over the rain)*. The fan belt is broken!

LADY MONTEFIORE. Oh dear! Oh dear!

DRIVER *(popping his head into the car)*. Madam, don't worry. I will get mechanic near the Bull Temple.

LADY MONTEFIORE. What do you want me to do in the meantime? Knit a sweater?

DRIVER. Good idea.

LADY MONTEFIORE. You can't leave me here!

DRIVER. What can I do?

LADY MONTEFIORE. How long do you think you will be gone?

DRIVER. Only five minutes.

LADY MONTEFIORE. You can't possibly walk to that temple and return in five minutes! Can't we stop a car or something?

DRIVER. Madam, who will stop in this rain? Don't worry. I will lock the car and you do not open your door for anyone. Just for five minutes.

LADY MONTEFIORE. If you'd said you will be gone for fifty minutes I wouldn't be worried. Oh Winston, what are we to do?

DRIVER. Madam, it is wet outside. Please listen to me.

LADY MONTEFIORE. Oh well . . . but do hurry! Here, you may use my parasol.

DRIVER. It is okay Madam. It is wet outside. It will get spoilt.

LADY MONTEFIORE. Well, whatever suits you best.

DRIVER. I am locking the door Madam.

LADY MONTEFIORE. Ooh er . . . all right. Good luck.

Car door shuts. Click of the lock.

Nothing seems to be going right for us, Winston . . .

Temple bells ring at a distance followed by the blowing of the conch. The sound of the rain persists as another car drives up and stops. The door opens and bangs shut.

Interior. Car.

Winston whines a little.

LADY MONTEFIORE. I am sorry but you will just have to wait. We have run out of them. See—no bikis. No more till we get back home.

Knock on the window.

Oh! Oh—how in the world? Thank God! I can't hear you! Wait, let me—how do you unlock this door? Oh I think I know . . . there!

The door opens letting in the fury of the thundershower.

Maybe you can take Winston and I back—what are you . . .?

Winston barks.

What in? Oh! Aaaaagh!

Winston's bark turns vicious and he snaps. The collective 'om' sound is heard. The sound from blowing the conch grows louder. Fade out. Fade in Swami.

Interior. Swami.

SWAMI. The body is but a garment that the soul discards, and wears yet another garment. So we are trapped in the cycle of birth and death because the soul desires new bodies just as our body desires material wealth. In order to liberate yourself from this endless cycle, you offer yourself to Lord Krishna. Surrender. So let go off your material wealth and begin your spiritual journey. Travel light . . .

Fade out Swami. Fade in the rains. Thunder. Winston whines.

Interior. Uma and Suresh in the bedroom.

The rain can be heard faintly through the window. The phone rings for quite a while.

SURESH *(sleepy).* Hello . . . Damn! Where? . . . Send Munswamy over. *(Hangs up.)* She has to go out in this weather.

Suresh gets out of bed and starts to wear his uniform.

UMA *(stirring).* What is it?

SURESH. Nothing much, go back to sleep. It's that English woman again.

UMA. What about her?

SURESH. She is dead. In her car somewhere on Whitefield road.

UMA *(getting up).* I'll make some coffee for you.

SURESH. Better hurry.

UMA. Can I go with you?

SURESH. What for?

UMA *(after a while)*. Just to keep you company.

SURESH. Look. I know you think you are very clever at this after that hijra case . . .

UMA. No, I didn't mean . . .

SURESH. Let me finish. I don't like you interfering in my work. I don't interfere in your work do I?

UMA *(speaking quickly to have her say before she is interrupted)*. You did. You never let me complete my thesis!

SURESH. Sweetheart, let us be clear about this. Your professor didn't like your work . . .

UMA. I couldn't submit . . .

SURESH. Hang on.

UMA. The full paper because . . .

SURESH. Let me finish. It's 1 a.m. and I don't want to argue with you. I didn't allow you to use the hijra murder because it was a sensitive case. Just listen . . . this is probably one of those robbery cases. She must have put up a fight so she got killed. Some of those Muslims in that area have been arrested before. They must have stopped the car.

UMA. How do you know?

SURESH. I haven't finished.

UMA. You never do! I just want to come because I met the lady once. She seemed a wonderful person and for this to happen to someone like her is . . .

SURESH. When did you meet her?

UMA. Tragic, to say the least. Oh I visited her once at her hotel. She wanted some help with her dog . . .

SURESH. Did Munswamy take you there?

UMA. No.

SURESH. Good. Because I don't want him helping you when he is supposed to be on duty.

UMA. Put on your shoes while I make the coffee. *(Pause.)* Winston!

SURESH. Huh?

UMA. What about poor Winston?

SURESH. Who?

Cut to more thunder and rain. Police siren fading out.

Interior. The police station.

CHARLES. Why wasn't I informed?

SURESH. We don't know who you are. And please lower your voice in my police station.

CHARLES *(with restraint)*. But . . . but surely you would have found some papers in her bag. My address. It is a bit odd that you didn't look in her bag.

SURESH. Who are you?

CHARLES *(after a pause)*. My name is Charles Montefiore. I live at the Swami's ashram in Whitefield.

SURESH. Let me see your passport.

CHARLES. Here it is, Officer.

SURESH *(examining his passport)*. So. How were you related to the deceased?

CHARLES. She was my sister. I cannot believe it! I had to read about it in the paper this morning!

SURESH. No we didn't find any address. Only a book with phone numbers, all foreign. Not a single Indian phone number or address, except a card of the hotel she was staying in.

CHARLES. Nothing else?

SURESH. Maybe there were other things. What papers did you expect us to find in her bag?

CHARLES. May I take a look at her belongings?

SURESH. They have been sent to the forensic experts . . Interesting.

CHARLES. What?

SURESH. Your profession.

CHARLES. No longer. I gave that up to come to India.

SURESH. You can't stay for very long you know. They are not going to renew your visa a third time.

CHARLES. That may not be necessary. I have applied for Indian citizenship. If I am to be a Hindu, I might as well live in India.

SURESH. Yes. Of course!

CHARLES. I thought that might please you. There's one more thing . . . I don't want my sister's body lying in that morgue. She must rest in our family graveyard.

SURESH. There is to be a postmortem I am afraid.

CHARLES. You will keep me informed.

SURESH. We will. As far as we know, you are her only relative. Is there anything else?

CHARLES. No. Well there is. Winston.

SURESH. I beg your pardon?

CHARLES. The dog. Where is he?

SURESH. One of our constables is looking after him. *(Ringing a bell.)* Munswamy!! Damn. I forgot. I gave him the day off to look after that dog.

CHARLES. I want that dog.

   Cut to:

Interior. Uma's kitchen.

UMA. What a sad dog! He has got the bug.

MUNSWAMY. Nobody in my house could sleep, Madam. We gave it some milk and biscuits. Didn't eat anything, crying all night.

UMA. Do you think the driver is in some way involved?

MUNSWAMY. No Madam. There is no proof.

UMA. Why did my husband arrest him then? Was there any money missing from her bag? All the money was still in her bag . . . Whoever killed her did not kill her for her money. Maybe not for the money in her bag . . . Let's meet the driver.

MUNSWAMY. I knew you will want to talk to him. Sir has gone to the headquarters this morning.

UMA. Then let's go! We'll drop Winston off at the vet's. And Munswamy!

MUNSWAMY. Sir!

UMA. Let's keep all information confidential, shall we?

MUNSWAMY. Yes, Sir!

　　Cut to:

Interior. The police station.

DRIVER. Madam, I tell you I am not having anything to do with her death.

MUNSWAMY. Listen to madam first.

DRIVER. What is my crime? Being a Muslim? I tell you they will not have arrested me if I was not a Muslim! Who will believe me? You are also a Hindu.

UMA. No. You misunderstand. I want you to help me find out who killed the English lady.

DRIVER. How can I help you? I don't know anything! I leave her for half an hour and when I come back she is dead. In my car. Couldn't she die somewhere else? Why don't you help me also? My life is not important?

UMA *(quietly)*. I understand Maqsood. I will try to help you. But you help me find out her killer and I am sure it will benefit you also . . . by proving your innocence.

DRIVER. I will try to help you. I don't know anything. I am just a Muslim. You should help me.

UMA. I will try. I am just a woman . . .

　　Cut to:

Exterior. Car driving on a busy road.

MUNSWAMY. After the Bull Temple, the next place the driver took her to is this man who found the dog. 16th Cross, Lakshmi Nivas.

UMA. What's his name?

MUNSWAMY. Sitaram Trivedi. A north Indian.

UMA. And a Vaishnav brahmin. Hmm. Wonder how he found Winston.

Cut to:

Interior. Living room of Sitaram Trivedi.

SITARAM TRIVEDI. I feed the poor people at the temple every day. I too have dogs. So one of the street boys who found the dog brought him to me. A very nice breed . . . Very unfortunate about the lady.

UMA. Yes.

SITARAM TRIVEDI. It is quite a privlege having the daughter-in-law of the Deputy Commissioner of Police visiting me. What can I do for you?

UMA. This isn't exactly an official visit. I am merely interested in finding the motive for her murder. It is for my thesis on violence in India.

SITARAM TRIVEDI. How did you meet her?

UMA. Well, my husband is the Superintendent and it was at his station that she registered her complaint when she lost Winston.

SITARAM TRIVEDI. What do you know about her?

UMA. Oh very little I am afraid. She must have spoken to you at length, considering she had lunch with you.

SITARAM TRIVEDI. How do you know she had lunch with me?

UMA. Her driver told me.

SITARAM TRIVEDI. Ah yes! The . . . Muslim gentleman.

UMA. Yes.

SITARAM TRIVEDI. She was very naive. Trusting anyone.

UMA. You mean she shouldn't have employed a Muslim driver?

SITARAM TRIVEDI. I didn't say that. Yes I did invite her to lunch. I read the announcement in the papers. I was thinking of putting in an advertisement myself after I found her dog. She talked about all kinds of things. The countries she had travelled to. Her charities. She did not live in England although she was English.

UMA. Why is that?

SITARAM TRIVEDI. Because of the dog. So she could travel with her dog. England has very strict rules about bringing in animals. She did say she lived in Lucerne or Laussane or somewhere. Are you interested in joining the Corps of Detectives?

UMA. Oh no! My interests are purely . . . well . . . somewhat personal. You are in no way obliged to talk to me about . . .

SITARAM TRIVEDI *(laughing)*. A woman with your fine background needs all the encouragement. I will be happy to tell you what I know of the dear departed English lady.

UMA. Thank you. I appreciate that.

SITARAM TRIVEDI. Let me see . . . I should draw a quick biography for you. She was an extremely wealthy woman. A spinster. Never married. From an illustrious English family from Hertfordshire. Was totally devoted to her dog. She was here in India to . . . let me see . . . what was she doing here? I believe she had someone here she wanted to visit . . . I can't remember the name.

UMA. Charles.

Silence.

SITARAM TRIVEDI. Yes. Did she talk to you about Charles?

UMA. Not at all. She just happened to mention that name. Who is he?

SITARAM TRIVEDI. I believe her brother.

UMA. You are not sure.

SITARAM TRIVEDI. No. You see I must admit that after a while I wasn't paying too much attention. I was more interested in her dog Wilson . . .

UMA. Winston.

SITARAM TRIVEDI. Yes. Where is he?

UMA. He is with me for the weekend. On Monday, he will be taken over to the British Embassy along with her body, which is in the morgue.

SITARAM TRIVEDI. Unfortunate. All this. The papers said that she was strangled.

UMA. Yes. With Winston's leather leash. Did she appear to be . . . spiritually drawn towards any guru?

SITARAM TRIVEDI. That wouldn't be very uncommon for a European travelling to India. I mean they don't exactly come here for the weather.

UMA. I got the feeling she was distinctly . . . if I can use the word Hindophobic. But I could be wrong.

SITARAM TRIVEDI. There are two types of Europeans. Ones who understand and appreciate the depth and complexity of Hindu philosophy and the others who feel threatened by it. The world will realize the greatness of the Hindu way of life. Wait and see. It is a question of time. They can't be blind for ever even if they choose not to see. They have to open their eyes sooner or later. We shall have our temples all over the world.

UMA. And at Ayodhya?

SITARAM TRIVEDI. Time will tell.

UMA. What if it leads to a civil war? The horrors of partition all over again. Is Hindu pride worth all that? Isn't there any other way of establishing Hindu pride?

SITARAM TRIVEDI. You are still young. What do you know of the horrors of partition? I have lived through it! Is there anything else you want to know about the lady? I believe I have said all that I can recall.

UMA. Did she seem antagonistic towards Hindus?

SITARAM TRIVEDI. No. No. But she was totally ignorant of Hindu rituals. She thought we sacrifice children to appease goddesses.

UMA. I guess she could be scornful of Hindu rituals and yet seek spirituality in this country.

SITARAM TRIVEDI. The two cannot be separated.

UMA. But she wasn't seeking spiritual growth? That wasn't her intention in coming here?

SITARAM TRIVEDI. No. I think she came here to visit Charles. He lives here in Bangalore now. At the ashram in Whitefield. He calls himself a Hindu. I suppose you will want to meet him.

UMA. I plan to visit the ashram this afternoon.

SITARAM TRIVEDI. He wasn't particularly looking forward to meeting her I could tell from her conversation.

UMA. Why?

SITARAM TRIVEDI. She wanted him to return to England.

UMA. Have you met him?

SITARAM TRIVEDI. Yes. And no.

UMA. What do you mean?

SITARAM TRIVEDI. I visit the ashram quite often. I have seen him there.

UMA. What kind of a person is he?

SITARAM TRIVEDI. You will soon find out. I wish you good luck in your efforts. Jai Sri Ram.

UMA. Er . . . Thank you for your time.

SITARAM TRIVEDI. Will you take some advice from someone older to you?

UMA. What is it?

SITARAM TRIVEDI. Don't take your Catholic school education too seriously. Jai Sri Ram.

Cut to:

Exterior. Driving on the Whitefield road.

UMA. A dangerous man.

MUNSWAMY. What Madam?

UMA. I said he is a dangerous man. He is a real right wing Hindu fanatic.

MUNSWAMY. Why do they want to create so much trouble?

UMA. They feel they know everything. And they feel superior because they feel they know everything. And feel threatened by the presence of Islam and Christianity.

MUNSWAMY. I did not like his face.

UMA. Why?

MUNSWAMY. Somehow, he seemed like a bad person . . .

UMA *(laughing)*. Was it because of his eye?

MUNSWAMY. I don't know . . .

UMA. Maybe you couldn't tell why you didn't like his face. Perhaps the reason is because he had a speck of white in his right pupil. It had a glint when the light shone a particular way. But that's no reflection on his character!

MUNSWAMY. I have seen many bad people. Criminals.

UMA. You've been watching too many Bollywood films.

MUNSWAMY. Where is his family? No wife, no children.

UMA. His wife is dead. There was a garland around her photograph in the corner of the living room.

MUNSWAMY. No children.

UMA. Maybe they are away. Maybe he doesn't have any.

MUNSWAMY. No wife, no children. He cannot be a good man.

UMA. I don't have any children. Does that make me a bad person?

MUNSWAMY. Madam, I did not mean like that! If God is willing . . .

UMA. Let's drop in on Winston first to see if he is all right. Then take me home. We will leave soon after lunch. We will think and feel better with some nice avarekai sambar inside us.

Cut to:

Interior. Uma on the phone.

UMA. Hello, Ratna aunty? . . . This is Uma calling from India . . . Oh I am so sorry, is it too early there? I never could figure out this daylight saving time . . . Well I just called to find out whether you attended Swami Jeevananda's discourse . . . Wasn't he there in London? . . . Oh. I just thought, since he was away in America he might have stopped over . . . You would know if he was there right? . . . Look I will call again. Sorry once again for disturbing you. Bye.

Dialling beeps.

Hello. May I speak with the Governer's secretary? This is Uma, DCP Rao's daughter-in-law . . . Hello Mrs Jairam . . . fine thank you. Well it's the wedding season all over again! *(Laughing.)* In fact I am helping the Chief Minister with his guest list! You and your husband are of course on the list. The reason why I called is I just want to do a security check on some of the invitees. You can never be too sure these days. So do you have a Mr Sitaram Trivedi in your files? . . . Oh any information to make sure he is safe? And whether he has any children I need to invite as well . . .

Cut to bhajans (hymns) from the temple, at a distance.

Exterior. On the Whitefield road.

The car comes to a halt.

MUNSWAMY. The car was parked here.

Uma gets out of the car.

UMA. Interesting that it stopped just a kilometre away from the temple.

MUNSWAMY. This is a very good place to kill the English lady. Only fields, no houses or shops. It was raining so heavily that there was no traffic on the road. The road was filled with water. We don't know whether he came in a car or from the fields.

UMA. Or from the temple.

MUNSWAMY. No tyre marks, footprints, nothing. What heavy rain! Two houses collapsed last night. It was written in her fate. If she had stayed at home . . . In England I don't think they have rains like this.

UMA *(after a while)*. In Hertford, Hereford, Hampshire . . .
Hurricanes hardly ever happen.

MUNSWAMY. What?

UMA. Nothing. Something silly.

MUNSWAMY. What was the need for her to go to the ashram in
such rains? Could she not wait?

UMA. Maybe she couldn't. I have a feeling her murder is
connected with whatever business she had come with to India,
to settle with . . . her brother. She certainly wasn't a Palace-
on-Wheels tourist or a devotee of the Swami.

MUNSWAMY. Shall we go to the ashram?

UMA. Those sugarcane fields are a perfect hiding spot. Come.

Uma walks towards the fields in a muddy ravine.

MUNSWAMY. Madam, the farmers don't like it . . .

UMA. There are some labourers there. Ooh! . . .

MUNSWAMY. Careful. The mud is all wet.

UMA. Maybe someone over here saw something. Has anyone
ever bothered to ask them?

MUNSWAMY. At night in the rains, who will be here?

UMA. But still . . . Oh!

MUNSWAMY. What Madam?

UMA. That scarecrow over there . . . is wearing a raincoat!

Walking towards the scarecrow.

MUNSWAMY. Madam wait. Let us first ask someone . . .

UMA. I just want to take a closer look. I am not disturbing
anyone. We are helping them by scaring the birds away.
Quick, why don't you ask the farmer there where he got this
raincoat from and whether he will loan it to us.

Munswamy walks away.

MUNSWAMY. Namaskara.

*The birds chirp madly as they fly away. Voices in the
distance. Fade out. Uma and Munswamy walking back
to the car.*

UMA. You see the level of trust the police department have built with people? Maybe somebody over here has actually seen it all happening. But they won't tell for fear of harassment from the police! Thank God you are not in uniform.

MUNSWAMY. What can we do? We have to follow our orders.

They stop.

UMA. Oh I didn't mean you. I am angry with . . . You know who I am talking about . . . This raincoat is from England. Burberry's. I know a Bollywood movie star who owns one.

MUNSWAMY. The lady's raincoat?

UMA. It belongs to a man.

MUNSWAMY. Oh. You mean . . . her brother?

UMA. I guess he is the only Englishman around. Unless there are more at the ashram, which is very likely. Charles can afford a coat like this one . . . look at the right sleeve. Torn. Poor Winston tried his best to save his mistress. That is why the murderer wanted to get rid of it. Probably some blood stains deep in the fabric. It's all washed off the surface by the rains.

MUNSWAMY. Shall we go back and tell Sir that we have found this?

UMA *(after a while)*. No. He didn't want us getting involved. So we are not helping him. We are helping the English woman. And Winston. So we will go to the ashram and find out the truth.

Drums can be heard approaching accompanied by chants of 'Jai Sri Ram, Sita Ram!'

Where did that procession appear from?

MUNSWAMY. Must be the nearby villages.

UMA. There isn't any festival on right now, is there?

MUNSWAMY. Not a Ram festival.

UMA. Why the procession? Those idols are gigantic!

The procession is quite close now and the din drowns out their conversation for a while.

SITARAM TRIVEDI *(driving up to them)*. Jai Sri Ram!

UMA. Mr Trivedi! What a surprise!

SITARAM TRIVEDI. You should not be. I am supervising this procession with my personal security guards.

UMA. Why? Do you expect trouble?

SITARAM TRIVEDI. There always is when we pass the Muslim areas.

UMA. How do you know it's the Muslims?

SITARAM TRIVEDI. I know you are trying to appease the minorities. I too believe in peace. After all we are very tolerant . . . up to a point.

UMA. It's so easy to start a riot. Anyone can throw the first stone.

SITARAM TRIVEDI. Yes. That is why I am here to protect our religion!

UMA. Anyone. Even a hired hoodlum.

SITARAM TRIVEDI. Perhaps. It is my dharma to protect what we hold sacred. We must re-establish Hinduism . . . Ah! I see you have been to the ashram already.

UMA. How do you know?

SITARAM TRIVEDI. Swamiji has loaned you his raincoat.

UMA. Does this belong to the swamiji at the ashram?

SITARAM TRIVEDI. Maybe I am mistaken. I thought I saw him wearing it . . . was it the same night? Yes . . . at the Bull Temple. Anyway, what are you doing here? Checking out the scene of the crime?

UMA. You could say that!

SITARAM TRIVEDI. Well, I wish you good luck.

UMA. Thank you. Oh I was meaning to ask you where is your daughter?

SITARAM TRIVEDI *(after a while)*. She is no longer with me. Killed by a . . . fanatic. A . . . non-Hindu. Has the driver confessed as yet?

UMA. He may be innocent.

SITARAM TRIVEDI. Quite a coincidence that the car should break down right here where there are no lights on the road. Excuse me, I must follow the procession. Jai Sri Ram.

He drives off. By now the procession is at a distance once again.

UMA. Surely he must be mistaken. It can't belong to the swami!

MUNSWAMY. Madam if you don't mind me saying . . . I think the truth is that the Muslim driver only planned it. Otherwise why did he stop the car here?

UMA. Hmm. He was driving an Ambassador, wasn't he?

MUNSWAMY. Yes.

UMA. A similar model to this one here?

MUNSWAMY. Yes. I think it is.

UMA. At what speed do you think you could drive this car at night? With a heavy monsoon shower?

MUNSWAMY. I think about forty to fifty kilometres per hour.

UMA. Take out the fan belt.

MUNSWAMY. Why?

UMA. Take it out and drive straight to the ashram. And drive between forty and fifty! Hurry! We have to get back home soon after that . . . before my husband returns! Otherwise we are both in trouble. So hurry!

MUNSWAMY. Yes Sir!

Music. The car chugs along and slowly comes to a halt.

Exterior. Outside the ashram.

MUNSWAMY. Madam we are near the ashram and the engine is overheated!

UMA. Just as I thought.

MUNSWAMY. So you are saying someone cut the fan belt when the car was here?

UMA. Possible isn't it? With some rough calculation you know the car will come to a halt at that lonely stretch. You also know that the driver will try to fetch help. How much time would you need to strangle someone? There's one more thing.

MUNSWAMY. What Madam?

UMA. She knew him. The driver had locked the car. There were no signs of a break in. She unlocked the door for him.

MUNSWAMY. Now what do I do?

UMA. Put the fan belt on and let the engine cool down. We will enter the ashram as visitors.

Cut to:

Interior. A large hall.

The Swami's lecture fades in. His voice is amplified with a public address system resulting in an echo.

SWAMI. The mind of man has lost the point of balance and harmony in every sphere of existence. We are so engrossed in material survival that we are no longer aware of what is happening to us. Today we are so preoccupied with our own sense gratification that we are unaware of the existence of our fellow human beings. We see our brothers and sisters, fathers and mothers, children—merely as means to fulfil our own needs. They do not exist for us unless they fulfil some need or want. That is the cause of violence today. Because we feel that anyone who does not fulfil our needs or wants is not required on this planet. And sometimes the death of fellow human beings may also fulfil some base need in us. Today, this base need of some imbalanced person has affected us in the ashram. I call upon shishya Charles to say a few words to us about how he has learned to come to terms with death. *(Chanting a Sanskrit verse from the Upanishad.)* Poornasya poornamadaya/ Poornamevavashyasishate. *(Translating.)* If Infinity is removed from Infinity/ Infinity still remains. Now, Charles will recite the Shanti path for us.

CHARLES *(clearing his throat before chanting).* Tamasoma jyotirgamaya Asatoma sadgamaya. *(Pause.)* Swamiji, may I say the rest in English? . . . Thank you, Swami. You are compassionate. *(Reciting.)* From darkness lead us to light. From untruth lead us to the eternal truth. From death lead us to immortality. *(Chanting.) Om. Shanti. Shanti. Shantihi. (After a while.)* My sister . . . my sole relative . . . 'sole' as in 'only' . . . came to India to visit me. She wanted me to go back to England with her. She loved me and she thought she knew what was good for me. She felt this somehow wasn't natural, for me . . . this life. Style. This madness, as she called it. I tried to explain to her that I was a deeply unhappy person in England. I didn't know it then . . . I know it now after Swamiji's blessings . . . I was too busy chasing all the wrong things. But here in this ashram I have found happiness, I have never experienced before. *(Applause from some members of the audience.)* I feel sad that someone got something out of killing my sister. Nobody would want her dead for any other reason. She was a warm and wonderful human being . . . Deep inside . . . I do miss her terribly, but India and Swamiji have taught me how to deal with this loss. I am still a happy person. Dhanyavada.

> *A round of applause. Distant thunder. There is a slight commotion in the audience.*

UMA. What is the matter?

MUNSWAMY. I think a woman there has fainted.

UMA. She needs some fresh air. Clear the crowds while I help take her outside.

> *Commotion fades out.*

Exterior. Under the banyan tree.

> *A lone bird chirping.*

UMA. Are you all right? . . . I have some homeopathy pills if you still feel that way.

CHARLES. She is not going to speak to you or anyone for a few days. She is practising mauna.

UMA. Oh. Maybe she could write down her symptoms in case she needs to be treated.

CHARLES. I think she will be fine. Thank you for your help.

UMA. You must be Charles Montefiore.

CHARLES. I might be.

UMA. You must be. I can see the resemblance. Although I expected you to be somewhat . . . older.

CHARLES. Did you know my sister?

UMA. Is there some place where we can talk privately?

CHARLES. That's one thing we don't have at the ashram. Privacy. I am on my way to the market. Care to join me?

UMA. I will be happy to.

MUNSWAMY. Madam. It is getting late. You have to be back.

UMA. When do you think we will be back?

CHARLES. In a couple of hours.

UMA. Oh.

CHARLES. Well, maybe you will like to come again.

UMA. No! There's not much time to lose. How are we going?

CHARLES. In my Rolls Royce.

UMA. We are going to the market in your Rolls Royce?

CHARLES. To sell our vegetables. I couldn't go in the morning. Don't want to waste all that good stuff. Follow me.

They start to walk.

MUNSWAMY. Madam!

UMA. Call up the home and tell them I will be late! *(As they walk.)* I guess the swami has made quite an impression on you.

CHARLES. He is a wise old boy. I like what he stands for.

UMA. What does he stand for?

CHARLES. Peace and love. And beauty.

UMA. India is hardly peaceful and lovely.

CHARLES. The ashram is.

UMA. That it is. Or so it seems. Were you really unhappy in England?

CHARLES. Good God, no! That was just PR work for the ashram. The crowds love it when I say I was deeply unhappy before I met the Swamiji.

UMA. Oh I see.

CHARLES. Well. Here it is.

UMA. This is your Rolls Royce?

CHARLES. Don't you believe me? Hop on.

UMA. Oh I do believe you. Except I didn't know Rolls Royce made bullock carts as well.

Charles hops on to the front of the bullock cart setting off the bells around the bullocks' neck and sides of the cart.

CHARLES. Here, I'll lend you a hand . . . It might help if you hitched that sari up a bit.

UMA. I've never been on one of these!

CHARLES. The vehicle of the future if you ask me. It won't be long before Rolls Royce makes them.

A few grunts and 'oh's from Uma as she finally climbs in to the cart. Uma laughs as she finally gets on board.

Hei! Hei!! *(Making a clicking sound from the back of his throat.)* Hei!

The bullock begins to move.

Drive on, Silver Shadow!!

An assortment of sounds—iron rimmed wooden wheels on a bumpy road, bells, music and the occasional clicks from Charles! They shout to be heard over the noise.

Don't hold yourself! Let go! Let your bums jump with the bumps.

UMA. Ooh! Aah!

CHARLES *(fading out)*. So tell me. Who are you? And what is your interest in all this?

*Music continues for a bit. Fade out. Approaching the
marketplace.*

CHARLES *(fading in)*. How interesting that you should want to
help me.

UMA. How so?

CHARLES. Unexpected. Most extraordinary.

UMA. What were you before you became a full time ashramite?

CHARLES. That would be telling.

UMA. You can't stay on in India for ever you know. They are
very strict about these things.

CHARLES. Swamiji sorted that one out. You see, technically I am
married. To an Indian.

UMA. Oh.

CHARLES. To Radha. The girl who fainted.

UMA. You mean you just left your wife in that condition to sell
vegetables for money you obviously don't need? I think you
are taking being an Indian man to an extreme level.

CHARLES. There are enough people at the ashram to take care
of her. That's what community is all about . . . Why? Does
your husband treat you badly?

UMA. That would be telling. Did Swamiji arrange your marriage?

CHARLES. Yes. I like this arranged marriage business. I get to
live here in India and she gets a husband. No illusions of love
and everlasting happiness. *(Fading out.)* No one wanted to
marry her because she is so thin.

*Fade in marketplace sounds of people talking. Cows
mooing. Bicycle bells. Bells from other carts.*

(Professional seller style.) Alugadde, bhindi, badnekai, eerooli!
Organically grown vegetables!

UMA. Oh! If only my husband should see me now!

Fade out marketplace.

Exterior. Outside the ashram.

*A couple of birds chirping. Peace. They are walking
towards the car.*

UMA. The ashram is quite beautiful. I can see why you want to
live here.

CHARLES. Is this your first visit?

UMA. No. Not recently . . . My mother was a devotee of the
Swami. I used to tag along with her as a child.

CHARLES. Anything you recall from your childhood about this
place?

UMA. Yes! Lots of things. There used to be a hut over there
which was like a creche. *(Laughing.)* It was one, in fact . . .
Someone has grown dhatoora bushes all along. Not a good
idea with children around. The leaves and stem are quite
poisonous . . . and . . . lots of other memories.

They stop walking.

How did you come to know of the ashram?

CHARLES. I met a man in London. An Indian. He talked a great
deal about Advaita philosophy and so on. I was impressed and
accepted his invitation to visit him in India. He turned out to
be the most bigoted, racist, casteist, classist man I have met.

UMA. There are a lot of those going around. Some of them in
very high positions of power.

CHARLES. Fortunately I discovered the ashram.

UMA. Did the man bring you here?

CHARLES. Not a hope! He hates the swami. Says he is up to no
good. I found out about this place.

UMA. From whom?

CHARLES. *The Lonely Planet.*

Uma laughs.

I nicked it from a tourist from Afghanistan!

UMA *(controlling her laughter)*. This is Munswamy. Of course,
he is not on duty.

CHARLES. How do you? Munswamy did you say?

MUNSWAMY. Yes sir.

CHARLES. Winston is with you!

UMA. How did you know?

CHARLES. I came to know at the station. Where is he?

UMA. Well now he is with me. I couldn't bring him I am afraid. Officially he is supposed to be with Munswamy.

MUNSWAMY. I will ensure you have custody tomorrow sir.

CHARLES. Thank you for looking after him.

UMA. We have something else though that may perhaps belong to you.

CHARLES. What is it?

UMA. Munswamy.

Munswamy gives Charles the raincoat.

CHARLES. Where the devil did this come from?

UMA. So you admit this is yours?

CHARLES. Admit! It was mine. I gave it away. As a present.

UMA. To whom?

CHARLES. Why do you look at me like that? Where did you find this?

MUNSWAMY. Madam. Please. Let us go back. It is better that this case is taken by the COD.

CHARLES. Where did you find my raincoat?

MUNSWAMY. Don't tell him Madam!

UMA. We found it on a scarecrow. In a field close to where your sister was murdered.

CHARLES. Well! I'll be gobsmacked!

UMA. The right sleeve is torn.

CHARLES. But. Why? . . . Surely you don't believe I killed her do you?

UMA. I don't. But you are the only one, it seems, who stands to gain from her death. You inherit her wealth and property. All five hundred acres of prime Hertfordshire land!

CHARLES. Nonsense. I don't want any of it. And I can prove it . . . Oh no, I can't.

UMA. What are you talking about?

CHARLES. The papers! Did they find any documents addressed to Barnsworth and Milling? In her bag?

MUNSWAMY. No. There were no papers like that.

CHARLES. I remember she put them in the centre compartment of her bag. Did you look there?

UMA. Wait a minute! You have to answer my questions first!

CHARLES. I didn't kill my sister for God's sake!

UMA. To whom did you give that coat?

CHARLES. To Swamiji!

UMA. Was he at the ashram that night?

CHARLES. No.

UMA. Do you know where he was?

CHARLES. At the Bull Temple.

MUNSWAMY. Madam. Please let us go back and inform the department. We will have the Swami arrested.

CHARLES. Arrest him? Just because he was at the Bull Temple and lost his raincoat when my sister died? You might as well arrest the scarecrow.

UMA. It depends on what he stands to gain. Now. This is important. You have to tell us what the contents of that document were.

CHARLES. I–I can't. I promised her I would keep it a secret. But I guess it doesn't matter now that she is dead. She wanted me to go back and look after our estate. I didn't want any of it. So we had to set up two trusts. For one of the trusts dealing with my share of the wealth, I had the ashram as the beneficiary, with Swamiji as the senior trustee. So you see, he had no reason to kill my sister. He has no motive to kill her.

UMA. But, as I understand it, you do stand to gain. Her share of the family wealth comes to you, doesn't it.

CHARLES. What do I need all that money for? I only want a couple of dhotis in a year which the ashram provides me with anyway. I grow my own vegetables . . . I don't want any of it. I . . . Yes. I see what you mean. All her wealth is now mine. Well, it's just a question of time before I draw up another deed. You wait and see.

UMA. So the Swami has twice as much to gain now!

CHARLES. No. I won't give it all to the ashram. I will split it between two trusts exactly the way my sister and I had worked it out before her death. It's all a bit overwhelming right now but I will get around to doing it.

UMA. What about your wife?

CHARLES. She gets nothing! She wants nothing. It's the ashram that gets my wealth. Without bumping anyone off.

UMA. I just don't understand. Something is not right.

MUNSWAMY. Madam, we must hurry. Sir will be very angry.

CHARLES. It is time for my private satsang with the Swamiji. Care to join?

MUNSWAMY. No Sir. Madam has to be at home before the guests.

UMA. I will stay. We are late anyway. Munswamy, I will never get an opportunity like this. Let's go . . . Wait. Give me the keys. You take the bus and go back. Tell my husband I am having a chat with the swamiji!

MUNSWAMY. But . . .

UMA. Munswamy.

MUNSWAMY. Sir!

Thunder.

UMA. Give me the keys. And hurry or you will miss the last bus back.

MUNSWAMY *(handing the keys to her)*. Yes Madam.

UMA. Take care. I will see you tomorrow.

CHARLES. And I want Winston tomorrow.

> *Cut to:*
>
> *Strains of a tanpura in the background.*

Interior. Swami's private chamber.

CHARLES. Swamiji, this is Uma.

SWAMI. Hari Om.

UMA. Namaste.

CHARLES. She is a bit of a detective. She's been sussing me out all evening. Now it's your turn.

SWAMI *(laughing a loud open laugh)*. If only it was possible to 'suss' people out like that, my child. Beware of Charles he is a wicked man.

CHARLES. Me? Wicked? I am just a simple vegetable grower. Look at my filthy dhoti.

SWAMI. And also the Calvin Klein underwear peeping out from your dhoti. *(Laughing again loudly at his discovery.)* You see? How he fools us that he is a simple farmer.

CHARLES. Well . . . I guess a man needs his little comforts.

SWAMI. And who is this lovely child?

CHARLES. Her mother used to visit you twenty years ago or so.

UMA. I remember coming here too.

SWAMI. Ah. Those were the days when there was none of this nonsense of Hindu supremacy and 'India for Hindus' movement. We were truly a secular nation.

UMA. We still are, I guess.

SWAMI. Perhaps it is not too late . . . The irony of Fate! I was at the temple speaking at an inter faith seminar, condemning the pulling down of the mosque. And at the same time, our Christian sister was brutally murdered.

UMA. Do you think her religion had something to do with it?

SWAMI. I hope not. I hope that this is not a sequence to the savage burning of the Australian missionary and his children. Where does our religion teach us to be so violent? It is all a power game.

CHARLES. They found our raincoat in the fields where her car had stalled. It was simply thrown there.

SWAMI. Just as I thought. Someone in the ashram is involved. I leave the raincoat in the main hall. Anyone can use it. Any of my aides or devotees . . . Look at these men. They never leave me alone. They know everything that is going on here. We do not beleive in secrets.

The door opens.

Yes my daughter?

UMA. Daughter? She is his daughter?

CHARLES. That's just a way of speaking. He called you his child, didn't he?

SWAMI. What have you brought for me? Milk?

CHARLES. How are you feeling now Radha? Better? . . . What's the matter?

SWAMI. Come say hello to Uma. She is the lady who helped you this evening. When you fainted?

UMA. Hello Radha. What have you got there in your hand?

SWAMI. You may break your vow of silence if you want to tell us something.

UMA. I feel as if I know you. I have seen you some . . . those eyes! I have been so stupid!

Radha falls to the ground.

Look, dhatoora leaves! She's consumed the poisonous leaves! We need to take her to a hospital. She must have a stomach wash immediately!

SWAMI. St Mary's hospital. I'll call and let them know you're coming.

CHARLES *(lifting Radha).* We'll take your car!

Thunder and downpour.

Interior/Exterior. On the Whitefield Road.

UMA. Keep slapping her face.

CHARLES. Come on! Come on!

UMA. I should have known.

CHARLES. What?

UMA. It's not your sister's death which is important to him. But yours.

CHARLES. Then why was my sister killed?

UMA. He had to stop her from executing your letter of intention to Barnsworth and Milling. That would leave the swami with everything. And he would get nothing. He wanted that raincoat to be found. That's why he threw it in the field, knowing it will be found. So he could put the suspicion on swami. Now listen to me. Once we get her to the hospital, you are going to move into a hotel in town and make sure that the police provide you with enough security until you have set up your trusts.

CHARLES. It wont be so easy getting . . .

UMA. He is a very influential person.

CHARLES. And who is this charming . . .?

UMA. One of Swami's aides must be his goon. He knows everything that goes on in the ashram. In Hertford, Hereford, Hampshire . . .

CHARLES. What are you talking about?

UMA. Property. That's what they are after. Your property.

CHARLES. They can't possibly . . .

UMA. To set up a township or a mega ashram, to get expatriate Indians, millionaires interested in donating to the ashram, which would be a facade of course, to raise funds for their grand election campaigns, to gather support . . .

CHARLES. Support?

UMA. For their pogrom.

CHARLES. Pogrom? Like the Nazis you mean?

UMA. Probably, I don't know. To eliminate Muslims, Christians . . . maybe not genocide but to disempower them, to build temples, to win the 700 million strong Hindu vote bank.

CHARLES. But then . . . why would she want to kill herself? She gets it all as I can see if they bump me off before I form the trust.

UMA. The poor woman doesn't want any of it. Beaten up by her father, forced to act according to his wishes. She couldn't take it any more . . .

CHARLES. And who might this charming gentleman be?

UMA. The man who got you interested in Hinduism and invited you here. Sitaram.

CHARLES. How do you know?

UMA. Let's say I saw it in her eyes. I checked him out this afternoon. He makes several trips to England. He is affiliated to the India for Hindus movement.

The car slows down.

Damn!

CHARLES. What's wrong?

The car comes to a halt with the engine still running.

UMA. Munswamy forgot to put the fan belt on again! Oh! How is she?

CHARLES. I didn't want to upset you, but she is sinking.

UMA *(getting out of the car)*. There's a car coming.

The conch blows far away. The rain is almost deafening. Another car approaches.

Stop! Please stop!

CHARLES *(getting out as well)*. Uma! Get back into the car! It's no use!

A gun is fired. The bullet hits the body of the car.

Get back into the car!

SITARAM TRIVEDI. Don't move or I will shoot you!

UMA. Take your daughter to the hospital!

SITARAM TRIVEDI. Get that man to come out! *(Yelling.)* Get out of that car Charles! Or I'll shoot her.

CHARLES *(getting out of the car)*. Leave her alone!

UMA. Didn't you hear me? Radha is in the car! Dying! If she dies, you get nothing!

SITARAM TRIVEDI. You dare to kill my daughter and I will . . .

CHARLES. She killed herself.

UMA. No! Liar! Your daughter was not dead. She is now. And she was killed by a fanatic. You! You killed your daughter!

Pause. The rain continues to pour.

SITARAM TRIVEDI. I don't believe you! Where is she?

CHARLES. In the car. She is dead. You get nothing!

SITARAM TRIVEDI. I don't believe you!

UMA. See for yourself!

SITARAM TRIVEDI. Get away from the car!

He walks to the car.

No! You will die for this.

Charles lunges at him.

CHARLES. You killed my sister for nothing!

The two of them fight a while before the gun goes off.

SITARAM TRIVEDI. Hold it! Or I–I . . .

He falls to the ground. They help him into the car.

CHARLES. How could you have killed her? How do you wake up in the morning and justify your actions to yourself?

SITARAM TRIVEDI. I–I didn't want any of it for myself. *(His breathing is heavy.)* I–I only wanted to help the Hindu cause.

UMA. You could have helped the Hindu cause by being a good Hindu yourself.

Fade out rain.

Interior. Uma and Suresh in the bedroom.

UMA. . . . by framing the swami, he would get rid of an opposer. The Swami is truly spiritual and wants none of this new brand of Hinduism. Radha was totally under her father's control, it would be very easy for Sitaram Trivedi to manage the property once she inherits it from Charles whom I am sure he would have killed in a way to make it look like an accident. He had grand plans. England would have been the perfect place to set up his own pseudo ashram.

SURESH. Did this man Charles shoot at Sitaram?

UMA. Sitaram had the gun all along. He meant to kill us!

SURESH. You don't know that for sure.

UMA. Of course I do. Why would he pull out a gun and shoot real bullets at us?

SURESH. In the court, I want you to say it was an accident.

UMA. That man tried to kill your wife!

SURESH. No he did not. That's just your imagination.

UMA. Oh come on Suresh!

SURESH. It was an accident, do you understand? He thought you were being attacked and so he stopped to help you. His gun went off accidentally.

UMA. I am not going to say that.

SURESH. Nobody is going to believe you anyway. You have no proof.

UMA. You are a supporter.

SURESH. What do you mean?

UMA. You do believe in it yourself. What people like Sitaram are trying to do to this country. You want it. I am going to say what I want to say in court.

SURESH. Oh. Okay. I was on to him anyway. I would have nabbed him alive if you hadn't interfered.

Fade in airport announcement.

Exterior. Airport.

ANNOUNCER *(background).* Please do not leave your baggage unattended. For security reasons, any unattended baggage will be confiscated.

CHARLES. Well. Thank you for everything.

UMA. You are welcome.

CHARLES. And thank you for offering to look after Winston. The laws have changed now—no quarantine for Winston when I take him back.

UMA. You could have taken him with you now.

CHARLES. Not right now. The inquest was stressful enough . . . I'll be back—soon after I set up the trusts and make sure she rests peacefully in our family graveyard.

UMA. She will, knowing that you are setting up the trust for Winston the way she wanted it. *(Sighing.)* I wonder what the outcome of all this will be.

CHARLES. Don't let your husband take all the credit.

UMA. The papers are full of it. At least we made a noise.

CHARLES. You did. You were marvellous in the courtroom.

UMA. What's the point? It's his story which will have more weight. The real issue is going to be sidetracked.

CHARLES. I am sure my colleagues are not going to ignore this one.

UMA. Your colleagues?

CHARLES. My ex-colleagues I should say. I worked for the London Metropolitan Police Force.

UMA. I don't believe you!

CHARLES. It's true.

UMA. You mean—you used to work at Scotland Yard?

CHARLES. That's right.

UMA. Oh sure, like you drive a Rolls Royce to sell vegetables!

CHARLES. You wait and see. And one more thing. The five thousand pound cheque which my sister had made out to Mr Sitaram for finding Winston . . . he never did get a chance to encash it . . . I want to offer that money to Munswamy for looking after Winston. Will you please let him know?

UMA *(pause)*. Charles?

CHARLES. Yes?

UMA. You are a remarkable man!

CHARLES *(pause)*. I'll come back. Soon!

UMA. Till we meet again!

Music takes over.

(Under the music.) Munswamy!

MUNSWAMY. Yes Madam!

UMA. I think Winston wants to go for a walk.

MUNSWAMY *(euphoric)*. I will take him for a walk. Come Mr Winston!

UMA. Take care, he is a very rich dog. As well endowed as the Swami!

Music. Credits.

MORNING RAGA

A Screenplay

A Note on the Play

I was beginning to get curious about Mahesh Dattani. His plays had well-etched characterizations with an overarching angst running through, that made them stand apart from the 'light comic' variety flooding the market. An original writer is a fast vanishing breed. Mahesh belonged to that rare species. I planned to meet him but couldn't.

And suddenly, out of the blue, I get a call in London, where I am holidaying, from Mahesh Dattani. He is directing a film! His words tumble out of him. 'It's about a meeting of two worlds,' he explains. 'A story that brings together the modern and the traditional, unites the past with the present, Carnatic music with Western music, fate and coincidence with individual choices.' He wants me to play one of the central characters, a Carnatic singer, Swarnalatha, who lives with an anguished past.

The film is to be produced by Raghavendra Rao, a producer–director I have shared a terrific rapport with since 'Kamyaab', a film we did together eighteen years ago. Mahesh has roped in Rajeev Menon, a cinematographer I have great respect for.

I evince interest and request him to send me the script. It arrives. Neatly bound. Running into what seems like a thousand pages! I turn the pages over quickly to read Swarnalatha's scenes. Very few lines. Lots of subtext. I am comforted. I now read the script carefully. An emotional current grips me as I read it, even though it is overstated in places. I have questions and Mahesh seems almost delighted to answer them. He comes over to meet me in Mumbai. 'Why me?' is the first question I ask. 'I don't know a thing about Carnatic music. Why do you want to take a risk with me when there are so many talented south Indian actors who would look and sound the part?' Mahesh replies: 'I know I have quite a choice of actors from the south who are more familiar with the milieu. But to me there are several booby traps laid out even before I start if I were to choose from them. Firstly, some gestures and mannerisms. They would be taken for granted. I want the inner movements, adding psychological dimensions that manifest themselves in gesture and behaviour. I need consistency in style. And my other principal actors Prakash and Perizaad have studied method acting at the Lee Strasberg School in New York.'

I am convinced this is worth exploring further. He has thrown up a challenge and I rise to the bait. I pick up the script and read it again. Mahesh's screenplay makes emotional transitions between the lines rather than through dialogue. For instance, in the scene where Abhinay's father confronts Swarnalatha in the fields and asks her to back off from his son because her music will take him nowhere, Swarnalatha is enraged at this insult to music. But she doesn't say a word to his father. She turns to Abhinay and says 'I will sing for you.' That one line says it all—it contains the entire history of the inter-personal relationships between the characters.

However, other scenes are not so clear. Mahesh and I disagree over the interior life of Swarnalatha. She seems to grieve over her friend's death much more than her own son Madhav's! We need to establish a deep friendship between Swarnalatha and Vaishnavi without devouring cinematic space. Swarnalatha holds herself responsible for Vaishnavi's death because she pushed a reluctant Vaishnavi into making that trip to the city on that fateful bus journey. It's a big back-story that continues to be discussed and reworked even after we have actually started shooting. Rajeev Menon suggests we compress it in the first song 'Maate . . .'

I try to persuade Mahesh to give up the Madhav track altogether but he can't bear the thought, so we struggle on . . . Mahesh wants Swarnalatha's sense of loss for her own son to be buried and forgotten. He wants the flood gates to open only towards the end after she comes to terms with her loss and guilt. What Mahesh has kept in the final cut is far less complicated than what he originally had in mind but I think it works.

A script must serve many masters and accomplish many purposes. Mahesh is generous enough to accept that it is a collaborative process. Ultimately the value of any script always comes back to its role as the plan or blueprint for the film. In Densham's words, 'It's the script that provides the magic that brings together a group of people and it all comes from the imagination of the writer. That's the purpose of a script. In a sense, it's a magic carpet, where everybody that you need will climb on board that idea or dream and bring it to reality on the screen.'[1]

---

[1]Linda Seger and Edward Jay Whetmore, *From Script to Screen: The Art of Collaborative Writing*, New York: Henry Holt & Company, 2003.

According to Frank Pearson, a screenplay means different things to different people. The producer 'weighs' it for 'audience appeal', the director visualizes it as a 'progression of images and scenes', the designer tries to fit it into locations and sets, the actor is intent to learn his lines and the assistant director sees it as a schedule. 'They read the screenplay like a flea lives on a dog, without caring much what the whole dog looks like.'[2]

I can't help but agree with what Frank Pearson says. But as a professionally trained actor with thirty years of experience behind me, I struggle to look at the larger picture which is what attracted me to the script of *Morning Raga* in the first place.

Mahesh enjoys working with actors. It helps that Perizaad and Prakash are professionally trained. (Much as I try, I find it difficult to deal with amateurs. I think directors who cast amateurs in lead parts are arrogant!)

Rehearsals with Prakash and Mahesh are fruitful in ironing out most of the creases: some of them are my own blocks and some have to do with the script. The three major scenes with Prakash are fine-tuned by Mahesh as we rehearse and improvise. The first meeting between Swarnalatha and Abhinay has seen several drafts. Mahesh is careful to keep the violin as a centre of attention in all the drafts to heighten the conflict of the past, suggesting rather than explaining what is on Swarnalatha's mind— that she holds herself responsible for the death of Abhinay's mother and suspects he might have returned to blame her for it. But Abhinay doesn't. He is too preoccupied with starting his music group. The invitation to sing takes Swarnalatha completely by surprise. With it come the demons from the past, a theme that recurs in Mahesh's work. Mahesh, like all writers, treats his script like he would treat his child. But he realizes that other people are needed to help his child grow up.

I figure that unless I get the Carnatic music totally right, no amount of obsessing over Swarnalatha's interior world will make her appear credible. Mahesh introduces me to an exceptionally gifted violinist, Ranjani (who he also casts as Vaishnavi, my friend in the film), to give me music lessons. I am scared to death when I first hear the music and am convinced I will never get it right. It is entirely due to Ranjani's painstaking efforts that I succeed in

---

[2]Pearson in *From Script to Screen: The Art of Collaborative Writing.*

lip-synching the intricate swarams. Carnatic music has rigid
mathematical equations which cannot be compromised even as the
singer improvises. Swarnalatha can hold her own with Western
percussions so effortlessly because of her rigorous training.

Rajeev Menon's mother is a Carnatic singer and he loves
Carnatic music to death. He helps me with the posture and the
gestures of the musician. Meanwhile Prakash has worked tirelessly
on learning to play the violin like a real professional. Perizaad is
a trained ballet dancer and doesn't fault on a single beat. Shaleen
is an actual drummer and Vivek does a convincing act of playing
the electronic guitar. The 'Pratibimb' band is ready and raring to
go.

The shooting of the climax song is scheduled for the last three
days. When I arrive on location, there is tension in the air. Mahesh
wants to redo the scene preceding the climax song. He decides to
go with the song first and then think of what the scene will be.
Mahesh is furiously writing out several drafts and looks a wreck.
Rajeev is screaming at his assistants. Perizaad's skirt is too tight.
Latha (the production designer) is unhappy because the vinyl she's
used for the backdrop is wrinkling up. Shobhu, the producer is
chewing up his nails. I find myself ticking off my make-up artist
for no fault of his. The tension in the air is so thick you can slice
it with a knife. I walk up to Rajeev and say, 'I'm really insecure
about doing this song because this is what will make or break the
movie.' He looks back at me, equally vulnerable, and says, 'I'm
scared to death myself.' And in that instant the magic happens.
The magic that lights up the screenplay. The magic that makes the
actors' adrenalin flow. The magic that is captured when all
elements rise together in harmony.

How appropriate that *Morning Raga* ends with a song. A
meeting of two worlds that come together through music. Life
takes over art. From the time Mahesh shouts 'Action' to the time
he says 'Wrap', a transformation has occurred, if even for a
fleeting moment, in the lives of all those who made *Morning Raga*
possible. Tan Eberhardt had famously moaned: 'You should
understand scriptwriting is like giving birth, then having the baby
stolen by a bunch of dirty gypsies, and then seeing this thing on
the street corner years later.'

It is for Mahesh to decide whether these 'dirty gypsies' made
'this thing' more than the sum of its parts.

Shabana Azmi
(Shabana Azmi is a renowned actor and political activist.)

The film was released in India on 29 October 2004. The international premiere was part of the Cairo Film Festival in December 2004.

Principal cast:

SWARNALATHA	Shabana Azmi
VAISHNAVI	Ranjani
ABHINAY'S FATHER	Nasseer
ABHINAY	Prakash Kovelamudi
PRIYANKA (PINKIE)	Perizaad Zorabian
MRS KAPOOR	Lillete Dubey
MR SHASTRI	T. Vijay
MUNNA	Vivek Mashru
BALAJI	Shaleen Sharma
APPA RAU	Dharmavarpu Subramanyam

The film was directed by the author.

Producer	K. Raghavendra Rao
Executive Producers	Shobu Yarlagadda
	Madhavi Polavarupu
Music	Amit Heri
	Mani Sharma
Director of Photography	Rajeev Menon
Editor	A. Sreekar Prasad
Production Design	Latha Kovelamudi
Audiography	Lakshminarayana
Choreography	Suchitra Chander Bose

An R.K. Teleshow presentation. An Arka Mediaworks production.

Exterior. Day. A village bus stand.

We see some villagers getting into the bus with their baggage. Swarnalatha is being helped by her husband taking in the tamburi with some difficulty. Swarnalatha is also carrying a child of about four years. Vaishnavi follows with her male child of about the same age as Swarnalatha's. She has a violin in a case with her. We cannot hear them over the chatter and excitement.

Cut to:

Exterior. Day. Outside a city home.

We see Mr Kapoor getting into a car with his briefcase. At the front door is Mrs Kapoor and her toddler girl. Mrs Kapoor pulls the daughter in and shuts the door even as Mr Kapoor is getting into his car.

Cut to:

Interior. Day. Bus.

The villagers scramble for seats and try to fit in their baggage on the overhead rack. Swarnalatha and Vaishnavi find a couple of seats in the last row.

Cut to:

Exterior. Car. Moving.

Mr Kapoor is driving out of the city.

Cut to:

Interior. Day. Bus.

Swarnalatha and Vaishnavi settle down and hold their children and their musical instruments closely.

Cut to:

Interior. Car. Moving.

Mr Kapoor puts on the stereo. A popular Western number of the seventies plays. We see his briefcase on the seat next to him. He flips it open with his left hand and fumbles around to find his hip flask. He places the flask between his thighs, and unscrews the cap.

Cut to:

Exterior. Car. Moving.

The car rushes past the frame as we swish pan to follow it moving fast into the countryside, leaving the music from the stereo in the background.

Cut to:

Interior. Bus.

We see Swarnalatha and Vaishnavi in close-up with their instruments and children in the frame, as the bus begins to move.

Cut to:

Interior. Bus.

The driver does a quick prayer to the picture of Lord Ganesh in front of him as he proceeds to drive his bus out of the village.

Cut to:

Exterior. Countryside.

The car is moving fast, weaving through some passing trucks.

Cut to:

Exterior. Day. Outside the village.

The bus with its passengers has left the village and is now picking up speed. We hear people singing and a fair amount of noise from the bus.

Cut to:

Interior. Bus. Moving.

Vaishnavi's child draws a pattern of the sun on the dusty window pane.

Cut to:

Interior. Day. Car. Moving.

The sun glares through the windscreen of Kapoor. A puff of smoke from his cigarette clouds the frame.

Cut to:

Exterior. Day. A bridge.

Long shot of a bridge over a flowing river. The bus is approaching the bridge.

Cut to:

Interior/Exterior. Car. Moving.

The camera moves stylistically from Kapoor's profile to the early morning sun, the birds flying across the sky . . . From the glare of the sun the camera moves towards the bus and into the passengers happy faces. The camera continues to caress their faces as it moves to the back of the bus and captures the happy children, their mothers, the musical instruments . . . The camera moves out of the bus and captures the car approaching from the opposite direction . . . Subject camera shots of car and bus drivers in high speed. The music continues as the two vehicles collide. The bus driver sees the collision about to happen. He swerves to avoid the impact. The car hits the side of the bus, sending Kapoor flying out of the windscreen. The back window of the bus shatters on the impact, sending the children and musical instruments in separate ways . . . The bus breaks the wall of the bridge and begins to keel over into the river. Inside we see the passengers world turning upside down even as the morning sun glows through the back of the bus. Quick cross-fade.

Exterior. Day. A bridge.

We see Kapoor's car overturned on the bridge. Kapoor is lying on the road in a pool of blood. The music from the stereo continues to play.

Cut to:

Exterior. Day. River.

We see a part of the bus as we follow the violin case flowing gently down the river even as the music from the car plays on . . . Fade out. Twenty years later appears on black screen.

Fade in:

Exterior. Busy morning city street. From Abhinay's window.

We see the city begin its activities. It is 8 a.m. An alarm clock (electronic) goes off. We pull back to see . . .

Interior. Morning. Bedroom/Bathroom.

The alarm goes off in Abhinay's small apartment. It is an annoying electronic alarm with a toneless voice announcing the time and saying 'rise and shine' with a long beep. Abhinay wakes up and sits up on his bed staring at the alarm clock. He jumps up and turns on his computer/keyboards. He goes into the bathroom as his computer boots up. His cell phone goes off. He comes back in and answers his phone as he undresses.

ABHINAY. Ya? . . . Of course I have it done . . . tomorrow? . . . okay, okay, just joking. How about three?

He goes into the bathroom.

(From the bathroom, hysterical.) In an hour? Shit!

He throws the cell phone out which lands on his key boards setting off some strong beat even as the alarm insistently announces the time with 'rise and shine' followed by a long beep.

Cut to:

Interior. Day. An advertising company office.

A chic advertising office. We follow the coffee boy around a corner even as the advertising jingle is playing. The coffee boy leaves us on Rajeev and Abhinay. The jingle is played on a computer. We finish on Abhinay. He looks on at Rajeev.

ABHINAY. So that's the tune. Find a singer with a squeaky voice and it should be a hit.

RAJEEV *(clearing his throat).* Well, it's nice but . . .

ABHINAY. Nice? What do you mean nice? It's a bubble gum jingle. Does it stay in your head or not?

RAJEEV. Where's the pop? I told you the client wanted a pop. It needs to go *(Singing.)* Dum—dum—pop—dum dum bubble gum—pop. Or something like that. We'd worked it out. Why don't you just save yourself a lot of time and follow the brief?

Abhinay looks at him as if he could throttle him.

ABHINAY. You want a pop?

RAJEEV *(sarcastic).* Is that too much to ask for from a creative genius?

Abhinay stands up.

ABHINAY. You can stick the bubble gum up the client's brief. I quit.

Abhinay moves to the door.

RAJEEV *(protesting).* Hey, Abhi—come on—I need this today.

ABHINAY. That's your problem now. I have had enough.

RAJEEV. Do you realize this is professional suicide. No agency will give you any work once this gets out!

ABHINAY. That suits me fine. You know what? I tried the bubble gum. It doesn't pop.

Abhinay leaves.

Cut to:

Exterior. Day. A village bus stand.

A bus drives in. A few people get off. Abhinay is the last to get off. He has a duffel bag with him. He begins to walk to a narrow road.

Cut to:

Exterior. A field.

We see an endless field of paddy. Abhinay walks on.

Exterior. Day. Another part of the village.

Some villagers recognize him.

OLD MAN. What Abhinay? Staying for a long time?

ABHINAY. Just a few days.

Abhinay is greeted by a man with a buffalo walking in the opposite direction.

APPA RAU. Oh, oh. Annapoorna, see. See who has come. Our Abhinay!

ABHINAY. Namaskara Appa Rau. *(Patting the buffalo.)* All these years and you are still milking Annapoorna!

Abhinay walks away.

APPA RAU. Give my regards to your father. *(To his buffalo.)* A nice boy from our village should not be roaming around unmarried.

Abhinay smiles to himself as Appa Rau rambles on walking away.

Cut to:

Exterior. Day. Outside Abhinay's village home.

Abhinay comes to the front door of his house which has a large veranda with big windows. There are workers in the front yard taking in cows, bundling hay, etc. He knocks on the old-fashioned wooden door. It is open and he walks in.

Cut to:

Interior. Day. Abhinay's village home.

Abhinay goes in and calls out 'appa' hesitantly. Abhinay comes to his father's bedroom door and he hears a tinkle of anklets and some hurried activity. His father's voice from inside.

FATHER. Who is it?

ABHINAY. It's me, Abhinay.

There is a flurry of activity inside.

FATHER *(from inside)*. Wait a while. You couldn't inform me you are coming?

ABHINAY. It's okay. I will come back later.

Abhinay walks away. The door opens and a young woman steps out. Abhinay stops and looks at her. The young woman passes him by a little sheepish.

YOUNG WOMAN. I will make dosa for you.

The young woman exits in the direction of the kitchen. Abhinay's father comes out. He heads straight for the dining table expecting Abhinay to follow him, which he does.

FATHER. So after three years you decide to show your face. Now that you are earning, why do you have to see me? Come, sit. So, too busy in the city to come to your village home?

Abhinay sits down as we hear noises from the kitchen. Abhinay looks at his father.

ABHINAY. Not half as busy—as you.

Abhinay's father is a little annoyed at this reference to his dalliance. But he manages a wistful laugh and gestures as if it is in the hands of God. Abhinay gets up and goes to his mother's photograph on the wall. He pulls it down and takes it to another room. His father watches his actions and shakes his head.

Cut to:

Exterior. Day. Abhinay's father's fields.

Abhinay and his father are walking alongside his paddy fields. A crop is being harvested on one side. His father yells out some instructions as the harvest is being loaded on to waiting bullock carts. Abhinay is distracted and is looking elsewhere, at some infants in their makeshift cradles of saris made by the women in the fields. Their conversation fades in as they approach. One of the babies in the cradle starts to cry.

ABHINAY. I am not coming back.

FATHER. Oh. Then what are you going to do?

ABHINAY. I want to start a music group.

His father stares at Abhinay.

FATHER *(yelling).* Whose baby is that? *(To Abhinay.)* Will you be able to support yourself?

ABHINAY. I will be spending what I have saved.

FATHER. You have also gone mad! Like your mother! She is controlling you from the other world!

In the background we see a woman running to her baby and picking it up.

ABHINAY. It has nothing to do with my mother! It's something I want to do.

FATHER. Then go to the city! Why did you come here!

ABHINAY. Does my mother's twentieth death anniversary mean anything to you?

Abhinay looks away. Father stares at him for a while and then turns his attention to the waiting bullock carts.

Cut to:

Exterior. Evening. Roadside.

A long shot of a row of bullock carts. Fade to night.

Exterior. Night. Coconut grove and water.

*The crickets take over the silence of the village as we
see the palm trees. The overcast sky prevents a reflection
of the trees in the still water body next to it.*

Cut to:

Interior. Night. Abhinay's village home. Bedroom.

*Abhinay has put his mother's picture up on the wall
with a sandalwood garland around it. Abhinay is
taking out some of his mother's photographs from a
chest. He shuts the chest (which is below the hanging
photograph) and places the framed pictures on the
chest, one by one. Abhinay switches off the light and
lies down on his bed. He tosses a bit. It is dark. He
opens a window and lies down with his eyes wide
open. The moon appears from behind a cloud. The
water body now reflects the palm trees. The moonlight
lights up his mother's garlanded photograph. In one of
the photographs, his mother holds a Carnatic violin.
Abhinay looks at it. He sits up on the bed and looks
at his mother in the picture. Abhinay gets up and goes
into the outer room.*

Cut to:

Interior. Night. Abhinay's village home. Living room.

*Abhinay enters the room and goes to an old trunk.
Abhinay opens the trunk which is a little rusty. He
goes through some articles in the trunk, but he doesn't
find what he is looking for. The noise wakes up his
father. His father enters the room and puts on a light.
Abhinay looks at his father.*

ABHINAY. Where is amma's violin?

FATHER *(not too sure he has heard right)*. Violin? *(Looking at
him as if he is crazy.)* Why do you want it in the middle of the
night?

ABHINAY. Where is it?

FATHER. I don't know . . . I gave it away.

>   *His father turns to go back to sleep.*

ABHINAY *(insistent)*. To whom?

FATHER. God alone knows. I can't remember all the things I gave away and to whom.

>   *His father exits. Abhinay sits down near the trunk.*
>   *Cut to:*

Exterior. Early morning. A part of the village.

>   *Appa Rau is walking with his buffalo. Abhinay is walking with him.*

APPA RAU. Only on∋ person knows and she won't tell you!

ABHINAY. Who is the person?

APPA RAU. Annapoorna!

>   *Appa Rau laughs at his joke.*

ABHINAY. Such a small village and you don't know where a violin went? The whole village will know what I ate for dinner but you don't remember where my mother's violin is?

APPA RAU. Everybody knows. But we forget. We forget all that we want to forget. Why remember all that which brings you pain?

>   *Annapoorna moos.*

Oh, oh. Are you feeling unwell, my mother? I am talking to your grandson only. Not any stranger from the city.

>   *Appa Rau walks away leaving Abhinay standing. We follow Appa Rau for a while.*

(To his cow.) Do you know where the Carnatic violin came from? France! Many centuries ago, the French people presented their violin to the great King Tipu Sultan. Very proud people.

>   *We cut to Abhinay looking at the fields. We see Appa Rau in the distance his voice fading away.*

The king gave it to his musician to do something with it as he was unhappy with the sound. 'What is this—ke, ke, ke sound?' he said. 'Make it sound better.' His musician retuned it and showed the French how to use it properly. That is how the Carnatic violin was born . . .

In long shot we see Abhinay wandering into the fields.

Fade to:

Exterior. Late morning. By the riverside.

Abhinay has with him some cooked rice and other paraphernalia for the crow feeding ritual. The morning sun is quite pleasant. The riverside has people washing their buffaloes, trucks or themselves. Abhinay calls one of the men in a cattamaran and request him to take him to the other side. Abhinay gets in and is ferried to the other side. We cut to another part of the river, where a similar ritual is being set up but we don't see the person. Abhinay goes down to the riverbank, away from the rest, under the bridge.

Cut to:

Exterior. Afternoon. By the riverside. Another spot.

We see the back of a woman (Swarnalatha) walking towards the river.

Cut to:

Exterior. Morning. By the riverside.

Abhinay sits down in the shade. The sun light dapples on the water.

Cut to:

Exterior. Morning. By the riverside. Another spot.

Swarnalatha bends over and washes her hands in the river.

Cut to:

Exterior. Morning. By the riverside. Another spot.

We see Abhinay putting down morsels of rice. The crows begin to caw.

Cut to:

Exterior. Morning. By the riverside.

At the river wistfully. She sings a few notes to the river as she stands on the bridge.

Cut to:

Exterior. Morning. By the riverside/bridge.

Abhinay is compelled by the voice and wants to find out the source. He walks up the riverbank and on to the other side of the bridge. Abhinay sees the woman on the other side. Swarnalatha stops singing and turns to go away. Abhinay steps on the road to talk to her.

ABHINAY. Wait!

As Swarnalatha turns, she is aghast at what she sees . . . A car is driving full speed on to the bridge heading straight at Abhinay. Abhinay turns to see a car coming straight at him.

SWARNALATHA *(screaming)*. Go back! Go back!

The car swerves to avoid him and ends up banging against the wall of the bridge. Swarnalatha is horrified but rooted to her spot. The car has come to a halt.

Cut away.

The villagers hearing the screech of tires rush to come to the spot.

Exterior. Morning. Bridge.

Abhinay rushes to the car even as the car door opens. Music plays from the stereo. A flustered Pinkie gets out of the car. Pinkie is an attractive young woman of the city in her early twenties.

PINKIE. I–I am sorry. Are you all right?

ABHINAY. I am fine. Are you all right?

PINKIE. I think so.

Abhinay stares at the source of the music.

The car stereo playing.

Pinkie notices that the music bothers Abhinay. She turns off the stereo. The villagers now gather around the car. An old woman stares at Pinkie. Pinkie is nervous now.

ABHINAY. Er . . . I think you better get in the car.

OLD WOMAN. Don't let him go! He is a murderer!

Pinkie is perturbed by this remark.

You city people! You are a curse to us. How many more people do you want to kill! Was my husband not enough? *(Pointing to Abhinay.)* Was his mother not enough? Swarnalatha looks at Abhinay in a new light. *(Pointing to someone else.)* Was his son not enough?

Abhinay stares back at Swarnalatha, hardly hearing what is going on. A villager consoles the old woman.

VILLAGER. Amma, that was twenty years ago. This is not the man.

OLD WOMAN *(very convinced)*. No. I tell you this is the same man. Don't leave him! Abhinay! He killed your mother! Wasn't she on the bus also? Huh?

VILLAGER. Yes, Amma. But this is not the person. This is a woman.

Pinkie is backing to her car. She looks pale. The old woman comes back to the present time. It begins to rain.

OLD WOMAN. Oh.

VILLAGER. Come, come on.

The villagers begin to go their way.

OLD WOMAN *(while going away)*. A curse be on the people who pass on this bridge.

Swarnalatha hears this and backs away from the bridge. Abhinay stares at her retreating figure barely hearing Pinkie's apologies. Suddenly Swarnalatha is gone and

Pinkie gains focus in his mind. She is holding an umbrella out to him. He accepts the umbrella.

Cut to:

Exterior. Day. By the bridge.

We see Pinkie and Abhinay walking in the rain holding the umbrella, followed by a bullock cart dragging Pinkie's Santro through the rain.

Cut to:

Exterior. Day. A part of the village.

Swarnalatha is walking in a daze. Although there is a mild shower, she seems unconcerned about getting wet. She is near a shop with a bench outside on the street. She feels faint and sits down holding her head. The villagers are concerned. Some women give her a glass of water. A little girl tugs at her mother's sari.

LITTLE GIRL. What happened Mummy?

MOTHER. Nothing. That poor woman is cursed.

LITTLE GIRL. Why is she cursed?

MOTHER. Because she did not take care of her child. Now enough. Come.

The mother drags the little girl away.

Cut to:

Exterior. Day. A village garage for trucks and buses.

A mechanic is working under Pinkie's car.

PINKIE. . . . What about you? You live here?

ABHINAY. Used to. I am just visiting.

PINKIE. I–I am sorry to hear about what happened. I–I don't know what to say but . . .

ABHINAY. It's okay. Things happen.

PINKIE *(stops saying what she started out to say)*. Yes. I know.

Abhinay looks at her wondering what she means. The coconut-seller gives them a coconut each.

Can I have a straw?

ABHINAY. A straw?

PINKIE. How am I supposed to drink it?

ABHINAY. Just follow me.

Abhinay puts his mouth to the hole in the coconut, tosses his head back and drinks it in one go. Pinkie tries to do the same. As she tosses her head back, the water pours down her face. Abhinay looks on slightly amused. Pinkie sputters and drops the coconut and wipes her mouth and dress, laughing with embarrassment.

Cut to:

Exterior. Day. Fields.

We see Pinkie's car in long shot driving through some mud roads.

Cut to:

Exterior/Interior. Car. Moving. Paddy fields.

They are on a mud road between fields. They look at the fields while they talk to each other.

ABHINAY. All that is my dad's. He wants me to live here but . . .

PINKIE. You have other plans for yourself.

ABHINAY. Maybe. What do you do?

PINKIE. Oh, I am just out of college. Did my Mass Communication. I help my mom a bit with her boutique but . . . And what do you do in the city?

ABHINAY. I composed jingles for some stupid commercials, now . . . I want to start a music group.

PINKIE. Oh really?

Pause. Pinkie looks at him.

I am sorry to hear about the accident with your mother. I just want to let you know that . . .

ABHINAY. I think I will get off here, if you don't mind. I do want to take that walk.

The car comes to a halt. He gets off.

PINKIE. Maybe I can help.

ABHINAY. Help?

PINKIE. With your music group. To start it I mean.

ABHINAY. How can you help?

Pinkie thinks for a while.

PINKIE. I can sing.

ABHINAY. Sing.

PINKIE. Yes, I can . . .

ABHINAY. I mean, sing for me now.

PINKIE *(laughing)*. What is this? An audition?

ABHINAY. Yes!

Pinkie begins to hum a song and then sings full throated.

Cut to:

Exterior. Day. Outside Abhinay's village home.

Background music. Abhinay jumps out of the car and runs in.

Cut to:

Interior. Day. Abhinay's village home.

Abhinay rushes past his dad who is reading a paper.

FATHER. Abhinay, sit down I want to . . .

Abhinay has rushed into his bedroom. His father turns to look at where he has gone.

Cut to:

Interior. Day. Abhinay's village home. Bedroom.

Abhinay throws his clothes into his duffel bag. He rushes out of the room . . .

Cut to:

Interior. Day. Abhinay's village home.

Abhinay goes past his dad. Comes back to him, quickly touches his father's feet.

ABHINAY *(going out of the house).* I am going back to the city! Will call you before coming!

His father gets up and goes out to see what is happening.

Cut to:

Exterior. Day. Outside Abhinay's village home.

Abhinay gets into the car. They drive away, leaving his father standing in the veranda.

Cut to:

Exterior. Day. A part of the village.

The car drives past Appa Rau and his buffalo.

APPA RAU *(to his buffalo).* He thinks he can leave the village so easily. He is a fool. He does not know that the village is his place. We know our place. But he is not wise and old like us . . . He will come back.

Cut to:

Exterior. Day. Outside the village.

The car drives past leaving a desolate Swarnalatha standing and watching the car leave the village and across the bridge into the city.

Cut to:

Montage.

The city scape. Their car driving through a busy road.

Cut to:

A café.

A college kid is jamming away on his guitar and singing 'yeah, yeah, yeah' with headbanging motions, throwing his hair back and forth. He finishes with a bang. He looks at Pinkie and Abhinay who are trying to look poker-faced.

COLLEGE KID. So. What do you say, man?

ABHINAY. Can you play the guitar?

Cut to:

A college hall.

A bald, tattooed, huge, bare chested muscular guy is pounding away on his drums. He has a good sense of rhythm. Pinkie and Abhinay nod their heads to the beat. They look at each other and smile in approval. The drummer stops.

DRUMMER. I want six lakhs cash tomorrow morning and I will play for you.

Abhinay and Pinkie slide away waving bye.

PINKIE. Sorry, we are a bit low on funds.

Cut to:

A home.

An elderly man strums a guitar. He stops.

ELDERLY MAN. Jesus loves you. Repent and you will be saved.

Pinkie and Abhinay look at him.

PINKIE. Hallelujah.

Cut to:

Exterior. Day. On a busy road.

They are driving on a narrow road, exhausted. We see a row of posters of a woman with huge thighs advertising some porn film. The car goes past a man with a guitar. The car goes back to catch him. Pinkie gets off. We see the back of a guy with a guitar slung over his shoulder. He is staring at a vulgar looking poster of a woman with thunderous thighs. Pinkie notices the guitar. Pinkie stands beside the guy and looks at the obscene poster as well. The guy notices

Pinkie. He is wiry and meek looking, wearing rounded spectacles, a clean white starched shirt and sober grey pants. He (Munna) is terrified.

PINKIE. Nice poster, no?

MUNNA. What? No! I mean . . . I don't know, Ma'am. I was looking at the view!

PINKIE *(smiles at him).* Nice view. *(Pointing at his guitar.)* Do you play that thing?

Cut to:

Exterior. Day. A music store.

Abhinay enters the store. The window displays a drum set.

Cut to:

Interior. Day. A music store.

Balaji, a young hep looking salesman gives him a demo of the drum set.

BALAJI. This baby packs in quite a punch. Oh man, your neighbours are going to love it.

Balaji gets a little carried away playing the drum set. People outside on the street gather around the window. Balaji does a little jig for their benefit. They applaud. Abhinay is very attentive.

(Finishes with a toss of the drum stick, and pats his back.) So. Where do you want her delivered?

ABHINAY. I'll buy her . . . I mean the set . . . On one condition.

BALAJI *(a little wary).* What's the condition?

ABHINAY. That you come with it.

Balaji withdraws his hand and steps back from Abhinay.

Cut to:

Exterior. Day. Outside Mrs Kapoor's boutique.

Long shot of Pinkie's car parking outside the boutique.

We see Pinkie, Abhinay, Munna get out of the car and start taking out the drum set, keyboards, etc.

Cut to:

Exterior. Day. The entrance to Mrs Kapoor's boutique.

A hand cart with the drum set is waiting outside the boutique. Pinkie drives into the parking area. Abhinay, Munna and Pinkie get off. Abhinay gestures to the hand cart guy to bring it in. The boutique has a very fashionable window display with high fashion creations on the mannequins. The trio enter the frame. Pinkie holds the door open. We can hear Mrs Kapoor's loud socialite voice through the open door.

MRS KAPOOR *(off-screen)*. Not at all! What makes you say that? You look absolutely fabulous.

Cut to:

Interior. Day. Mrs Kapoor's boutique.

We see a large lady in an outlandish costume, two sizes small for her. Mrs Kapoor, an attractive woman in her mid forties is admiring the large lady. Mrs Kapoor wears Go Go earings, her hair piled up on top held by a chop stick. She wears chunky jewellery with stones and beads. She wears flared pants and a sleeveless top.

MRS KAPOOR. It's taken at least five years off your—everything.

LARGE LADY. You think so?

MRS KAPOOR. Of course!

Pinkie comes in with her gang.

Munna almost drops his guitar when he sees Mrs Screwwalla.

PINKIE. Hi mom! These are my . . .

MRS KAPOOR. Oh darling! Please tell Mrs Screwwalla how she looks. Now be honest dear. She is a very dear friend after all. Be honest.

PINKIE. I can just see Mr Screwwalla taking it off the minute he sees you in it! Oh Mrs Screwwalla, be kind to him. Don't buy the dress! Think of his blood pressure!

Mrs Screwwalla is delighted.

MRS SCREWWALLA. Nonsense. I'll take it. A little excitement won't do him harm.

PINKIE. Don't say I didn't warn you.

Abhinay looks at Pinkie slightly amused. The drum set is brought in.

Er–Mom. This is Abhinay and this is Munna.

MRS KAPOOR. Oh yes! Your wonderful talented friends. So pleased to meet you! Go right in. Pinkie dear, go ahead. I'll call if I need you.

Mrs Kapoor turns her attention on Mrs S. The rest go into a backroom with their equipment.

(To Mrs S.) Oh I just love encouraging young talent. I want to be surrounded by art and beauty and culture.

Cut to:

Interior. Day. The boutique's store room.

As the trio enter, we can still hear Mrs K.

MRS KAPOOR *(off-screen).* Oh let me show you this new painting I am working on. It is . . .

The store room is filled with racks of clothes and mannequins, some of them without any clothes. The drum set can barely fit in. Munna looks at the mannequins and his jaw drops. Abhinay looks at the space. There is hardly any room for the equipment.

ABHINAY. This is it?

PINKIE. We'll manage. Just you see. Why don't we just put down the stuff where you want it and . . . *(To Abhinay.)* Oh careful, you are leaning on Simran's dress.

Abhinay backs out of a rack and looks at the dress.

Cut to:

Interior. Day. Mrs Kapoor's boutique.

Balaji walks in with a bundle of clothes. Mrs Kapoor is working away on a painting. She notices Balaji and puts down her palette, greeting him warmly.

MRS KAPOOR. Oh hello! I knew it. I knew. I had this premonition that a handsome young man is going to walk in and I am going to make him look like a prince. It's Destiny!

BALAJI. Really? That's cool, man. Guess he is late. I am looking for this chick called Pinkie? I guess I have the wrong address.

MRS KAPOOR. You've come to the right place all right!

BALAJI *(suddenly wary)*. Are you Pinkie? Shit man! I knew that guy was a weirdo!

Mrs Kapoor's enormous smile freezes. She points to the store room.

Cut to:

Interior. Day. The boutique's store room.

The group have set up their equipment. Munna has found himself a place close to a busty mannequin. Balaji storms in.

ABHINAY. Ah! Good timing. Balaji—this is Pinkie—and Munna.

BALAJI. Call me Bals.

MUNNA. Pleased to meet you.

PINKIE. Hi balls.

BALAJI *(upset)*. It's Bals, not balls. Call me Bals.

PINKIE. Sorry . . . *(Trying it out.)* Bals.

BALAJI *(looking at the clothes racks)*. What's all this crap?

PINKIE. If you don't mind, leave that dress alone. Mrs Nene is extremely fussy. Can we start? I have other things to take care of.

ABHINAY. Right. Let's try out the first section.

BALAJI. Right. Let's begin with something important.

ABHINAY. Such as?

BALAJI. The look.

PINKIE. The look?

MUNNA *(who was staring at the naked mannequin).* I wasn't! I wasn't looking at anything!

BALAJI *(he has taken out some costumes from his knapsack).* Looks are everything. We gotta look cool guys. Attitude.

Balaji wears a bandana and a thick dog chain. He poses for the group to give their approval. He gives an attitude as well.

PINKIE *(taking his trip).* Kewl!

BALAJI. I like her, man. She's cool. Yeah, what? Maybe some leather? Or streak our hair? How about some rudraksha beads? Seventies Hippie Hare Rama stuff. How about that? That's where it all began folks. Goa. The home of trance!

PINKIE. How about playing some good music?

ABHINAY. Good idea. Let's try something out.

Abhinay plays the first section on his keyboard. Abhinay assigns the sections to Munna and a beat to Balaji.

BALAJI. Sure. *(Patronizingly to Abhinay.)* That's cool stuff.

ABHINAY. Thanks.

They play for a while. Pinkie hums a few bars. Just as they are grooving . . . Mrs Kapoor sneaks in quietly. She sneaks past Munna who is distracted by her presence. Mrs Kapoor picks up an outfit and sneaks past Pinkie who gives her mother a look.

MRS KAPOOR *(whispering to Pinkie).* The old bat is here.

Mrs Kapoor gestures to Pinkie to say 'I'll take care of her.' Mrs Kapoor leaves. They finish the section once again.

ABHINAY. That's great. Now let's try a variation. Pinkie, could you do a little groove after the melody?

Pinkie tries it out. Abhinay okays it.

Okay, 1,2,3,4 . . .

They start to play again for a moment before they hear a high pitched scream and a woman's sobbing. Mrs Kapoor pops in and out while the sobbing continues.

MRS KAPOOR *(in a panic).* Pinkie! Help!

PINKIE *(moving to the door).* I take it she doesn't like the dress.

Abhinay looks on a little annoyed.

Cut to:

Interior. Day. Mrs Kapoor's boutique.

Pinkie rushes to her mother, even as Abhinay comes storming out.

ABHINAY. This isn't working out!

He storms out.

Cut to:

Exterior. Day. Outside Mrs Kapoor's boutique.

Abhinay goes out. Through the glass we can see Pinkie concerned and following him out. Abhinay leans against a wall. Pinkie goes to him.

PINKIE. What's the matter?

ABHINAY. I am sorry I can't work in a place like that.

PINKIE. What do you mean a 'place like that'?

ABHINAY. We can't have a decent rehearsal in there without *(Imitating Mrs K.)* 'Oh darling, won't you help me with Mrs Screwalla' and all that shit.

PINKIE. Hold it. Hold it right there mister better than the rest. My mother gave us that place for free. You can't afford a place. That's the way my mother earns an honest living. If you don't like it, pack your stuff right away.

ABHINAY. I thought you wanted to help.

PINKIE. I thought you wanted to start a music group.

We leave them gesticulating at each other as the music picks up.

Montage.

The scratch tune they were practising is now the background music for this montage.

Interior. Day. Mrs Kapoor's boutique.

Slow speed shots of Pinkie consoling a weeping customer while a helpless Mrs Kapoor looks on.

Cut to:

Interior. Day. The boutique's store room.

The group in one of Balaji's outfits, playing and trying to look cool.

Cut to:

Interior. Night. Abhinay's apartment bedroom.

Abhinay working out some music on his keyboards and saving it on his computer.

Cut to:

Interior. Day. The entrance to Mrs Kapoor's boutique.

The group walk in wearing another strange uniform by Balaji.

Cut to:

Interior. Day. The boutique's store room.

Abhinay is giving Pinkie some notes. We see Munna patting one of the mannequin's bottom. The moment Pinkie turns around he withdraws his hand.

Cut to:

Interior. Day. Mrs Kapoor's boutique.

Mrs Kapoor is on the phone, while Pinkie and Abhinay are waiting to hear the result of that conversation. Mrs Kapoor hangs up and gives them good news which makes them jump with joy.

Cut to:

Interior. Day. The boutique's store room.

A middle-aged man (Manager) in an African shirt is listening to their music. Mrs Kapoor is standing next to him encouraging the group by swinging to their music. After they finish, Mrs Kapoor applauds wildly and turns to the Manager. The Manager shrugs his shoulders and nods. They are all elated and hug each other. Mrs Kapoor hugs Munna spontaneously. Munna staggers away. Abhinay hugs Pinkie spontaneously.

Cut to:

Interior. Night. A coffee shop.

We start with the band name Pratibimb as the music now has a source. We pull back to see our group playing. Pinkie is singing a sweet romantic song. We pull back further to see the party. Some people are at the buffet, some are by the drinks and mostly chatting with each other. Mrs Kapoor is the only one swaying to the music. She chats with someone and points to the group. The person politely excuses herself. The group finish their song and wait for an applause. The crowd continues to chatter away oblivious to the group's presence. Mrs Kapoor applauds and whistles loudly and tries to get the others to join in. At the most, some people in the crowd smile at her politely. The group is crushed.

Cut to:

Interior. Night. A banquet hall.

We see some of the workers stacking up the chairs, cleaning the ashtrays, etc. We see the group seated at a table very depressed. The kitchen is in the background. The swinging doors keep swaying crazily as the workers go in and come out. Noises from the kitchen disturb them as they finish a basic meal served to them.

BALAJI. Maybe we can try a different look.

MRS KAPOOR *(annoyed by a waiter who bumps into her).* You played wonderfully well! Oh Pinkie darling, you will be a hit I tell you. It's just finding the right gig . . .

The Manager comes to them. He tosses a pay packet on the table.

MANAGER. As agreed, here is the balance payment. I think that settles the accounts, right?

ABHINAY. What do you think of our music?

MANAGER. Nobody complained.

ABHINAY. What do you think?

MANAGER. It's good.

ABHINAY. No. I want an honest opinion.

The Manager looks at Abhinay.

MANAGER *(still on Abhinay).* You want an honest opinion?

The group look at him.

There are hundreds, thousands of young musicians in this city and they all think they are different or unique, but they are not . . . You are one of them. *(Abhinay is hurt at this.)* Good or bad, they are all pretending to be Whites who are pretending to be Blacks. *(Imitating their body language and tone.)* Kewl! Yo!

BALAJI *(taking offence).* What's wrong with being cool?

MANAGER. Hey. You asked me what I thought of your music. I told you.

ABHINAY. If you don't like our music, that's your problem.

Abhinay walks away. Pinkie looks in his direction.

MANAGER. No. If I don't like your music, that's your problem.

Pinkie gets up.

PINKIE *(to the Manager).* Give us time.

MANAGER *(walking away).* Take your time. Just don't waste mine.

Pinkie looks on concerned. Mrs Kapoor is puzzled.
Fade out.

Exterior. Night. The city from above.

We see Abhinay walking aimlessly amidst the late night bustle.

Cut to:

Exterior. Night. Beach or park bench.

Abhinay walks slowly into frame and sits down. There are couples around him necking. A woman slowly walks past him giving him the eye, hoping to earn some money out of him. Abhinay is lost in thought. He begins to walk. He comes to a a row of sewage pipes. He peeps into one of them. It is a home. A boy in rags is singing a lullaby to his baby sister. Abhinay is taken out of his mellow mood by the song. He fishes out a few rupees for the boy. The boy begins to sing again rocking his sibling to sleep. Abhinay stares after the boy and walks away.

Cut to:

Interior. Night. Car. Moving.

Mrs Kapoor is driving. Pinkie is staring out of the window. Mrs Kapoor rambles on but Pinkie is hardly listening.

MRS KAPOOR. Darling I didn't know that singing meant so much to you. I will speak to Mr Khatri and see if I can arrange a solo for you . . .

Pinkie remains silent. After a while she looks at her mom.

Cut to:

Exterior. Night. The driveway of Kapoor's home.

The car enters the driveway after a watchman opens the gate for them. They park the car and get off.

Cut to:

Interior. Night. Mrs Kapoor's bedroom/bathroom and balcony.

Mrs Kapoor is taking off her make-up in the bathroom.
Pinkie enters her bedroom tentative. She is about to
withdraw. Mrs Kapoor senses her presence and calls
from the bathroom.

MRS KAPOOR. Pinkie? Darling?

Mrs Kapoor comes out just as Pinkie is leaving.

Did you want something? *(Looking at her.)* What's the matter?

PINKIE. Oh nothing really I . . .

MRS KAPOOR. You are not going to sleep with all that make-up
on. Come here and I'll take it off.

Mrs Kapoor disappears into the bathroom while Pinkie
sits down on the bed.

(Rambling on from the bathroom.) You must watch out.
Before you know it, those wrinkles will appear and you are a
has-been.

Mrs Kapoor goes to her with the cleansing milk and
begins to apply it on her.

PINKIE. I went to that village last month.

MRS KAPOOR. Which village?

Pinkie gently takes her mother's hand away from her
face.

(Realizing what she means.) Oh . . .

PINKIE. I had to go . . . It doesn't seem very important to you
does it? That I lost my father on that day twenty years ago?

Mrs Kapoor gets busy with the make-up stuff, putting
it away.

MRS KAPOOR. That's not true . . . Oh, how can I explain to you?
I am trying to forget a lot of things . . . I just want to get on
with my life.

Mrs Kapoor goes into the bathroom. Pinkie follows
her.

PINKIE. You didn't love him, did you? All you care about is yourself.

MRS KAPOOR *(slamming the stuff in the sink).* Pinkie that's unfair to me. You are being very very unfair.

PINKIE. You think you are being fair to me? Every time I try to talk about my father you change the subject! You didn't love him, but I did!

Mrs Kapoor turns away and busies herself with her hair.

MRS KAPOOR. You were a baby when he died.

PINKIE. All my childhood memories have him, mom. All I remember about you is you would drag me away from him. Why did you hate him so much?

MRS KAPOOR. I didn't hate him. Oh no, I didn't in spite of . . . *(Exercising great restraint.)* You loved your father and . . . I want you to have good memories of him.

Pinkie looks at her mother. Mrs Kapoor is in tears. Pinkie comforts her.

PINKIE. Tell me.

MRS KAPOOR. He used to beat me up.

Pinkie is perturbed to hear this.

MRS KAPOOR. He would start in the morning and . . . I tried to protect you . . . and I did. Pinkie, that's all that mattered to me. That you didn't see any of it. I don't want you to hate your father. He was sick, but—he loved you a great deal. He did.

Pinkie slowly holds her mom and hugs her. Mrs Kapoor smiles at her reassuringly.

MRS KAPOOR. It's okay. I am all right. I am a tough woman.

PINKIE. And . . . the accident?

MRS KAPOOR. He–he was responsible for it. He was drunk. He killed those villagers.

Pinkie is shocked. She walks out of the bathroom.

The scene where she almost hits Abhinay, the old woman's curse. She is overwhelmed. She rushes out to the balcony overlooking the city. Mrs Kapoor comes to her and comforts her.

Cut to:

Exterior. Night. A busy part of the city.

Abhinay is walking on the streets. Party revelers spill out of pubs and get into their cars.

Cut to:

Exterior. Night. Mrs Kapoor's home.

Pinkie gets out of her home and into her car. She drives out after the watchman opens the gate for her.

Cut to:

Exterior. Night. A busy part of the city.

Abhinay bumps into a group of friends.

FRIEND 1. Hey Abhi! How is it going?

ABHINAY. Fine.

FRIEND 2. How is the music scene?

FRIEND 1. Come on. Join us. We are going to my place. Come on.

Cut to:

Exterior. Night. Pinkie in her car.

Pinkie looks up at Abhinay's flat from her car. She gets her cell phone out and calls him . . .

Cut to:

Interior. Night. Abhinay's apartment.

The phone rings in an empty apartment.

Cut to:

Interior. Night. A wild party.

Loud music. People dancing and smoking. Abhinay is seated on a crowded sofa. He seems to like being there.

His cell phone is ringing. He looks at the caller and switches it off.

Cut to:

Exterior. Night. Pinkie in her car.

Pinkie puts away her cell phone and gets out. She walks into the building.

Cut to:

Interior. Night. Stairs.

Pinkie is greeted by the watchman.

PINKIE. Abhinay's flat please.

WATCHMAN. 2nd Floor. 201. But he is not in.

Pinkie hesitantly starts to climb the stairs.

He is not there madam.

Cut to:

Interior. Night. A wild party.

A woman is now talking to Abhinay over the loud music. We can't hear any of it. The person seated next to Abhinay gets up and the woman sits next to him. He enjoys it when she makes a pass at him.

Cut to:

Interior. Night. Stairs.

Pinkie sits down on top of the stairs.

Cut to:

Interior. Night. A wild party.

Abhinay is now necking the girl and soon they are kissing.

Cut to:

Interior. Night. Stairs.

Pinkie sits there lost in thought. Again the images of Abhinay on the bridge and Swarnalatha flash in her mind.

Cut to:

Interior. Night. A wild party.

Abhinay gently pushes the woman away, finishes his drink and leaves.

Cut to:

Interior. Night. Stairs.

The watchman comes up to the first floor landing to check on Pinkie. He looks at her. Pinkie sighs and gets up to go. Abhinay walks up and notices her. He is quite drunk. Pinkie notices that he is drunk.

ABHINAY. What is it?

PINKIE. I–I wanted to talk to you, to tell you . . .

ABHINAY. I don't need your sympathy.

PINKIE. I–Abhinay, your . . .

ABHINAY. Good night.

PINKIE *(walking past him)*. Good night.

Pinkie leaves. Abhinay fumbles with his keys to open his door. The watchman comes to his help.

WATCHMAN. She was waiting for two hours.

Abhinay sighs and leans against the wall wishing he hadn't been so rude.

Fade out.

Interior. Day. Abhinay's apartment. Kitchen/living room/front door.

The radio is playing an FM station in the background. We see Abhinay in the kitchen preparing his breakfast. Occasionally he takes a sip of his orange juice. The doorbell rings. Abhinay puts the stove on simmer, takes another swig of orange juice and comes into the living room and the front door. He opens the front door. A postman with a huge parcel.

POSTMAN. Parcel for you. Sign here please.

Abhinay looks at the parcel not having a clue what it is or where it's from. He signs for it and accepts it. Abhinay shuts the door and puts the parcel on the dining table. He gets a pair of scissors from his desk and begins to open it . . . The parcel is wrapped in gunny cloth. It takes some unravelling. It is a worn out violin case. There is a patch on one side. Abhinay clicks open the case and finds a violin with a note attached to it. Abhinay picks up the note and reads it. We hear the Carnatic notes that Swarnalatha sang at the riverside. Abhinay holds the violin in his hand, a sense of excitement building up inside him as he feels the texture of the violin. We see the picture of his mother bathed in moonlight transforming into a memory of Abhinay's mother, Vaishnavi playing the violin. The camera moves quickly though and we only see her back and part of the bow as it moves over the strings. The camera moves further to reveal Swarnalatha next to Vaishnavi singing while Vaishnavi is accompanying her. We come back to Abhinay looking at the violin.

Fade out.

Exterior. Day. Outside Swarnalatha's house. Main door.

POV of Abhinay as he walks to Swarnalatha's main door. Intercut with Swarnalatha's pot going down the well. Flashes of young Abhinay walking on that same path. We see Abhinay's hand, knocking on the door. The door is opened by Swarnalatha's husband. He looks at Abhinay.

Cut to:

Exterior. Day. Backyard of Swarnalatha.

Swarnalatha is drawing water from the well. Nagamma, her maid, comes to her.

NAGAMMA. That boy is coming here, Amma!

Swarnalatha has removed the rope from the pot and is about to pick it up.

Vaishnavi's boy!

Swarnalatha drops the pot and it falls into the well.

Cut to:

From the well. The pot falling in.

Cut to:

Exterior. Day. Backyard of Swarnalatha.

Swarnalatha is flustered.

SWARNALATHA. Oh! Call someone, quickly before it goes right down! Oh! *(Nagamma leaves. Swarnalatha frets over the pot. Calling.)* Somu!

Abhinay comes to the backyard. Swarnalatha begins to sweep the area around the tulasi plant.

What do you want from me?

ABHINAY. I—just came to thank you.

SWARNALATHA. For what?

ABHINAY. For sending me the violin.

Swarnalatha stops sweeping. A little boy comes running in and jumps into the well.

SWARNALATHA *(turning to him)*. I came to know you were looking for it.

ABHINAY. Don't you want to keep it?

SWARNALATHA. No.

ABHINAY. Why did you keep it for so many years then?

She begins to sweep again.

SWARNALATHA. Why didn't you ask for it all these years?

ABHINAY. I didn't know where it was.

SWARNALATHA. And now you have come here to blame me for your mother's death and stealing her violin.

ABHINAY. I am not here to blame you for anything. I just came here to thank you for sending me my mother's violin, and also to . . .

Swarnalatha looks at Abhinay.

SWARNALATHA. And also . . .?

ABHINAY. To ask you to sing for me.

The little boy throws the pot out of the well. The boy pops up spitting water and laughing at his accomplishment.

SWARNALATHA. What do you mean?

ABHINAY. I am starting a music group and I want you to be a part of it.

SWARNALATHA. No. I can't.

The boy has come up to her with the pot. He holds out the pot to her.

ABHINAY. It's what you wanted to do.

BOY. Amma, your pot.

ABHINAY. Please, you must come with me to the city.

BOY. Take your pot, Amma.

Swarnalatha grabs the pot from the boy and yells at both of them.

SWARNALATHA. Go away! Just go!

The little boy is frightened and runs away. Abhinay too leaves. Swarnalatha resumes her sweeping. She picks up the pot. Abhinay is at the door with the violin. He begins to play it.

(*Shouting.*) That is not the way to play it!

Abhinay stops to play.

You cannot hold a Carnatic violin like that. Come here.

Abhinay walks to her.

Sit down.

Abhinay is about to sit on a low stool.

Sit down on the floor!

Abhinay sits on the floor, cross-legged. Swarnalatha instructs him on how to hold the violin correctly.

Now play.

Abhinay plays a simple scale.

Swarnalatha's husband, Mr Shastri comes to the doorway and stares at his wife's rediscovered passion. Swarnalatha looks on as Abhinay plays.

Fade out.

Interior. Day. The boutique's store room.

MUNNA. What?

BALAJI. What?

Interior. Day. Swarnalatha's living room. Intercut.

SWARNALATHA. No.

Interior. Day. The boutique's store room.

ABHINAY. I am fed up of this place anyway. A change of scene won't do us harm.

Interior. Day. Swarnalatha's living room.

MR SHASTRI *(to Swarnalatha).* Do it.

Interior. Day. The boutique's store room.

PINKIE. I think it's a great idea.

Interior. Day. Swarnalatha's living room.

MR SHASTRI. She hasn't stepped out of this village in twenty years.

Interior. Day. The boutique's store room.

BALAJI. But why?

ABHINAY. I will explain everything when we get there. Come on. Let's move.

Mrs Kapoor comes into the store room with coffee.

MRS KAPOOR. Here you are boys. Mind. Don't spill any on the clothes.

Everyone is busy packing. Mrs Kapoor looks on.

Pinkie dear, is there something I ought to know.

PINKIE *(excited and delighted).* Oh mom! You are not going to believe this! Guess where we are going?

Cut to:

Exterior. Day. Car. Moving.

They are driving in Pinkie's car to the village. They cross the bridge and Appa Rau.

Cut to:

Exterior. Day. Outside Swarnalatha's house. Main door.

They begin to unload their stuff out of the car. Abhinay is excited as he takes his keyboard in. A brief flash of the young Abhinay going to the front door. Pinkie goes in.

Cut to:

Interior. Day. Swarnalatha's bedroom.

Swarnalatha is seated on her bed as she hears the intrusive sounds of the people in her backyard.

Cut to:

Exterior. Day. Swarnalatha's backyard.

They have set up their equipment. Nagamma stands there fascinated by all this. Munna resists the temptation to put his hand on her butt.

BALAJI. I can't believe this! *(To Pinkie.)* Could you explain to me once again what we are doing here?

MUNNA. Is this your mother's place?

Abhinay reacts sharply to that innocent remark.

ABHINAY. No.

BALAJI. Maybe when we cut the music video we could use all this shit. And I have a surprise for you guys too. I have the look for the group.

With a flourish he takes off his jeans and overshirt to reveal some tight leather outfit that looks obscene. Nagamma covers her face. Swarnalatha walks in. Pinkie looks at Swarnalatha. Balaji is embarrassed. He moves away to hide behind a bush. Swarnalatha looks at Balaji with disapproval.

ABHINAY. Er, everyone this is Auntie . . . I mean Mrs Swarnalatha Shastri.

PINKIE. Hello, Mrs Shastri. I am Pinkie.

SWARNALATHA. Pinkie? What kind of name is that?

PINKIE. Er. Well my name is Priyanka but Mummy calls me . . .

SWARNALATHA. Priyanka . . . What a nice name.

ABHINAY. This is Bals.

BALAJI *(putting on his trousers)*. Balaji. Call me Balaji. Pleased to meet you Mrs . . .

SWARNALATHA. Please call me Auntie.

PINKIE. But you don't look that old Mrs Shastri.

SWARNALATHA. Please don't flatter me. I am as old as I am. In the village we are proud of our advancing years. So call me auntie.

An embarrassing pause.

ABHINAY. So . . . Auntie has agreed to sing for us.

BALAJI *(flabbergasted)*. What?

Swarnalatha stares at him.

ABHINAY. Aren't you going to at least thank her for it.

MUNNA. Thank you, Auntie.

BALAJI *(resigning)*. Thank you, Auntie.

ABHINAY *(taking charge)*. Okay. Let's get to work please.

Balaji quickly puts on his jeans and overshirt. Abhinay gives Pinkie a look. They take their positions.

Swarnalatha rolls out a mat and sits cross-legged. Balaji gets up to adjust his drum, we see the pattern of a woman's hands on the back of his jeans, that Swarnalatha would notice if she turned around. Abhinay quickly stands in between them while Balaji settles down.

Right. Now, we will play the groove we worked on yesterday. We will play it once for auntie's benefit.

SWARNALATHA. I don't need to listen to your music. You please tell me when to start.

ABHINAY. Okay. You can come in after the fifth bar.

SWARNALATHA. Hmm. Which raga are you playing?

ABHINAY. Right. Good question. Which raga would you like to sing in?

Swarnalatha looks at him warily. She opens a book that she has with her, putting on her reading glasses.

SWARNALATHA. You must always start with a Ganesha sthotram. *(Looking at Balaji.)* He is the God that will remove all your obstacles. *(To Abhinay.)* Can you play in raga Todi?

ABHINAY. Sure.

He plays the scale on his keyboard.

Something like that?

SWARNALATHA. Something like that. *(Sighing.)* Anyway, you play what you can.

Also he switches on a recorder that is placed near Swarnalatha. They play. Pinkie now has lyrics which she sings in perfect key and manages to join in with Swarnalatha. When it is time for Swarnalatha's cue, as she is about to come in, Balaji gives a heavy crash of drums. There is a pause as Swarnalatha covers her ears at the noise.

Pause.

Swarnalatha starts a scale. Abhinay complements it with his composition on the keyboard. They finish as

Pinkie looks at this new relationship developing which the others are oblivious of.

BALAJI *(spontaneously)*. Hey that's cool shit.

Swarnalatha goes to him and twists his ear.

SWARNALATHA. What is all this nonsense language?

BALAJI *(wincing in pain)*. Ow! Leggo, man—I mean Auntie!

SWARNALATHA. What will you call me?

BALAJI. Auntie! Auntie!

SWARNALATHA. And wear some decent clothes if you are in my house, understand?

Swarnalatha turns to Munna. Munna backs away in fright.

MUNNA. Mummy!

Nagamma runs away frightened.

Cut to:

Interior. Day. Abhinay's apartment.

Abhinay is on the keyboard, listening to the tape and trying to get the melody on his keyboard. Balaji, Munna and Pinkie are in the background.

BALAJI. She almost cut off my ear man!

PINKIE. You shouldn't have called her singing cool shit.

MUNNA. My mother also sings in the Church.

Pinkie gestures with patience.

PINKIE. It seems to me that there might be something in this . . .

BALAJI. It's not cool.

PINKIE. Look. Let's just give it a shot. What have we got to lose?

BALAJI. Our image. At least mine. Might as well bring in my grandmom.

PINKIE. Do you or do you not want to make a recording?

BALAJI. How is she going to help?

Balaji goes to Abhinay.

Look if you really want fusion, keep the Carnatic stuff in the background. Write in some good sections for me. People like the punch. It's the drums man. It's all about drums.

MUNNA. No. The bass guitar is the speciality of the group. I will jam a bit more. It's the guitar that works.

PINKIE. Oh sure. I could say it's my singing. Where does all this . . .

ABHINAY. It's the raga.

BALAJI. Huh?

ABHINAY. It's the raga. I need the raga to make it work.

He plays the melody on his keyboards.

Cut to:

Interior. Day. A rehearsal hall or stage.

Abhinay and the rest have set up their equipment and are waiting for the manager to come with the record company director. The manager walks in with Rajeev from the advertising agency.

MANAGER. Meet Mr Rajeev Ramnathan from Magic Sound.

Abhinay looks at him.

And this is . . .

RAJEEV. Hello Abhinay. Fancy meeting you again!

MANAGER. Oh, I didn't know you knew each other. That makes things easier.

RAJEEV. Not necessarily.

ABHINAY. Hello Rajeev. I guess you don't want to listen to my stuff.

RAJEEV. Not at all. I want to hear what you have been up to since you gave up doing bubble gum jingles. Let's hear what you have got, I don't have much time.

He sits down. Abhinay cues his group and begins to play. Rajeev is apparently bored with the music. Abhinay plays the Maha Ganapathy melody on the keyboard. Rajeev looks at his watch. He gets a call on his cell phone. He gets up to leave. Abhinay stops playing, so do the rest of the group.

I am sorry Abhinay, let me be blunt—you are better off composing jingles. You were really good.

ABHINAY. Rajeev, you were better off as an advertising general dogsbody than a programme director of a record company. Why don't you go back to your previous job? Do you know that melody is five hundred years old? And you prefer a bubble gum jingle to it?

RAJEEV. I didn't hear it. You reduced a Carnatic raga to a melody on your keyboard and I suppose you think you are being different.

ABHINAY. Wait till you hear it with the singer. Live.

RAJEEV. I am sorry. I am not coming to yet another audition.

ABHINAY. It won't be an audition. It will be a concert.

   Cut to:

Exterior. Day. A city street.

   They are walking to their car.

PINKIE. Try for another singer.

ABHINAY. We will get her.

PINKIE. How? She's never moved out of her village in twenty years.

ABHINAY. I will get her.

   Abhinay gets into the car. We stay on Pinkie.

PINKIE. Abhinay, why do you want her?

   Abhinay looks at her.

ABHINAY. You won't understand.

Cut to:

Interior/Exterior. Swarnalatha's backyard.

Swarnalatha is pouring the water from the pot onto the tulsi plant. She then begins to spread some chillies for drying. She hears the strains of the violin. She goes towards the interior of the house. She looks in to see Abhinay and Shastri chatting while he plays the violin casually. She goes in. Abhinay stops when he sees her.

SWARNALATHA. What do you want?

ABHINAY. I just came to say hello.

MR SHASTRI. Swarnu—why don't you sit down while I make some coffee for our guest. Come sit . . .

Before she can say anything Mr Shastri has vanished. She sits down.

SWARNALATHA. Why do you bring your mother's violin here?

ABHINAY. Don't you like it?

He picks it up to play again.

SWARNALATHA. No don't play it, please.

ABHINAY. Will you sing for me in a concert?

SWARNALATHA. No.

ABHINAY. You must. I cannot do the concert without you.

Swarnalatha is perturbed.

SWARNALATHA. Why?

ABHINAY. I don't know. It somehow makes sense.

SWARNALATHA. I don't go to the city.

ABHINAY. You must.

SWARNALATHA. Why?

ABHINAY. Because it's me who is asking. Vaishnavi's son.

Swarnalatha looks away.

My mother played for you. You can sing for me. Or don't you want to return the favour because she is dead and it doesn't matter any more?

*Abhinay storms out leaving a disturbed Swarnalatha.
Mr Shastri appears.*

SWARNALATHA. He wants me to sing in a concert!

MR SHASTRI. Do it! Do it and get it over with.

Swarnalatha looks on perturbed by his remarks.

Cut to:

Interior. Night. Swarnalatha's Bedroom.

*They are asleep. We hear some groans. We see
Swarnalatha is in pain. She is clutching her abdomen.
Shastri gets up and goes into the kitchen. Swarnalatha
is crying. She mutters to herself 'I won't do it.' Shastri
comes in with a hot water bottle and gives it to her.*

MR SHASTRI *(whispering to her)*. Do you need anything else?

Swarnalatha shakes her head. After a while.

(Softly.) Swarnu . . . I am sorry.

*Swarnalatha opens her eyes thinking about what he
said.*

Cut to:

Exterior. Day. Outside a temple.

*The temple is fairly crowded. Swarnalatha is going
round the temple praying. As she comes to the main
entrance, she bumps into Abhinay's father.*

ABHINAY'S FATHER. I hear my son is learning music from you?

SWARNALATHA. Maybe.

ABHINAY'S FATHER. Please leave him alone. Music will take him
nowhere.

*Swarnalatha is offended at this remark against music.
Abhinay appears out of the temple. He sees his father
and Swarnalatha together and is perturbed. Abhinay's
father puts some money in the hundi and walks away.
Abhinay looks at Swarnalatha and she goes to a
beggar and gives him some fruit. Abhinay follows his
father.*

Cut to:

Exterior. Day. Ferry.

Swarnalatha is coming out of the temple. She gets into a ferry full of people. Abhinay and his father are already in the ferry. She sits opposite them. Abhinay's father stares at her. Swarnalatha slowly nods at Abhinay. Abhinay is elated and gets up almost knocking himself over.

Cut to:

Exterior. Day. City street.

Abhinay drives to his apartment. Parks his car on the road and runs in talking on his cell phone . . .

Cut to:

Exterior. Day. Outside Mrs Kapoor's boutique.

We see Balaji and Abhinay struggling to put the drums in a waiting tempo. Pinkie comes out with a whole bundle of clothes. Mrs Kapoor is behind her.

MRS KAPOOR. Don't forget to pull up the hem and take enough gel for the boys.

PINKIE. Got it Mom.

MRS KAPOOR. I'll be there early to wish you good luck.

Cut to:

Interior. Day. Manager's office.

The Manager is on the phone.

MANAGER. Ya . . . ya, ya. By the way, Rajeev you might want to come to the Music Utsav tonight. I've got some interesting music playing there . . .

Cut to:

Exterior. Day. A part of the village.

Appa Rau is walking Annapoorna to his next customer.

APPA RAU *(to Annapoorna)*. Here is some news that will get rid of your stomach ache . . . Our Swarnalatha is going to the city

to sing! Yes, I heard it only this morning. That boy Abhinay
has asked her to sing with some modern band . . . What she
will do singing there God alone knows . . .! After all that
happened, she still wants to sing in the city. Let us see . . .

    Cut to:

Interior. Day. A banquet hall.

    Balaji is setting up his drums. Abhinay is checking out
    the acoustics. Pinkie gets their clothes ready.

PINKIE. Come on boys. Let's try these out.

    Cut to:

Interior. Evening. Swarnalatha's home.

    Swarnalatha is trying out appropriate saris.

    Cut to:

Interior. Evening. Mrs Kapoor's boutique.

    Mrs Kapoor is wearing an evening dress. Looking
    smart. She is rushing a customer.

MRS KAPOOR *(escorting the customer to the door).* I am sorry,
but I am closing early today. It's a special day you see . . .

    Cut to:

Exterior. Evening. A road in the village.

    Mr Shastri and Swarnalatha are in the car. The car
    comes to a halt, stopping a bullock cart from going
    through. Swarnalatha looks a little troubled by this.

    Cut to:

    The phone inside the house begins to ring.

    Cut to:

Interior. Evening. A banquet hall.

    Pinkie is on the phone trying to reach Swarnalatha.

PINKIE. I think they've left already.

    Pinkie hangs up.

Cut to:

Exterior. Evening. A road in the village.

Swarnalatha looks at her husband.

MR SHASTRI *(reassuring her)*. Don't worry, we will make sure you will get there in time.

Mr Shastri gets out of the car.

SWARNALATHA. How will we get there?

MR SHASTRI *(opening her door)*. I'll get the car repaired and pick you up after the show.

SWARNALATHA. I can't go all by myself!

MR SHASTRI. Swaru . . . Trust me! Everything will be all right.

Swarnalatha gets out of the car reluctantly.

Cut to:

Interior. Evening. A banquet hall.

The Manager comes up to them.

MANAGER. Is everything okay? Where's the lady?

PINKIE. She is on her way. We will get ready.

Cut to:

Exterior/Interior. Evening. Near the village bus stand/inside the bus.

Mr Shastri and Swarnalatha walk to the bus.

MR SHASTRI. Don't worry, I will call Abhinay and ask him to receive you at the station.

SWARNALATHA. Come with me!

MR SHASTRI. Don't worry. I will follow in the car.

Mr Shastri puts her on the bus. There is a general chatter from the passengers. The bus is quite full. The bus driver honks to signal he is ready to leave.

(Waving to her and shouting.) I will see you at the show. All the best!

Before Swarnalatha can respond, more people come in.

Take a seat! There!

Swarnalatha finds a seat at the back of the bus. The bus begins to move. There is a woman next to her with a baby in her arms. As the bus leaves the station, Swarnalatha turns around to see Mr Shastri waving and walking away. Exterior of bus leaving the station. Inside the bus, people settle down but the chatter continues. Swarnalatha stares at the child in the woman's arms. The child is drawing a pattern on the dusty window pane. Swarnalatha looks away as she feels a panic attack coming. She looks back at the child . . .

Flashback: Day. Bus.

Swarnalatha's child is drawing a pattern on the window pane. Present time. Evening. Bus. Moving. Swarnalatha looks around. Everyone is busy chatting or settling down to sleep. A small group begins to sing. This makes Swarnalatha even more edgy. The bus approaches the bridge. Swarnalatha can see the bridge now. She panics. Swarnalatha gets up and tries to go to the front. But there is a lot of stuff in the aisle. Swarnalatha looks at the bridge approaching . . .

Flashback. Interior. Bus. Falling over the bridge.

Swarnalatha's tanpura cracks as the passengers are jolted out of their seats as the bus begins to keel over. Swarnalatha's child is torn away from her with the impact. Vaishnavi reaches out to Swarnalatha's child. Vaishnavi's child is pulled away.

Present. Bus. Moving.

Swarnalatha leans forward. She sees the river.

SWARNALATHA *(screaming)*. Stop it! Stop the bus!

The bus stops on the bridge. Everyone looks at her as she tries to get off with her bag. The bag comes apart

*as she gets off the bus. Swarnalatha gets off the bus
and runs back towards her village. The bus starts up
and begins to leave as a tearful Swarnalatha runs away
from the bridge. Swarnalatha turns around to see the
ghostly figures of Vaishnavi and her son. Swarnalatha
looks away. We pull back on the empty bridge.*

Fade out.

Interior. Night. A banquet hall.

*The guests have arrived. Rajeev makes a grand entrance.
Mrs Kapoor makes a bee line for him.*

MRS KAPOOR. Oh hello Rajeev. We met at Ramya's party. What
a surprise to see you here. And a pleasure. Let's find a cozy
spot . . .

*Rajeev succumbs to her charms and allows to be led to
his seat by her. Abhinay, Balaji and Munna are all
waiting in the wings. The Manager comes up to them.*

MANAGER. Rajeev is here and so are a couple of record company
managers. He is looking forward to . . . Where is the lady?

ABHINAY. She is on her way.

MANAGER. Well, I am going to announce you in a few minutes.

ABHINAY. Ten minutes, please . . .

*The Manager nods and walks away. Pinkie comes in
looking very anxious. Mrs Kapoor is making small talk
with the guests. Pinkie looks at a worried Abhinay.*

PINKIE. She wasn't there.

ABHINAY. Maybe Mr Shastri is to bring her after all.

Cut to:

Interior. Night. Swarnalatha's backyard.

Swarnalatha sits on the steps not moving.

Cut to:

Interior. Night. A banquet hall. Entrance.

*Mr Shastri walks in to the party and looks around for
his wife. Pinkie notices him.*

PINKIE. Oh there he is!

Pinkie walks up to Mr Shastri.

Oh thank God! We are delayed already.

MR SHASTRI. Why haven't you started?

PINKIE. Where is auntie?

MR SHASTRI *(shocked)*. You mean she isn't here?

PINKIE. She wasn't on the bus.

Cut to:

Interior. Night. Another part of the hall.

The Manager walks up to Abhinay.

MANAGER. I am announcing you.

The Manager walks towards the stage.

Cut to:

Interior. Night. A banquet hall.

Mr Shastri is on Pinkie's cell phone, waiting for a reply.

Cut to:

Interior. Night. Swarnalatha's backyard.

The phone rings, but Swarnalatha is wandering in her backyard listlessly. She goes inside. We follow her.

Cut to:

Interior. Night. The stage in the banquet hall.

The Manager gets up on the stage.

MANAGER. Ladies and gentlemen. A few announcements before our first group . . .

Cut to:

Interior. Night. Swarnalatha's living room.

The phone is still ringing. Swarnalatha picks up the phone and puts it back in the cradle.

Cut to:

Interior. Night. A banquet hall.

*Mr Shastri hears the click of the phone. He turns to
Pinkie and shakes his head.*

MANAGER *(off-screen)*. And now for the event that I am proud
to present . . .

Cut to:

Interior. Night. The stage in the banquet hall.

MANAGER. A new group with a new sound—Pratibimb!

*There is a round of applause. Rajeev applauds looking
for Carnatic singer. The Manager turns to Abhinay in
the wings, gesturing for him to come on stage. Balaji
and Munna get on stage. Pinkie goes to Abhinay.*

PINKIE. She isn't coming.

*Balaji rolls the drums. Abhinay is crushed that she
can't make it. He looks at Mr Shastri.*

Flashback. Interior. Bus. Falling over the bridge.

*Abhinay as a child is reaching out to his mother
Vaishnavi. Vaishnavi moves to reach out to
Swarnalatha's child. From the young Abhinay's POV
we see Swarnalatha also reaching out to her child.*

Present. Abhinay in the banquet hall.

ABHINAY *(troubled)*. She let me down!

*Pinkie pulls him up on stage. They take their positions
as the audiences wait. Balaji and Munna begin their
instrumental sections. It is Abhinay's cue to bring in
the piano. Abhinay strikes the first chord.*

Flashback. Exterior. Morning. Village.

*Young Abhinay running outside while we hear a
morning raga playing faintly. (Intercut this scene with
Abhinay playing on the keyboards). The Intercuts end
with young Abhinay finding his way into Swarnalatha's*

home from where the music is coming. Nobody opens the door. His banging on the door is 'match cut' with his pounding on the keys. Pinkie's cue comes in. She begins to sing while she observes Abhinay on the keyboards working himself to a frenzy. The young Abhinay is now trying to peep through a window. He slips and falls. The older Abhinay stops playing. Pinkie continues to sing for a while. When her section is over, all eyes are on Abhinay.

ABHINAY *(looking at Pinkie)*. I can't . . . I can't . . .

Abhinay gets up and begins to walk away. The crowds begin to murmur. Mrs Kapoor is disconcerted. Rajeev holds his head in his hands. Mr Shastri looks on and leaves. The Manager rushes to Abhinay. Rajeev shakes his head. Pinkie signals to Balaji and Munna who start to play a popular tune just to keep the crowds busy.

MANAGER. Are you crazy? What's the matter with you?

ABHINAY. I am sorry. I just couldn't. I am sorry.

Abhinay leaves. Pinkie follows him. Rajeev does a wash out sign to the Manager.

Cut to:

Exterior. Night. Parking lot.

Abhinay comes to the parking lot, followed by Pinkie.

PINKIE. Abhinay!

ABHINAY. Don't ask me why, please!

PINKIE. It's okay. It's okay.

ABHINAY. No it's not okay. I let you down. I let myself down.

Abhinay leans against a wall.

It's not there. Whatever I am looking for. It's not there.

PINKIE. I understand.

ABHINAY. How can you understand?

PINKIE. I do.

*Pinkie looks away and walks to her car. She turns
around and looks at Abhinay.*

When I was small, I took my time to learn to walk . . . I
remember my father. Every morning he would put me down
on the floor and stand in front of me with his arms wide open.
When I walked to him he would hug me. If I crawled to him
he would move away . . . *(Her eyes going moist.)* When he
died . . . I couldn't walk. I refused to walk because . . . he
wasn't there . . . any more.

Abhinay looks at her with new eyes.

You see. I do understand.

Abhinay goes closer to her. Abhinay kisses her gently.

(Patting him on the cheek.) Abhinay . . . I did learn to walk
. . . When are you going to start?

*Pinkie gets into her car leaving a very thoughtful
Abhinay.*

Cut to:

Interior. Night. Swarnalatha's living room.

*Mr Shastri walks in through the main door to find
Swarnalatha crouched on the sofa. Swarnalatha looks
at him tearfully.*

SWARNALATHA. I just couldn't go.

Mr Shastri sits next to Swarnalatha.

MR SHASTRI. He needs you.

SWARNALATHA. Why?

MR SHASTRI. He is a musician. And so are you.

SWARNALATHA. You never . . .

*Swarnalatha cries softly. Mr Shastri holds her in his
arms as she sobs.*

Fade out.

Exterior. Morning. Marketplace.

*Swarnalatha is buying flowers, coconuts and puts them
in her bag. She walks away from the market.*

Cut to:

Exterior. Day. A part of the village.

Flashback. Music. Subjective shot of little Abhinay walking through the fields, looking for something or somebody.

The scene ends with present day Swarnalatha startled at seeing Abhinay. Abhinay has his duffel bag with him.

ABHINAY. You let me down!

Swarnalatha is flustered by this direct accusation.

SWARNALATHA. I–I am sorry but I am helpless. There are some things I can't do even if I wanted to . . .

Swarnalatha begins to walk. Abhinay follows her.

ABHINAY *(sighing).* It's the same with me. *(After a while.)* I can't play without your voice.

SWARNALATHA. You can find another Carnatic singer . . .

ABHINAY. It's not just that!

SWARNALATHA *(stopping).* Then what is it?

ABHINAY. I don't know. All I know is that I want you in the group.

SWARNALATHA. But I . . .

ABHINAY. You don't have to say anything now. I will wait. Think about it. But remember, I am waiting for you to sing for me. I know you will. You want to sing. And I can help you fulfil your ambition. I am not leaving the village till you agree.

Abhinay turns around and walks away. Swarnalatha watches him.

Cut to:

Exterior. Day. Outside Abhinay's village home.

Abhinay walks to his front door. The door is locked. He notices a woman's footwear. He goes around the corner of the house and enters through the back door.

Cut to:

Exterior. Day. By the riverside.

Mr Shastri and Swarnalatha are seated by the river opposite a poojari who is guiding them through the whole ritual. Poojari chants the mantras and stops to ask for the name and gotram.

POOJARI. Name of the deceased and *gotram*.

MR SHASTRI. Madhavan, *gotram* Kashyapasa.

The poojari continues with the ritual using the name.

SWARNALATHA. Vaishnavi.

The poojari stops and looks at Swarnalatha.

Vaishnavi.

MR SHASTRI *(to the poojari)*. Add one more name—Vaishnavi.

POOJARI. Relation?

(No response.)

How was she related to your family?

Mr Shastri looks at Swarnalatha. She does not respond.

Oh. I will say sister . . . And her *gotram*.

Swarnalatha does not respond.

MR SHASTRI. We don't know. Use the same *gotram* as my son's.

The poojari looks at them warily and chants using both names. Swarnalatha is lost in thought as the ceremony progresses. We pan to see Abhinay not too far away with moist eyes, looking at Swarnalatha as he puts the rice dumpling into the river.

Fade out.

Interior. Day. Mrs Kapoor's boutique.

Mrs Kapoor is flattering a customer as usual. Pinkie is a little distracted.

MRS KAPOOR. . . . It's just the right colour for your complexion. It makes you look so much fairer, don't you think so Pinkie?

PINKIE. Huh?

MRS KAPOOR. Pinkie, dear. Doesn't Mrs Naidu look fairer in this fabulous creation?

PINKIE. Yes. She does.

The phone rings.

MRS KAPOOR. Could you get that please? *(Turning her attention on to her customer.)* Now, why don't you step in and . . .

PINKIE *(on the phone).* Hello?

Pinkie is surprised as she recognizes the caller's voice.

Yes . . . It's okay.

Intercut:

Interior. Day. Swarnalatha's living room.

Swarnalatha is a bit hesitant with what she wants to say.

SWARNALATHA. I hope one day you will understand why I . . .

PINKIE. I was meaning to call you too. Just to let you know, that it's okay.

SWARNALATHA *(after a while).* Thank you. I want to help you. And Abhinay.

PINKIE. Looks like we all want to help each other but don't know how.

SWARNALATHA. You really want the group to succeed, don't you?

PINKIE. More than anything else.

SWARNALATHA. Because you like to sing or . . . because of Abhinay.

PINKIE. Well . . . a bit of both I guess.

SWARNALATHA. How long have you been singing?

PINKIE. Oh I don't know, ever since I was a child but . . .

SWARNALATHA. Then it won't be too difficult.

PINKIE. What?

SWARNALATHA. To teach you Carnatic singing.

Pinkie takes a while to think about it.

PINKIE. Okay.

SWARNALATHA. So, when would you like to start?

PINKIE. Depends.

SWARNALATHA. On what?

PINKIE. On how long it takes me to get there.

Pinkie hangs up, just as her mother comes out of the dressing room. The customer leaves without buying anything.

MRS KAPOOR. Oh damn! You weren't much help. Now I want you to rush these clothes to Mrs Khanna and . . .

PINKIE. Mom. I won't be able to help with the boutique for a while.

MRS KAPOOR. I don't believe it! Why?

PINKIE. I have other important things to do.

MRS KAPOOR. More important than the boutique? More important than your mother?

PINKIE. Oh Mom be reasonable.

MRS KAPOOR. If there is anything that has kept us going, it's the boutique. How do you think I paid for your education?

PINKIE. I am not working here any more Mom.

Pinkie leaves the boutique. Mrs Kapoor follows.

Cut to:

Interior. Day. A basement parking lot.

Pinkie goes to her car, followed by Mrs Kapoor.

MRS KAPOOR. Pinkie, I need you. I can't handle this by myself.

PINKIE. There is a whole world outside your boutique.

MRS KAPOOR. Don't preach to me about the world outside the boutique!

Pinkie walks away.

Pinkie, help me! You are all I have.

PINKIE. And you are doing all this for me, I know. Mom, I have helped you enough. Now I want to do something that will help both of us.

MRS KAPOOR. Which is?

PINKIE. Helping those people in the village.

Mrs Kapoor softens.

(Going to her mom.) Mom. You owe it to yourself too. Let me go.

Mrs Kapoor looks at her daughter.

You can do a lot. If you want to.

Pinkie gives her a hug, gets into the car and drives away. Mrs Kapoor is lost in thought.

Cut to:

Exterior. Day. The countryside.

The car moves past the frame. The sun lights up the countryside with a warm glow.

Cut to:

Exterior. Day. Outside Abhinay's village home.

A hand knocks on the door. Abhinay's father opens it. He is taken aback at the visitor. Swarnalatha speaks to him matter of fact.

SWARNALATHA. Is Abhinay here?

Before he can respond, Abhinay appears.

Please come to my house in one hour.

ABHINAY'S FATHER *(beginning to protest).* Now, you can't expect him to . . .

SWARNALATHA. And bring your mother's violin.

Abhinay's father is stunned into silence.

ABHINAY. I'll be there.

Abhinay goes in.

SWARNALATHA *(to his father).* I can teach him raga. I can teach him tala. Let us see whether he has inherited some bhava from his mother.

Swarnalatha walks away, leaving a stunned father.

Cut to:

Exterior. Day. Outside the village.

We see Pinkie's car approaching the bridge. The car crosses the bridge and we see Appa Rau and his buffalo. Appa Rau sees Pinkie's car drive by and shakes his head knowingly.

Cut to:

Interior. Day. Swarnalatha's living room.

Swarnalatha makes Pinkie and Abhinay do a prayer to an idol of goddess Saraswati and to Lord Ganesh. They sit in front of her. Abhinay is poised with his violin. Swarnalatha sings the basic notes of a simple raga. Abhinay follows it on his violin. Pinkie repeats the notes. Swarnalatha sings a traditional Saraswati or Ganesh sthotram. This accompanied by Abhinay on the violin and Pinkie following Swarnalatha but with a more Western voice than hers.

Montage.

Slow dissolves. Under the song. Abhinay playing the violin. Pinkie referring to the lyrics from a book. Swarnalatha's hand as it taps the rhythm on her thigh. Pinkie following the rhythm the same way. From Swarnalatha's POV—Abhinay playing the violin, cuts to Vaishnavi playing the violin. Pinkie leaving for the city in the evening. Abhinay at night playing the violin in front of his mother's photograph. Pinkie arriving the next morning. More singing lessons. Appa Rau giving them fresh milk. (Note: In this montage we see Pinkie slowly wear more traditional clothes. Abhinay too wears a dhoti. Some shots of Abhinay and Pinkie walking by the river in traditional clothes. Mr Shastri will also figure in this montage. Swarnalatha will offer some valuable insight into the Carnatic style).

Cut to:

Interior. Day. Abhinay's village home.

Abhinay is pacing with a phone in his hand, waiting . . .

ABHINAY. Ya . . . This is about a loan . . . No it's not a housing loan . . . It's for a concert . . . ya, you heard right . . . well, a music concert . . . stop laughing . . . Oh you are coughing, I am sorry I thought you were . . . Wait. I can offer a collateral . . . my apartment . . . Fine I will come over with the papers—tomorrow? . . . What time? . . . Sure. Thanks.

His father overhears this conversation.

ABHINAY'S FATHER. Do you think you will get back all that money? From a music concert?

ABHINAY. Yes. It will come back to me.

ABHINAY'S FATHER. And if it doesn't?

ABHINAY. It will. I know . . .

ABHINAY'S FATHER. If it doesn't come back, you will return to my home and fulfil your duties as a son.

ABHINAY. I am so sure it will, I can even agree to those terms.

Abhinay heads towards his room. He turns around to face his father.

You must have said that to my mother too . . . fulfil your duties. But I am certain my mother didn't question you about your role as a husband or father. Neither will I.

He goes in.

ABHINAY'S FATHER. I brought you up! Not your mother! She never cared for you, she never cared for me! I knew on my wedding night that she didn't love me! She only cared for that woman and her music!

Abhinay comes out with his duffel bag.

And now, you!

Abhinay leaves.

Cut to:

Exterior. Day. Outside a city building.

We see the logo of a bank. Abhinay walks out, looks around and lets out a deep breath taking in the city. He takes out his cell phone as he walks away . . .

Cut to:

Exterior. Day. Country road.

We see Mrs Kapoor driving with Abhinay, Munna and Balaji.

Cut to:

Exterior. Day. A part of the village.

We see Mrs Kapoor driving into the village.

Cut to:

Exterior. Day. A part of the village.

Pinkie and Appa Rau are having a chat. Mrs Kapoor in the car passes them by. She comes to a halt and reverses.

PINKIE. Mummy!

They get out of the car.

MRS KAPOOR. Oh Pinkie darling. Just look at you!

PINKIE. What are you doing here Mom?

ABHINAY. I just got her to drive us here. We are doing a concert!

PINKIE. A concert!

MRS KAPOOR. Abhinay told me all. We are going to make you rock! I am taking advance bookings faster than I can sell clothes!

Appa Rau looks on.

APPA RAU. What is that? Her hair is like your hair Annapoorna!

BALAJI. Hey man! Look at all that shit on the walls!

MRS KAPOOR. Nonsense. I love that ethnic look. It will be the rage in the city in a year.

PINKIE. What are you guys doing here?

ABHINAY. We need to rehearse. Right here.

MRS KAPOOR. Now you people run along and practise while I soak in the atmosphere a bit before I leave.

Appa Rau and his buffalo are now really close to Mrs Kapoor. She looks at the buffalo warily.

Er–not too much atmosphere. Just a wee bit . . .

BALAJI. Come on man. Where's the auntie? She is not getting out of this one, is she?

Abhinay looks at Pinkie.

ABHINAY. She is. It's Pinkie—Priyanka who will sing the Carnatic sections.

Munna is staring at a village belle who is bending over to pick up some dung on the ground. Abhinay turns Munna's face away from the belle and leads him away.

Come on, let's rap. *(To Munna.)* That's the real stuff, not a plastic dummy!

Pinkie looks at her mother.

PINKIE *(smiling).* I don't know what the hell you are up to. But I am glad you came.

Pinkie suddenly hugs her mother tightly and runs to join Abhinay and the others. Mrs Kapoor looks on for a while before being aware that Appa Rau and his buffalo are right next to her.

MRS KAPOOR. Er—maybe you can help.

APPA RAU. Would you like some milk? Fresh milk from Annapoorna.

MRS KAPOOR. Who?

APPA RAU. My buffalo, Annapoorna.

MRS KAPOOR. Oh. No thank you. *(Patting the buffalo with great trepidation.)* Er–no offence meant. Actually, I am looking for some weavers. I hear there are some in this village.

Cut to:

Interior/Exterior. Day. Swarnalatha's living room. Backyard.

Balaji, Munna have brought some of their equipment.

SWARNALATHA. Stop! I am not going to have all that noise in my house!

PINKIE. But auntie, we must practise with you.

SWARNALATHA. I told you I am not singing!

ABHINAY. It's only a recording! I could record your track right here in the village!

SWARNALATHA. No! And take those noisemakers out of my house.

Cut to:

Exterior. Day. Another part of the village.

Mrs Kapoor is walking along with Appa Rau and his buffalo. She is clearly uncomfortable in her high heels walking on a muddy road.

MRS KAPOOR. How much further? Ow!

Mrs Kapoor twists her ankle.

APPA RAU. Madam, why don't you remove those circus shoes?

MRS KAPOOR. I can't walk any more. What do I do? Help me!

Mrs Kapoor puts an arm around Appa Rau. He is clearly embarrassed.

APPA RAU. Annapoorna! Look that side! *(They walk for a while.)* *(Pleading.)* Madam! The house is here. Please Madam, walk properly. I am a respectable man with grandchildren. I will take your leave now.

MRS KAPOOR. How will I get back? No. You can't leave me here! Wait.

Cut to:

Exterior. Day. A field.

A whole group of villagers are staring at something. We see that they are staring at Balaji and Munna. One child points to Munna.

CHILD 1. Look! That is Michael Jackson.

The other child points to Balaji.

CHILD 2. No, no! That is Michael Jackson.

They set up their instruments. Balaji and Munna start tuning their instruments. The birds on the field fly away making a racket. The villagers laugh.

VILLAGER. Let them think they are playing music. Their noise will keep the birds away from our grains!

The villagers laugh louder. Munna is staring at the village belle who is gawking at this strange bunch. Abhinay gives the cue on his violin.

Cut to:

Exterior. Day. Outside the weaver's hut.

Appa Rau is sitting on his haunches with his buffalo beside him. Mrs Kapoor's voice is heard from inside.

MRS KAPOOR *(off-screen)*. Fabulous! Oh this one is exquisite!

APPA RAU *(to his buffalo)*. See. Remember what my father said? He said it in front of you only. Never trust a city person or a woman. She is both.

Cut to:

Interior. Day. Weaver's house.

Some old women have gathered expectantly around Mrs Kapoor who is examining some woven fabrics. There is an old handloom in the background. The old woman who had cursed Pinkie in the accident scene is next to Mrs Kapoor.

OLD WOMAN. This one sari will cost you three hundred rupees.

MRS KAPOOR. Nonsense!

OLD WOMAN. Madam, we are all poor people. Okay give us what you think is best.

MRS KAPOOR *(pretending to be businesslike)*. Well, if you change the border the way I want it, I could give you seven hundred for a sari. Not one rupee more.

All the women can hardly contain their excitement.

OLD WOMAN. Yes. Yes Madam! You tell us what you want. You will look very beautiful in this sari Madam.

MRS KAPOOR. Don't flatter me! That's the same line I use in the city. It's not for me.

OLD WOMAN. Er—one sari is enough, Madam?

Mrs Kapoor looks around and sees a photograph of a middle-aged man. The photograph has a garland around it.

MRS KAPOOR. How many can all of you make in a month?

Cut to:

Exterior. Day. A field.

Pinkie has started on her Carnatic scales. Balaji and Munna get carried away and start jamming wildly. The crowds are even more amused by this.

Cut to:

Exterior. Day. Outside the weaver's hut.

Mrs Kapoor comes limping out of the hut followed by the women who are helping her. The women are all smiles.

MRS KAPOOR *(to Appa Rau)*. Kind Sir, now if you will assist me back to my car.

APPA RAU *(looking at the other women)*. Madam, you can ask these women to help you.

MRS KAPOOR. Why? Don't you want to help me?

OLD WOMAN. Appa Rau, help her. We will all help you Madam. Come.

Cut to:

Exterior. Day. A field.

The band have finished their song. The villagers are heckling.

VILLAGER. Useless fellows!

ANOTHER VILLAGER. What is this music? Some city monkeys singing together, taught by a village sparrow.

VILLAGER. That sparrow left her baby and went to sing!

Suddenly one of the villagers notices Swarnalatha. Swarnalatha is hurt by this remark. Abhinay notices this.

ABHINAY *(angry)*. Keep quiet! All of you!

There is a silence. Suddenly, Mrs Kapoor's voice is heard.

MRS KAPOOR *(off-screen)*. Yoo hoo!

They all turn in the direction of the voice. Mrs Kapoor is riding on the buffalo led by Appa Rau followed by the woman. The villagers start laughing again. Pinkie shakes her head as she looks at her mother.

Yoo hoo! Anyone for a ride?

While the villagers are laughing, Swarnalatha leaves. Abhinay looks at her leaving. As Swarnalatha leaves, she sees Abhinay's father.

ABHINAY'S FATHER. They are laughing at my son, because of you!

SWARNALATHA. They are laughing at your son today. Tomorrow they will salute him for his talents. But then he will be Vaishnavi's son.

Swarnalatha leaves. Abhinay's father looks on in despair.

Fade out.

Interior. Night. Abhinay's village home.

Abhinay is practising on the violin. Abhinay's father comes in and sits down.

ABHINAY'S FATHER *(interrupting)*. Very good. Very good.

Abhinay looks at his father and gets back to practising.

FATHER. Just like your mother. But . . .

Abhinay stops playing.

ABHINAY. But?

ABHINAY'S FATHER. Is it enough to make you famous?

ABHINAY. If she had lived she may have been a famous musician.

FATHER. Is Swarnalatha a famous musician?

ABHINAY. She doesn't want to be famous.

FATHER. You are very innocent. You are going to lose all your money, and she is not going to help you when you go knocking on her door.

Abhinay is disturbed by this remark.

Cut to:

Interior. Day. Swarnalatha's living room.

Swarnalatha is teaching a complicated raga to Pinkie. Abhinay walks in. Swarnalatha is completely engrossed in trying to get Pinkie to sing it correctly. She doesn't notice Abhinay. Abhinay makes some noise opening his violin case. Swarnalatha without even looking at him tells him 'Shhh'. Abhinay walks out leaving his violin behind. Swarnalatha continues to persist with Pinkie, both of them oblivious of Abhinay's entry and exit.

Cut to:

Exterior. Day. Outside Swarnalatha's house. Main door. Yard.

Abhinay sits under a tree.

Cut to:

Interior. Day. Swarnalatha's living room.

Swarnalatha keeps pushing Pinkie. Pinkie finally gets it. Swarnalatha is pleased.

PINKIE. Auntie, I can never sing like you though.

SWARNALATHA. Of course you can. You just need more practice.

The two women smile at each other, bonding in a special way. Swarnalatha notices the violin. She goes to the violin and picks it up. She sits down again and fingers the violin.

This belonged to Abhinay's mother . . .

Pinkie looks at the violin.

Sindu Bhairavi.

PINKIE. What?

SWARNALATHA. That is the name of the raga I am going to teach you now. It's a morning raga. It's—very special to me. It was Vaishnavi's favourite raga. It was the raga I was planning to sing . . . *(Collecting herself.)* Please note down the ascending and descending scale.

Pinkie takes out her notebook. Swarnalatha starts to sing it. Pinkie is making notes in her book. Swarnalatha plays the scale on the violin.

Cut to:

Exterior. Day. Outside Swarnalatha's house. Yard.

The strains of the violin drift into the yard where Abhinay has fallen asleep. We close in on Abhinay.

Cut to:

Flashback. Day. Outside Swarnalatha's house. Main door. Yard. Jump cuts.

The young Abhinay running towards a window. He bangs on the window. The raga continues to play in the background. The young Abhinay looking through

the window. The young Abhinay yells 'Mummy'
through the window. Swarnalatha continues to sing as
she comes to the window and shuts it. He falls down.
The young Abhinay on the bus, separated from his
mother as Vaishnavi reaches out to save Swarnalatha's
child.

Cut to:

Present. Day. Outside Swarnalatha's house. Main door. Yard.

Abhinay wakes up with a start. The raga continues.
Abhinay rushes to the main door. It is open. He goes
in.

Cut to:

Interior. day. Swarnalatha's backyard.

Intercut with the flashback, where the little boy finally
comes in to the same room to see his mother playing
the violin.

In present time Swarnalatha is playing the raga, still in
a daze. Abhinay comes running in.

ABHINAY. That's it!

Swarnalatha stops playing.

That's the raga I want! That's what I was looking for, don't
you see! *(To Pinkie.)* My mother never played that for me! She
only played it for her. *(Pointing to Swarnalatha)*!

Swarnalatha is hurt at this remark. Pinkie is shocked.

PINKIE. Abhinay!

Swarnalatha gives a sad smile.

SWARNALATHA. Yes. You are right. I took your mother away
from you.

PINKIE. No!

ABHINAY. I didn't mean it that way, I . . . I want you to sing
that! You have to!

SWARNALATHA. I am cursed!

Cut to:

Flashback. Day. Outside Abhinay's village home.

The strumming of the tanpura spills into this scene with her voice. We see Vaishnavi feeding Abhinay as a child. The young Swarnalatha runs to her gate and gestures to Vaishnavi to join her. Vaishnavi leaves her child after a peripheral wiping of his mouth, picks up her violin and rushes to Swarnalatha, running behind her.

Cut to:

Flashback. Day. Swarnalatha's living room.

A venerable old man is teaching Swarnalatha the morning raga. Vaishnavi is accompanying her on the violin. Swarnalatha's child is being looked after by Mr Shastri. Abhinay's father comes in with Abhinay. He leaves his son there and walks away. They continue to play.

Cut to:

Flashback. Day. Outside Swarnalatha's house. Main door.

Swarnalatha is dressed up and with her tanpura. Her son is throwing his food around. Mr Shastri can't control him.

SWARNALATHA. How can you let him do that?

MR SHASTRI. Look, if he is in my care, I will look after him my way!

SWARNALATHA. You can't! I will take care of him. I will take him with me.

Cut to:

Flashback. The accident in slow motion or step freeze.

Swarnalatha and her son. Vaishnavi and young Abhinay get on the bus. Mr Sharma and Abhinay's father help them on. The bus leaves the station. Swarnalatha's son doing the pattern on the window. The accident. The bus keeling over.

Cut to:

Exterior. Day. After the accident.

The bodies have been retrieved and shrouded. The wind blows at Swarnalatha's sari to reveal a bandaged abdomen and bruised arm.

MR SHASTRI. You killed my son!

ABHINAY'S FATHER *(to the other villagers).* These lives were lost because of that woman!

Close in on Mr Shastri's face as he looks at his wife, blaming her for the loss of their son.

Cut to:

Present. Day. Swarnalatha's living room.

We see a remorseful Mr Shastri listening to the story. Pinkie is moved by this story. Her eyes are moist. Swarnalatha is in a daze.

PINKIE. It's not your fault.

SWARNALATHA. Then whose fault is it?

PINKIE. I . . . It's not your fault.

Swarnalatha gives a sad smile. Swarnalatha gets up.

SWARNALATHA. I wish you all the best. I won't give you my blessings. Since they would be more of a curse. But please believe me. I want you to be happy. I do.

ABHINAY. I–I am sorry. I didn't mean that . . .

Swarnalatha restrains him with a gesture while she walks away.

SWARNALATHA. Now if you will excuse me. *(Stops and looks at Pinkie.)* I have taught you enough. I have nothing else to give you.

Swarnalatha goes in, a tired old woman. Pinkie looks at Abhinay.

ABHINAY. I don't know why I said it. I didn't mean it.

PINKIE. You are wrong. You are both very wrong. There is something you ought to know.

ABHINAY. What is it?

Pinkie leaves taking Abhinay by the arm. They go in.

Cut to:

Interior. Day. Swarnalatha's living room.

PINKIE. Please auntie. There is something I ought to tell you.

Swarnalatha stops.

SWARNALATHA. Tell me.

PINKIE. Come with me, please.

Cut to:

Exterior. Day. Outside Swarnalatha's house.

After a while, Swarnalatha gets in to the car. Pinkie and Abhinay get in as well. Pinkie drives on. Pinkie presses the central lock system. Swarnalatha notices it.

PINKIE. First there is something I must do.

SWARNALATHA. What is it?

Abhinay looks at Pinkie.

PINKIE. I hope you will find it in you to forgive me.

Pinkie puts the car in top gear and speeds towards the bridge. Swarnalatha realizes that she is going over the bridge. Her panic attack starts.

SWARNALATHA. No! Please! Stop the car!

PINKIE. I just want to show you that it is not your fault!

ABHINAY. What are you doing?

PINKIE. To show you that there is no curse on you!

Swarnalatha holds on to Pinkie to prevent her from driving further.

SWARNALATHA. Stop it! Stop the car! We will all die!

ABHINAY *(holding Swarnalatha back)*. Calm down! Stop the car!

*Swarnalatha looks outside and sees the bridge
approaching. A truck passes by in full speed.*

SWARNALATHA *(gasping for breath)*. No!

*Swarnalatha watches in horror as they cross the bridge.
Her head spins. The car reaches the other side of the
bridge and Pinkie pulls over. Abhinay opens the door
for Swarnalatha. Swarnalatha rushes out gasping for
air. She runs to a tree and sits down, not looking at the
bridge. Pinkie follows her.*

PINKIE. You see. Nothing happened. It is not a curse on you! I
knew that nothing would happen, because you are not to
blame. Look at me please . . . Pinkie holds Swarnalatha so that
they are looking into each other's eyes. Abhinay joins them on
the edge. It was my father . . . He was driving the car.

*Swarnalatha is still dazed but is listening to Pinkie
now. Abhinay stands still at this revelation.*

He . . . my father . . . was a very unhappy man. I—was too
small then to know that. I thought he was happy. He loved
me. He really loved me. I know that. But he was unhappy
. . . and he took to drink . . . *(Pleading now.)* I know that if
he were alive he would beg for your forgiveness . . . Please try
to forgive him . . . He made a big mistake. He shouldn't have
been driving but . . . he did . . . If you cannot forgive him, at
least don't blame yourself for what happened . . .

*Pinkie looks on at Swarnalatha, waiting for a response.
Swarnalatha slowly stands up and walks towards the
bridge. She sees the bridge in a new light. She takes in
a deep breath. Pinkie comes closer to her awaiting
forgiveness. She hugs Pinkie. Swarnalatha breaks away
from Pinkie and goes to Abhinay.*

SWARNALATHA. It doesn't matter whose fault it was. The truth
is that your mother is gone and so is my son. Can any force
bring them back to us? Can any force bring back her father?
No.

Abhinay looks at her fighting his tears.

SWARNALATHA. So, go to the city and don't think about these things. Go. *(To Pinkie.)* You have my blessings, if that is what you want.

Swarnalatha slowly begins to walk back home. Abhinay follows with his gaze, lost in thought. Pinkie comes to Abhinay.

PINKIE. Abhinay–I wanted to tell you but . . .

Abhinay looks at Pinkie and then at the diminishing figure of Swarnalatha.

ABHINAY. It's okay . . . It's—not your fault . . . It just happened . . . it just happened to your father . . . It's okay.

Pinkie is overwhelmed by this remark. She moves closer to him. Abhinay opens his arms out and they embrace. We open out to see them standing at one end of the bridge in a tight embrace. At the other end of the bridge is Swarnalatha looking at them. She turns and begins to walk away.

Dissolve to:

Interior/Exterior. Day. Backyard of Swarnalatha.

Mr Shastri takes a letter to the backyard where Swarnalatha is working on her garden.

MR SHASTRI. A letter for you. From Abhinay.

Swarnalatha continues with her gardening.

SWARNALATHA. Read it.

Mr Shastri opens the envelope. It is a card with a mother and child. Mr Shastri takes the card and holds it in front of Swarnalatha. Swarnalatha tries to take the card but her hands are soiled. Mr Shastri opens the card and reads out.

MR SHASTRI *(reading).* 'You are wrong. There are forces that can bring back your son and my mother to us. I hope one day I can help you understand how proud your son would be if you

sang for him. I don't know how to make you see that, but I
will keep trying.' *(Taking out some tickets.)* He has invited us
to his concert. Do you . . .?

> *Mr Shastri stops mid sentence when he sees . . .*
> *Swarnalatha cries silently. Mr Shastri gently puts the*
> *card on the plant she was tending to.*

Cut to:

Exterior. Day. Outside the village.

> *Mr Shastri is driving Swarnalatha across the bridge.*
> *Swarnalatha is joyous. They drive past the countryside.*
> *They enter the city. Swarnalatha looks on at the city*
> *scape in wonderment. Like a little child, pointing out*
> *to big buildings.*

Cut to:

Exterior. Evening. Outside the auditorium.

> *Mrs Kapoor drives in with Rajeev.*

RAJEEV. I thought we were going over to your place!

MRS KAPOOR. Later, darling. A little bit of music won't do you
any harm. Would it? Surely you can do that for me! No?

> *We see a poster of the group. Rajeev notices the*
> *poster.*

RAJEEV. Oh no! Not him!

> *There is a crowd of young people coming in.*
> *Mrs Kapoor is taking Rajeev right in.*

MRS KAPOOR. Here you are. You know Priyanka is my
daughter, Pinkie . . . Well, I can't call her Pinkie any more I
suppose . . .

RAJEEV. Oh! What did I do to deserve this?

> Cut to:

Interior. Night. Auditorium.

> *The crowds begin to take their seats. People are yelling*
> *for their friends. It is quite thin.*

Cut to:

Interior. Night. Stage.

The curtains are drawn. The equipment is all in place. Abhinay is pacing up and down, a little nervous. He peeps through the wings into the auditorium. Mrs Kapoor comes to him.

MRS KAPOOR. You better rock mister. Rajeev is here. You only have this one chance.

ABHINAY. I wish there was more of a crowd.

MRS KAPOOR. Don't worry about that.

Abhinay looks out.

Cut to:

Auditorium

There are a stream of villagers coming in.

Cut to:

Interior. Night. Stage.

ABHINAY. I can't believe it. The entire village is here!

MRS KAPOOR. Well, I did sell a few tickets while I was there. Where is Pinkie? Oops. I better rush. There is Rajeev slinking away.

Mrs Kapoor leaves. Abhinay looks out.

Cut to:

Cutaway. Auditorium.

There are two empty seats right up in front. We see Abhinay's father along with the villagers in the front row. Abhinay looks at the entrance. Abhinay sees Mr Shastri, alone, walking down the aisle and takes his seat. The one next to him is empty. Abhinay is disappointed. Pinkie comes on stage from the wings.

PINKIE. Looking for someone?

ABHINAY. Huh? . . . My father is there but . . .

PINKIE. Turn around.

Abhinay turns and looks beyond the wings. Backstage in the wings is Swarnalatha. Abhinay rushes to her beaming.

ABHINAY. I am glad you could come!

PINKIE. Why not? She is our guru after all.

ABHINAY. Yes.

Swarnalatha is a little overwhelmed. Abhinay bends down and touches her feet. So does Pinkie. A Stage Manager walks up with a walkie talkie.

STAGE MANAGER. Positions on stage please. We are ready to start.

Stage Manager walks away speaking into the walkie talkie.

PINKIE *(to Abhinay)*. You better hurry. I'll be with you in a moment.

ABHINAY *(leaving)*. Right. *(To Swarnalatha.)* Do stay after the performance.

PINKIE. We will take them out to dinner. Now go on.

Abhinay goes on stage. Pinkie looks at Swarnalatha.

Cut to:

Interior. Night. Stage.

Abhinay enters stage. Balaji and Munna are already in place. Balaji does a good luck clap with Abhinay and Munna. Abhinay checks out the violin on the stage.

Cut to:

Interior. Night. Backstage.

A bell goes off.

SWARNALATHA *(to Pinkie)*. I won't be able to stay for long after the show so . . .

Swarnalatha makes to leave.

SWARNALATHA. Auntie . . .

Swarnalatha turns around.

STAGE MANAGER. Priyanka, please take your position.

PINKIE *(dismissing him)*. A minute.

STAGE MANAGER. You have less than a minute.

Pinkie goes to Swarnalatha.

PINKIE. This was your dream, wasn't it? To sing in the city?

SWARNALATHA *(smiling weakly)*. You fulfil it for me.

PINKIE. No. I can't.

Another bell goes off.

STAGE MANAGER. Madam, please!

PINKIE. I cannot fulfil it.

Swarnalatha turns to exit.

No, wait! You gave up a lot for your music. Now is your chance.

SWARNALATHA. What do you mean?

PINKIE. The first number we play is called Morning Raga. It is the raga you wanted to sing! The one you taught me.

SWARNALATHA. Go ahead and sing it.

PINKIE. Don't do it for anyone else. Not because I am asking you, not for Abhinay, not for your son or anyone else. Do it because you want to!

The third bell goes off.

Please!

STAGE MANAGER *(coming to Pinkie)*. I will have to insist you get on that stage now! *(To Swarnalatha.)* Madam, please take your place, we are starting.

PINKIE. You decide your place.

Abhinay gestures to Pinkie to come on stage. Pinkie walks to the edge of stage. She turns around and looks at Swarnalatha. Swarnalatha remains frozen as she digests what Pinkie has just said. Pinkie walks on stage as the curtains open. Balaji gives a roll of the drums. They are greeted with a loud applause. Just as Abhinay is about to cue them in, Pinkie gestures to him to stop. There is an awkward silence. Pinkie looks at Swarnalatha. Swarnalatha makes a decision. Swarnalatha walks towards the stage. Pinkie is relieved. Abhinay looks on. Swarnalatha touches the stage with her hand in salutation.

The lights go off and a follow spot comes on Swarnalatha. One stays on Pinkie as she gestures to Swarnalatha to take her place. Swarnalatha walks slowly to the mike. She looks at the audience. She is truly overwhelmed to be there. It is a dream come true. When she takes her place Pinkie makes an announcement. Swarnalatha begins with the scale of raga Sindu Bhairavi, going into intricate patterns. Rajeev sits up. Mrs Kapoor is pleased. There is a warm applause to this. Swarnalatha is touched.

SWARNALATHA. Thank you. It has been a difficult raga for me to learn. Twenty years is a long time. Music is a never ending journey.

Abhinay and Pinkie look on.

It has been my dream to sing for an audience such as you. But . . . *(Finding it difficult to get the words.)* tonight, I will sing this song for my son who, like my music, has returned after a very long journey. *(Looking at Abhinay.)* Abhinay, I sing this raga for you—my son.

Another spotlight picks up Abhinay who is so touched by this tribute. Swarnalatha begins to sing once again. Abhinay picks up his violin and begins to play. Pinkie joins in on the English lyrics. The three are lit in individual follow spots. Swarnalatha looks at Abhinay as he plays. A flashback of Swarnalatha imagining singing this song to her son. They are playing by the river. Abhinay when he plays the violin . . . A flashback where Abhinay imagines his mother Vaishnavi singing and playing with him. Pinkie sings and imagines (flashback) her father rocking her to sleep. The three of them come together in one spot. Flashback of Swarnalatha and her son, Vaishnavi and young Abhinay running in slow motion across the bridge. The song ends to a thunderous applause. They take their bows and look at each other. The music picks up as the credits roll.

We see Rajeev enthralled by the performance. The villagers are whistling for Abhinay. Abhinay's father is touched. The villagers carrying Abhinay outside the auditorium. Swarnalatha and Pinkie embrace. Abhinay and Swarnalatha embrace controlling their tears.

UMA AND THE FAIRY QUEEN

A Radio Play

A Note on the Play

Played out against the backdrop of a hot and bustling Bangalore, a third case, for Uma Rao, intrepid sleuth and wife of Suresh Rao, the Police Superintendent.

And the play's the thing—in this instance a special production of Shakespeare's *A Midsummer Night's Dream* put on to mark Independence Day. Things go horribly wrong when Michael Forsyth, the leading actor playing Oberon is kidnapped, only to reappear just in time to play his part. But he disappears again before the end, and is found shot dead in the greenroom by Nila Ahmed his famous Pakistani wife and co-star. To make matters worse, it's rumoured that their marriage is on the rocks.

Uma Rao is intrigued by the whole affair, gets to know Nila, finds out that she's been married before and suspects that there's more to this than either political intrigue or marital problems. It seems to Uma as she tries to sleep through the long hot night, after her husband has once again been berating her because she has no children, that the clue lies somewhere in the play, and a certain line 'I do but beg a little changeling boy' goes round and round in her head.

With the help of Liam Tate, British Cultural Ambassador, Uma outwits her husband as usual, and gradually unravels the mystery of why Michael Forsyth was killed, although she is left finally with her own very personal dilemma.

Jeremy Mortimer
(Jeremy Mortimer is Executive Producer,
BBC Radio Drama.)

Uma and the Fairy Queen was first broadcast on 16 August 2003 at 3 p.m. on BBC Radio 4. The play was directed by Mark Beeby. Cast for first production:

UMA	Priyanga Elan
SURESH	Ajay Chabra
NILA	Souad Faress
FEROZ	Akbar Kurtha
MALIK	Kaleem Janjua
LIAM	Gerard McDermott
MICHAEL	Stephen Critchlow

Exterior. A busy street.

We hear the honks of impatient drivers as a car has stopped to pick up its passengers.

MICHAEL. Where are we going? Listen I have to be at the hall by six! Hey! Take it easy! Stop pushing me! Oh I say!

They get into the car. Slam of doors and they drive away.

Fade out. Credits.

Interior. Liam's home.

The doorbell goes off followed soon by a loud knocking on the door. Liam opens the door.

LIAM. Nila! What are you . . .? Are you all right.

NILA. Oh, Liam! Can I come in?

LIAM. Yes of course. Sit down and I will get you something to . . .

NILA. Liam!

They embrace. He kisses her.

LIAM. There! What is the matter? Some ruffian in the bazaar?

NILA. No. No! Oh I don't know how to tell you!

LIAM. Calm down. Let me fix you a drink and then you can tell me.

NILA. It's, it's Michael! I am so afraid, I don't know what to do! Liam, you are the only one I can turn to.

LIAM. Oh, Nila!

Fade to:

Interior. Malik's home.

MICHAEL. It was very silly of you to do that.

FEROZ. I don't care. I mean it. I will do it.

MICHAEL. Look, if you promise to behave, I won't find it necessary to report you.

FEROZ. That's what you would like, isn't it? To see me locked up safely so you can carry on with your life, not caring about what other people have had to go through to survive!

MICHAEL. Oh for God's sake! I have to go now. They will miss me and it will cause a panic, you know.

FEROZ. All right. I will let you go now. But don't say I didn't warn you.

MICHAEL. Look. Why don't we all meet in a more proper manner and sort things out?

FEROZ. No!

Cut to:

Interior. Car. Moving.

The noise from the cars, autorickshaws, scooters fade in and out as the car drives through a busy but clear road.

SURESH. Put up your window.

UMA. I can't bear the air conditioning.

SURESH. I want to talk to you.

A click of the button as Uma presses the power switch. The window slides up cutting off the noise instantly.

UMA. What is it?

SURESH. Just wanted to let you know that we are on high security alert. They caught some terrorists in Delhi.

UMA. Anything I can do?

SURESH. I want you to stop coming over to the police station and going through our files. I know you think you are smart especially after that Scotland Yard guy gave you a pat on the back.

UMA. You don't think I deserved it? Besides Charles didn't pat me on the back, he sent me a thank you note for helping him nab the man who murdered his sister.

SURESH. I don't want my superiors to think I give you classified information, that is all.

UMA. But you don't! Things would be a lot easier if you did.

SURESH *(sarcastic)*. You seem to be doing pretty well without my help anyway.

UMA. I think there are people who trust me enough to assist me with information . . .

SURESH. Oh give me a break! Everyone likes a pretty face! Do you really think they respect your intelligence? Those foreign cops, and all those diplomats you seem to enjoy socializing with?

UMA. I am looking forward to the play tonight. Please don't spoil it for me.

SURESH. You fancy yourself to be a detective do you?

UMA. Keep your eye on the road, Suresh.

SURESH. From now on I am keeping an eye on you. No more sleuthing around, understand?

UMA. The air conditioning is giving me a headache.

Uma presses the button. As the window slides down the noise from the traffic takes over once again.

Fade to:

Interior. A busy foyer.

There is a general buzz that accompanies a crowd in the foyer when the doors haven't been opened yet.

UMA. Is everything okay?

SURESH. Should be. We have a shortage of staff. Nowadays you can't take a chance with security. With all these foreigners around . . . We have enough on our hands as it is with crime in the city, now we have to provide protection to all these foreigners!

UMA. Softer. They might hear us. It's a special occasion. I think it was a nice gesture from the British Council.

SURESH. Bringing a Shakespeare company to mark our Independence Day! If you ask me, they only want to remind us that they ruled over us once.

UMA. Shh! It's a lovely play and a rare privilege to have such a famous theatre company from London perform in our home town. But something is wrong.

SURESH. What?

UMA. It's five past seven and they haven't opened the doors yet. They usually start on time.

> *The crowds swell and we hear Liam Tate's 'Pardon.*
> *Sorry' as he works his way towards Uma Rao.*

LIAM. Uma Rao?

UMA. Yes. Mr Tate?

LIAM. Yes! So pleased to meet you finally! Charles Montefiore speaks very highly of you.

UMA. Er–this is my husband Superintendent of Police Suresh Rao.

LIAM. Ah yes! . . .

UMA. Suresh this is Liam Tate, the British cultural ambassador to India.

SURESH. Hello.

LIAM. We have put you through a lot of trouble I know. Er . . . May I have a word with Uma in private if you don't mind. Uma?

UMA. Er . . .

SURESH. Sure. Excuse me.

UMA. What is it?

LIAM. Not here. In private. If that is possible . . . Follow me.

The noise from the crowds chatter seems to increase.

Hello—hello there—not right now I am busy . . . *(To Uma.)* Damn!

UMA. Why don't we go backstage?

LIAM. What a good idea! Let's . . .

UMA. Through this door and down the passage.

They open a creaky door that shuts loudly behind them. They walk down a passage. Their footsteps echo in the empty and large passage. So do their voices.

I know this hall very well, we did our school plays here and this is where we would hide from the teachers just before showtime, to scare them a bit . . .

LIAM. Oh I hope this too is just a prank that will be over with soon! We might as well talk here.

They stop.

UMA. What is it, Mr Tate?

LIAM. Michael has been kidnapped.

UMA. Michael Forsyth? . . . How do you know?

LIAM. It's pretty certain. His wife saw some men push him into a car.

UMA. Have you received any letter or phone call from . . .?

LIAM. No, and until we do I want this to remain confidential! I don't want our government to panic and start recalling all the British expats! That's the last thing I want after so many years of building bridges between our cultures. I need your advice, Uma.

UMA. How may I help you?

LIAM. Without Michael, we cannot perform. They don't have an understudy. How do we cancel the performance without creating too much of a suspicion? We need to keep the press out of this and I notice there are quite a few of them outside.

UMA. That shouldn't be too difficult. The main fuse for the stage lights are right here.

She opens the fuse box and yanks out the fuse.

LIAM. What on earth . . .?

UMA. Now you can announce that the stage lights have failed and nobody would suspect a thing. We'll blame it on the Bangalore Electric Supply. Everybody does.

LIAM. But won't the management call the electricity department and have them fix it right away?

UMA. Your faith in the Indian bureaucracy is touching Mr Tate. Now, I will keep this fuse right here. I hope you resolve this issue. Now, if I may be of assistance . . .

LIAM. Oh, that would help although I am not sure what you can do. We have to be discrete about it you understand.

UMA. All the more reason why you should seek my assistance and not my husband's.

LIAM. I hope it doesn't come to that.

UMA. One thing at a time. Can I meet his wife?

LIAM. She is in a bad way.

UMA. Understandable.

LIAM *(sighing)*. All right. She is in the greenroom.

They walk.

UMA. She is playing Titania, the fairy queen isn't she?

LIAM. Not tonight though.

UMA. I read a review at the British Library. The *Guardian* I think. Michael and she have received rave notices, haven't they?

They open a door.

LIAM. As the Fairy king and queen they certainly share a destructive chemistry on stage, like they do off it. Uma, I think you ought to know . . . Their marriage is falling apart. It's an open secret in London, but—it's not something they like to talk about.

UMA. I understand.

Liam knocks on a door.

NILA *(from within).* Go away!

LIAM. Nila. It's me, Liam. It's important.

After a while the door opens.

NILA. Have they found . . . his body? Tell me the truth.

LIAM. No, my dear, we don't know anything yet, but I would like you to meet Uma Rao. She is a detective of sorts.

NILA. A detective?

UMA. Of sorts. Let's just say, I have my uses in finding out the truth.

NILA. Oh . . . I don't know.

LIAM. There's no harm in talking to her.

NILA. All right. Come in. I am afraid the lights are out. There is just the emergency lamp.

LIAM. I will leave you two alone, while I make the announcement about the cancellation—owing to technical reasons. I will be with you shortly and we will do the best we can.

NILA. Thank you, Liam.

Liam leaves shutting the door.

UMA. Mrs Forsyth, I am so sorry.

NILA. Call me Nila. Everyone knows me as Nila Ahmed. Oh, I look ridiculous in this costume now! I might as well take it off. Could you please help me . . .

UMA. Yes of course. Let me.

Uma goes to Nila and helps her with the costume which is made of silk.

NILA. The last time I wore silk before this part came along was . . . We had a Christian wedding. Michael's parents insisted. Instead of a conventional gown, I wore a dazzling white silk gharara . . . I don't like our first scene. I don't like it at all . . . Tell me, are there many Pakistani's living here in Bangalore?

UMA. Why do you ask?

NILA. Oh, no particular reason. You know I am of Pakistani descent.

UMA. I know you were quite famous in Pakistan too, weren't you in a TV serial . . .?

NILA. Please! That is all behind me now. I–I didn't know the serial was shown here in India.

UMA. No it wasn't. I just happened to be visiting a friend in Pakistan and . . . read about it.

NILA. Look this is a trying time for me, and I really don't want to talk about all that, you understand?

UMA. Yes, I do. It must have been tough on your parents.

NILA. What?

UMA. The marriage?

NILA. With Michael? Oh. No, no. My parents were fine . . . No. It wasn't my parents at all. *(Changing the subject.)* This dress has been in far too many performances. I could ask for a replacement I know, but . . .

UMA. I am sure they would oblige.

NILA. I–I don't want them to think I am behaving like a star.

UMA. But you are. People are here to see you and Michael. Not for Shakespeare!

NILA. Well, I am sorry they will be disappointed. I feel awful.

UMA. It's not your fault.

NILA. It is! It is my fault!

UMA. Really? How?

NILA. I . . . I shouldn't have allowed Michael to wander off on his own. I saw them! I saw them push him into a taxi. I could see it all from my hotel balcony.

UMA. Did he receive any calls in his room?

NILA. None that I know of. And I would know. We were together all the time.

UMA. Did he make any calls?

Pause.

NILA. No. I don't think so. But who would he call apart from room service? Or the British Consulate. He doesn't know anyone in this city.

UMA. What did these people look like? The ones with him when they drove off in a taxi.

NILA. There were three of them. I–I can't remember what they looked like. About medium height . . . They all had beards . . . I think. Ow! I forgot about the safety pin on that sleeve! I . . . Oh! *(Nila breaks into sobs. After a while.)* He received a note. It simply said—I will kill you . . . I love him! I don't want another divorce!

The door is flung open.

Michael!!

There is a silence.

MICHAEL. I love you too, Nila.

NILA. Oh, Michael!

They embrace.

I love you. I love you.

UMA. Mr Forsyth, we really were worried . . .

NILA. I am sure he can explain everything after the performance. Now if you will excuse us Uma, quick! Get into your costume!

There is a flurry of activity.

UMA. Well, what can I say? Break a leg.

Uma shuts the door and opens the passage door and shuts it behind her. Uma's footsteps echo. She can hear their voices through a ventilation shaft.

MICHAEL. Oh for God's sake, Nila, listen to me. Don't you care?

NILA. Shut up! Just let me be!

MICHAEL. We will talk later. I am sure Liam would want to know the truth too.

Cut to:

Mendelsohn's music continues to play.

LIAM. Ladies and gentlemen! I am happy to announce that the electricity has been restored and we will, after all, have the performance tonight. Please be in your seats. We will begin shortly.

Music continues.

Interior. Inside the auditorium.

The music continues to play.

SURESH. What did he want from you that could be so important?

UMA. Oh, nothing at all. They were just concerned about the electricity and wanted me to speak to the electrician in Kannada. That's all.

SURESH. Such a fuss. They are so fussy, the English.

UMA. Liam Tate is Irish.

SURESH. Huh?

UMA. Oh never mind. You know I played Titania in my school production . . .

The music takes over.

Fade in:

Titania's entry. Music.

There is a mild applause at her entry. Shakespeare's dialogue between Oberon, played by Michael and Titania, played by Nila moves in and out of focus in this scene.

MICHAEL *(as Oberon).* Ill met by moonlight, proud Titania!

NILA *(as Titania).* What, jealous Oberon? Fairy, skip hence. I have forsworn his bed and company.

MICHAEL. Tarry, rash wanton! Am not I thy lord?

NILA. Then I must be thy lady. But I know when thou hast stolen away from Fairyland

And in the shape of Corin sat all day

Playing on pipes of corn, and versing love

To amorous Phillida. Why art thou here

Come from the farthest step of India

> *Laughter from the audience.*

But that forsooth, the bouncing Amazon,

Your buskined mistress and your warrior love,

To Theseus must be wedded?—And you come

To give their bed joy and prosperity.

MICHAEL. How canst thou thus, for shame, Titania, Glance at my credit with Hippolyta, Knowing I know thy love to Theseus?

> *We hear Suresh snoring.*

UMA *(whisper)*. Wake up.

NILA. These are the forgeries of jealousy!

SURESH *(waking up)*. Huh? Sorry. I am tired.

UMA. Try not to snore.

NILA. . . . And this same progeny of evils comes from our debate, from our dissension. We are their parents and original.

SURESH. Are you enjoying it?

UMA. I don't like this scene. I don't like it at all.

MICHAEL. Do you amend it, then! It lies in you. Why should Titania cross her Oberon? I do but beg a little changeling boy To be my henchman.

SURESH. Changeling?

UMA. A child. Secretly substituted by the fairies for the parents' real child.

NILA. Set your heart at rest. The fairy land buys not the child of me.

His mother was a votaress of my order,

And in the spiced Indian air by night

Full often hath she gossiped by my side . . .

SURESH *(whispering)*. What are they going on about?

UMA. They are fighting over this boy.

SURESH. What boy?

NILA. But she, being mortal, of that boy did die,

And for her sake do I rear up her boy;

And for her sake I will not part with him.

UMA. It's a boy she adopted.

SURESH. Why does he want the boy?

UMA. Good question.

MICHAEL. Give me that boy and I will go with thee.

NILA. Not for thy fairy kingdom! Fairies, away.

We shall chide downright if I longer stay.

Music begins.

MICHAEL. Well go thy way. Thou shalt not from this grove

Till I torment thee for this injury.

The music fades out.

Fade in:

Finale.

This is greeted with a huge round of applause as the actors take their curtain call.

SURESH. Let's go.

UMA. Wait. Michael and Nila have to take their curtain call.

The applause continues.

SURESH. These stars will take their time in coming on stage. I'll check with the VIP security.

UMA. Something's wrong. Something is going on backstage!

A gun shot is heard, followed by Nila's scream. There is a murmur amongst the audience.

Suresh! Quick! Clear the way. We must go backstage!

SURESH. Oh no! You stay right here Uma. This is serious. *(Into his phone.)* Hello, Suresh Rao. Contact control tower. Get me the Commissioner, quick.

> *The crowds begin to panic as they rush to the exit. Mendelsohn's music continues to play as the mayhem increases. Suresh's voice on a megaphone goes 'Please do not panic, leave through the nearest exit, please do not rush.'*

Uma! Go to my car! It's a stampede. Take my keys and—Uma! Don't go there! Uma!

> *We follow Uma as she opens the passage door leading backstage. As she shuts the door, we lose the crowds and the music. Uma's footsteps echo as she runs down the passage. She opens another door.*

LIAM. Uma. Oh, it's a nightmare come true . . . Michael's been murdered.

UMA. God! Nila!

> *Fade out.*

Interior. Suresh and Uma's home.

> *The television set is on and we hear Suresh's voice from the TV.*

SURESH *(on TV)*. At this point it is a little difficult to say but yes, we cannot rule out the possibility of cross-border terrorism. No one has claimed responsibility for this act of terror but it appears to be the work of a larger network . . .

> *Suresh switches off the TV.*

I won't be home for dinner. We are having a meeting with the Commissioner.

UMA. Oh fine. I will see you in the morning then.

SURESH. What are you planning to do?

UMA. Just the usual stuff . . .

SURESH. I don't want you meddling around.

UMA. I am not meddling . . .

SURESH. By the way, what was the important thing that Liam personally wanted to talk to you about? And don't give me that line about the electricity.

UMA. It's a secret. I promised not to tell.

SURESH. Do you know it's against the law to hold back relevant information?

UMA. So, are you going to arrest me?

SURESH. Uma, stop playing games. If it has anything to do with all this I want to know.

UMA. I was told Michael was kidnapped.

SURESH. What? You mean, before the show? And what do you mean 'you were told'? Was he or wasn't he?

UMA. Nila saw him get into a taxi with three other men. She said the men were about medium height. Michael was a tall and strong man.

SURESH. So you are saying that he went of his own accord? What if they were pointing a gun behind his back?

UMA. Look if you want me to help you, I have to get something in return.

SURESH *(laughing)*. And what would you want in return?

UMA. The forensic reports. And access to the greenroom. You have specifically instructed your subordinates not to allow me in there.

SURESH. How did you know that?

UMA. I went there this morning.

SURESH. No you did not. I would have known if you had stepped out of the house.

UMA. I have my ways.

SURESH. Has my constable Munswamy been giving you information again?

UMA. Maybe, but don't take it out on him, he . . .

SURESH. Munswamy is my subordinate, and I won't have him do your work.

UMA. What he does in his spare time is his business. He is not our changeling boy to fight over!

SURESH. What the hell are you talking about?

UMA. Simply that he is not a child and can make up his own mind.

SURESH. Look Uma. You may think you are very clever and smart, but really you need to focus on other things.

UMA. Such as?

SURESH. Oh! I don't know what to do with you! Why don't you join a cookery class like all normal women? The problem with you is that you have too much time and nothing to do since you don't have any children!

UMA. Suresh, that bothers you more than it bothers me.

SURESH. It doesn't bother me! I was thinking of how bad you must feel about it.

UMA. No. I don't feel bad at all. But I think you do. You want to talk about your feelings?

SURESH. I have to go. Running late already. My uniform is never ironed properly. Please tell the dhobi he isn't doing his job properly.

Suresh leaves, slamming the door behind him.

Cut to:

Exterior. Outside Suresh and Uma's home.

Suresh walks down in a hurry to his car.

SURESH *(yelling)*. Driver! Driver!! Where the hell are you?

The driver runs to him.

Come on, you lazy swine! Don't stare at my face! Get in the car!

The driver gets in. Suresh gets in slamming his car door shut.

Fools! All of you!

The car starts and they drive away.

Fade to:

Interior. Uma's home.

Dial tones as Uma dials a phone number.

UMA *(tentative at first, softly).* Hello, Charles? . . . This is Uma
. . . I am so sorry to call at this hour, it must be 5 a.m. for you
I know but . . . I am fine. And you? . . . And Winston? . . .
I am glad that's sorted out, well the reason why I called
is . . . Oh so you know all that. Did Liam tell you? . . . Oh
. . . Well it is very strange . . . Charles, I need your help . . .
It appears the Indian Government would rather have our
police investigate this just to keep it low profile, although I
don't see how after today's headlines, but there is something
not quite right about it . . . well, don't laugh, but I find it
oddly relevant they were playing Oberon and Titania . . . I
knew you would take me seriously . . . Well, to start with, I
met Nila briefly in her make-up room before the performance.
She said she hated playing Titania. 'I don't like our first scene.
I don't like it at all', she said soon after she mentioned her
Christian wedding to Michael . . . Which made me pay
attention to her first scene, but before I come to that, there
were some other quirks that I noticed in her behaviour. Nila
said they received a note that read 'I will kill you' . . . well after
she brought that up she cried to me 'I don't want another
divorce.' Implying she has had a previous marriage but . . .
really! What an odd thing to say at that point! If my husband
were to receive a death threat, I would say 'I don't want him
dead', . . . or 'I want him dead' but you wouldn't in the least
expect me to say 'I don't want another divorce.' . . . It set me
thinking that she probably knew where he was going and his
life wasn't in danger after all despite that note. But of course,
I was proved wrong in my thinking . . . I wouldn't rule that
out entirely, it seems she has a motive . . . she is hiding
something that she doesn't want out in the open. A secret so

big that she would kill to keep it a secret . . . Her own husband. *(Reflective.)* Yes, I can see how that can be a possibility for some women. Hmm. That makes sense . . . why she brushed Michael aside when he suddenly showed up. As if she didn't want him to say anything till she had had a talk with him. Which she never did. Or did she? . . . Charles, I am afraid I am clueless, unless I can get to some information. Which is where I need your help . . . The scene? Oh something about the way it was performed. I did pay attention to their first scene, maybe I am reading too much into it because I was looking for some meaning in their actions. When Oberon says the bit about glancing at his credit, or simply put, Titania's accusation of his dalliance with Hippolyta, Michael—as Oberon—pointed at Liam in the audience at the line 'knowing I know thy love for Theseus', and she responds with tears in her eyes—'These are the forgeries of jealousy.' Again she was choked with feeling later in the scene where she talks of various vicissitudes—'and this same progeny of evils comes from our debate, from our dissension'. Then her left hand, the one away from the audience clutched—almost involuntarily—her womb when she said 'We are their parents and original.' Whereas in the play Titania is speaking metaphorically.

Pause.

There is more but I will hold on to it till I am more sure, and know more about the gun, fingerprint reports, etc . . . Precisely. Where is the gun? . . . Now this is what I need you for . . . but first tell me a little bit about Liam.

Cut to:

Interior. Liam's office.

Opening a door.

LIAM. Uma! Do come in. My office seems to be the last refuge after all those press people. Let's talk before the packers and movers come in.

UMA. I am so sorry about all this.

LIAM. Me too. Won't you sit down? I simply had to see you before I leave.

UMA. I read the *The London Daily* online.

LIAM. Our Foreign Office has instructed all of us to leave this country in forty-eight hours. After all that we have achieved in cultural relations . . .

UMA. It is hard on you I know . . . But no one has claimed responsibility, so we don't know how political this murder is.

LIAM. Precisely. We don't know.

UMA. If I belonged to a militia or terrorist organization, I think I would gain more mileage by murdering you.

LIAM. But why? Why would anyone want to murder a British actor? No, don't tell me!

UMA. Hmm. Why would Titania cross her Oberon?

LIAM. Eh?

UMA. Good question. Why? I think the answer to that lies in where Michael went that afternoon and who he met.

LIAM. That's another mystery. Why did they kidnap him and why did they let him go? Only to murder him a few hours later.

A knock on the door.

That must be the packers. I hope they are kind on the dowry chest I picked up at the bazaar. Well, Uma. I don't know how this is all going to end. But I do hope I get to come back and keep the collaborations going.

UMA. Goodbye, Liam. I only hope things don't get worse . . . what with the war on Iraq and our tensions with Pakistan, it can lead to a . . .

The door is flung open.

LIAM. Good God! Nila! What is the matter?

NILA. I am being detained for questioning! I can't leave this country . . . I–Oh! Do something! They think I killed him!

Cut to:

Interior. Suresh's office.

SURESH. She was the only one backstage at that time. I have spoken with the cast. They were all on stage for the curtain call. The crew were in the properties room putting things away. The lighting and sound people were in their cabins. It had to be her.

UMA. Where's the gun?

SURESH. We are working on that one.

UMA. She couldn't possibly shoot him and hide the gun in the greenroom.

SURESH. Maybe she had an accomplice.

UMA *(thinking)*. The secret passage.

SURESH. Hmm?

UMA. There's no motive!

SURESH. They fought a lot. And she is from Pakistan after all.

UMA. What is that supposed to mean?

SURESH. You know they want to create trouble here.

UMA. They think the same of us! Oh, what's the use? So you suppose the Pakistan government hired a famous artiste to shoot her famous English husband?

SURESH. Why not?

UMA. Because it sounds ridiculous!

SURESH. You don't understand these matters. They don't want us to have good relations with UK. Look I understand you are fond of this Nila woman because you played the same part in school or whatever. But leave the real work to me. Now please don't make me raise my voice at you in front of my officers. Go home, Uma.

The phone rings. Suresh answers.

Yes? . . . I do have some leads, I . . . *(A little disconcerted.)* Oh . . . Well . . . That changes things a little . . . Okay . . .

Will have it sent to him right away . . . Yes . . . You are welcome.

He hangs up.

(*A little shaken.*) The case is transferred to the commissioner's office. Interpol is now involved. I guess you can gloat over it now.

UMA. No. I don't want that. All I want to do is help resolve this.

SURESH. There is one more thing.

UMA. What is it?

SURESH. I am to hand over copies of the forensic reports to you.

UMA. Oh! . . . Thank you.

SURESH (*quietly*). You are welcome . . . If you can wait for a while, I will have them printed out.

UMA. Certainly.

SURESH (*on the phone*). Get me a print out of the Forsyth file.

Puts down the phone.

UMA. Suresh. It is you who don't understand. It is not in our interest that this murder gets to be more political than it really is. The relations between Pakistan, India, UK are at stake. That is the real issue.

SURESH. Now you want to save the world.

UMA. Is that such a bad thing to do?

SURESH. No, not at all. Not if you are doing it just to be one up on me.

UMA. Do you really believe that's why I am doing all this?

SURESH. You used your influence to get the case out of my hands.

UMA. Your department almost arrested a British citizen of Pakistani descent without substantial evidence against her! What do you think that will do to our diplomatic relations? I am sorry but I had to get Liam to use his diplomat status to get things under control.

SURESH. Was it Liam? Or that fellow from Scotland Yard, Charles whom you had a soft corner for?

UMA. Both. And yes, I like Charles.

SURESH. Why are you being so cruel to me?

UMA. Well . . . I don't know. Maybe—because it's my turn.

Cut to:

Interior. Uma's home.

Dial-pad tones as Uma dials a telephone number.

UMA *(flipping through the pages in the file)*. Hello, Mr Menon? . . . this is Uma Rao, my husband is the Superintendent of police, I think the commissioner spoke to you about me . . . good . . . Yes I do have a copy of the reports, thank you. There is just something that I want a clarification on . . . it's to do with the note, is that the only scrap you have or am I missing a copy of something? . . . I see . . . and one more question for now. It says there were three sets of fingerprints found on the note and one set belongs to a woman and one of the deceased, anything on the criminal records matching the third? . . . When will you know? . . . Thank you so much. I appreciate your cooperation.

She hangs up.

(Contemplating.) These are the forgeries of jealousy?

She dials again.

Hello? Mumtaz? . . . *(Laughing.)* Yes, it is! How are you? . . . I wish I was, except now they have made it so difficult for us to get a visa to Pakistan! . . . Yes, it's awful all this talk and diplomatic one upmanship . . . Mumtaz, I was doing some research for a magazine and I thought I could use your help. I couldn't find anything much on the internet. Remember Nila Ahmed? . . . The TV star, yes . . . Oh! You read about it? Yes it's awful. Right here in my hometown . . . *(Laughing.)* You are clever. Yes I must admit I am doing some sleuthing on that . . . oh good. To start with, what's the name of the serial she acted in? The one that made her really famous? . . .

(Scribbling down on paper.) Right . . . No I never got to see
it. We didn't get it here . . . *(Scribbling down the name.)*
Wasn't she married when she met Michael? . . . But Ahmed is
really her screen name? What then was her married name? I
see . . . Tell me, there was some scandal about her wasn't
there? . . . Hmmmm. There was quite a bit of gossip around
her I remember . . . Oh . . . Right, it's coming back.

   Cut to:

Exterior. Outside the auditorium.

   Uma drives up to the security.

UMA. Uma Rao. I have permission to examine the greenroom
and stage . . .

   She drives in.

Interior. Auditorium passage.

   *Uma opens the door leading to the passage. She walks
   slowly across the passage. Her footsteps echo. She says
   Titania's lines more or less to herself but with also a
   bit of a performance. The words echo.*

UMA. And this same progeny of evils

Comes from our debate, from our dissension.

We are their parents and original.

   (As Oberon.)

Do you amend it, then! It lies in you.

Why should Titania cross her Oberon?

I do but beg a little changeling boy

To be my henchman.

   (As Titania.)

Set your heart at rest.

The fairy land buys not the child of me.

   Pause.

Hmmm.

She walks quickly to the door to the greenroom and opens it.

Bang! *(Running to the passage door.)* Run, run, run, open the secret door. *(She opens it.)* Throw the gun to someone standing there. Shut the door. *(Shutting the door.)* And scream.

She screams.

Hmm. Not quite right. Not quite . . .

Fade to:

Interior. Night. Uma and Suresh's bedroom.

Uma enters from the bathroom, shutting the door, humming to herself.

SURESH. You seem to be in a good mood.

UMA. Yes. I have had a fruitful day.

SURESH. What did you do?

UMA. Oh just a few phone calls.

SURESH. And a visit to the theatre.

UMA. Yes.

SURESH. Any luck? Have you cracked the case as they say?

Uma gets into bed.

UMA. If you are not reading could you turn off the light?

Pause, as Uma settles in. Suresh turns in bed to face her.

SURESH. Uma.

UMA. What?

SURESH. Would you be happier if we had children?

UMA. Don't know, Suresh. Happier? I really don't know.

SURESH. Well, a friend of mine—they couldn't have children of their own—you know what they did? . . . they stayed in his village for a few months . . . a poor distant cousin of his was expecting a seventh child and they couldn't afford to keep her . . . so my friend and his wife, they brought the child with them and . . . everyone acknowledged the baby to be theirs.

UMA. Why all the secrecy? Can't they just adopt legally?

SURESH. You know how people are.

UMA. I am sorry Suresh. I am not ready for it.

SURESH. You don't want a child.

UMA. No. I don't think I do.

SURESH. That's not a very nice thing for a woman to say!

UMA. Good night.

SURESH. It's all the attention you are getting because of your detective work. If you didn't have all that attention, you would be happy to be a mother.

UMA. Suresh. I am not a mother. I don't know whether I will be happy being one or not. Believe me, it really isn't an issue.

Pause, as Uma turns off the light. She lies down.

SURESH. Do you love me?

UMA *(under her breath)*. Oh for goodness sake!

SURESH. What did you say?

UMA. Don't be such a child.

SURESH. No. No. You are getting me wrong. What I want to know is, if you hated me enough would you kill me? I–I am merely thinking about that Nila woman.

UMA. Well . . . The question did occur to me too.

SURESH. What? To kill me or not?

UMA *(impatient like with a child)*. No, no! Whether, if I hated you enough I would kill you.

SURESH. Would you?

UMA. I don't know. I don't hate you enough.

SURESH *(turning around)*. No children. That is the problem. If there were children there wouldn't be all this talk of murder.

Pause. Suresh begins to snore lightly. The voices of Oberon and Titania play in Uma's mind, they resonate and sound distorted at times.

NILA *(as Titania)*. We are their parents and original.

MICHAEL *(as Oberon)*. Do you amend it, then! It lies in you,

Why should Titania cross her Oberon?

I do but beg a little changeling boy

To be my henchman.

NILA *(as Titania)*. Set your heart at rest.

The fairy land buys not the child of me.

His mother was a votaress of my order,

And in the spiced Indian air by night

Full often hath she gossiped by my side . . .

> *The last line 'Full often hath she gossiped by my side' repeats and grows to distortion as her innocuous word to Mumtaz on the phone 'There was quite a bit of gossip around her' take over and grow. Uma wakes and sits up.*

UMA *(softly)*. The changeling! Of course!

> *She goes back to bed. Suresh's snores continue.*

> *Fade out.*

Interior. Liam's office.

> *Liam is arranging his books on a shelf. He drops some of them.*

LIAM. Damn! I was so sure those books belonged there. Never mind, I will just leave them in their boxes in case something happens and I need to start packing again.

UMA. Thank you for staying on.

LIAM. Against my government's advice. *(Trying to be casual.)* So tell me, what do the forensic experts say?

UMA *(evasive)*. Oh, lots of interesting things . . . First of all, it is clear that he was not kidnapped.

LIAM. How so?

UMA. He ordered the taxi. I checked with the hotel.

LIAM. Oh. So Nila was lying.

UMA. Not necessarily. She may have thought he was being forced into the car. That's what she saw from her balcony. That's when she panicked and called you.

LIAM. Yes.

UMA. But you didn't call the police.

LIAM. I didn't inform the police because . . .

UMA. You didn't want it publicized.

LIAM. Exactly. I got in touch with Metropolitan Police in London and Charles told me to get in touch with you.

UMA. Right. Now comes the interesting part. He did receive a death threat.

LIAM. What?

UMA *(fishing out a paper)*. Here's a copy of what they found in his wastebasket.

LIAM *(reading it)*. 'I will kill you'.

UMA. Notice that it's torn at the last word.

LIAM. What does that mean?

UMA. That it's not the last word. If you look at the size of the paper it just feels that . . . there's more. It would be extremely difficult to tear up this page just so, unless you wanted to. That brings us to two questions.

LIAM. One of them being where is the rest of the note?

UMA. Absolutely.

LIAM. And the other?

UMA. Where did Michael go, after deliberately tearing up the note, destroying a part of it and throwing the rest in the wastebasket, and calling for a taxi? Also, who were the three men who joined him outside the hotel? Let's go.

Uma gets up and walks to the door.

LIAM. Where to?

UMA. I called the taxi service this morning and the driver gave me the address he took Michael to.

LIAM. Let me call for the car.

UMA. Are you crazy? Your embassy's car will bring us too much attention.

LIAM. How will we go?

UMA. In all your years in India, Liam, have you ever sat in an autorickshaw?

Cut to:

Exterior. Inside an autorickshaw.

The noise from the autorickshaw driving at a reckless speed of fifty kilometres per hour drowns their conversation eventually.

LIAM. How much longer will it take?

UMA. I told him to take the scenic route for your benefit!

The autorickshaw driver takes over by blowing his horn. Fade out autorickshaw. Fade in children playing on the streets.

Exterior. A street.

The autorickshaw approaches and comes to a halt.

UMA. Thank you . . . Are you all right?

LIAM. Oh I will be fine as soon as my ears stop ringing.

The autorickshaw starts again.

Oh!

The autorickshaw drives off.

UMA. Now. Where would 36 be?

LIAM. That's 34. So it should be the one next to it.

UMA. Don't be silly, Liam. That's number 2, after 34.

They begin to walk.

LIAM. Yes of course, how silly of me . . .

Their conversations begin to fade out slowly as they walk away.

I can't believe we are on a case that potentially endangers the relations between three countries. I mean, it's just the two of us!

UMA. You never know. If the bureaucracy that the English left us with wasn't so efficient in delaying work, the Central Investigation Department would have done all this by now.

The children continue to play. Fade out.

Exterior. A quieter street.

A cycle passes by ringing a handbell. A street dog barks.

LIAM. What do you plan to tell these people? Tell us about your English visitor?

UMA. If they have nothing to hide, they will tell us. If what I think is right . . . Oh I completely forgot. How much money do you have? In pounds.

LIAM. Oh, about two hundred quid.

UMA. Remember, you are a friend of Michael's and you know everything.

LIAM. I do?

They open a rusty iron gate which creaks loudly.

UMA. Hello!

The main door of the house opens. A man (Malik) speaks to them.

MALIK. Yes?

UMA. Hello. This is Liam Tate, a friend of Michael's.

MALIK *(after a while)*. And you are his wife?

UMA. No. I am Uma Rao. Just accompanying him you see . . .

MALIK. Why? Can't he speak English?

LIAM. How do you do?

MALIK. What can I do for you Mr Tate?

LIAM. Well . . . you see. Michael was a good friend of mine and . . . I know everything.

MALIK. He was a good man. He shouldn't have been murdered.

LIAM. Yes I agree.

UMA. We just wanted to talk to you. You see he told Liam he was visiting you . . .

MALIK. He told you why he was visiting us?

LIAM. Well er . . .

MALIK. What did he tell you?

LIAM. That he . . . It was Nila actually who told me.

MALIK. I don't believe you. Why will Nila say anything? . . . Come inside.

UMA. Thank you.

The street dog barks some more as a scooter passes by.

Cut to:

Interior. Inside Malik's home.

MALIK. There is nobody home. I cannot offer you anything.

UMA. That's okay. Thank you.

MALIK. So what do you want from me?

UMA. Liam wants to write about his friend's visit to India and the people he met. He is willing to pay for it.

MALIK. What did Nila tell you?

UMA. Oh she didn't know much about his visit here.

MALIK. Oh (*After a while.*) There is nothing much to tell. You are wasting your money. He came here because he was sponsoring my son's education. He came here to meet him.

LIAM. That would be interesting to know more about. He never told me that. Er–Uma, you want me to take notes?

UMA. Go right ahead, Liam.

MALIK. He saw my son through his school and now plans to pay for his higher education abroad.

UMA. Fifteen years?

MALIK *(correcting her without thinking)*. Twelve.

UMA. Exactly twelve?

MALIK *(after a while)*. Yes.

UMA. You knew he was in India?

MALIK. Yes. He did inform us.

UMA. He did? Or did you read about it in the newspapers?

MALIK. No. He called to say he will be here.

UMA. I notice you get the *Bangalore City Reporter*. Surely you must have seen their picture on the front page!

MALIK. No. He called me from London a week before they came here.

UMA. A week before they were performing in Japan.

MALIK. Are you calling me a liar?

UMA. Now I know. I understand why you need to lie.

MALIK. Please leave my house!

LIAM. Now look here, Sir. I am sure there is no need for us to get emotional.

UMA. I am afraid, Liam, there is every reason to get emotional. Mr Malik, I know who you are and who your son is. I understand your reasons for secrecy. It is not something our society approves of. But believe me, all I am interested in is finding out some more details that will help us solve this crime. If you don't cooperate, it will leave me no option but to send the CID over, and they will not be so understanding about your family matters.

LIAM. Uma, I do hope you know what's going on, because I certainly don't.

UMA. In good time, Liam. You can put away that note pad, there's no need.

MALIK. Please. I am sorry. I will cooperate. What is it you want to know?

UMA. To start with, who were the men who received him at the hotel and brought him here?

MALIK. I went to the hotel to bring him here.

UMA. And who else?

MALIK. Nobody.

UMA. And the other two?

MALIK. What other two? There was just me, Michael and the taxi driver.

UMA. I see . . . What did Michael and your son talk about?

MALIK. Feroz was telling him about his future plans. How he wanted to go to London for higher studies, etc.

UMA. Michael almost missed his performance to hear that? Couldn't he have done it another time?

MALIK. I don't know. He is not here to answer that question.

UMA. But your son is. May I talk to him please.

MALIK. He is very shy.

UMA. It's only us.

MALIK. No. Please.

UMA. Mr Malik, please. It is important that I speak to him.

MALIK. He isn't keeping too well, you see. He is away.

UMA. Can I speak to his . . . mother?

A voice from within.

MALIK. My wife died five years ago.

FEROZ. I don't have a mother.

MALIK. Feroz! Go to your room!

FEROZ. He is my father. I only have him.

UMA. You are lucky to have him as a father, Feroz.

MALIK. Feroz, please. Go back to your room.

FEROZ. What do they want from us?

UMA. We just want to talk to you.

FEROZ. I heard. You have come to throw mud on our face. You are no different than the others.

UMA. No. I am here to help you.

FEROZ. You can help by going away and leaving us in peace.

UMA. Not until I find out what you and Michael talked about.

FEROZ. We talked about India. We talked about my education. We talked about a lot of things.

UMA. Did you talk about his wife?

FEROZ. No! Get out of here!

UMA. Feroz, this is important. You liked Michael. Don't you want to help us find out who killed him!

FEROZ. He was a good man! I don't want to talk about her!

UMA. Why not?

FEROZ. It's none of your damn business! Go away!

UMA. Please don't hate her so much. She was helpless.

FEROZ. She is a whore! She killed him! She was responsible entirely for his death.

UMA. How do you know she killed him?

FEROZ. Because . . .

UMA. Because?

FEROZ. I just know.

UMA. Feroz, how do you know your mother killed him?

FEROZ. She is not my mother!

UMA. No matter how much you may deny it, she still is your mother. And will be.

FEROZ. I hate you, you bitch!

MALIK. Feroz! Please leave now. I told you he is unwell.

UMA. Where do you think she got the gun from?

MALIK. Enough!

UMA. Why do you think she would kill her own husband?

Malik starts beating Feroz.

MALIK. Go! Enough!

LIAM. I say . . .

UMA. Tell me Feroz! Why?

FEROZ. Because she is in love with this white man!

LIAM. Now really!

FEROZ. I saw them! I saw them together!

UMA. Where? Where did you see them?

Malik is pushing Feroz to his room.

FEROZ. Everywhere! In the hotel! In his room! She is a whore! Michael died because of her!

A door slams. We hear a loud whack and a cry.

LIAM. Don't believe him! Don't believe a word of what he said! It's not true.

UMA. More strange than true. Oh, what a tangled web!

The children playing outside grow louder as they yell and scream at each other. The sound of the autorickshaw driving away drowns their cries.

Fade in:

Exterior. Hotel lobby.

They walk to the lift. Suresh joins them.

SURESH. What are you doing here?

UMA. It is absolutely important that I speak to Nila now. You can't stop me since I have authorization.

SURESH. Your authorization may not be any good. I am here to remove my security men. Nila Ahmed is no longer held back for questioning. She may return to her country.

UMA. Who gave those orders?

SURESH. You should know, since you are the smart one.

UMA. Suresh, I have no time for games. Where is the order? Show me.

SURESH. Yes, Ma'am. Officer!

An officer approaches.

(Sarcastic.) Please show Detective Uma Rao the papers.

The officer leaves for a while and returns while Liam is still speaking.

LIAM. Oh, the British Embassy may have spoken to the Commissioner. I think it has all worked out fine. Hopefully, things will return to normal and we can continue with our cultural relations programme.

UMA *(snatching the papers).* Give me those.

She tears them up.

SURESH. Who do you think you are! This is serious contempt of law!

UMA. So arrest me.

SURESH. I might. One of these days I might!

UMA. You are too scared about what the neighbours will say!

The lift bell goes off signalling the arrival of the lift.

Now, your officers are to remain here because your bureaucratic office will want papers to release her and you don't have them. Come on, Liam.

They get inside the lift.

SURESH. You are going to be in serious trouble! You are . . .

The lift doors shut on Suresh.

Cut to:

Interior. Inside the lift.

LIAM. Uma, do you really think she killed him?

UMA. We will soon know. Everyone is lying. I want to know who is telling the truth. Liam, why did you say she called you after she saw Michael being taken away?

LIAM. She did contact me.

UMA. I checked the hotel phone records. She made no call to your office, home or cell phone.

LIAM. She was with me that afternoon. She ran away from Michael. That's what she told me. Believe me, I was only trying to comfort her.

UMA. You could have told me that if you had nothing to hide. The police along with my husband are downstairs. By the time we go down, we should know who is guilty of murder.

The lift bell gives a short tinkle as their floor arrives and the doors open. They get out and walk down the corridor.

LIAM. Would you rather I wait outside?

UMA. No, Liam. I would rather you are there. I want to speak to you both. Some of the pieces just don't fit in.

Uma rings the doorbell.

Only the fairy queen can help us.

LIAM. Fairy queen?

UMA. He said 'Michael died because of her.' He also said to me 'I hate you, you bitch.' *(Realizing.)* Oh my God! I wondered why that sentence stayed in my mind. Of course!

The door opens.

NILA. Oh, Liam! I have been trying to get hold of you all day!

LIAM. May we come in?

NILA. Yes, of course. Uma, won't you come in?

UMA. Thank you.

Nila shuts the door after they are in.

NILA. I am sure they don't mind me having guests. I don't know what my rights are. I wanted to speak with you Liam. That awful police officer told me that I couldn't leave my room without a police escort. Can't the British embassy get me out of here?

LIAM. Yes, and we almost succeeded.

NILA. Almost?

UMA. Nila, you will soon be free to go. Unless you are arrested on the charges of murdering your husband.

NILA. What do you mean? How can you possibly think I would kill Michael? He was all I had. Why would I . . . it's unthinkable.

UMA. Unfortunately it is a bit thinkable in the eyes of the law. You were the only one near him when he was shot dead. You didn't get along with him. Maybe you have found someone else.

NILA. Not true!

UMA. And you lied about his kidnapping. You sent him on a mission. After he completed it for you, you killed him. He knew about your son. Is that why?

Silence.

Why? I want the motive.

NILA *(quiet)*. Is there an extradition treaty between India and UK?

UMA. I am afraid not. You will be tried in an Indian court. But I can help you leave. It's very simple.

NILA. How?

UMA. You tell me who killed Michael.

NILA. I don't know! I wasn't in the greenroom! I was prepared to come on stage for the curtain call. I was waiting for Michael to come out and join me for the curtain call! I heard the gun shot, I went in and saw him lying on the floor with blood all over.

UMA. By then the murderer had escaped!

NILA. Yes!

UMA. Nila, it was impossible for the murderer to leave the greenroom without bumping into you!

NILA. I was too shocked, I didn't notice!

UMA. Nila, you are still lying. None of the actors on stage noticed you in the wings waiting for your curtain call as you said. When they looked around for the two of you they didn't see you.

NILA. I was out there! I tell you I was.

UMA. No you weren't. You were in the room with Michael. So, you either killed him yourself or—you know who killed him and you are not telling.

Silence.

NILA. I killed him.

UMA. Why?

NILA. I wanted a divorce and he wouldn't give me one. I also inherit all his wealth.

LIAM. Good God! And you told me you loved him and would never leave him.

UMA. And the note? Who wrote the note?

NILA. I did.

UMA. It doesn't look like your handwriting.

NILA. I got one of the waiters to write it for me.

UMA. 'More strange than true'.

NILA. I don't know what you mean?

UMA. 'We are their parents and original'. You know perfectly well what I mean.

NILA. I am done with the play! I never want to play that part again!

UMA. I am afraid you will have to relive the past once again.

NILA. I don't want to. I have made my confession to you. If you want me to sign a statement or anything . . .

UMA. But first the past, as always. Seventeen years ago when you were Mrs Nila Malik and pregnant. It certainly made the news, since you were a popular TV star, every household in Pakistan knew you as Ruksana the ideal housewife. Everyone was happy until Malik's first wife discovered that she could not conceive not because of any problem with her, but a routine test showed that your mutual husband Mr Malik was unable to become a father.

NILA. I never hid anything from him. I told my husband the child was not his when I came to know. He was understanding and promised not to tell anyone.

UMA. That suited him all right since he could then save face, by producing a child. A healthy child. A son. Everyone was happy. His parents, his friends, his aunts.

NILA. We loved him. We did. We still do.

UMA. But Sohaila, his first wife had a problem. Society would point a finger at her. If the other wife could produce a child, then the problem lay with her. In her anxiety to prove her innocence she showed her husband's medical report to a few friends. So the scandal broke out. The journalists smelled a scoop. Except in Nila's culture this is a serious crime, Liam, as serious an offence as say, in your culture, if you were to have a second wife while still married to the first.

NILA. More grave than that. Overnight I became the adulteress from an ideal housewife! Public anger built up and there was a fatwa on me! That I should be stoned to death in public!

UMA. Those are the kind of headlines that make it here to India from across the border.

NILA. What could I do?

UMA. Like all resourceful people, you managed to flee the country and seek asylum in UK. Where of course you met your fairy prince. Your rescuer? The first creature that you woke up to see?

NILA. Michael was more than a rescuer. We were in love.

UMA. But first, the changeling.

NILA. I wanted to take him with me! Believe me, I wanted to! But Aman and Sohaila wanted the baby too. I thought that maybe later I could ask them to send him over! But after the divorce, he didn't want to part with him. We fought.

UMA. But Michael was understanding and found a solution. He offered to sponsor the child's education and living expenses, knowing full well that Aman Malik wasn't earning anything at all after he lost his job. That way you would feel less ashamed about leaving him behind.

NILA. Yes. Yes! The shame is something I will live with for the rest of my life!

UMA. Don't be so hard on yourself, Nila.

NILA. I wanted the child! I could easily have . . .

UMA. But you didn't. You did what you thought was best, under the circumstances. Now about your arrest. Since you have confessed to the crime, tell me what you did with the gun.

NILA. I–I threw it away.

UMA. And where did you throw it away?

NILA. I can't remember?

UMA. And how did you acquire the weapon? A Derringer?

NILA. I–brought it with me.

UMA. Do you have a license for it?

NILA. No.

UMA. Nila, it's no use. You have never used a gun in your life. You've never even held a gun before have you? It wasn't a Derringer, but a country pistol that was used. That message was for you, wasn't it? What did it say? I will kill you, you whore?

NILA. Just arrest me and get it over with!

UMA. You covered up. You wanted to give the impression Michael was kidnapped so that the suspicion will fall on some unknown terrorist organization. After Michael was accidentally shot at, you went back to your room and tore that message in a way that it would appear someone wanted to kill Michael and not you. You covered up for your son. You are even ready to go to jail for him.

Nila begins to cry softly.

NILA. Michael never told me they were here! He desperately wanted him to meet me and—find his peace.

UMA. But he didn't. He followed you and was ready to kill you, but Michael rescued you for the last time at the cost of his life.

NILA. He died because of me! My son suffered because of me. I just wanted to get away. I can't. I've given up. I can't.

LIAM. Nila . . . I am so sorry.

A knock on the door.

I'll get it.

He goes to the door and opens it. The door is flung open.

What the . . .?

Liam is pushed aside and a gun is fired. A glass window pane shatters.

FEROZ. Nobody leaves the room. You! Shut the door!

LIAM. I—yes.

Liam shuts the door. Feroz walks to Nila.

UMA. Feroz, no!

NILA. Go ahead. Kill me if that brings you any peace.

FEROZ. I won't kill you so easily. Michael wanted us to meet and talk. So now we talk!

UMA. Feroz, listen to her.

FEROZ. No! You listen! All of you.

LIAM. I am listening.

FEROZ. I know what you were telling these people. How tough you had it. How you were a victim of your society. Right?

(Turning to Uma.) Isn't that what she was telling you? Well, you two wanted to know the truth. I will tell you. She had it all. She was a famous TV star. Everyone knew her face! She thought she could do whatever she wanted to do. But she was wrong. She was an immoral woman and that is something we do not forgive! She slept with her actor friends! For money, for pleasure, or just to please the Devil. And I was born out of her cesspool of lust. *(To Nila.)* You! You don't know what I had to suffer. In school I was known as the bastard! At home I was the unwanted child. We had to move to India and live in hiding to run away from the disgrace, but you won't let us live in peace. Unless you are dead you won't let me live in peace. So die. Prepare to go to hell, mother!

A banging on the door.

SURESH *(from outside).* Open the door!

UMA. Feroz, she loves you. She is prepared to go to jail for you.

FEROZ. Jail is not hell enough for you.

The door is broken open, as Feroz fires. Suresh and his officers storm in.

SURESH. Drop the gun, or I'll shoot!

FEROZ. Die.

Feroz fires once again, Suresh shoots at him too.

SURESH. Arrest him!

There is a scuffle as the cops take Feroz away. A police siren takes over.

Fade out.

Exterior. Inside a car.

The Bangalore traffic at its worst.

LIAM. Uma, dear, do you mind rolling up your window.

Uma presses the button on her side to roll up the window. The noise vanishes.

UMA. Quite a change from the autorickshaw.

LIAM. What do you think will happen to Feroz?

UMA. He is still a minor. So he will be sent to a juvenile home . . .

Liam's cell phone rings.

LIAM. Excuse me. *(On his phone.)* Yes? . . . Oh that's good. Yes . . . Will be right there, thank you. *(To Uma.)* The surgery went off all right. She is in the ICU.

UMA. Thank God . . . I guess all our cultures have one. Yours, mine, Nila's.

LIAM. What?

UMA. A fairy queen.

LIAM. Yes. I suppose so.

UMA. And we all want to pin her down. We just won't let her fly in peace . . . You can take a right turn there and that will take us to the hospital.

Fade out.

Interior. Hospital.

The hospital corridor. Liam walks up to Uma.

LIAM *(whispering).* She wants to talk to you.

Uma walks into the Intensive Care Unit.

Cut to:

Interior. ICU.

Silence.

NILA *(weak).* I need your help.

UMA. Whatever I can do.

NILA. I want to take him with me.

UMA. That would be very difficult.

NILA. I will wait.

UMA. I will see what I can do.

NILA. He is young. He needs me.

UMA. And you?

NILA. I need to make amends.

UMA. Yes. I will try. Now rest.

> *Cut to:*

Exterior. Outside the hospital.

> *An ambulance siren can be heard fading out. Uma and Liam walk to the parking lot.*

LIAM. I guess my dowry chest is safe for sometime now. I think it will make a splendid coffee table.

UMA. Who knows what stories lie hidden in there!

LIAM. I hope things will be okay between you and your husband.

UMA. I think I can handle him. It's the same for us isn't it? In your part of the world too.

LIAM. What do you mean?

UMA. Damned if you have children, and damned if you don't.

> *Another siren approaches as the ambulance drives in to the hospital entrance.*
>
> *Music. Credits. End.*

EK ALAG MAUSAM

A Screenplay

Ek Alag Mausam was released in India on 4 February 2005. The film was produced and directed by K.P. Sasi.

Principal characters:

APARNA	Nandita Das
GEORGE	Rajit Kapur
DR MACHADO	Anupam Kher
PARO	Gargi
RITA	Renuka Shahane
GEORGE'S FATHER	Gopi
Cinematography	M.J. Radhakrishnan
Music	Ravi
Lyrics	Kaifi Azmi/Sushma Ahuja
Art	Shashidhar Adappa
Editor	Ajit Kumar
Sound Engineer	Hari Kumar
Playback singers	Hariharan, Anuradha Paudwal, Usha Krishnadas and Anupam Kher

The film was supported and presented by Actionaid India.

Interior. Aparna's home. Morning.

Aparna is filling up a flask with orange juice. She brings the flask over to an assortment of bags packed and ready to travel. Paro is putting on her school shoes.

APARNA'S MOTHER. Arre! Why are you putting your shoes so soon?

Paro kicks them off.

Come here.

Paro gets up and goes to Aparna's mother who is ready with the pooja thali. Aparna's mother removes 'nazar'.

May God keep you happy, wherever you are.

PARO. Why? Why are you sending me away?

Aparna's mother turns away to hide her tears. Aparna looks at Paro.

(*To Aparna.*) I don't want to go, you know that and yet . . .

Aparna is determined not to allow her emotions to get the better of the situation.

APARNA. Put on your shoes.

Paro looks at Aparna's mother who still has her back to her. Paro goes to her and hugs her from behind. Paro puts on her shoes.

Cut to:

Exterior. Aparna's home.

From far we can see the front door opening and Paro, Aparna and a domestic help carrying the bags make their way to the car.

Fade in music. Aparna and Paro drive off, leaving Aparna's mother at the door waving out to them. Credits over the car getting on the Bombay Highway to Panchgini.

Interior. Car.

Paro reaches out for the orange juice flask and drinks out of it.

APARNA. I'd like some of that too.

Paro twists the cap on the bottle and stares at her.

(Looking at Paro with some authority.) May I have some of that juice?

PARO *(looking back at her with equal poise)*. Is this like the end of our relationship?

Aparna focusses on her driving. She speaks after taking a sharp curve and when there is a straight stretch of road ahead of her.

APARNA. I never pretended to be your mother. You will have enough money to see you through college. After college, you are on your own. I have left my flat to you so you won't have to worry about not having a home . . .

PARO. A home without you.

APARNA. Yes. Better get used to the idea.

Paro unscrews the cap of the flask and offers the flask to Aparna. Aparna takes it while still concentrating on the road, or pretending to. While she is drinking from the flask . . .

PARO. You are running away from me now . . . the way you ran away from George.

A truck appears from nowhere.

Flash of George driving a truck. Surreal.

Aparna swerves to avoid the truck, spilling the orange juice. The truck driver honks madly at her and drives on. She pulls over to the side of the road and stops the car. Aparna reaches out for some tissue and begins wiping the seats. She gets out of the car to wipe off the stains on her sari. Paro gets out too and walks away from the car. Aparna looks at Paro sitting under a tree. Aparna sighs and leans against the car.

Cut to:

Interior. Aparna's home. Surreal.

Suresh is lying on the sofa with his arm covering his face. Aparna walks in through the main doorway.

APARNA. Suresh! *(Going to the sofa.)* Suresh! It is confirmed. I am pregnant!

Suresh mumbles something and rolls over and goes to sleep. Aparna picks up the bottle of rum that has fallen down and props it on the table.

Cut to:

Exterior. Car. Road. Tree.

Aparna walks towards Paro sitting under a tree.

APARNA. You don't want to miss the first assembly at your new school, do you?

PARO. Yes.

APARNA. I'll visit you. As often as I can.

PARO. And when you can't, you don't want me visiting you, right?

Aparna nods.

And what about me? What if I want to visit you?

APARNA. You will concentrate on your studies and your career. You said you wanted to be an engineer. You are not going to become one by spending time with me.

PARO (*matter of fact*). I want to be with you when you are dying.

APARNA. I want to be left alone.

Paro looks at her. Paro gets up and walks towards some bushes.

Where are you off to now?

PARO. Behind the bushes.

APARNA. Want me to come?

PARO (*turning back, sarcastic*). No. I want to be left alone when I go.

Aparna sighs and smiles.

APARNA. Make sure nobody can see you from the road.

Paro disappears behind the bushes. Aparna looks out on to the road. Another truck rushes by honking madly.

Cut to:

Soundtrack only as we stay on Aparna looking out on the road. Cooper's voice through phone.

Fade in.

We haven't met. My name is Rosalynd Cooper. I am a volunteer nurse at the Central Hospital where I am calling from. Your gynaecologist Dr Sanyal and I wish to meet with you and your husband . . . It is extremely important that we meet as soon as possible . . .

Fade out.

Interior. Aparna's home.

Aparna and Suresh. Suresh is a bit nervous.

APARNA. She said we should both go.

SURESH. I–I am not so sure I want to go.

APARNA. It's something about our baby. I am scared Suresh. I want you with me.

SURESH. You will be fine. I don't feel too well.

APARNA *(really concerned).* I think it is important we both go. Please!

SURESH *(not meeting her eyes).* Please.

Aparna is really hurt that he does not want to go with her.

Cut to:

Exterior. Outside a clinic or hospital.

Aparna gets out of her car and walks slowly to the clinic. She hesitates for a while outside and then picks up the courage to go in.

Cut to:

Interior. Office of the doctor.

Dr Sanyal, her gynaecologist is seated at the desk. Rosalynd Cooper, a volunteer nurse, is seated opposite him/her.

APARNA *(entering).* Sorry, I am a bit late.

COOPER *(rising, moving to Aparna—trying to pronounce her name correctly, but doesn't quite get it right).* Aparna? *(Offering her hand.)* I am Rosalynd Cooper. We spoke on the phone.

Aparna shakes her hand and manages a smile.

Won't you come in and have a seat?

Aparna walks in to the room.

SANYAL *(a large authoritative voice).* Where is your husband? *(Without waiting for a response, turning to Cooper.)* Didn't you tell her to bring her husband as well?

COOPER. Maybe it's a good idea to have a chat with Aparna first.

APARNA *(trying to collect herself).* He couldn't make it.

SANYAL *(looking at her).* Sit down.

Aparna sits down. She looks at Cooper for support. Cooper gives her a smile.

APARNA. Am I going to lose my baby?

Pause.

Cooper looks at Dr Sanyal.

COOPER. Aparna . . . I would strongly advise you to . . . give up your baby.

APARNA. Why? What's wrong with my baby?

SANYAL. Look here. I think it is better for you to come with your husband some time when he is free . . .

APARNA. No. It's my baby too and I want to know why I can't have it.

Pause. Cooper speaks after some thought.

SANYAL. Your blood samples were sent to us for some routine tests. I believe we have your consent for these tests.

APARNA. Nobody asked me for my consent. They just took the samples.

Cooper looks at Dr Sanyal.

SANYAL. There is no question of consent. Hospital policy. So that patients may not claim they were infected after they were admitted.

APARNA *(hanging on to every word)*. And . . . what are the results?

Dr Sanyal shakes his/her head.

COOPER. Aparna . . . Have you heard of HIV?

Aparna looks at her with disbelief. She laughs a little.

APARNA. Are you saying that my child . . .? But that's impossible! The child can only get it from its m . . .

Aparna stops midsentence as the shock of what she is saying hits her.

COOPER *(moving to Aparna)*. It's you, Aparna.

APARNA. It's not possible. How could I be HIV positive?

SANYAL. We are certain.

APARNA. It just can't be! . . . I haven't had a sexual relation with anyone but my husband, I haven't had any blood transfusions, I always make sure the doctor uses a disposable syringe . . . No, it can't be. Isn't there a different kind of test? That's more accurate?

COOPER. We have done the Western Blot. Aparna, I am a trained counseller. I suggest we talk . . .

APARNA. But . . . How?

SANYAL. It is very clear to me that you got it from your husband.

Aparna thinks about it for a while. Tears well up in her eyes.

APARNA. And . . . how did he . . .?

Silence.

Aparna turns away. She takes out a handkerchief from her bag.

SANYAL *(clearing his/her throat).* I am sorry, but I don't have much time . . .

Aparna looks at him/her, totally vulnerable. Cooper puts a hand on her shoulder.

I will get to the point. We have not yet formally admitted you into my nursing home, so as far as we are concerned, we are refusing to admit you on the grounds that it will upset our nurses and other patients . . .

APARNA. My baby?

SANYAL. You can't have it.

APARNA *(getting up, shaking her head).* No. This can't be true.

COOPER. Do sit down Aparna.

SANYAL *(to Cooper).* Show her the report.

Cooper hands over the report to Aparna. Cooper steps back ready to offer her support at any moment. Aparna looks at the report.

Fix an appointment with Cooper. She will deal with you at the Aids counselling centre. There is no need to come to this hospital any more.

Aparna rushes out of the office.

COOPER. Aparna! Wait! You must talk to us!

SANYAL *(dismissing Cooper).* I will handle this.

Dr Sanyal rushes out as well. Cooper looks on, unsure.

Cut to:

Exterior. Corridor. Near the lift.

Aparna is punching the button for the lift. Dr Sanyal catches up with her.

SANYAL. Aparna . . . Now listen to me carefully . . . *(Giving her a card.)* Go here. They will risk doing an MTP.

APARNA. I want to keep my baby!

SANYAL. Don't be a fool . . . No proper nursing home is going to touch you. And either your baby or you will die soon.

The lift doors open. Dr Sanyal helps her into the lift, presses the ground floor button and quickly steps out of the lift. The doors close on a helpless and bewildered Aparna.

Cut to:

Interior. Lift going down.

Aparna leans against the wall of the lift. The lift comes to a halt. The doors open and a whole group of young people walk in chattering. They hardly notice Aparna. The lift goes down again. Aparna cringes from the others, not wanting to touch them. The lift stops at the ground floor. The doors open and everyone files out. Aparna looks out of the lift, at the crowds and she cannot get out. The lift doors close again only to open immediately as someone has pressed the button from outside. The person waits for Aparna to get out. She gets out slowly.

Cut to:

Interior. Reception and exit/entrance of nursing home.

Aparna walks to the exit. A lab technician and a nurse are chatting. They suddenly stop chatting when they notice Aparna. They look at her with a mixed feeling of pity and disgust. Aparna rushes out of the nursing home, to the parking lot and into her car.

Cut to:

Interior. Aparna's home.

Aparna enters her home. She rushes to the phone and calls her mother.

MOTHER *(through phone)*. Hello?

APARNA. Hello, Mother?

MOTHER. Aparna?

Aparna does not respond immediately as she is trying to find the right words.

(Panic.) What's wrong? Aparna?

APARNA *(after a while)*. Nothing.

MOTHER. Your voice sounds so different. Are you keeping well?

APARNA. Mother . . .

MOTHER. Is the baby all right? Hey Ram! Has something happened to you? I told you to come here! It is not right for you to do the delivery there!

APARNA. I–I will call you back . . . Mother.

Aparna hangs up even as her mother's 'hello's can be heard. The bedroom door opens and Suresh enters the living room. Aparna looks at Suresh. Suresh speaks after a while, with difficulty.

SURESH. I–I am sorry.

APARNA. You knew!

SURESH. I wasn't too sure myself . . . They tested me at the alcoholics' clinic.

APARNA. And you didn't tell me.

SURESH. I–I didn't know how to . . .

APARNA. And–how . . . do you think you got it?

Suresh looks away.

How often?

SURESH. Please!

APARNA. All those business trips! Those late nights. How many women have you infected so far?

SURESH. I don't know!

APARNA. You are too drunk to know.

SURESH. What are you going to do now?

APARNA. I don't know. Help me, Suresh . . . What am I to do?

Suresh is frightened at the prospect of making these decisions.

They want me to lose our baby. Suresh, you are responsible for ruining my life! Help me now.

SURESH *(edging his way to the main door)*. How can I help you? I am dying too.

Aparna realizes that he is just as helpless as she is.

APARNA. Suresh, don't leave me now.

SURESH. I–I have some important work. I am leaving the city . . .

APARNA. Suresh, stay for a while! Just talk to me for a while!

SURESH. No. I can't . . . I am sorry, Aparna.

Suresh leaves in a hurry. Aparna rushes to the door. She is about to call him back. She decides to slam the door instead. She bolts the door from inside and leans on it.

Fade out.

Exterior. Car. Road. Tree.

Aparna and Paro walking back to the car.

PARO *(looking at some shrubs)*. Auntie, look! Touch-me-nots!

Paro runs towards the plant.

Come on.

APARNA. We are running late . . . Oh all right. But quickly . . .

Paro touches the leaves and watches them cringe. One by one.

PARO. Remember at Jeevan Jyoti there were so many. All over the place.

APARNA. I am sure there will be plenty at the boarding school.

PARO. How do you know?

APARNA. There must be.

PARO. You know, George called you a touch-me-not.

APARNA. He did? When?

PARO. Oh some time ago. At Jeevan Jyoti.

APARNA. You were too young. How can you remember?

PARO. He is right.

APARNA *(hugging Paro)*. There. See. I am not a touch-me-not.

PARO. Let's go back home to nani.

APARNA *(getting up and walking to the car)*. Come on. Enough of this idle chatter.

PARO. There see. He is right. You are a touch-me-not!

Paro runs to her and tickles Aparna's tummy.

You are!

APARNA *(reacting to the tickling)*. No I am not.

PARO *(tickling her some more)*. Yes you are.

APARNA *(tickling Paro in the tummy)*. No I am not. You are!

PARO *(squealing and cringing with delight)*. No I am not!

APARNA *(tickling her some more)*. Yes you are!

PARO *(with uncontrollable laughter)*. No I am not! No!!

Paro laughs while she clutches her stomach, leaning against the car. Aparna laughs as she watches her double up with laughter.

Cut to:

Interior. A sleazy looking operation room.

Aparna is lying on the table, clutching her abdomen. The sheets are bloodied. We dont hear her scream. The doctor and nurse stay far away, not wanting to touch her. The nurse throws an extra sheet to her.

Cut to:

Interior. Aparna's home.

A very weak Aparna is speaking on the phone. She can barely hold the phone in her hand.

APARNA. Mother! Please come here! I am dying! I am dying, mother!

Aparna breaks down sobbing.

Cut to:

Exterior. Car. Road. Tree.

Aparna is smiling as Paro continues to laugh. Aparna tickles her some more.

PARO *(pleading now).* Enough, enough!

APARNA *(holding her hands near Paro's tummy and making a tickling gesture).* Then get in the car!

PARO *(laughing).* No!

Aparna 'attacks' her with her fingers going for her tummy. Paro screams with delight and gets into the car laughing. Aparna gets into the driver's seat again. They both look at each other for a moment, their eyes bright with the fun and games.

APARNA. I am so glad that at least you are all right.

Paro's smile fades a little. Aparna starts the car and they drive off.

Fade out.

Interior. Car.

The stereo is on. A love song is playing. Paro hums along with it. Aparna joins in. Aparna smiles a little as the song gets a little sentimental. The song ends. Paro applauds.

PARO. Did you and George sing songs together?

APARNA *(embarassed by the question).* Don't be silly. *(After a while.)* Yes we did.

PARO. When I am in love, I will write a song, and he will have to sing it for me.

APARNA. You have a long way to go before you start thinking of all that.

PARO. I am not going to wait as long as you have.

Aparna reaches out and ruffles her hair. They drive in silence.

Cut to:

Exterior. Entrance to Jeevan Jyoti. On campus.

Aparna drives into Jeevan Jyoti. She parks her car near a beautiful garden. She follows a sign to where it shows the office is. She looks inside. Nobody there. There is a pretty child feeding the pigeons.

APARNA *(to the child).* Hello.

No response.

Do you know where I can find Dr Machado?

The child smiles and points towards a hall. Aparna walks in the direction the child pointed out. Aparna looks back at the child, concerned.

Cut to:

Interior. Day. A group therapy session in progress.

Aparna comes to a room from where a loud booming voice is heard. The door is open so she walks in to the group therapy session in progress. The inmates are

*seated in a circle on chairs or on the floor. Dr Machado
is at the centre of the circle. He moves around with
grace and energy. Aparna steps in quietly. She hangs
around the door and observes.*

DR MACHADO *(moving around).* You are not alone in this world.
There are hundreds of thousands of people like you suffering
in silence. Why? Because they all think that they are going to
die. Of course they will die. Of course you will die. We will all
die one day. Who is to say when? Then why this fear of dying?
What is important is that we are alive today. We are alive right
now! Am I right or am I wrong?

There are a few mumbles of approval.

Aren't we all dying? Isn't everyone in this world dying?
(Pausing for effect.) I am not HIV positive but I am also dying.
But do I think about my death all the bloody time? . . . No.
I think of each moment that I have. Each day. Each month.
Each season that I have. So why don't you. You all have these
moments, months, seasons . . . Will somebody give me some
water, yaar?

*A little boy who doesn't look too well gives him a
bottle of water.*

(Patting the boy.) Thank you. And some of us have a very
short and very special season.

Dr Machado gulps down some water.

(Wiping his mouth with his sleeve.) Ah . . . Now where was
I?

Someone prompts him.

Ah . . . yes. So let us all say together—'I am alive, this moment,
this day!' Come on.

*He moves around in the circle encouraging people to
join in.*

Come on! Say it. 'I am alive. This moment, this day!' Come
on. 'I . . .

They join in halfheartedly—'I am alive, this moment, this day.'

Together!

More people join in—'I am alive, this moment, this day.'

Louder and together!

The best response this time. Aparna observes all this and now she is unsure. She remains at the door wondering whether she should leave.

Good. Now let's share some positive experiences. Anyone with positive experiences?

Some hands go up, including the little boy who gave him the bottle of water. The doctor points out to the little boy.

Let's have Suraj's story. Tell us Suraj. What happened to you today that made you very happy?

SURAJ. I had a very bad cough. There was blood, and I thought I will join Mummy and Daddy in Heaven very soon . . . but I am much better after the medicine you gave me!

Silence. Suraj coughs a little but he supresses it.

DR MACHADO. Keep fighting. Seize the moment!

A young man raises his hand.

Manoj. Let us hear what Manoj has to share with us.

MANOJ. I went to the dentist the other day . . . He said I needed gum surgery to save my teeth. I thought I should tell him the truth. So I told him that I am HIV positive, so that he will be more careful during the surgery. The dentist looked at me strangely . . . He ordered me to wait outside. I waited for an hour before his assistant came out to say the doctor was not free to do the surgery and I should go somewhere else. She did not even take money for the consultation. Okay. I said. I went to another dentist across the street. I didn't tell him anything. I just let him do the surgery. *(Showing off his teeth.)* And now I have perefect gums.

Some of them laugh.

And today I sent him a `letter telling him that I am HIV positive!

More laughter and some applause.

Let him know that any of his patients could be HIV positive.

DR MACHADO *(to the group in general)*. So what do you all feel? Did Manoj do the right thing?

Silence at first. Then a murmur as they begin discussing it amongst themselves. Aparna turns to leave. Dr Machado beckons to her.

Don't go yet young lady. Why don't you join us?

Aparna gets a little shaky now since everyone has stopped talking and look at her.

APARNA. I–I didn't mean to disturb you . . .

DR MACHADO *(going to her)*. Hello, I am Dr Machado. You must be Aparna.

APARNA. Yes. Hello.

DR MACHADO *(leading her into the room)*. Everyone—this is Mrs Aparna . . .

APARNA. Miss Aparna Verma.

DR MACHADO. And Aparna is here . . . just to visit us or . . .?

APARNA. No. I mean—yes. I am here just to volunteer, that is if you need my services. That is all.

DR MACHADO *(his smile freezing)*. Ah. I see.

APARNA. There is no other reason why I should be here.

DR MACHADO. Ah. And you want to help us?

APARNA. Yes. If you need my help. I–I am sorry if it is improper for visitors to drop in.

DR MACHADO. Why not? We have nothing to hide.

Aparna looks at the doctor, wondering if there was an innuendo in that statement.

(To the group.) Do we need this lovely young lady's help?

Some nods of approval especially from the men.

SURAJ. Can you cure us?

APARNA. Er. No. But maybe I can help you . . . seize the moment as the doctor said.

Murmurs of approval.

MANOJ. What do you think, Madam? Did I do the right thing?

APARNA. I beg your pardon?

DR MACHADO. You heard his story. He wants to know whether he did the right thing by not telling the second dentist that he is HIV positive.

APARNA *(looking at Manoj, after a while).* Yes. You did the right thing.

Fade out.

Interior. Dr Machado's office and clinic.

Dr Machado is busy with different coloured pills. He is preparing dosages and putting them in little paper bags. Aparna sits across the table sipping her tea.

DR MACHADO. Damn! That George is never around when you need him . . . Just give me a minute while I sort these out . . . See these green ones? I smuggled some in from America. They will help them live just a little longer. Can't bring them in without heavy duties . . . But I–I manage . . . Hah! Those customs officials are fools! Or maybe I am just too clever for them . . .

APARNA. Doctor . . .

DR MACHADO. Just a minute . . . *(Making a tune with 'just a minute' while he finishes sorting out the pills.)* Just a minute . . . just a . . . there!

He clears up all the little packets and then turns his attention on Aparna.

Yes. What can I do for you?

APARNA. Like I said I would like to volunteer.

DR MACHADO. Why?

APARNA. I–I am now separated from my husband and I–don't have any children so . . .

DR MACHADO. Doctor Sanyal told me about you.

APARNA *(almost dropping her tea cup)*. Oh! I am sorry . . .

DR MACHADO. That's okay. I was going to call you, but you showed up instead.

APARNA. Maybe I should leave. I have a headache.

DR MACHADO. Don't worry. I won't tell anyone.

APARNA. She shouldn't have told you or anyone. It's unethical.

DR MACHADO. It's my job to know. Well—I respect your need for confidentiality. You have my word. No one will know about it from me. But why have you come here?

APARNA. I told you. I want to be of some use to people with . . . people who have the disease.

DR MACHADO. And yet you don't want others to be of use to you.

APARNA. What do you mean?

Doctor Machado looks at her. After a while . . .

DR MACHADO. Aparna . . . Are you afraid of death?

Aparna looks away.

APARNA. I am afraid of a lot of things . . . *(Collecting her thoughts.)* I didn't come here to be counselled. Doctor do you need my services over here, or don't you?

Doctor Machado thinks about it for a while. Suddenly springing to life.

DR MACHADO. Come with me.

APARNA. Where?

DR MACHADO. Come.

Doctor Machado dashes out, gesturing to her to follow him.

Let me see how useful you are.

Cut to:

Exterior. Outside a special ward.

Doctor Machado enters frame followed by Aparna.

DR MACHADO (*stopping midstep so that Aparna almost bumps into him*). I just remembered I have some important work. You go in there.

APARNA. Wh–what do you want me to do?

DR MACHADO. Ramnath, who has been with us for four years is now dying.

APARNA. Oh!

DR MACHADO. No sympathy. Now this is your test. Go in there and try to entertain him.

APARNA. Entertain him?

DR MACHADO. If you can make him smile before he goes, you can stay.

APARNA. But what do I do?

DR MACHADO. I don't care what you do. Make his journey a little easier.

APARNA. But–where are you going?

DR MACHADO. I told you . . . I have some important work.

APARNA. What could be more important than this?

DR MACHADO. I have to cut my toe nails. Later on I won't get any spare time—we will get busy with the cremation. In there . . . Call me when he is gone. Bye . . .

Dr Machado leaves without a second glance at her. She has no option but to go in . . .

Cut to:

Interior. One of the wards where a man is dying.

Aparna goes in to a room filled with natural light. In a corner is a bed where a group of men are huddled.

Aparna approaches the bed with a great deal of trepidation. She is quite horrified to see . . . A man who is all skin and bones. Trying very hard to breathe. The rattle is very strong. It could be heightened. The others are playing a game of cards around him. One of the men is Manoj.

MANOJ *(dealing the cards).* Come on. One more game.

The dying man raises his hand feebly to say no.

MAN A. Yes you can. Come on. Try to beat us.

MANOJ. You can't beat death. But you can beat us. Try!

APARNA. Give him something! Some drug to ease his pain!

MAN B. We can't. We don't have any.

MAN A. Look!

The dying man is trying to reach out to grab the cards dealt to him. He manages to hold them.

MANOJ. What will you bet on?

The man looks at Aparna. His breathing gets more and more desperate. He turns the cards around.

Two Aces and a King! He won.

The breathing stops.

MAN A. What a way to go! We all owe him something. When we meet him next.

Aparna looks at the still figure. She can't take it. She rushes out.

Cut to:

Exterior. The clinic, etc.

Aparna rushes out and runs towards the office.

Cut to:

Interior. Dr Machado's office and clinic.

Aparna runs into the clinic/office. A man is seated with his back to the door. There is a stethescope around his neck.

APARNA. I think I have failed, doctor.

The man turns around. He is mixing some kind of coloured concoction. He is pleased to see an attractive woman in front of him clearly distressed.

GEORGE *(not really concerned about the cause of her distress).* You have failed? Never mind. Try again.

APARNA. I am sorry. I thought you were Dr Machado.

GEORGE *(still focussed on her).* Why did you fail?

APARNA. I really don't know. I just couldn't joke with him. I tried to play cards with him but . . . Now he is gone.

GEORGE. You mean he left you for that? Never mind. *(Taking out a pack of cards.)* You will find someone else to play cards with. What kind of a man is he? Refusing to play cards with you?

APARNA. What are you talking about?

GEORGE *(coming back to reality but only for a while).* Can I ask you the same question?

APARNA. I am talking about what's his name? The man who died. Dr Machado told me to entertain him but I failed. I am not really competent to work here.

GEORGE. Of course you are.

APARNA. No I am not doctor. I feel miserable.

GEORGE. Now, now. Of course you are useful to the centre.

APARNA. I am? How?

GEORGE *(at a loss—then handing her the solution).* Here. Why don't you stir this?

APARNA. I am not so sure. I will probably spill this lifesaving medicine.

GEORGE *(going to her, sitting on the edge of the table).* No. No you won't. Just handle it very carefully.

Aparna handles it as if it were an explosive.

APARNA *(stirring very carefully).* I will probably stir it all wrong and it will be useless.

GEORGE *(eyeing her while she is stirring it)*. No. No. You are doing a very good job . . .

APARNA *(aware of his presence, backing her chair a little)*. Have I stirred it enough?

GEORGE *(leaning forward)*. Let me see . . . Hmm. No just a little bit longer.

> *Aparna stirs it, but now she is aware of him leaning over her. She suddenly looks up to catch him looking at her.*

(Seriously.) Come on. Stir.

APARNA. I think I have stirred it enough. See . . .

GEORGE *(pretending to examine it seriously)*. Oh yes. Perfect.

APARNA *(placing the container carefully on the table)*. May I go, doctor?

GEORGE. Yes. *(Quickly.)* No. No.

> *Suraj walks in.*

SURAJ. Ei, Georgie. Is it ready?

GEORGE *(trying to be authoritative)*. Not now. Can't you see I am busy?

SURAJ *(impatient as children can be)*. But everyone is waiting! You told us it will be ready! *(Spotting the container Aparna was holding.)* There it is!

GEORGE. Suraj! No! I will give it to you later.

> *Suraj picks up the container, spilling some of the contents.*

APARNA. Oh, No! You have spilt it. Dr Machado will never forgive me, we . . .

> *Aparna stares at Suraj who has dipped a straw in the container and is blowing pink soap bubbles.*

That is the lifesaving drug?

GEORGE. I never said it was.

SURAJ. Come soon Georgie.

> *Suraj walks out with the soap solution.*

APARNA. You are not a doctor!

GEORGE. I never said I was.

APARNA. Who are you?

GEORGE. Er–excuse me. I have some important work.

APARNA. How dare you?

GEORGE *(at the door)*. Tell Dr Machado that you passed the interview with George.

Aparna moves to give him a piece of her mind but he is gone.

Fade out.

Exterior. Garden.

Dr Machado is working on a vegetable patch with some young people.

DR MACHADO. Ah! I hope Shyamu, you will be around to taste these radishes!

SHYAMU. Wan't to take a bet? I will be around.

DR MACHADO. Don't bet too high with me, silly boy. I can make sure you lose the bet.

Laughter as they progress with the gardening. Aparna is searching for Dr Machado. She finds him.

APARNA. Oh! Dr Machado! I failed.

DR MACHADO. Is he still hanging in there?

Aparna shakes her head.

(To Shyamu.) Tell George to keep the truck ready.

SHYAMU. Will we have a get together tonight?

DR MACHADO. We will have to. It's a promise I made to Ramnath.

Shyamu leaves.

(To Aparna.) Help me pull out these weeds.

Aparna helps the doctor pull out weeds.

Not those. Those are radishes planted by Shyamu.

APARNA. Sorry. These?

DR MACHADO. Yes. So have you decided?

APARNA. What? Oh. Well I am not so sure how useful I will be to you.

DR MACHADO. Good. That's a start. At least you are not here to dole out sympathy just so you can feel good about yourself.

APARNA. Doctor Machado. I am not pretending to be doing an act of charity. I am doing it for myself. And I have no intention of doling out sympathy just as I have no intention of seeking sympathy for myself.

DR MACHADO *(impressed)*. Good. Better and better in fact. So when would you like to start and what would you like to do?

APARNA. I would like to work with the children, as soon as possible.

DR MACHADO. I think that is a good idea. But we already have someone working with the children. Maybe he can do with some help.

APARNA. I will be happy to just assist.

DR MACHADO. Yes. Why do you want to work with children?

Aparna looks at him for a while. She looks away and uproots another plant.

You just uprooted a rose sapling.

APARNA. Yes. One bloom lost to the world.

The doctor looks at her, understanding her pain.

DR MACHADO. I know it is against my religion to say this. I hope Jesus will forgive me . . . I think you did a wise thing by losing your child.

Cut to:

Exterior. Jeevan Jyoti. Truck.

George drives the truck around to where the body is kept. Aparna and Dr Machado come to the spot.

DR MACHADO *(to Aparna).* Come and meet one of our really energetic volunteers.

George hops out of the truck.

APARNA. You! Doctor, this man . . .

DR MACHADO. I see the two of you have met. Let me look into the arrangements.

The doctor leaves them alone.

GEORGE. So have you decided to stay?

APARNA. And what business is that of yours? Yes. I have decided to work with the children. You know—I really didn't think it was funny the way you took advantage and made me feel like a fool, especially when I had just seen a man die in front of my eyes.

GEORGE. I didn't do anything. I was just trying to make you feel comfortable and useful. What was it you said, when you came in? 'Doctor I have failed!'

APARNA. So you drive a truck.

GEORGE. The way you say that, it seems it is a great sin to drive a truck.

APARNA. No, there is nothing wrong in driving a truck—doctor!

GEORGE. Look. Just because you thought I was the doctor . . .

APARNA. Never mind. What are you doing here with your truck. Are you really a truck driver or do you just clean them?

GEORGE. Your first day here and you are asking so many questions! Who do you think takes the bodies for cremation? The municipality van won't even enter the compound. Before me they had to bury or burn them all right here. So be careful. If you come here often enough people will think you have Aids also.

Aparna looks away. She walks to the other end of the truck just in time to see them carry the dead man's body. She turns away . . . George notices her reaction.

I am sorry. I didn't know . . .

498   *Collected Plays Volume Two*

APARNA *(recovering, her defences up)*. Don't know what? What? There's nothing wrong with me . . .

Pause, as George looks at her, softening a little.

GEORGE. And I don't clean the trucks. And I don't just drive it. I own it. *(Deliberately changing the mood, to the others.)* Come on. Hurry up. I don't have all day for social service, like some poeple.

George walks away before Aparna can say anything.

Fade out.

Interior. Aparna's home.

The doorbell rings. Aparna's mother comes to the door. She opens it to Aparna.

MOTHER. Do you want some tea?

Aparna shakes her head. She walks into the living room and takes off her sandals.

(Concerned.) Did you meet the doctor?

APARNA. Yes.

MOTHER. What took you so long?

APARNA. Mother, he knows that I am HIV positive.

MOTHER *(sitting beside her)*. How did he know? Can people tell just by looking at a person?

APARNA *(laughing)*. Don't be silly mother.

MOTHER. Are you still planning to work there?

APARNA. I start from tomorrow.

Her mother looks at her for a while.

Mother, there are children there who are even more sick than I am . . .

MOTHER. And their parents?

APARNA. Sick. All of them. Or dead.

MOTHER. I want to see you happy . . . If helping them makes you happy . . .

APARNA. I want to make the children happy. They can be happy, not I . . .

MOTHER *(fighting her tears, smiling weakly)*. If you can't be happy, at least be strong . . . I will help you be strong . . . *(Patting her head.)* Be strong.

Fade out.

Interior. Night. Aparna's bedroom.

Aparna is asleep. She tosses a bit and goes back to sleep. She dreams.

Cut to:

The dying man. Surreal.

The man is actually playing cards with Aparna. He picks up his cards and holds them out to her. He holds up three Aces and laughs. She has lost.

Cut to:

Interior. Night. Aparna's bedroom.

Aparna wakes up with a start. She turns on the bed light and catches her breath. She leans forward to pick up the glass of water, but it topples and breaks. Aparna's mother's door can be heard opening. We hear her faintly.

MOTHER *(off, faintly)*. Aparna? Aparna? Are you all right?

APARNA *(calling)*. Mother!

Aparna leans back and lies on her bed, eyes wide open, beads of perspiration. Her mother comes in.

MOTHER. What happened?

APARNA. Mother. Will you sleep here next to me?

MOTHER. Are you all right?

APARNA *(smiling weakly)*. Yes.

Aparna's mother gets into bed next to Aparna. Aparna snuggles up to her.

MOTHER *(patting her)*. I am here for you. But be careful of the world. Don't let anyone know of your illness. I remember when people thought my uncle had TB, nobody even came to visit us . . .

Fade out.

Exterior. Outside Jeevan Jyoti.

Aparna drives into Jeevan Jyoti. Again we focus on a sign that says 'Leave Your Prejudice Outside'.

Cut to:

Exterior. Another part of Jeevan Jyoti.

Manoj and Aparna are walking towards the children's area. Manoj is carrying a tape player.

MANOJ. Madam, the doctor won't admit it but we can do with a lot more help.

APARNA. Aren't there enough volunteers?

MANOJ. Are you joking? Only George has remained here. Others are too scared that people will think they have Aids . . . You seem to be very educated, so you are quite broadminded.

APARNA. Maybe.

MANOJ. Then tell me Madam. Did I really do the right thing by not telling the dentist that I am HIV?

APARNA. Maybe not . . . *(Thinking about it.)* Maybe you did the right thing by telling the first dentist that you were HIV positive. And maybe you did the right thing again by not telling the second one.

They come to the playground. There are about a dozen children waiting there patiently. They all stand to attention when Aparna appears.

MANOJ. Everyone. This is Aparna didi. Say hello to Aparna didi.

The children do a sing song 'hello'. Clearly their heart's not in it.

APARNA. Hello.

MANOJ *(pointing out).* This one is positive, so is this one, this one is negative, those two are positive, negative—all the older ones are negative.

Pause as Aparna digests all this. She is overwhelmed.

So. What do you want to do?

APARNA. I don't know. *(To the children.)* What would you like to do?

The children stare at her.

I am here to take care of you. I don't know how though . . . Let's all learn a song to sing. Shall we do that?

Not much enthusiasm.

MANOJ *(shaking his head).* I have other work . . . *(Handing over the tape player to Aparna.)* Here . . . Please return it to the office afterwards.

Manoj leaves. Some of the children look at him leaving, helpless.

APARNA *(deciding to take charge of fun and entertainment).* Okay. Let's learn a tune. Then we can have some fun putting words to it. Ready? Okay. Sing after me. *(Singing a tune.)* La, la, la, la . . .

No response.

Okay. Sing with me . . . La, la, la *(Pleading.)* Won't you try? You will enjoy it I promise you. *(Self-conscious now.)* La, la, la . . .

SURAJ. Okay, auntie, we will try just to make you happy.

APARNA *(not too sure how to take it).* Thank you. Okay. La la la la . . .

Some of the children join in.

Good. La la la la—then—dee de dee de dee.

The children join in on the dee de dee de dee.

Good. Now together.

Together they scratch out a rough tune.

(Pleased with their progress.) See, it is not that difficult is it?

SURAJ. We never said it was, Auntie.

APARNA. Okay. Now I will play a cassette . . . *(Inserting a cassette in the player and presses the play button.)* Listen to this alaap.

We hear the alaap of the tune she was teaching them. A honk from a truck is heard. The children suddenly get some life in them. Aparna looks in the direction of the truck to see George driving in, some music blaring from his truck. Aparna sighs and looks at the kids.

SURAJ. Auntie, can we please go play with Georgie uncle?

There is a chorus of 'please Auntie' from the children.

APARNA *(resigned).* If that's what you want. Go.

The children all cheer and run towards the truck. Some of them run faster than the others. George hops out of his truck in his characteristic style with a 'ghetto blaster' playing a pop folk song. The children run to him wanting to hug him. Suraj runs for a while but he stops as he is short of breath. He coughs for a while. Aparna notices Suraj is having difficulty and goes to him.

(Kneeling.) Are you all right?

SURAJ. It hurts very much in my chest. I have Aids that's why.

Aparna is overwhelmed by his frank logic. She hugs him.

Aunty, will you do something for me?

APARNA. Yes! Anything you say. Anything I can do.

SURAJ. Will you please take me to Georgie uncle?

Aparna is at a loss for words. She picks him up and walks towards George. George turns up the volume of the player and places it on the bonnet of the truck. He begins to do a hip-hop which the children join in on.

Suraj joins them, but very soon he is exhausted. He coughs some more and collapses. George does not notice it. Aparna notices that Suraj has fallen down and panics. She picks him up and yells to George and the others but the music is too loud. Aparna runs to the player and turns it off. Everyone stops to look at her.

APARNA *(hysterical by now)*. Suraj! Take him to Dr Machado. Quickly.

GEORGE *(casual)*. Oh Suraj. You spoilt our fun and I told you not to do that.

APARNA *(furious)*. How can you be so uncaring? *(Picking up Suraj.)* I will take him to doctor.

GEORGE *(taking Suraj from her)*. What will Dr Machado do? He is not God. *(Going to the truck.)* Here, Suraj. I have something for you. *(Taking out a wooden soldier.)* I made it for you. Soldier. You wanted to be a soldier? This is you. Now show me how you can fight. You will fight? Yes?

Suraj nods weakly. George takes him away and hurries to the clinic. Aparna is left dumbstruck. The rest of the children stare at her. One of them tugs at her dress.

CHILD. Aunty. Play the music.

Aparna stares at the child. She backs away.

Fade out.

Interior. Clinic.

Dr Machado gives Suraj a combination of pills.

DR MACHADO. You are lucky. This is the last of the stock I have. There . . . Do you want to go to your room?

SURAJ *(weak)*. No.

Aparna is at the door.

GEORGE *(placing the toy soldier next to him)*. You will stay here and learn to be a soldier.

SURAJ. Yes.

DR MACHADO. Good. I will make you some Ayurvedic powders. *(Busying himself.)* Whenever you have a cough you can have it with water.

GEORGE. Arre forget about all this medicine. He will go when he has to go. But he won't go without putting up a fight. Right? *(Punching Suraj lightly.)* Come on, fight.

SURAJ. It hurts very badly.

GEORGE *(punching him again).* Come on. Make a fist.

APARNA. Leave the boy alone. Can't you see he is in pain?

GEORGE. He is fine.

APARNA. Where are his parents? Maybe he should be with them.

DR MACHADO. All right, you two get out of my clinic and shut the door. Don't want all these powders flying away. Go, go. Both of you.

> George and Aparna step out of the clinic. George shuts the door of the clinic.
>
> Cut to:

Exterior. Clinic.

APARNA. Call Suraj's parents! Don't you think he should be with them at this stage?

GEORGE *(going to her).* I don't think so.

APARNA. Why not?

GEORGE. They are both dead.

APARNA. Oh. *(Embarassed.)* Somebody should have told me.

GEORGE. Death is not news over here. Life is.

APARNA. Don't preach to me!

GEORGE. You are right. I am just a truck driver. What will I know?

APARNA *(regretting it).* I am sorry. I am very upset as you can see.

GEORGE. What about?

APARNA. What about? About Suraj. About the lack of facilities. About the casual way everything is done here. And above all I am deeply concerned about the welfare of these children.

GEORGE. And you think I am not?

APARNA. No. I don't think you are. A child is dying and all you can think of is yourself. You are here just to have a good time yourself.

GEORGE *(now a bit angry)*. Madam. Do you think I enjoy being around dying people? I am here to have fun? Why don't you ask the children what they feel about me? Is it too much to hope for that the last few days they have that they learn to laugh, to think of their life. To seize the moment as the doctor keeps saying? *(Now getting at her.)* You know what I think? I think you are jealous of me because the children like me more than they will ever like you.

Aparna is dumbstruck.

(Regretting it.) I am sorry. I am upset as you can see.

APARNA. I jealous of you?

GEORGE. I didn't mean . . .

APARNA. I think you are right! I am sorry about everything I said. The fact is that I do resent it that I have nothing to give to the children, while you seem to be their hero.

GEORGE. Would you like to be their hero?

APARNA. Oh, what's the use! They don't really need me.

Aparna leaves. Dr Machado calls out for George from inside the clinic. George goes inside the clinic.

Cut to:

Interior. Clinic.

Dr Machado has finished making the Ayurvedic powders. George enters the room.

GEORGE *(to Suraj)*. How is our soldier doing?

SURAJ *(holding the toy soldier up).* Attenion! The soldier will kill all enemies of the country.

GEORGE. Live like a soldier, die like a soldier.

DR MACHADO. Here. Make packets out of these.

George helps him fold up the pieces of paper the powders are on.

Aparna is a very nice girl.

GEORGE. Too much of a memsahib.

DR MACHADO. Be nice to her.

GEORGE. Why? . . . Doctor.

DR MACHADO. Hmm?

GEORGE. Is she HIV positive?

The doctor looks at him.

DR MACHADO. Tell Mariamma to make sure Suraj takes these every morning on an empty stomach. Or when he has a cough. Also we need to get more vitamins for everyone. I hope that pharmaceutical company will continue with their donations . . .

George looks at him as the doctor rambles on. He has got his answer.

Fade out.

Exterior. Playground.

George is walking by, when he spots the tape player left out in the open. He picks it up to return it. He decides to check out the cassette in it. He presses the play button. We hear the alaap that Aparna was trying to teach the children. He sits down listening to it, getting a bit dreamy over her voice. He doesn't notice the children creeping up to him. Suraj presses the stop button.

SURAJ. I am feeling better already. Play something else, Georgie.

GEORGE. Why? What is wrong with this cassette?

SURAJ. It is boring. Like that aunty.

GEORGE. She is not boring.

SURAJ. Leave her. She is not coming back.

GEORGE. How do you know?

SURAJ. We didn't give her any bhav.

GEORGE. Why?

SURAJ. We know you don't like her.

GEORGE. Who told you that?

SURAJ. Oh. You like her? More than you like us?

GEORGE (*laughing and punching him lightly*). Oh, so you are jealous now! I like her in a different way than I like you . . . But she doesn't like me. She likes you.

SURAJ. Oh, so you are jealous of us? Say that!

GEORGE. Chup! Now help me think of a way of getting her back here.

SURAJ. How can we help?

GEORGE (*looking at all the children*). Come here, all of you . . .

They huddle up . . .

Cut to:

Interior. Aparna's home. Kitchen

Aparna's mother is cutting vegetables. Aparna is leaning against the wall.

MOTHER. Are you going to stand there all day?

APARNA. I am not going there again.

MOTHER. But what happened? Did anyone say something?

APARNA. Yes.

MOTHER. What did they say to you?

APARNA. The truth. That the children don't really want me. I don't think they need my help.

MOTHER. You were there only for two days. It will take time.

APARNA *(moving to her)*. Let me help you in the kitchen.

MOTHER. I can manage.

APARNA. Mummy, don't you start making me feel useless too!

MOTHER. No, no. I didn't mean it like that. All right. Wash these vegetables properly. I will put the cooker on the stove.

They begin their activity when the doorbell rings.

Must be the milkman. *(Picking up a book.)* Trying to match accounts with him will take one hour.

The doorbell rings again.

(Entering living room.) Arre bhai, I am coming! What is the hurry?

She opens the door to the children and George standing very sheepishly.

I am sorry children. I don't give any donations like this.

SURAJ. We havent come here for a donation.

MOTHER. Then what do you want?

SURAJ. We want to meet aunty.

MOTHER. Aunty? Whose aunty?

GEORGE *(clearing his throat)*. You see, these children want to meet Aparna aunt . . . I mean Aparna ji.

Aparna appears at the door.

APARNA. I will handle the milkman, mummy. You go in.

She stops when she notices the children first and then George.

Why have you all come here? *(To George.)* Why have you brought them here?

MOTHER. Oh! So these are the children! Come in. Come in.

Before Aparna can protest, her mother shows them in. George follows trying to avoid looking at Aparna.

They don't look bad going by their faces.

SURAJ. You also don't look bad going by your face.

MOTHER. My! Look how he talks! What will you have? Some ladoos? *(To George.)* And you, doctor?

GEORGE. Ladoo.

APARNA. He is not a doctor.

GEORGE. And some tea.

APARNA. Tea? At this hour?

GEORGE. I am sorry but we can't stay for lunch. I have a delivery.

MOTHER *(going to kitchen).* I will make the tea. You sit and talk with your guests.

The mother exits to kitchen.

GEORGE. They all forced me to bring them here . . . *(Trying to appear sheepish.)* All right, all right, I admit that I am wrong. The children prefer to be with you than with me . . .

APARNA. I don't believe you. You are up to no good.

GEORGE. Look. I admit I was wrong.

Forget it. It was a bad idea going to the centre. I have nothing to offer you.

George pushes Suraj in front.

SURAJ. Aunty. Please come. We all want to learn that song you were teaching us.

APARNA. May I ask why this sudden interest in good music?

SURAJ. Afterwards we all liked it.

The children all nod in agreement.

APARNA. There's something wrong over here and . . . *(Looking at George.)* I strongly suspect you have something to do with all this.

GEORGE. Me? Why would I want you back? I can look after the kids, I don't need you.

SURAJ. No. But we don't want him. We want you.

APARNA *(still suspicious)*. Why?

> *The children all look at George. George looks away, whistling.*

GEORGE. Tell her. Tell her why you want her back. I don't want her back.

SURAJ. Because you have such beautiful eyes.

CHILD 1. And such lovely hair.

CHILD 2. And such a nice voice.

APARNA. You taught them to say all that!

GEORGE. Oh so you think I think that you have such beautiful eyes, such lovely hair and such beautiful lips and a graceful walk and . . . and . . .

SURAJ. Ei, Georgie, we never said all that ha.

APARNA. Enough! No more. You may eat all your ladoos and drink your tea and then leave!

> *Aparna tries to make a dramatic exit into the kitchen. George makes an urgent gesture to the kids to start.*

GEORGE. 1-2-3 . . .

> *The children sing as a perfect chorus the first part of the song that Aparna was trying to teach them. Aparna cannot believe her ears. She turns around mesmerised. Aparna's mother comes with the tray of ladoos also mesmerised. Her eyes go moist when she hears the song. The children stop.*

SURAJ. Aunty, we don't know the rest of the song.

MOTHER *(almost moved to tears)*. Aparna used to sing that song as a child.

SURAJ. We don't know the rest of the song.

GEORGE. So? She doesn't want to teach you all. You can learn some other song. I will teach you some other song, better than that one.

MOTHER. How well they sing! Here have these ladoos. Have all of them. There are more.

She puts the tray on the table and gestures to the children to eat. The children refuse to eat them.

SURAJ. First aunty must agree to come to Jeevan Jyoti again.

MOTHER *(to Aparna).* Are you mad? You were telling me nobody wants you there! Look at these children and this nice man.

GEORGE. George.

MOTHER. Yes. They have come all the way here for you.

Suraj coughs a little. All eyes turn to him. Aparna softens.

SURAJ *(smiling).* Please say yes so we can eat the ladoos.

MOTHER. Of course she will say yes. There is no need to ask her. Go on. Eat the ladoos.

The children cheer and grab the ladoos and devour them as if they have never seen ladoos before. Aparna's mother fusses over them. Aparna and George stand staring at each other.

Fade out.

Night. Aparna's bedroom. Dream.

Aparna is sleeping next to her mother as usual. She dreams about the song. She is singing it as a little girl. She dreams of the children at Jeevan Jyoti singing that song. She dreams of George telling her he doesn't think she has beautiful eyes, hair, lips, etc. She smiles a little in her sleep.

Fade out.

Exterior. Night. Truck.

George is driving his truck. He is listening to some popular Hindi song on his player. Passing trucks honk in acknowledgement. He pulls over at a dhaba. Not too far from the dhaba is a little shack with a red sari hanging outside.

GEORGE *(hopping out of his truck).* Ei Sukhiya! What have you brought from Calcutta?

SUKHIYA. George! Where are you these days?

GEORGE. What are you eating? Butter chicken! Hmmm!

> *George reaches out to dip a roti in his butter chicken, but Sukhvinder smoothly takes it away from him.*

(Choosing to ignore it.) I am in Bombay only these days. I am thinking of giving my truck to someone else to run.

SUKHIYA. Why what is the matter? I hear you spend most of your time in some hospital.

GEORGE *(guarded).* Maybe.

SUKHIYA. Why what has happened to you?

GEORGE. I have fun playing with the kids.

SUKHIYA. I hear they are all very sick.

GEORGE. Yes. Some of them have Aids.

SUKHIYA. George bhaiyya. If you don't mind me saying this . . . why don't you sit there?

GEORGE. Why? If I sit there you won't get Aids? What if the breeze blows in your direction?

SUKHIYA. Huh? Don't come near me!

GEORGE. What if I look at you long enough? You might get Aids!

SUKHIYA. You are making fun of me? I will beat you to a pulp.

> *A woman from the nearby house swaggers out.*

WOMAN. Ei Sukhiya! Are you coming? Don't waste my time!

SUKHIYA. Coming!

> *The woman goes in.*

GEORGE. Oh! So first you feed your stomach and then what's below your stomach.

SUKHIYA. Not everyone is a saint like you.

> *Sukwinder gets up to go to the hut.*

GEORGE. Finish your chicken.

SUKHIYA. My stomach is full, and now . . .

GEORGE. You forgot your cap.

George hands him a monkey cap.

Why do you wear this cap?

SUKHIYA. When I drive my truck, the cold wind gets into my ears.

GEORGE *(slipping the cap on Sukhiya's head).* So when you are driving your truck in there, wear your cap. Understand?

SUKHIYA. Yes. Yes. Nowadays all this Aids is in the news. You don't do any such masti so you are saved. But us . . .

Sukhiya takes out the bottle of rum and takes a large swig from it before going in. George walks to his truck. He hears someone speaking in whispers. He looks around. The voices are from behind the bushes. He walks towards the sound.

Cut to:

Interior. Inside the hut.

The woman lies inviting on a mat. Sukhiya comes in and takes another swig from the bottle, looking at the woman. He puts fifty rupees on a table closeby. The woman takes out a packet of condoms from under the pillow.

SUKHIYA *(drunk).* What's this? There's no fun in that?

WOMAN *(frightened).* George had said . . .

SUKHIYA. Even my wife cannot tell me what I should do, who are you? *(Taking his money.)* If I drive twenty miles, I can go to Champa. She gives me complete pleasure.

WOMAN *(laughing nervously).* Arre, I was just teasing. Come. Come on.

Sukhiya takes off his cap. The woman throws away the condom packet.

Cut to:

Exterior. Truck.

George gets into his truck, starts it and drives it close to the bushes. He turns on his headlights. The lights catch two men behind the bushes.

GEORGE *(loudly).* You two should wear your caps also!

George drives away.

Fade out.

Exterior. Lake. Truck. Sunrise.

George is in the lake washing himself. There is a pail of water near the truck and a towel. The player is playing the song which Aparna is trying to teach the children. Aparna drives past. She hears the song faintly. Stops and reverses and gets out of her car on the opposite side of the road.

APARNA *(calling).* George?

George doesn't hear her. He is finished with his little swim. He slowly steps out of the lake . . . Aparna notices him and is transfixed as he slowly emerges from the water, his wet body shining a golden yellow in the morning sunlight. He has nothing on except a very tiny langot. George notices her and waves out to her first. He notices that she is staring at him. He is suddenly aware of his body and the effect it has on her. He moves to the truck and picks up the towel and begins to wipe himself while dipping his feet in the pail of water to wash the sand from his feet. He shakes off the water from his hair . . . Aparna is flustered. She steps back into the car and drives off without a word. George looks at his face in the rear view mirror and smiles.

Cut to:

Exterior. A new shed coming up or an old one being repaired.

Dr Machado is cutting some wood for the frame. Aparna looks on.

DR MACHADO. The children will be here after their lunch.

APARNA. Are you going to do all this work by yourself?

DR MACHADO. No labourer wants to work with us. Don't worry, George is helping me.

APARNA. Is there anything I can do?

DR MACHADO *(thinking about it)*. Hmm. Maybe you could put some nails on the doorway for the curtains. You will find the hammer and nails near the door.

Aparna moves around the corner to the other side of the shed. She finds the hammer and nails. We see a huge asbestos sheet, George's hands holding it from behind, and his feet approaching. He can't see Aparna. He places the sheet so that Aparna has to back up against the wall. Their faces meet once he has put the sheet down. He grins. She wriggles out from the side. Aparna places the nail on the door frame but stops short of hammering it in.

APARNA. I–I can't do this.

GEORGE. Why?

APARNA. I am afraid of hitting my fingers.

GEORGE. Let me hold the nail for you. *(He does so.)* Now hammer it in.

APARNA. I can't. I am afraid of hitting your fingers.

GEORGE. No you won't. Just look at the nail and hit. Go on. 1–2–hit!

She hits his fingers instead with the hammer. He lets go waving his fingers in pain.

OOOOw!

Aparna immediately takes his finger and brings it to her mouth about to suck it. She freezes. He stops yowling. She slowly puts his finger in his own mouth and looks at him sucking his finger like a baby. She laughs and ruffles his hair.

Cut to:

Exterior. Playground.

Aparna begins to teach the song to the children. A montage of the children with George and Aparna. Singing the song in the playground. Dr Machado joins them. In the garden, etc. They finish the song in the woods.

APARNA. Very good!

DR MACHADO *(applauding)*. Very good! I know what we should do! We should have a show. The children will sing for the public!

This is met with general excitement.

GEORGE *(pretending to be disappointed)*. What is there to do a public show about? It is just a silly song. I don't know why these children are so excited about it?

APARNA. Now don't pretend. I don't think the children would have learnt the song if you hadn't forced them to.

GEORGE. Why should I force them to learn your silly song?

APARNA. Suraj told me everything.

George looks away embarassed.

DR MACHADO. Suraj? Where is Suraj?

They notice Suraj isn't around.

APARNA. Suraj? *(Worried.)* Find him George.

Cut to:

Exterior. Montage.

George and Aparna search for him, calling out his name. Aparna spots him fallen down under a tree.

(Clinging to George.) George!

George runs to Suraj. Dr Machado appears from another direction. Suraj smiles weakly at them, but he can barely do little else. His breathing is heavy and painful for him.

GEORGE *(to Suraj).* Come on. We are going to do a show for the public and you will be the star! Come on. Fight!

APARNA. Take him to the clinic.

DR MACHADO. Take him to the clinic but . . . It is a miracle from God that he is with us for so long . . .

SURAJ *(beckoning to George to come closer, whispering).* Soldier.

GEORGE. Yes. Yes. *(To Aparna.)* He wants his soldier.

APARNA. Where is it?

GEORGE. I took it back to repair it.

APARNA. Hurry! Get it! *(Taking Suraj in her arms.)* I will take him to the clinic!

GEORGE. George runs towards his truck.

He gets in to the truck but the truck refuses to start.

God! Where are your miracles now?

APARNA *(tossing him her car keys).* Take my car. Go!

George gets out and goes towards her car. George gets in and starts the car.

DR MACHADO. Stop!

George slams the brakes.

It will be a lifetime for Suraj before you bring him his soldier. Take him with you.

Aparna rushes into the car with Suraj in her arms.

APARNA *(slamming the door shut).* Let's go!

George drives off as if he is in a race with the devil. Dr Machado looks at the rest of the children.

DR MACHADO. Oh Jesus! Why did you give some flowers such a short season?

Cut to:

Interior/Exterior. Car driving on a highway. Sunset.

Aparna is holding Suraj close to her bosom.

APARNA. Suraj? We will get you your soldier soon. Okay? *(To George.)* How far do we have to go?

GEORGE. Another mile. The longest mile I have ever driven.

SURAJ. Is the sun setting?

APARNA. Yes. It is a beautiful sunset. Look.

GEORGE. Don't show him the sunset.

APARNA. Why not?

GEORGE. Something I told him once.

SURAJ. God is playing football with the sun. He always scores a goal.

GEORGE. Sometimes when he has a clever goalkeeper like you, he can lose. So keep the goal carefully. God is going to keep trying to kick the ball in.

Distant thunder.

And when there is thunder, all the children of the world are shouting—'Too bad! You missed!'

SURAJ. You never said that before.

A long shot of the car racing across as if fighting the setting sun.

Cut to:

Exterior. George's home. Twilight.

The car drives up to his modest shack somewhere on the outskirts of the city. George gets out and rushes to the door.

GEORGE. I never bother locking it.

Aparna still carrying Suraj steps out and follows George into the house.

Cut to:

Interior. George's home. Twilight.

George looks around for the wooden soldier. Aparna puts Suraj down on a makeshift bed.

GEORGE *(finding the toy).* Here! At last the soldier triumphs!

George gives the toy to Suraj. Suraj clasps it to his bosom and smiles.

Thunder.

SURAJ. God missed a goal!

APARNA *(relieved).* Oh! Thank God!

GEORGE. Thank God!

Aparna is so relieved that she laughs and hugs George. George reciprocates by embracing her with more feeling. Aparna stiffens. George breaks away.

APARNA. I–I must take Suraj back.

She picks up the sleepy Suraj who is clutching his toy and takes him out.

Cut to:

Exterior. Outside George's home.

Aparna puts Suraj in the car. She looks at George who is standing near the doorway. George walks up to her. Aparna stands looking at him. George takes the cue and moves to her and kisses her tenderly.

GEORGE. Aparna. I love you.

Aparna gently breaks away.

APARNA. I–I can't . . .

GEORGE. Because you are HIV positive?

Aparna looks away.

Aparna . . . It can still work. It can. You see . . . I am HIV positive.

Aparna recoils. She is shocked at this news. George moves towards her. She runs to the car.

(Following her.) It is a miracle for us! Aparna!

Aparna gets in the car. George gets in front of the car.

Aparna. You are running away from life!

Aparna backs up the car and speeds away.

Thunder.

(*Shouting after her.*) What is wrong in it? Tell me what's so wrong?

Fade out.

Interval.

Interior. Kitchen at Jeevan Jyoti.

Aparna is busy preparing sandwiches. George comes in.

GEORGE (*cheerful*). Hello.

APARNA (*not looking at him*). Is the van here?

GEORGE. Yes. Need some help?

APARNA. No I will manage.

GEORGE. Have you filled the drinking water?

APARNA. Yes. Everything is taken care of.

GEORGE. Did you boil the water?

APARNA. Er–no. I forgot.

George begins to pour the water into a large pan on the stove.

GEORGE. Can't take a chance with bacteria in this place.

APARNA. No.

George looks at her while he waits for the water to come to a boil.

GEORGE. I am sorry about last week.

APARNA. I am sorry too.

GEORGE. Maybe I should have told you before. About me. But now you know.

APARNA (*turning to him*). Look. Do me a favour. Let's just forget what happened last week, okay?

GEORGE. Why?

APARNA. I don't have to give you a reason. Just forget everything. I want to forget it, so don't keep reminding me.

GEORGE *(covering up by being casual)*. Okay.

Fade out.

Exterior. Van. On the road.

The van is full of children. Aparna and George driving makes its way uphill. Singing from the van.

Dissolve.

Exterior. On a hill near Jeevan Jyoti.

A van is parked closeby. Laughter and noise from the picnic crowd can be heard even at a distance. George is sleeping on the grass with his cap covering his face. Aparna and the children are seated closeby. Lots of food being passed around from picnic baskets.

APARNA. Arre, arre. Don't grab like that. You should always offer to others first. Pass these sandwiches around.

They pass the food around. General chatter.

Do you know the story when God stopped the devas from eating?

There is a chorus of no.

You see the devas were very happy with themselves. So they ate, drank and slept. They didn't do any work. Soon they became very lazy and selfish. All they did was think of themselves and how much they could eat at every meal. God was very angry with them. So he put a curse on them. As a result of that curse, the devas could not bend their elbows.

CHILD. Could not bend their elbows?

CHILD 2. Why did he put such a curse on them?

APARNA. You see. When you can't bend your elbows—how do you eat? Try eating without bending your elbows.

The children try doing it. They laugh at how silly they all look and feel. Naturally, they can't do it.

And so they couldn't eat. All the devas were extrememly upset. As upset you would be if you couldn't eat all this delicious food. They begged God to take back his curse. And God said—If you can eat without bending your elbows, then only shall I lift the curse. So they tried and they tried, until finally they succeeded!

CHILD 2. They succeeded? How? By magic?

CHILD. Did the food fly into their mouths?

CHILD 1. Did they lick it off their plates like cats?

CHILD 2. Why don't you show us how they succeeded?

George is watching through the corner of his eyes.

APARNA. I will. It is possible. First you all think about it.

CHILD 2. No. We don't know. Tell us aunty!

APARNA. Think. You are not thinking.

CHILD. George will know.

CHILD 1. Yes. Georgie will know!

APARNA. Perhaps he doesn't know either.

GEORGE *(coming to them).* Let me see. Straight elbows right?

APARNA. That's right.

George straightens his right arm.

GEORGE. Like this?

APARNA. Yes.

George kneels and picks up a wada from the plate with straight arm.

GEORGE. Now, with a straight arm, I may not be able to eat this nice tasty wada, but . . . *(Turning to Aparna.)* I can feed somebody else this tasty wada.

George feeds Aparna the wada. The children applaud.

CHILD. But Georgie, you will still be hungry.

GEORGE. No. Not if aunty, I mean Aparnaji, feeds me the same way. Applause!

The children applaud.

CHILD 2 *(to Aparna)*. He fed you, so you have to feed him now.

GEORGE. Yes. That is the moral of the story isn't it? Take care of each other and God will take care of you.

APARNA. Yes. But . . . This is silly. It's just a story.

GEORGE *(sing song)*. Practise what you preach! Practise what you preach!

The children join George in chanting 'practise what you preach'.

APARNA. All right. All right.

Aparna picks up a sandwich with a straight arm.

GEORGE. Not that one. The egg sandwich.

Aparna reluctantly picks up the sandwich of his choice with a straight arm and drops it in his mouth. The children applaud.

CHILD. If Suraj were here, I would have fed him and he would have fed me.

GEORGE. But Suraj is here.

CHILD. Where is he?

George points to the sun.

GEORGE *(lightening the mood)*. Did I tell you about God playing football?

APARNA. Don't be silly.

CHILD. Tell us. Tell us.

GEORGE. Imagine that God is playing football. And the sun is his ball. When he kicks the ball, it is sunrise. The ball goes high in the air. That is noon. When it lands in the goal, it is sunset. God always scores a goal.

APARNA. Why do you want to teach all that nonsense to little children?

GEORGE. One kick of the ball for God and we get a whole day.

APARNA. Nonsense.

GEORGE. The sun goes down into the ocean and cools off.

APARNA. Everyone knows it is the Earth that goes around the sun.

GEORGE. Every morning God has a new football.

APARNA. God playing football! That is all you can think of. It's neither poetry nor science. There's no sense in it.

GEORGE. Can one make sense of Destiny? Why bother even trying?

APARNA. Eat up children. It is getting late.

Fade out.

Exterior. Car. On the road.

Aparna and Paro are singing away tunelessly a Hindi film song. 'Suhana safar aur yeh mausam haseen . . .' They finish the song with laughter.

APARNA. When I was your age, I had a massive crush on Dilip Kumar. I used to watch all his old films over and over! He was really the hot hero in my mother's time.

PARO. I like Shahrukh Khan. I fell for him when he stuttered 'I love you K-Kiran'. I wish my name was Kiran. Who thought of my name I wonder.

APARNA. Your mother of course.

PARO. It could have been my father.

APARNA. I don't think so . . . Your mother didn't know who your father is.

PARO. Do you think he is still alive?

APARNA. Who knows? Probably not, if he gave the virus to your mother.

PARO. I get so angry. Thinking about this nameless faceless man who killed my mother.

APARNA *(reaching out and patting her)*. Now don't get so angry. Your father is not an important person in your life. Your mother is.

Paro thinks about it. She smiles.

PARO. How did you first meet my mother?

APARNA. I have George to thank for that.

Cut to:

Exterior. Truck. Outside brothels.

George, Manoj and Shyamu have converted the truck into a makeshift stage. George has a megaphone. Prostitutes have gathered around the truck.

GEORGE. So to conclude . . . Can HIV be spread through touch?

MANOJ AND SHYAMU *(forming a chorus).* No!

GEORGE. Can HIV spread through mosquitoes and flies?

MANOJ AND SHYAMU. No!

GEORGE. Can HIV spread through living, eating sleeping with an infected person?

MANOJ AND SHYAMU. No!

GEORGE. Then how can you get infected?

MANOJ AND SHYAMU. Through unprotected sex with a man or woman.

GEORGE. Any other way?

MANOJ AND SHYAMU. Through infected blood and contaminated injection needles.

GEORGE. Any other way?

MANOJ AND SHYAMU. From infected mother to newborn.

GEORGE. Any other way?

MANOJ AND SHYAMU. No.

GEORGE. If there are any questions please ask them. We are here to answer . . .

George is interrupted by a commotion not too far away. A woman, Rita, is being dragged out of her house.

RITA. Don't touch me you mother fucker!

MAN A. Get out! Go die somewhere else.

MAN B. Take your filth with you!

The second man drags a five-year-old girl out of the house. The little girl is bawling due to all the commotion.

RITA. Ai! Don't touch my daughter! I will make you a hijra!

MAN B *(hitting her)*. I will break your bones! Now get out of here!

George, Manoj and Shyamu manage to get through the crowd that has gathered around watching the drama. Rita kicks at the man's crotch. He screams with pain. The first man picks up a stone and hits her with it. He picks up another stone.

GEORGE *(stopping the man)*. Wait, wait! Why are you hitting her?

MAN A. You keep out of this.

The second man has gone in and he starts throwing her things out.

MAN B. Take all your things and go die somewhere else!

RITA. Where I die is not your father's decision.

The men begin to beat her up again. George, Manoj and Shyamu manage to separate the men from Rita.

GEORGE *(pacifying the men)*. Why do you want to get arrested by killing her? There are ways to beat a woman so the marks don't show. Now tell me what's wrong.

RITA. What will they tell you. They have finished making money out of me so they want to throw me out.

GEORGE. She is still young. You can make lots of money out of her.

MAN A. Are you mad? She has Aids. She went and told all those journalists and now we are losing customers. Why don't you take her from here? Why do you socialists kick our stomachs like this?

RITA *(turning on George)*. All your fault! Now how will I feed my daughter? Why do you go about telling these loafers about Aids? Before you came here they didnt know anything. If you want to be so helpful, will you look after my daughter? Will you feed her? Educate her? No? If you can't do all that then don't pretend to help.

GEORGE. I was just trying to save you! Not take on all the problems of the world!

MAN B. If you want to save her then you take her out of here.

MAN A *(addressing the crowd)*. Nobody will be able to do any business over here if Rita stays here. You will all have to leave and beg on the streets for scraps of food! You all tell me what should we do?

> *The crowds unanimously feel that she should leave. Some of them say—'Let her go away somewhere else', 'Why did she have to tell all those people', 'She should have thought of her girl at least if she didn't care for us', etc.*

RITA *(pushing her child into George's arms)*. At least take her away. I will die here. But put my daughter in some orphanage.

> *George looks at the little girl. The little girl slaps him.*

> *Cut to:*

Inside the truck. Moving.

> *Rita is seated next to George who is driving. Little Paro is on her lap.*

MANOJ *(grumbling)*. That Dr Machado wants us to do all this good work but look at the mess it gets us in.

RITA. Ai! If you all didn't do all this good work I would still have my livelihood. Now where are you taking me?

GEORGE. I am taking you to Jeevan Jyoti. There you will be looked after.

RITA. And what do I have to do in return?

GEORGE. Nothing.

RITA. Oh. I don't believe you. I have met many men who wanted nothing in return. That's how I got into this business.

GEORGE. No. No. It is a hospital for people with Aids.

RITA. Oh. There are such places? Why don't you say all this when you come to give us free condoms?

GEORGE. Are you mad? People will have it closed down in one day. You saw what they did to you.

RITA. Oh. That is also true . . . *(Thinking about it shrewdly.)* Will I get meals three times?

GEORGE. Yes.

RITA. For my daughter also?

GEORGE. Yes.

RITA. And after I die, my daughter can stay there?

GEORGE. Yes.

RITA. Oh! Thank God I have Aids.

   Cut to:

Interior. Clinic.

   Dr Machado has just examined Rita's condition. Aparna and George await his diagnosis.

DR MACHADO. She has all the symptoms of TB. Probably due to Aids. If that is so she may not have long to live.

APARNA. What about the child?

DR MACHADO. I have taken a blood sample for testing. *(To Aparna.)* Take her to the special room. Don't want to put her with the others.

APARNA. And the child?

DR MACHADO. Put her in with the other children.

GEORGE. It is quite late. Maybe I can take you home.

APARNA. It's all right. I can manage.

GEORGE. I will wait outside.

APARNA. It doesn't make a difference to me.

DR MACHADO. Now, now. We have enough on our hands without your petty squabbles. *(Helping Rita up from the examination table.)* Come on child. Aparna will show you to your room.

George looks at Aparna hoping for her to say something. She doesn't. He walks away.

Cut to:

Interior. A small room.

Aparna fluffs out the pillow for Rita and makes sure there is enough drinking water.

APARNA *(opening the window)*. Leave the window open. You will feel good with the fresh morning air waking you up.

RITA. And what about my daughter? I heard the doctor say she will stay somewhere else?

APARNA. Yes. She will be fine with the other children.

RITA. Let her stay with me just for tonight please.

APARNA. But the doctor said . . . All right. I guess it won't make much of a difference.

RITA. Tell me one thing. After I am dead you will look after my daughter, no?

APARNA. There are many orphan children over here.

RITA. Look after her like your own child. Please. I will tell God to bless you with happiness!

APARNA. I–I don't have any children. I don't want any.

RITA. Lies. You want children very badly. I can see it in your face.

APARNA. No! I don't. Not any more. I dont want anyone. I don't want to end up like you! Begging others to take care of your loved ones!

APARNA *(realizing)*. Oh. So you too . . .?

APARNA. Excuse me. It's getting late. I have to go home.

Cut to:

Exterior. Outside the clinic.

George is waiting near Aparna's car. He is smoking a cigarette. He hears footsteps. Dr Machado approaches him.

DR MACHADO. How many times have I told you not to smoke? You are tired of living?

GEORGE. I promise I won't smoke ever again. If only she would talk to me.

DR MACHADO. Do you think she loves you?

GEORGE. I know she loves me as much as I love her.

DR MACHADO. Ah! But she doesn't know it you see.

GEORGE. How do I make her see it?

DR MACHADO. You two are travelling in different trains. Hers is travelling non-stop to the final destination and yours is stopping at all the small towns. Besides . . . has it ever occurred to you that she is travelling first class and you . . .

George looks away.

(Sighing.) Give me a cigarette.

GEORGE *(fumbling in his pocket).* I didn't know you smoked.

DR MACHADO. I need one now. I wish I could get drunk tonight.

GEORGE. Too much work?

George lights Dr Machado's cigarette.

DR MACHADO *(smoking).* We may have to leave Jeevan Jyoti.

GEORGE. What do you mean?

DR MACHADO. George. This could be the end of our dream.

GEORGE. What are you saying?

DR MACHADO. The lease runs out this year. I was hoping that the landlord will renew it. But he won't. He wants too much money.

GEORGE. How much time do we have?

DR MACHADO. It's no use.

GEORGE. Tell me—how much time and how much money?

Cut to:

Interior. Room.

Little Paro is crying.

RITA. Shut up!

LITTLE PARO. Mummy, don't lie on that bed. You will die.

RITA. Just shut up! Listen to me.

Little Paro continues with her sobs. Rita slaps her lightly.

Keep quiet and listen to me.

Little Paro stops crying.

Now I am going to die very soon . . . don't cry I said! . . . But you are going to live. That social worker told me that you don't have any disease. They won't let you stay here very long. So be nice to that aunty. Keep going to her and say very sweetly *(Talking like a little child.)* aunty you are soooo nice. I wish you were my mummy. *(Normal voice.)* And shake your head like this . . . Understand? Did you understand?

LITTLE PARO *(eyes wide with fear).* Yes.

RITA *(lying down on the bed with a sigh of relief).* Thank God for places like this.

Cut to:

Interior. The children's ward.

Aparna tucks a child in bed. There are rows of cots. She looks at one of the empty cots. It has the wooden soldier on the pillow. She picks up the wooden soldier. A child from the cot next to it wakes up.

CHILD. Where are you taking Suraj's soldier?

APARNA. I am returning it to him.

Aparna puts the wooden toy next to an altar which has a picture of Jesus.

Tomorrow you will have a new playmate. Who won't leave you like Suraj did. She will stay with us for a very long time.

Cut to:

Exterior. Near Aparna's car.

It appears that George and Dr Machado have had a serious conversation about the future of Jeevan Jyoti. Dr Machado throws away his cigarette butt, just as Aparna approaches them.

APARNA. Is everything all right, doctor?

DR MACHADO. Yes. Things are just fine.

APARNA. You look a little tired.

DR MACHADO. Maybe we all need a good night's rest. I will see you tomorrow.

APARNA. Yes. I am starting to practise for the charity show.

DR MACHADO *(after a beat)*. Yes. Good night.

APARNA. Good night doctor.

GEORGE. Good night doctor.

The doctor leaves. Aparna and George again have an awkward moment. Aparna moves to her car.

Aparna you still haven't answered my question. Do you feel you don't deserve happiness?

APARNA. I am happy as I am.

GEORGE. Look at me and tell me that.

APARNA *(stopping and turning to him)*. Yes. If there is anything that has meaning to me in my life it is this place. Jeevan Jyoti. I give to it what I can and I take whatever it gives me. There are no other demands.

GEORGE *(looking at her, not wanting to tell her the news now)*. What—what if Jeevan Jyoti wasn't there for you?

APARNA. Then I have nothing else to live for.

GEORGE. . . . And what if I am there for you?

Aparna looks at him.

APARNA. You won't be. You and I won't be here for very long, but we must make sure that Jeevan Jyoti lives on for ever.

GEORGE. I am not talking about the time when we won't be here. I am talking about now. All these years that we have left in us. We can be there for each other.

APARNA. To watch each other die? I see my mother observing my every move. My every cough, my every sneeze is painful to her. I can see the terror in her eyes when she is thinking this is the beginning of the end. I can't do this to anyone else. And what makes you think that just because we are both HIV positive, we will be happy together?

GEORGE. Forget for a moment that we are HIV. Forget that we have five, seven, ten, twelve years to live. Forget that and then think of our lives together.

APARNA. How can I forget? It is there! Written in our medical reports. Our death warrant. We can have those tests done over and over again but the truth is we will one day have Aids!

GEORGE. You have branded yourself Aids, Aids, Aids! You have put a big red stamp on yourself. I thought only an uncaring, unfeeling society would do that to us. But no. We don't have to worry about society. We are doing it to ourselves! I refuse to brand myself. All I know is that I love you and I want to marry you.

APARNA *(avoiding the issue)*. I think we are fooling ourselves that we love each other. You don't even know me properly.

GEORGE *(hurt)*. How can you say that, Aparna. That is totally untrue! I know your every mood, your every movement. I know your fears of death. I have seen you with the children. You want to be close to them; but any demands of affection and you are suddenly as distant as the stars. I can see the fears in your eyes and also the desperation to love something without the fear of causing it harm. Yes. I know you Aparna. I think of you all the time. I want to think of ways to make you feel happy. I have never felt this way about another woman before.

APARNA. You want me to believe that I am the only woman in your life?

GEORGE. That is the truth.

APARNA. Oh come on, George! You are a truck driver and you are HIV positive! Nobody needs to guess very hard how you got infected! How can I marry you knowing that you have been infected by another woman. That you have in turn infected several others. Why do you think my husband left me? Because he couldn't face me after I knew the truth. But you are even more shameless than him. You dare to ask me to marry you?

Aparna swivels around dismissive, to get into her car.

GEORGE (*really hurt, trying to supress his anger*). That's right. I am a truck driver, so I go to whores! Brand me also. (*Turning her around a little violent.*) It is you who don't know me.

APARNA. You are hurting me. Let me go.

GEORGE. Don't you even want to hear the truth?

APARNA (*breaking away from him*). Just leave me alone!

Aparna gets into the car.

GEORGE. Aparna! Give me a chance to explain! Once you know the truth . . . Aparna! I can't lose both Jeevan Jyoti and you!

Aparna drives away, tearstruck.

Cut to:

Exterior. Around Jeevan Jyoti/Intercut with Aparna in her room.

A background song. George wanders around Jeevan Jyoti, with a feeling of losing the two things he holds most precious—Jeevan Jyoti and Aparna. While Aparna in her room feels that her only refuge now is her solitude. The song ends with George sitting under a tree overlooking Jeevan Jyoti, which ironically looks as if it is at peace with itself.

Fade out.

Exterior. A village.

George stops his truck at the village square and walks towards his home. His mother is cleaning rice outside their home. His father is on the charpai with some elderly men. His mother sees him first. She gets up and he rushes to her. They embrace.

GEORGE'S MOTHER. Oh my son! Where have you been? You have never been away from home so long! I was going to come to the city to look for you.

GEORGE. I have been very busy mother. I missed you.

GEORGE'S FATHER. Son! Come here.

George walks to where his father is. The other people with his father look at each other. They get up.

VILLAGER ELDER 1. We shall take your leave now.

GEORGE'S FATHER. No. Stay for a while. My son is here after a long time. You must talk to him.

VILLAGE ELDER 1. No. Let's go.

They leave in a hurry. George watches them leave. He joins his father.

GEORGE. How are you?

GEORGE'S MOTHER. We are all fine. How are you?

GEORGE. Me? I am fine.

GEORGE'S MOTHER. Why do you look so sad?

GEORGE. I am very tired mother. I have had a long journey. I want to rest.

Cut to:

Interior. A room in George's parents' home.

George is lying down on a mat. His mother is fanning him with a punkha.

GEORGE'S MOTHER. I am not going to be around all the time. You understand what I am saying?

GEORGE. Yes, Mother.

GEORGE'S MOTHER. Then what are you waiting for?

GEORGE. I don't want to get married.

GEORGE'S MOTHER. Stop this nonsense talk and just do it. If you don't have any girl in mind I will find one for you right here in the village. Such a handsome strong son I have, not a blemish on his character, a good business—I can find hundreds of matches for you. First you stop driving the trucks yourself. Give them to someone else.

GEORGE. I like driving the truck, Mother. I like to move. I am most happy when I am moving.

GEORGE'S MOTHER. Whatever you wish my son. Just be happy.

> There is a commotion outside. Someone shouts out for George to come out.
>
> Cut to:

Exterior. Outside George's parents' home.

> George comes out followed by his mother. His father is already outside facing a small group of villagers.

GEORGE. What is this? Why are you all here?

VILLAGER 1. Don't pretend. You know why we are here.

GEORGE (going to them, rolling up his sleeves). No. Tell me.

VILLAGER 2 (moving back). Don't come near us!

VILLAGER 1 (picking up a stone). I said stay away from us. (To the rest of the crowd.) We all heard what Sukhiya had to say! He swore on his mother it is the truth.

VILLAGER ELDER 1. You will have to leave town George. We cannot tolerate you living with us!

GEORGE'S MOTHER. What nonsense are you all speaking about my son? Don't you see he is fine? You are all jealous of him. Your son is an idiot so you turn the whole town against my son?

GEORGE'S FATHER. Tell them son. Tell them this is not true.

GEORGE. So what if I have Aids? You can't get it by talking to me or by touching me! You can eat my leftovers and you still wont get it you understand!

A stone is hurled at him. George picks up a stone and throws it back at the crowd. The crowd backs away frightened.

VILLAGER ELDER 1. Go away George. And take your parents with you. We don't want you here. You will contaminate the whole village.

GEORGE. Yes! I will leave and I will take my parents out of this hell! But it is not I who will contaminate this village. Ask your son where he goes when his work in Bombay is over. Ask your brother what he does when he visits his uncle in Kanpur. It is they who will destroy all of you. They will pass on the infection to their wives, their wives will give it to their newborns and soon this whole village will be a graveyard. Where are you running now? Answer me! Speak to me you cowards!

The crowds slowly begin to disperse.

Why do you run away now? Stay and fight!

George turns around to say something but he is struck dumb by his mother's grief-stricken face.

Mother. I will be fine. Don't worry about me. I can live for another seven eight years, mother. I will take care of you.

His mother cannot bear it any longer. She breaks down and cries. She runs inside the house. His father collects himself and speaks.

GEORGE'S FATHER. You may live for another seven years. But you have killed us before we have entered our graves. What face do we have left in this village? (With great effort.) Don't come back. Leave. Go George! (Making a gesture as if to a beggar.) Go!

George cannot believe what he has heard. He just backs away. He manages to compose himself and smiles.

GEORGE. Won't you even say 'God bless you' to your son whom you shall never see again?

Fade out.

Exterior. Playground.

The children are making posters for the world Aids day concert. Aparna is guiding them.

APARNA. That is lovely. It will make such a good card. *(Turning to little Paro.)* And what's this you have drawn?

LITTLE PARO. Aunty, this is my mother. And these are all uncles who come to see my mother. One of them is my father, but I don't know which one.

APARNA. What is your name?

LITTLE PARO. Paro.

APARNA. Paro. We are going to send your painting to UNICEF. They will print it on a card and millions of people will see your painting.

LITTLE PARO *(the way her mother had instructed her)*. Aunty you are sooo nice. I wish you were my mother . . .

APARNA *(freezing)*. Well. I am not your mother.

A truck drives up into Jeevan Jyoti. Little Paro looks at the truck a little frightened. Aparna notices her reaction. George appears. He comes to the children with his player.

GEORGE. Hey! Come here all of you! I really missed my children! *(Hugging and kissing the children with a new passion.)* You are the only ones I love. Do you want to listen to some music?

The children cheer. He is about to play a tape.

APARNA. Trust you to disappear when there is so much work. And now when you do come here, you disrupt the children's activities by playing your silly music.

George presses the play button. He plays Aparna's song.

GEORGE. Do you still call it silly music?

APARNA *(taking the player from him)*. And I wish you wouldn't take the player when I need it to teach them the new song.

GEORGE. It happens to be mine.

APARNA. Look. I don't think you realize how important this is. We have to earn enough money through this charity event to save Jeevan Jyoti. I am trying to get these children to do some paintings that we could sell. Every bit will help to save this place. Of course, that may not be such an important thing to you . . .

Again George is left speechless.

Come on, children we have a lot of work to do. Come on!

GEORGE *(to the children)*. Go. What are you staring at my face for? There are more important things to do than playing with me.

LITTLE PARO *(doing her act again with Aparna)*. Aunty, you are sooo nice! I wish you were my mother.

APARNA. For the last time, I am not your mother!

GEORGE *(to little Paro)*. Sorry. Wrong number.

Cut to:

Interior. Telvision room at Jeevan Jyoti.

The entire group is watching television.

TELEVISION ANNOUNCER. December 2nd is known all over as World Aids Day and in our special bulletin we bring you a highlight of the cultural events planned for December 2nd. First we take a look at the children at Jeevan Jyoti a hospice for people living with HIV and the children of Aids victims will put up a special show at the Kala Kendra on the 2nd. Talking with us is the coordinator Ms Aparna Verma.

APARNA *(on television)*. I just want to say that these children have really worked hard for this event. The proceeds of this show will go to keeping Jeevan Jyoti afloat. So please, all of you out there do come and see it. I assure you that the children are very talented and will entertain you.

TELEVISION ANNOUNCER. Thank you Aparna, and here are some behind the scenes shots of the rehearsals at Jeevan Jyoti.

We see the children rehearsing. The children watching squeal and clap with delight. There is a brief shot of little Paro dancing. Rita is so thrilled she rushes to the TV and kisses it.

RITA. Oh! My little Paro came on TV! She looks like a little princess.

APARNA. Speaking of princesses, Rita did you get the cloth that you promised for the costumes?

RITA. I will go now Memsahib. How can I miss seeing my Paro on TV?

APARNA. You can see her dressed up at the show on 2nd. But there won't be one if we don't have their clothes ready in time. Go right now.

RITA. Yes Memsahib.

APARNA. And children, go to the playground for practice!

As Rita is leaving, she looks at George who was watching from the corner of the room.

RITA *(whispering to George)*. She is quite nice! Pretty too.

GEORGE. Who?

RITA. Memsahib, who else?

GEORGE. She may be a memsahib for you. To me she is . . .

George stops mid sentence and looks away.

RITA. And to you she is what? A princess?

Rita leaves laughing to herself. The children all file out and Aparna is left picking up some papers and the tape player.

GEORGE. Thank you Aparna.

APARNA *(turning around and noticing him)*. For what?

GEORGE. The children are happy. You have made them happy.

APARNA. They have made me happy. Jeevan Jyoti is the only thing that matters now. Isn't it ironic? We wanted to find ways to keep this place running to help the children. Now the children are keeping this place running with their shows so that we can be happy. I hope a time will come when they don't need us at all. I will be most happy when that day arrives.

GEORGE *(making light of it)*. They don't need me now. And neither do you. So I guess I am the happiest man around by your standards.

APARNA. When did we ever need each other?

GEORGE. If everyone felt that way, the world will come to a standstill.

APARNA. Well, we are not everyone are we? Excuse me.

Aparna leaves.

GEORGE. No. We are not like others. We are special.

Fade out.

Exterior. Dress material shop.

Rita is at the store buying cloth. She exclaims when she looks at some bright pink material.

RITA. Give me this one! My daughter will wear this one!

SHOPKEEPER. This is eighty rupees a metre.

RITA. Take this back and give me two metres of that one.

SHOPKEEPER. Do you have another hundred rupees?

RITA. Please give it to me! It's for my daughter.

SHOPKEEPER. No. No. I don't run any charity over here.

RITA *(leaning over the counter)*. Who is asking you to give it for free?

The shopkeeper looks around. He goes to the back of the shop behind piles of cloth and beckons to her to join him.

(Whispering to him.) Do you have a condom?

SHOPKEEPER *(annoyed).* Do you want the cloth or not?

RITA. Yes *(Muttering to herself while going to him.)* Die you pig.

> *Cut to:*

Exterior. Airport.

> *Dr Machado comes out with his baggage on a trolley. George is in Dr Machado's car. He trots over to the doctor.*

DR MACHADO *(hugging him).* Hey Georgie! How are you?

GEORGE. Welcome back home to India, doctor!

> *George takes the trolley from him.*

DR MACHADO. Mind. *(Taking a small case from the trolley.)* There is some precious cargo here.

GEORGE *(smiling).* Aha! Looks like some of the children will just have to live a couple of years longer!

> *They walk towards the car.*

DR MACHADO. So how is everyone at Jeevan Jyoti?

GEORGE. We have some new people and almost all of the old people are hanging in there.

DR MACHADO. A miracle.

GEORGE. So do you have some good news or what?

DR MACHADO. Good and bad. The good news is that there is a Dutch organization that is ready to give us all the funds we need.

GEORGE. And the bad news?

DR MACHADO. Because of our government's procedures we cannot accept the funds till we are registered. And you know how long that is taking us. It will be too late and we will have to give up the land.

GEORGE. Aparna is arranging a charity show.

DR MACHADO. Innocent girl.

GEORGE. Doctor, I haven't told her it won't be enough. It means a lot to her, this show.

DR MACHADO. All the society types will be there, pretending to help. But they will take their publicity and do little else.

GEORGE. Doctor I have thought of something.

DR MACHADO. What?

They have reached the car and George is putting the baggage in the boot.

GEORGE. But please don't tell anyone. I want Aparna to feel she managed to save Jeevan Jyoti.

DR MACHADO *(sighing)*. It's true what they say. All lovers are fools. I will promise anything to save Jeevan Jyoti and you know that. Now what is it you have on your mind?

They get into the car. We can see them talking but we don't hear them. Dr Machado softens. He pats George on the shoulder.

Cut to:

Exterior. Outside an auditorium.

We see some socialites getting out of their cars and generally hanging around the foyer. There are some television crew who are filming some of the socialites.

Cut to:

Interior. Make-up room.

All the children are ready and excited to go on stage. Aparna is putting the finishing touches to their clothes. The children look well turned out in their new clothes. George comes backstage looking for Aparna.

GEORGE. Aparna. Can I speak to you for a moment?

APARNA *(a little annoyed)*. Can't it wait till after the show?

GEORGE. No. *(Pulling her aside where they can't be heard.)* Rita died. Her last words were 'Tell Memsahib to take care of Paro'.

APARNA. Oh! Why? I just can't deal with all this. Why did you tell me now?

GEORGE. Because I won't be around after the show.

APARNA. Why? Where are you going?

GEORGE. I'm leaving Aparna. I am leaving for good.

APARNA. Leaving? I thought Jeevan Jyoti was your home.

GEORGE (*casual*). I'm a truck driver. I like to be on the move.

Paro comes to Aparna and tugs at her sari.

LITTLE PARO. Aunty, I am scared.

APARNA (*kneeling down*). Oh, don't be. They will all love you. Just—just think of your mother and you will be fine.

LITTLE PARO. Aunty, you are soooo nice.

Aparna waits for her to say the rest of her line but little Paro doesn't. Aparna hugs her tightly. Aparna looks up for George but he is gone. Manoj comes to her.

MANOJ. Madam we are starting in three minutes.

APARNA. George? Where is George?

MANOJ. He just left. He went out that way.

APARNA. Why didn't he stay for the function? Does he have some urgent business?

MANOJ. He has no business any more.

APARNA. What do you mean?

MANOJ. Don't you know? He sold all his trucks and his godown to pay for the lease agreement on Jeevan Jyoti.

Aparna is totally moved by this. Aparna moves towards the exit door.

Madam!

Cut to:

Interior. Corrirdor of hall.

Aparna comes looking for George. He is about to walk out into the street.

APARNA. Oh, George! Thank God I found you.

GEORGE. What is it?

APARNA. Why are you leaving so suddenly?

GEORGE. Suddenly? I have been around for years.

APARNA. But, but you can't leave Jeevan Jyoti!

GEORGE. Everyone comes to Jeevan Jyoti to leave it.

Manoj comes out.

MANOJ. Madam we are starting now! Hurry up!

APARNA. The children will miss you.

GEORGE. They have you.

APARNA. I will miss you.

GEORGE. You have the children.

MANOJ. Madam! The curtain has gone up.

APARNA. Get the children on stage, I am coming!

Manoj rushes backstage.

GEORGE. Goodbye. And all the best . . .

APARNA. George . . . I know you are leaving because of me
. . . If only . . . we were not HIV positive. Then maybe . . .

George laughs out loudly.

GEORGE. If you and I were not HIV positive I would be driving
my truck and you would be in your ivory tower. And we
would never have met.

There is applause heard from inside the auditorium.

Hurry up. I will watch a little bit till it's time for my train. And
oh yes—look after Paro. She is a nice girl.

Aparna can only nod.

And Aparna . . . Don't feel ashamed for being positive. It's not
your fault. It's your duty to make the world understand that.
Now go.

Aparna just stands there not moving.

(Imitating Paro.) You are sooooo nice. Now go.

> *Aparna smiles through her tears. George walks away.
> Aparna rushes in.*

> Cut to:

Interior. The stage.

> *The children are on stage. The chief guest has finished
> lighting the lamp. Dr Machado is stepping down
> escorting the chief guest back to their seat. Aparna
> enters. She heads straight to the mike.*

APARNA. Good evening and welcome to this evening's
programme. On World Aids Day we remember those whom
we loved but have left us because of Aids. All of us here today
on stage are people who have lost their loved ones to Aids or
will leave loved ones behind in this world because of Aids.
(Looking out to George who is right at the back.) I too am
living with the fear of losing someone whom I love. And I too
am not ashamed to say in public, am infected with the virus.
There is a murmur in the audience. Dr Machado is surprised
at this public disclosure. Aparna's mother is shocked and
embarassed. Aparna motions to the children.

We will now light a candle each for all the people we have
loved and lost to Aids.

> *One by one the children bring their candles and light
> them from the lamp. When everyone has lit their
> candles, Aparna picks up one candle, lights it and gives
> it to Paro. The children and Aparna sing a song. The
> audiences are moved to tears. By the end of it, they
> receive a standing ovation. Aparna is looking out for
> George. But he isn't there. Aparna looks at Paro who
> is crying by now. She goes to her and picks her up and
> hugs her very tightly.*

> Fade out.

Exterior. Car. On the road.

> *Aparna and Paro are enjoying the music playing on the
> stereo. Aparna stops at a diversion.*

PARO. Why have we stopped?

APARNA. I am just thinking . . .

PARO. What?

APARNA. That road, I am sure goes to . . .

PARO. Where?

APARNA. We will be late for the assembly anyway. Would you like to meet? No let me surprise you.

PARO. Aunty!

Aparna swerves onto another road off the main road.

Cut to:

Exterior. Car. Outside Dr Machado's house.

They get out of the car and walk to the front door. Aparna rings the doorbell. Dr Machado, now a bit older and slower opens the door.

DR MACHADO. Aparna! Miracles do happen! (*Hugging her.*) Come in. I was thinking about you and here you are! (*Noticing Paro.*) And who is this young lady? No, no! It can't be. Is it little Paro?

PARO. Yes it is.

DR MACHADO. Come in. I remember the first day you came to the centre. You made quite an impression. And you sang so well . . . I won't ask you if you want any tea because I don't have any. I have a little whiskey though.

APARNA. No thanks. We just came to see if you are keeping well. And we don't have much time.

DR MACHADO. Where are you all going?

PARO. Panchgini. She is packing me off to boarding school so that she can be rid of me.

DR MACHADO (*chiding Aparna*). Now. Now. I see you haven't changed much.

APARNA. I know. And it's too late for me to change.

DR MACHADO. That's what you said five years ago. And here you are still hale and hearty.

APARNA. Now it's really too late. Anyway, I just dropped by to say hello. I am glad to see you looking well, doctor. We must be on our way.

PARO. Look aunty! Your photograph.

On the shelf along with a dozen other photographs is one of Aparna with George.

APARNA. Now when did you take that? Doctor!

PARO. Can I keep it?

DR MACHADO. You may if you can get the two of them to pose again. But I have another picture to give to you.

Dr Machado gets another picture of little Paro and her mother. He gives it to Paro. Paro looks at it with disbelief. She looks at Aparna.

APARNA. That's your mother, Paro. And you as a little girl.

PARO. I–I wish you had given me this picture before.

APARNA. It's my fault. I never thought of taking one for you.

DR MACHADO *(to Aparna)*. You can't deny people their sentiments just because you are running away from your feelings.

APARNA. What do you mean?

DR MACHADO. You and George. Why did you run away and break his heart?

APARNA. How could I carry on with him? How could I when I knew he was HIV positive? The same feeling of betrayal I had with my husband. The same question that plays in my mind— How did he get it?

DR MACHADO. Didn't he tell you?

APARNA. Was there any doubt? He wasn't a drug user. And being a truck driver, it was very clear to me.

DR MACHADO. My child, you have been very foolish. So foolish. He didn't get it through a prostitute.

APARNA. How can you be so sure?

DR MACHADO. Because–because . . . *(Picking up another photograph which shows George with another young man.)* he got the virus from him.

APARNA. Who is this man?

DR MACHADO. This man—Joseph—was my son. He died of Aids seven years ago. I started Jeevan Jyoti in his memory. My son and George were best friends. People thought they were brothers . . . Joseph got involved with some antisocial elements from Bombay. He became a drug addict. It was George who dragged him to the hospital and got him treated . . . One day, they were coming back in George's truck. The truck fell into a ditch. George was seriously injured. Joseph escaped unhurt. George needed blood. Joseph gave him his blood. And— unknowingly—gave him the virus. When Joseph died of Aids, I knew that George was also infected. I told him to get himself tested . . . I owe a lot to George. I can never repay him . . .

> Silence as Aparna digests this and the doctor composes himself.

APARNA. Why didn't he tell me?

DR MACHADO. Did you give him a chance to? *(Putting his arm around her.)* It is still not too late.

APARNA. I don't know. I just don't know . . . I have nothing to give to him. I am too selfish. *(Going near Paro.)* Even by being Paro's guardian. I did it more for myself.

PARO. You gave me a lot Aunty. Even if you stopped me from calling you Mummy.

APARNA. What can I give you or anyone now? Yes. I can give you something. A photograph of me and you, like the one you have of your mother. That is all.

> Paro hugs Aparna and cries.

(Patting her.) Come. We still have some distance to cover. *(Turning to Dr Machado.)* Goodbye, doctor. I wonder if we shall meet again.

DR MACHADO. We don't know. We don't know. Miracles are known to happen.

Cut to:

Interior/Exterior. Car.

Paro is clutching the photograph that the doctor gave her of her mother and herself.

APARNA *(not looking at Paro)*. You know. Looking at you, I always felt that maybe, just maybe if I had not lost my child, she may have been HIV negative. But now, when I look at you holding that picture I don't regret it. I don't have to think about what you may go through when I am gone.

PARO. If for once you can think of me as your daughter, think of the pleasure I will have while you are still here. You are so silly, aunty. You did the same with George—

APARNA. Now no more talk of George. Hey! What music do you want to listen to?

Fade out.

Exterior. Panchgini boarding school.

They drive into the hostel. There is a matronly woman with a chart ordering people around. Aparna gets out of her car.

APARNA. Er—Excuse me.

MATRON. Yes?

APARNA. I am Aparna Verma.

MATRON. Is this a new admission?

APARNA. Yes.

MATRON. Goodness! Why are you so late. The principal will be displeased. You missed her speech.

APARNA. I am terribly sorry. I drove from Bombay. My ward is in there.

MATRON. She can check in to the hostel later. Give me the letter of acceptance.

APARNA. Right. It's right here. *(Looking in her bag.)* Somewhere.

MATRON. Not a very good example to your ward, are you?

APARNA. No. I am a terrible example. *(Giving up.)* I am sorry. I think I left it home.

MATRON. I can't do anything then. You will have to take her back.

APARNA. Oh please! Do something Ma'am!

MATRON. Look I have two hundred new admissions to handle . . .

APARNA. Please. I have spoken with the principal.

MATRON. You really shouldn't be losing important things, you know. It puts others through great inconvenience. Why don't you wait there while I sort out the others . . .

APARNA. Please . . .

MATRON *(stern)*. Wait there and I will see what I can do. Excuse me.

> *The matron walks away. Aparna walks back to the car. Paro has got out by now.*

PARO. What did she say?

APARNA. We will have to wait.

> *They go to the bench where they have been told to wait.*

PARO. You forgot something didn't you?

APARNA. Yes the silly letter of admission.

PARO. Which means that you really don't want me to leave you but you don't know that.

APARNA *(tired)*. Oh shut up. Now we will have to wait for ever.

> *While Aparna rambles on, Paro is looking around.*

(Rambling on.) I know them. They will make us wait and plead for hours before they take any action.

> *Paro's eyes pop out as she notices someone approaching.*

After all what did I lose but a letter. I am sure they have it in their files . . .

> *Paro stops Aparna by holding her arm. She points out in the direction she is looking. Aparna is surprised to see Dr Machado standing there.*

DR MACHADO. Alone and helpless as usual.

APARNA. Doctor! Why didn't you tell us you were coming here?

DR MACHADO. I decided to surprise you. I have a special present for you.

> *He points out to George sitting further away. Aparna's face softens as she sees him. He is much thinner and paler than before. Paro runs to him. He gets up and they embrace.*

He needs you. But he loves you too much to admit it.

GEORGE *(trying to pick up Paro)*. Hello my little pari.

PARO. I am a big girl now. You can't carry me.

DR MACHADO *(to Aparna in private)*. And you love him but you hate yourself too much to accept him.

> *Aparna runs to him. She smiles at him. George looks at her without betraying any emotion.*

GEORGE. I came to see Paro.

APARNA. Oh. Of course. How have you been?

GEORGE. Oh, I am fine. Haven't felt better in years.

APARNA. You look a little thin.

GEORGE. I have been exercising. I was eating too much butter chicken. So this is where our Paro will study. Quite fancy. Not like Jeevan Jyoti eh?

APARNA. No. Not at all like Jeevan Jyoti.

GEORGE. Okay. *(Offering his hand for a handshake.)* Well. I don't know whether we will be seeing each other again.

APARNA *(refusing to take his hand)*. Don't say that.

GEORGE. Whether I say it or not. It is the truth, isn't it?

The matron calls from a distance.

MATRON. Oh, Mrs Verma! I am sorry but if you have lost it there is little we can do.

Dr Machado approaches the matron.

Oh hello Dr Machado. When did you come?

DR MACHADO. Just a while ago. I came with George.

MATRON. George? Where is he?

The matron walks towards George ignoring Aparna.

Oh George! I want to tell you how much the principal appreciated your talk to the students on Aids.

GEORGE *(flirting with her)*. Never mind the principal. What did you think of it?

MATRON *(laughing and patting her hair)*. Oh I did too. Maybe I could tell you exactly what I thought when there aren't so many people around.

GEORGE. Yes.

MATRON *(looking at Paro)*. Now. Who is this child?

GEORGE. This is Paro.

MATRON. Hello Paro. And whose child are you?

Paro looks around.

GEORGE. She is my child.

PARO *(hugging George)*. Yes. This is my father Georgie.

MATRON. Oh, why didn't you say so before? *(Looking at Aparna.)* And this is . . .

PARO *(dismissive)*. Oh she is my guardian. She pays the fees.

MATRON *(to Aparna)*. Why didn't you say so that she is Georgie—I mean George's daughter? Never mind if you have lost it all. I will admit her anyway. I will be with you in fifteen minutes. *(To George, syruppy sweet.)* Bye.

GEORGE. Bye! *(To Paro.)* I have brought you something. Maybe you are too big for it.

He gives her the tin with soap solution and a bubble blower.

PARO. Soap bubbles! Let's go to the park. No let's go where we can climb the mountains.

APARNA. Wait a minute! What about me?

PARO. You can stay here and deal with the matron. *(To George.)* I will race you to it! Come on.

Paro runs. George runs but he stops as he feels a pain in his chest. He decides to run anyway. Aparna watches. She turns to Dr Machado.

APARNA. Do you think his time has come?

DR MACHADO. This is a very bad habit of yours. Why do you have to lose something to realize you want it?

APARNA. I am a fool. That's why.

DR MACHADO. So are you going to do something about it? Or remain a fool?

APARNA. I may be wiser now. But what is lost is lost.

Parking attendant near the car.

PARKING ATTENDANT. Madam! Move your car.

Aparna goes to her car to move it. When she opens the door she notices something on the floor of the car. She picks it up. It is the letter of admission. She runs to Dr Machado.

APARNA. Give this to the matron. *(Giving him the keys to the car.)* And move my car as well. I am taking a walk.

DR MACHADO. Do me a favour.

APARNA. What?

DR MACHADO. You are still wasting your time. Go!

APARNA. Yes Sir!

DR MACHADO. They went that way!

Aparna runs in the direction pointed out by the doctor. The doctor goes to the car. He sighs and asks the attendant.

Why is it that we understand the value of things only when there is a danger of losing them?

PARKING ATTENDANT *(wisely).* In old age we value youth. In death we value life. In summer we value the rains . . . Look at me. If I were younger, that matron would have been mine . . .

He goes away sighing wistfully.

Cut to:

Exterior. Hills.

A fog slowly begins to wrap the landscape. Aparna is lost. She has no idea where they could be. She begins to panic. She finds herself in a similar situation as in her nightmares.

APARNA. Paro! Paro!!

She is short of breath. She has to stop for a while. The fog begins to lift. She can see two figures in the distance.

(Almost to herself.) George!

Cut to:

Exterior. On a hill.

George and Paro are seated on a log of wood. Paro is blowing bubbles.

PARO *(stops blowing bubbles).* Look, the sun!

GEORGE *(squinting at the sun).* Yes. Do you remember what I used to say about the sun? Why do we have sunrise and sunset?

PARO. Mmm. No. I can't remember. That was so long ago Georgie. Why?

GEORGE *(thinking about it).* No. Forget it. It's too silly.

APARNA *(her voice from behind them).* Imagine that God is playing football.

*Paro and George turn around to find Aparna walking
towards them.*

And the sun is his ball. When he kicks the ball, it is sunrise.
The ball goes high in the air. That is noon. When it lands in
the goal, it is sunset. God always scores a goal.

GEORGE *(taking on her role)*. Why do you want to teach all that
nonsense to little children?

APARNA *(sitting next to him on the log)*. One kick of the ball for
God and we get a whole day.

GEORGE. Nonsense.

APARNA. The sun goes down into the ocean and cools off.

Everyone knows it is the Earth that goes around the sun.

APARNA. Every morning is a new football for God.

GEORGE. God playing football! That is all you can think of. It's
neither poetry nor science.

*Aparna rests her head on his shoulders. George looks
at Paro and gives her a big wink. Paro blows bubbles
on him.*

Cut to:

Interior. School hall. Stage (this scene is optional).

*Dr Machado is at the dias addressing a hall of earnest
looking school children.*

DR MACHADO. On World Aids Day. Let us remember the lives
of those who died of the virus and respect the dignity of those
who are living with HIV. Today's enemy is not other human
beings from another country or people of another religion or
race. The real enemy today is a tiny invisible creature—a virus.
The Aids virus knows no barriers of caste, creed, religion, age,
gender, race. It is not prejudice, fear or ignorance that will win
the battle against Aids. But understanding, precaution and
above all love. Today the world over doctors and scientists are
trying to find a cure for Aids. In the interest of mankind we
hope they succeed. While waiting for that cure to be invented

or discovered, let us not forget—that miracles are known to happen.

Cut to:

Exterior. On a hill.

Aparna and George are in each other's arms. Paro is blowing bubbles. We follow the bubbles till they all break except for a few strong ones.

THE TALE OF A MOTHER
FEEDING HER CHILD

A Radio Play

A Note on the Play

This short play was commissioned as part of *2000 Tales*, a landmark drama series marking the six-hundredth anniversary of the death of Geoffrey Chaucer, poet and author of *The Canterbury Tales*, and was produced by BBC Radio Drama and broadcast across BBC Radio 3 and 4 in the last week of October 2000.

Twenty-one writers were commissioned, and their starting point was to write a story which might be re-told to a group of travellers who are forced to spend the night together at a service station on a motorway in England.

2000 Tales created a vibrant, entertaining and challenging piece of contemporary drama which reflected topical concerns as defined by the leading writers of today.

In *The Tale of a Mother Feeding Her Child*, Mahesh Dattani created the character of an English woman, Anna Gosweb who tells the story of her journey back to a village in India where, twenty years earlier, she had had an affair with a local man. She arrives to find the village in drought and resolves to save the man's family.

Jeremy Mortimer
(Jeremy Mortimer is Executive Producer,
BBC Radio Drama.)

The Tale of a Mother Feeding Her Child was first broadcast on 29 October 2000 at 6.30 p.m. on BBC Radio 3. The play was directed by Jeremy Mortimer.

Cast for first production:

ANNA GOSWEB   Penny Downie

A monologue for a female voice.

'The journey from Delhi to Gujarat seemed to me at that time, an ordeal like I had never faced before—looking back on it though, it was in fact, the most comfortable part of my visit to India . . . yes . . . I had read about the drought even before I received his letter—his plea to save his life . . . a man whom I had met several years ago in Goa—one of those wild trips that, at nineteen, you think will take you to paradise and nirvana—I didn't really remember anything of what he said about his background. I could barely understand the few English words he spoke. At that time, I must confess I wasn't really paying attention. All that mattered was that I was having a wonderful time with him. He escorted me to the beaches and the old part of town. He protected me from drug peddlers and con men. I didn't take down his address when we parted. But he wanted mine . . . I was touched . . . he had preserved that piece of paper I had scribbled my address on . . . I thought of it a joke that he wanted my address . . . but there it was . . . the paper napkin with my handwriting on it, beside his prayer book. He hadn't written to me before ever. The village postman, I discovered, wrote the letter to me, for him. He didn't know how to write. Not in Gujrati nor in English . . . in perfect English, it said. "Dear Miss Anna Gosweb, I hope your God has been kind to you and favoured you with a good husband and many children. Our Gods have failed us, or should I say that they did not succeed in reaching us. They were too busy favouring our brethren in the cities and of course, the higher caste people of the villages. I have never begged you or anyone else for anything in all my life. I cannot bear the humiliation any longer of seeing my wife and child suffer so. If you could send me a thousand rupees, I assure you I shall pay it back as soon as we have a good harvest next year. Your friend in need. Jaman Gopalia. Jaman." The name brought the face back to me. A handsome man, short and well built. A labourer, who lit a fire for me on the beach and helped me find a good hotel . . . a farmer from Gujarat who made visits to Goa to earn enough money to pay off the debts his father owed. A story I didn't quite believe in then but after twenty years I know to be as true as the one I tell you now . . . I had to meet him again. To help him, yes. But also to tell him something I feel he had the right to know about. I thought of taking Jennifer with me. I am sure she should want to meet him if she knew . . . but she hasn't been keeping well. That's another story . . . I drew all the cash I had in my bank account. About four thousand pounds. I wasn't too sure whether traveller's cheques would be of any use where I wanted to go. I got on a plane and left for India . . . it was like stepping inside a furnace. I wanted to rush right back into the airport . . . the face of Jaman came back to me. I took the train to Gujarat . . . the air conditioning helped me sleep a little. I can't remember how long it took to get there—it seemed like for ever. The next thing I know is I was peering through the thick glass to look at hell itself. The land was tawny, deathly and broken down to flakes of dunglike . . . just bits of dried earth. The number of carcasses strewed around increase as the hours go by, and we get closer to Saurashtra. The relief workers travelling with me played cards. To preserve their sanity I suppose. There were patches of green land, the ones I came to know that belonged to higher caste farmers. But I knew that they didn't belong to Jaman or his family. Lakes that have been known to contain water for hundreds of years have dried up now. The water table has dropped to levels that make it impossible to access. I knew all this before I set off on my journey . . .

The train stopped at Kapileshwar. The relief workers got off with their stuff and vanished before I could ask them for directions to Kapaswadi. I can't tell you how I got to Jaman's village. I passed out at least twice on the bus. You would too at 43° celsius. I think the woman sitting beside me helped me get off at Kapaswadi, I can't remember very clearly now . . . if it weren't for the villagers I would never have found his home. People walked with me endlessly to guide me to the next settlement or ever a rough patch of land. Only to find out I was at the wrong person's home. Some were curious, some took pity on me. I parted with my bottle of mineral water to save a child from dehydration and certain death. Water was available in bottles and sachets, at a price . . . about twenty-five paisa bottle. Finally an old woman knew who I was talking about. They all knew. Except I wasn't pronouncing his name correctly. Once they got the name, there was a murmur of recognition followed by a long silence . . . I knew, looking into her eyes, that my trip had been a waste. I asked her whether he was fine. I could tell she understood some of my words. She nodded wisely. Of course he was fine. I didn't have much strength left in me and yet I cried. I wanted to tell him about Jennifer. I wanted to show him pictures of our daughter and perhaps invite him to England to meet Jennifer. At that point I simply wanted to come back to England. If only I had tried to contact him earlier. If only I had arrived a week earlier . . . my outburst was received by the villagers as a sign that I had known Jaman intimately. No words were necessary for them to understand that we were linked sometime in the past. They wouldn't think of letting me go without first meeting his family. The old woman turned out to be his aunt. She consoled

me by offering me some water with sugar in it. I didn't want
to deplete their resources any further and gestured to the old
woman to drink it. She brought another cup and poured half
the contents into it. She drank that and offered me the other
half. I felt much better after drinking it. Every eye that was on
me was filled with sympathy for me. I was frightened that very
soon the frantic pleas for help would start and I would be
compelled to hand out whatever money I had in my bag. I
understood their pride and sense of dignity after I met his
wife . . .

Jaman's aunt and some other woman. Took me to her
hut . . . I–I don't think I ever got to see her face entirely. Her
sari draped over her head fell on her face. I could see her lips
and the beads of sweat on her upper lip and chin. The aunt
said something to her. The lip tightened. I knew that this was
all wrong. Somehow they had the wrong idea. Or maybe they
had the right idea and I was naive enough to think it didn't
matter. It did. Of course it did. To her it mattered a great deal.
I was her late husband's girlfriend. Nobody can be mature
about such things. I didn't have the words tell her that it was
just one of those one night things. I wanted to tell her that he
slept with me only for the money, probably to buy her a new
sari or something. That's why he travelled all the way to Goa,
right? To earn some money to bring back to his family. I got
a great deal more out of it. More than I wanted really. I–I was
only nineteen! Of course I am glad I have Jennifer . . . such a
lovely girl . . . Shanti. When she called out her name, I almost
passed out again. That was my new age name! That's what I
told him but he didn't believe me. Shanti came out. I thought
she was ten. She was, in fact, fourteen; I came to know later.
She could barely walk. Jaman's daughter, Shanti . . . the
deathscape I had seen earlier was reflected in her face, her
body. Mother earth had given up on her. All at once, she was
a part of me. I was connected to it all . . . Jaman's wife, I never

did get her name, maybe I preferred calling her just that, Jaman's wife. She was civil enough to invite me into her home. We sat on the floor, silent at first. I didn't know what to say or do. I brought out Jennifer's picture and showed it to her. I had to let her know. She looked at the picture for a while and then looked at me. Shanti came over and took the picture from her mother. Shanti looked up at me and said 'Sister?' I am sure I heard right. Believe me, they knew. I really didn't know what to say. I saw tears streaming down Jaman's wife's face. She must have been crying for some time now, for the tears to show below the veil. That veil was the greatest barrier between us. She didn't make a sound. I cried again and looked to Shanti for help. Shanti kissed the photograph, looking at me all the time. She was telling me that it was okay. Once again, I felt connected. Until Jaman's wife gestured to me and then to the door. Clearly she wanted me to leave. She spoke and her tone was harsh . . . I looked at Shanti. Shanti spoke to her mother. I could tell she was pleading with her probably to let me stay for a while. There was an argument between the two of them. I just watched them. What they were saying to each other I will never know. All I knew was, I wanted to help them. I had enough money in my bag to help them tide over several droughts from what I could tell. I wanted to speak to them in Gujarati, to learn more about Jaman. To tell them that Jenny is in university. She has her troubles, but everything will be fine. I could take care of everyone . . . but it didn't appear at that time that I would be able to do all that. I simply looked around the little room at the mud walls while they talked endlessly. Once again I felt dizzy and thirsty, but I didn't have any more water with me. I asked Shanti whether I could have some water. I repeated the word water. She stared at me. I thought she hadn't understood, but she had. She pointed to an earthen pot nearby. I scooted over to where the pot was and looked inside the pot. How in the world did they ever drink that water? I went out and into the streets. I imagine every home in that settlement belonged to low caste people. They were not allowed to draw water from the well closeby. Now that the wells had dried up it didn't matter any way. They had to walk three miles every day to fetch a pot of water from the relief tankers. There were too many villages affected by the drought and not enough tankers to go around. They only made it to the upper caste neighbourhood. They had to wait their turn. Which came after the others had their fill . . .

I found a shop that had some bottled water. I bought about four bottles and took them back to Jaman's. Shanti appeared to be asleep. Her mother wasn't to be seen. I didn't know what what to do next. I hadn't a clue where I would spend the night. I heard a moan. I looked at Shanti. Death stared back at me. Shanti raised one frail arm towards me. I knew she was dying. I have seen that look before on . . . I know that look of starvation. I couldn't allow it to happen. Not in front of my eyes. I poured some water down her throat but she just couldn't take it in. Her mother arrived with some other women. They had seen enough of this and were prepared for it. Jaman's aunt tried to pour sugary water down her gullet but she just couldn't swallow any of it. She could barely cough. I picked her up in my arms and started to walk away from the group. They couldn't help her any more, but maybe I could. At that moment I hadn't a clue where I was going with her. The women followed me around waiting for me to tell them something. I walked aimlessly for a while before I turned around and waved for Jaman's wife to go with me. I said one word and they understood. I repeated the word 'Kapileshwar' till they understood that I wanted to take her with me to Kapileshwar. Jaman's wife ran alongside me. We were both very weak too and I imagine we weren't moving very fast. But at that time it felt like I was scaling the Himalayas. Jaman's wife led the way to the bus stop. Luck was with us. A bus was about to leave. Jaman's wife stopped a little away from the bus. I felt annoyed with her for taking this caste thing so seriously but I didn't know any better then. I grabbed her arm and rushed to the bus, yelling 'women and children first! women and children first!' I must have kicked and pushed or done something so we could get on the bus. We managed to find two spots together after I elbowed out a young man who was heading for the seat before us. An upper caste man looked at Jaman's wife sitting next to his woman. He raised his voice and ordered her to get out. He turned around to gather support from other people. I planted my foot on his butt and pushed him hard down the steps and out of the bus. His woman started screaming and rushed out to help him up. I yelled to the driver to get moving. I dug out a note—must have been a hundred pounds—from my bag and threw it in his direction. He started the bus and drove more out of fear. I suspect than for the strange looking money lying by his feet. Jaman's wife was terrified and clung on to me for the rest of our journey into Kapileshwar.

Fortunately the volunteers weren't too far from the bus station. We took Shanti straight into one of those tents. The smell of disinfectants has never been so comforting as it was when we entered that tent. They took Shanti from us and put her on drips right away. We sat beside her on the cot, waiting for her to say something. Her fever subsided eventually. The nurse brought some rice gruel and told Jaman's wife to feed her daughter . I grabbed the bowl from her—I must have appeared to be rude, I am sure but I didn't care, I had to do it—I propped Shanti's head up on my bag and help a spoonful of the gruel close to her mouth. Her lips closed on the edge of the spoon and she sucked the liquid in slowly. I looked at her while she swallowed the gruel. Spoon after spoon. I felt— relieved.

I stayed on with them for months. I brought them food from the local sweet shop. Day after day we gorged on samosas, jalebis, kachoris . . . the whole hut was filled with bottles of mineral water. The postman visited us often and translated for us. We played in the sands, Shanti and I. Jaman's wife and aunt taught me some songs. They laughed at my Hindi. Soon the monsoons arrived. We danced in the rains. I helped them plough their land. We ran through the fields and bathed in the pond. Mother Earth's breasts were swelling up once again with nourishment for her children. I could have stayed on for ever. But I had to come back to Jennifer. I got a call from the hospital . . .

I saved them. At least I saved Shanti. I fed her every day and will do so as long as I live.

I am as helpless with Jennifer as Jaman's wife was with Shanti. There is a veil between us. But it is Jennifer who wears it. She can't see me, she can't see herself . . . I hope somebody will save my Jennifer. By making her accept my help. She just won't eat. She just won't eat. At least I saved Shanti.